# MEDICAL
## Pulse-racing passion

**His Cinderella Houseguest**
Charlotte Hawkes

**Her Secret Rio Baby**
Luana DaRosa

MILLS & BOON

DID YOU PURCHASE THIS BOOK WITHOUT A COVER?
If you did, you should be aware it is **stolen property** as it was reported
'unsold and destroyed' by a retailer.
Neither the author nor the publisher has received any payment
for this book.

HIS CINDERELLA HOUSEGUEST
© 2022 by Charlotte Hawkes
Philippine Copyright 2022
Australian Copyright 2022
New Zealand Copyright 2022

First Published 2022
First Australian Paperback Edition 2022
ISBN 978 1 867 25883 4

HER SECRET RIO BABY
© 2022 by Luana DaRosa
Philippine Copyright 2022
Australian Copyright 2022
New Zealand Copyright 2022

First Published 2022
First Australian Paperback Edition 2022
ISBN 978 1 867 25883 4

® and ™ (apart from those relating to FSC®) are trademarks of Harlequin Enterprises (Australia) Pty Limited or its corporate affiliates. Trademarks indicated with ® are registered in Australia, New Zealand and in other countries.
Contact admin_legal@Harlequin.ca for details.

Except for use in any review, the reproduction or utilisation of this work in whole or in part in any form by any electronic, mechanical or other means, now known or hereafter invented, including xerography, photocopying and recording, or in any information storage or retrieval system, is forbidden without the permission of the publisher, Harlequin Mills & Boon.

This book is sold subject to the condition that it shall not, by way of trade or otherwise, be lent, resold, hired out or otherwise circulated without the prior consent of the publisher in any form or binding or cover other than that in which it is published and without a similar condition including this condition being imposed on the subsequent purchaser.

All rights reserved including the right of reproduction in whole or in part in any form. This edition is published in arrangement with Harlequin Books S.A..

This is a work of fiction. Names, characters, places, and incidents are either the product of the author's imagination or are used fictitiously, and any resemblance to actual persons, living or dead, business establishments, events, or locales is entirely coincidental.

Published by
Harlequin Mills & Boon
An imprint of Harlequin Enterprises (Australia) Pty
Limited (ABN 47 001 180 918), a subsidiary of
HarperCollins Publishers Australia Pty Limited
(ABN 36 009 913 517)
Level 13, 201 Elizabeth Street
SYDNEY NSW 2000 AUSTRALIA

MIX
Paper from
responsible sources
FSC® C001695

Cover art used by arrangement with Harlequin Books S.A.. All rights reserved.

Printed and bound in Australia by McPherson's Printing Group

**His Cinderella Houseguest**
Charlotte Hawkes

MILLS & BOON

Born and raised on the Wirral Peninsula in England, **Charlotte Hawkes** is mom to two intrepid boys who love her to play building block games with them and who object loudly to the amount of time she spends on the computer. When she isn't writing—or building with blocks—she is company director for a small Anglo/French construction firm. Charlotte loves to hear from readers, and you can contact her at her website: charlotte-hawkes.com.

Visit the Author Profile page
at millsandboon.com.au.

# CHAPTER ONE

THE MUSCULAR MOTORBIKE hugged the bend tightly and skilfully hurtled along the quiet A roads as Dr Lincoln Oakes—Lord Oakes to those who knew his family—raced to work on time.

He was never late. *Never.*

Strictly speaking, he supposed he wasn't late now. The crew weren't due on the air ambulance base until seven o'clock and it was still only six-forty. But that didn't make him feel any less agitated; it was a full ten minutes past the time he usually liked to be in work—always the first one in.

As if timings—not never-ending nightmares of that hellish night in the last war zone he'd been in—were the sole cause of his agitation.

Shifting on his motorbike, Linc accelerated harder and drew down from the sense of satisfaction that slid through him as the sleek machine emitted another throaty roar as it surged smoothly along the road.

As if that would change anything.

As though tearing along these country lanes meant he could somehow outpace the ghosts that haunted him, or silence the voices that whispered their accusations to him in the witching hours.

The nightmares were turning his head into a battle zone so that every time he jerked awake he could practically hear the gunfire, smell the acrid smoke, and feel the scorching Afghanistan sun.

Anniversaries of that terrible night were always painful, but this one—the fifth one—was hitting him harder than usual. No doubt because it had only been a month since the funeral of the old Duke of Stoneywell—the man who had been not only his father but his guide for the first two decades of Linc's life, but who had been more like a stranger these latter fifteen years, and not just because of the cruel disease that was Alzheimer's.

Without warning, memories closed in on Linc, making the scraping inside him all the more intense, and raw. He pushed them forcefully away; the last thing he needed was to be late for his job as an air ambulance doctor and miss a shout. How many more people could he fail to help?

Rolling the throttle as he leaned his bike, Linc powered around another tight bend—as if he could somehow escape his demons. As if he didn't know by now that it was impossible. But if he could just get through the next few days, after that they would grow weaker, and he'd be able to stuff them down for another year.

Finally, the roof of the Helimed hangar pulled into view. The glint of the morning sun off the harsh metal coverings. Down this straight, and a left into the entrance road, and he'd be there—into yet another shift that could mercifully occupy his thoughts for the next twelve hours.

Skidding his rear tyre as he drew to an abrupt halt, Linc threw his leg over the seat and yanked his helmet off as he moved. Another few strides and he was hurrying into the building where the close-knit team relaxed in between shouts, and he waited for familiar sounds to chase his ghosts away; letting them slink off at the door the way they always did when he was around his crew.

But today, instead of everyone being gathered in the kitchen, the usual mouth-watering breakfast cooking smells filling the air, his attention was drawn to the rec room—their recreation space— where there seemed to be something of a meeting going on.

Spinning sharply, he strode down the corridor and slipped into the room alongside Tom, one of the two paramedics on his crew.

'What's the story?' he asked, jerking his head towards the air ambulance charity's regional co-ordinator. 'What's he doing here?'

'You just got here?' Tom craned his neck around in surprise. 'You're always the first one in.'

'First time for everything.' Linc tried to shrug it off, even as he hated to do so. 'So, what's going on?'

'It seems Albert and Jenny were in a car accident on their way home last night.'

'Hell.' Something walloped into Linc, hard and low. 'What happened?'

Albert had been their Helimed crew's pilot for as long as anyone could remember and was like a father figure to the rest of them. They had a standing joke that the older guy had been installed along with the oldest parts of the rec room's ratty furniture.

Even Jenny, Albert's real-life daughter, had started as second paramedic on the team on the very same day that Linc himself had begun, four years ago. So, in a tight crew like this they weren't just colleagues, they were also like family.

'Not sure exactly what happened.' Tom shook his head. 'But apparently it's serious but not life threatening.'

'Well, that's something at least.' Linc blew out a deep breath.

'Yeah. We're just waiting on more news.'

'And that's what the chief came to say?'

'That and the fact that he's managed to get hold of an outside pilot for today's shift.'

'Why an outside pilot?' Linc frowned. 'Echo team's pilot is our go-to standby. What about a second paramedic?'

'We haven't got echo team's pilot—not unless he's turned into one of the hottest females I reckon I've ever seen.'

Linc snorted. 'Playboy Paramedic Tom's on heat again.'

Though to be fair, Tom's flirting always came second when he was a shout. Playboy or not, Tom was a damned good paramedic.

'Yeah, yeah.' The other man laughed now. 'I can't help it if women love me. They love you too, only you're too damned prickly to ever notice. As for our second paramedic, it's Probie.'

Linc eyed the lad across the room. In an air ambulance unit like theirs, they almost always had a trainee with them, whether it was a trainee doctor, or a trainee paramedic, and they almost always got the nickname Probie. This particular lad had been a land ambulance paramedic for years before he'd joined their Helimed crew. Making him up to a full-blown second paramedic to cover Jenny seemed like the good decision.

The new pilot, on the other hand, was a different matter.

'Fair enough re Probie,' Linc muttered. 'But I still don't see why they don't just bring in echo team's pilot. At least we'd all know how this particular crew works.'

'You know that Albert had started to talk to the powers that be about retirement, right?'

'Damn, I knew he was thinking about it,' Linc conceded. 'I didn't realise he'd actually spoken to anyone outside our team, though.'

'Apparently HQ already had feelers out for a new permanent pilot.'

'Yeah, well, they've got big shoes to fill replacing Albert. He was a top-notch RAF pilot with countless missions under his belt.'

'And apparently this new pilot is Army Air Corps. Plus she has over a decade's experience.'

Something slammed into Linc before he had time to think. A memory that punctured his chest and then bounced around, rattling at his ribcage, and evading his attempts to capture it.

'Army Air Corps?' he echoed, more sharply than he'd intended.

'Yeah. HQ were desperate when the call came in about Albert so they ended up phoning the regiment up the road to see if the military could lend us a pilot even for the day.'

'It's about eighty miles away,' Linc pointed out jerkily. 'Hardly *up the road*.'

'You know what I mean.' Tom brushed it off. 'Anyway, from what I can gather, the AAC told HQ that they could lend us a pilot, and that she's even getting ready to leave the military for Civvy Street. Regional have been falling over themselves all morning at the idea of securing her as a permanent replacement for Albert.'

The memory rattled harder in Linc's chest. There was no rational explanation for it, yet it was there all the same.

A feeling.

An image.

*Piper.*

He hadn't thought of her in years. No, scratch

that—he hadn't *allowed* himself to think of her in years. Which was a slightly different thing.

An Apache pilot within the Army Air Corps, Piper had served on several tours of duty with him—including that last one. Her skill and passion for her career had made her a guardian angel of the skies, and a glorious light illuminating the darkness of that hellhole.

And if it hadn't been for Piper's fast thinking and even faster flying, then those enemy leakers would have slipped the lines and managed to get into the hospital where he and his team had been holed up with the civilian patients. Which would have simply meant more numbers added to the body count that final hellish day.

But more than her skill and dedication to her career, the two of them had grown close on that tour, seeking each other out during downtime, sharing war stories, or simply trying to make sense of the events of a particular day or week.

Not to mention the *almost-kiss* the two of them hadn't quite shared.

If his responsibilities to his brother—the acting Duke of Stoneywell—hadn't left him no choice but to leave his beloved army a matter of weeks later, Linc had often wondered what might have happened between him and Piper.

Linc shoved the memories away, the way he had on those few occasions when she'd sprung, unbidden, to mind over the past few years. Whoever the new female pilot was, it wouldn't be Piper. The woman had always been married to her career above all else—there'd be no way Piper would be leaving the AAC for Civvy Street. She'd always joked that they'd probably have to carry her out of that job in a wooden box.

'Linc?' Tom's voice dragged him back to the present and he forced himself to focus on his colleague.

The last thing he needed was another haunting by his past right now.

'Yeah? Oh, right?' His voice sounded scratchy, but that couldn't be helped. 'Well, I guess an ex-AAC pilot wouldn't be a bad stand-in for the crew.'

'And if Albert's finally ready to enjoy a bit of retirement, then we can't exactly begrudge him that, can we?'

'Right,' Linc grated, his mind still racing despite his attempts to calm it.

It was almost a small mercy when a flurry of movement in the corridor negated the need for him to add more, as the charity's regional co-ordinator bustled cheerfully back in, a figure at his back.

'Okay, team, I'm delighted to introduce you to your new pilot. This is Piper Green.'

Linc's entire world—his entire being—went suddenly, somehow…liquid, and yet granite hard, all at the same time. It was a miracle his diaphragm could even move enough to allow him to keep breathing.

For a moment, he had to wonder if he was seeing things...if she'd been conjured up by the fact that he'd just been thinking about her. And the morning sun shining at her back like some kind of prophetic halo only made it seem all the more as though the image from his head had somehow slid out into the real world.

But slowly, *slowly*, his brain began to process what his eyes were seeing.

*'Legs?'*

Linc was hardly aware of uttering her name—well, nickname, anyway. He certainly didn't recognise his own voice, and the fact that he hadn't uttered it loudly meant that she oughtn't to have heard him from her position across the room. But he didn't think it was his imagination that she turned her head slowly and she looked straight at him, those familiar, all too expressive rich amber depths seeming to pierce right through him.

The five years fell away in an instant. It might as well have been yesterday that they'd last seen each other. There was no denying that...*thing* that still coursed between them, as powerful, and greedy, and urgent, as it had once been. For several long moments, Linc simply drank her in. As if he were back in that parched, bone-brittle desert, and she were his only source of crystal-clear water. He might have known it couldn't last long.

Abruptly, something followed the attraction; something that was far more potent—and unwelcome—than mere chemistry. It punched through Linc in that split second before he quashed it, and it was all he could do to stay standing in the doorway—affecting a casual air—as he folded his arms across his chest. As though that could somehow protect him from the emotions charging through him.

Attraction. History. But worst of all, *guilt*. For leaving at the end of that last tour without even a word. Because he didn't let people get close and he didn't get attached.

And Piper had threatened to do both.

Dimly, Linc became aware of his crewmate talking, but it was impossible to process anything over the roar in his head.

'Say again?' he murmured.

He wasn't sure he could have dragged his gaze from Piper, even if he'd tried. And by the way she was staring back at him—slightly wide-eyed and just as dazed—he thought perhaps she was finding it just as surreal. But if he didn't get a grip quickly, the entire crew was going to know that something was up and that might lead to questions he wasn't prepared to answer.

Even to himself.

With a concerted effort, Linc forced a more neutral expression onto his face, and lifted his voice to something approaching a normal tone.

'Hello, Piper, it's been a long time. Welcome to Heathston Helimed, otherwise known as Helimed hotel one-niner.'

*Linc was here?*

Somehow Piper resisted the compulsion to shake her head. As if that could somehow dislodge the apparition that stood in front of her.

'*Doc?* Major Lincoln Oakes?' she heard herself say. Casually. Teasingly. Somehow conveying the impression that she was in total control, when the reality was that her legs thought they might buckle under her at any moment. 'It can't be.'

This was the man who had haunted her across time, and the planet, for the past five years? Even as she eyed him, it felt as though their history was unrolling between them—as rich as any eleventh-century tapestry—for the entire Helimed base to see, if she wasn't careful.

For the better part of six months, on the worst tour of duty she'd ever been on, he'd been her go-to. The person she'd most looked forward to seeing—in the mess hall, in the officers' tent, or even just on the sandy perimeter line that made for a makeshift running track in that godforsaken camp—to offload the events of the day.

In an environment like a theatre of war, bonds could be forged quickly. Tightly. It was entirely possible for a colleague to know and understand you better than your own family. And it had been like that with Linc. They'd somehow...*clicked*.

Until their *almost-kiss* had nearly ruined it all.

They'd agreed it was a mistake—a line they would never again risk crossing—and still, a month later he'd left the armed services altogether, leaving her feeling vulnerable, and foolish.

If she'd known he was part of this crew, she would never have taken the post—emergency or not.

Okay, that wasn't precisely true. But she would surely have been better prepared for the inevitable encounter. A strong pep talk maybe—that reminded her just how she could resist Lincoln Oakes's particular brand of all things male. Thank goodness she'd already changed into the armour of her heavy-duty flight suit.

Not that it seemed to matter. Somehow, she still felt half naked and completely exposed in front of him.

'You two know each other?'

Piper blinked, startled. She turned her attention to the paramedic standing next to Linc, with his practised smile and easy charm. The guy was clearly accustomed to women falling at his feet, and he was certainly good-looking. But she hadn't even noticed him, standing next to Linc. From the instant that Linc had spoken, her entire world had zoomed in on just the two of them—like the narrow shot of one of those photographs she'd taken out in that bleak war zone.

She didn't care to analyse what that said about her. Or her unresolved feelings for a man she hadn't seen in half a decade, and hadn't really expected to ever see again. No matter what little fantasies her subconscious had conjured up sometimes, in the dead of night.

But now wasn't the time to dwell on that. Piper dredged up a bright smile and tried to remember what the guy had even said. Nothing came to mind, and it was a relief when Linc's rich, steady voice answered instead.

'Piper was an Apache pilot back when I served. We did a couple of tours together.'

'Apaches?' The other guy nodded with another practised grin. 'Sweet.'

And Piper couldn't help noticing the way Linc's jaw tightened. Was he remembering the undeniable chemistry that they'd once shared? Even if they'd deemed it too inappropriate for their respective military roles? Or was that purely in her own head?

Even now, as she watched him smooth his chin with his forefinger and thumb, a delicious shiver rippled over her back. How insane was it that she could still recall precisely how it had felt when that calloused thumb had once skated over her cheek to brush away the desert dust that seemed to get into absolutely everything? The way her breath had caught as his head had dipped, ever so slightly, towards hers.

And then the camp's shrill sniper alarm that had ripped them apart.

Piper tried telling herself that it was that particular all too vivid, adrenalin-pumping memory that made her blood pound through her body right now. A physiological reaction to that alarm call, rather than to the man standing right in front of her.

Maybe she would have believed the lie, had regret not still rippled through those nights when the ghosts of that almost-kiss would tiptoe through her dreams. A muted sorrow that the single moment five years ago had been shattered, their one chance gone.

No, she'd certainly never expected to see Linc again. Yet suddenly, here he was. Here *she* was.

It didn't matter how hard the logical, practical side of her brain told her that it was merely coincidence, it didn't silence the low, deep hum inside her. A hum that told her it wasn't just chance—it was something more. Something she didn't dare put a name to, but if she had dared, she might have called it...*fate*.

'So she's a good pilot, then?'

The colleague's question brought her crashing back to reality—to the here and now. She watched as Linc did that thing with his head that wasn't a shrug, precisely, but was just as non-committal. Standard, unreadable Major Lincoln Oakes.

'Yeah, Piper's a good pilot, and what we called army barmy,' he confirmed evenly to his colleague before turning back to her. 'So you can't seriously be thinking of jacking it in and heading to Civvy Street?'

There was something strangely comforting in his words, although his question set off the pounding in her chest again. Though this time for a different reason. He was right, the Army Air Corps had been her life—*flying* had been her life—but the army had its own drum beat, and it was her time to move on from Captain and get her Majority. But a Captain flying helis was appropriate—a Major flying them was not. And you couldn't exactly tell the Army that you didn't want a promotion.

Besides, running a flight-training wing would have taken her further from her mother and brother, for longer. And they both needed her; now as much as ever.

Still, Linc didn't need to know any of this.

'Not thinking of.' She wasn't sure where the nonchalant laugh came from, but at least it sounded a lot more natural than it felt. 'Already done. Paperwork went in three months ago and I'm officially out the door within this next month, hence why they were happy to loan me out to your air ambulance when they got the emergency call this morning.'

'You drove down this morning? It's a ninety-minute drive.'

'One of my colleagues flew me in,' she explained, awkwardly. Though she couldn't have said why.

It was almost a relief when the paramedic inadvertently rescued her.

'Who cares whether she drove, or flew in?' he clucked, making her smile despite everything. 'Allow me to be more welcoming than my colleague here. I'm Tom, Heathston Helimed's most eligible bachelor—August edition. It's great to meet you, Piper.'

There was such an easy likeability to the guy that she couldn't help grinning. At least it was easier than all the sizzling tension between her and Linc.

'Hi, Tom. Nice to meet you.' She grinned, shaking the paramedic's outstretched hand. 'Sorry about your crewmate, Albert. I hope he makes a speedy recovery.'

'We all do,' Tom agreed. 'Though, in the meantime, it looks as though you're the newest member of Helimed hotel one-niner—*Legs*, was it?'

'Old army nicknames,' Linc dismissed smoothly. 'Shared tours of duty. That's it.'

Tom looked greedily from one to the other.

'Nah, there's a story here, right? I can feel it in my bones.'

'Your bones are just going to have to wait, then.'

Piper whirled around as another crewman, who she'd seen manning the air desk in the room across the hall, now stepped through the doorway. 'Nine-nine-nine call just came in; not a lot of info, just that there's a kid on a bike somewhere near Roughston Lake. He's gone over and it sounds like there's an arterial injury; he's bleeding from his groin.'

'Piper,' the regional coordinator followed the crewman. 'I appreciate we haven't finished your briefing yet but...'

'No problem, I'll get the heli started.' Piper nodded grimly, heading rapidly out of the room and to the hangar. At least she'd already prepped the bird earlier that morning, and taken it out to the tarmac.

She didn't need to wait for anyone to tell her that they needed to get up into the air. She could practically hear Linc's voice in her head, reminding her that every second mattered. Here, as much as on the battlefield.

Which was exactly what she needed to also remind her of the other rules they'd had out there, in that war zone. Namely, steering clear of whatever it was that still arced between them. Because the truth was that they would never act on it.

They couldn't.

It wouldn't be professional. Which was why nothing had ever *really* been going to happen whilst they served together, and nothing would happen now. Better to eject all unsolicited thoughts about Lincoln Oakes out of her head, and try instead to reinstate the banter, and the old rapport they'd once shared.

Anything to protect her mother and brother and stop questions about why she'd turned her back on her army career—the career that had always meant so very much to her.

# CHAPTER TWO

'This is Helimed hotel one-niner,' Piper confirmed to the region's air traffic control a few minutes later. 'We have four on board and we're ready for lift; heading for Roughston Lake, just a few minutes up the road.'

None of them were dwelling on the fact that if it was an arterial injury then the kid could bleed out before they even arrived.

A moment later, the radio crackled and her flying permission was granted. Lifting the helicopter into the sky, she circled it around and headed off into the skies.

'Do you know where you're heading?' Linc's voice came over the internal helicopter intercom, from his seat in the cockpit beside her.

As she understood it, he would usually travel in the rear of the craft, being the critical care doctor, and one of the paramedics would sit up front with her as the navigational pilot, but she wasn't surprised he was up here now. Assessing her on this first run. Typical Major Oakes-style. By the easy acceptance of the rest of the crew, they didn't seem to be finding it all that startling, either.

'Yeah, with the barracks just up the road, I've flown around this region for years. Besides, I was going to head for Roughston Lake until more info comes through.'

She saw, rather than heard, Linc's nodded grunt of agreement.

They didn't have to wait long for their update. A couple of minutes later, the air desk crewman's voice came over the system from back at the base.

'Helimed hotel one-niner, this is hotel zero seven, we have an update on the casualty, over.'

'Go ahead, hotel zero seven.' Piper automatically flipped her comms to respond, her years of training kicking in despite the unsettling feeling of having Linc back on the scene.

'Seems the patient was taking part in some unofficial dirt-bike races in the woods to the north side of the lake when a collision occurred. They're quite deep in and the land crew are having trouble reaching them. The patient was propelled approximately six feet up into the air, along with his bike, and when he landed the handlebars of the bike fell onto him. He was bleeding profusely, but the other racers have allegedly managed to staunch it.'

Without even realising what she was doing, Piper cast Linc a look. They both knew that the injury was serious. The patient could bleed out in a matter of minutes, so it was up to them to find a way to get to them. Fast.

'Message received, hotel zero seven,' Linc acknowledged. 'We're about two minutes out but the area to the north is quite densely wooded. Can you get someone to step into a clearing and try to signal to us, over?'

'Roger that, Helimed hotel one-niner. Will ask now. Out.'

'Best landing area?' Piper asked over her headset as the air desk clicked out.

'There are only a couple of possibilities.' Linc's voice was tight, but it was the expression on his face that told her a fuller story.

Evidently, if she wanted to land close then she was going to have to do some pretty nifty flying.

Sure enough, Tom's voice crackled over the headset from his seat in the rear, next to a probationary paramedic lad who had only been introduced to her as Probie.

'No, you can't land on the north side. We've been here before and the main race humps are deep into the woods. It's too dense to land so Albert had to ground us close to the lake and we had to trek in. It takes about ten minutes.'

'The lad likely doesn't have ten minutes,' Linc noted grimly. 'Can you get us any closer, Piper?'

Focussing on the woods, she looked for anything that might work.

'Look for a track or a clearing,' Piper urged, nosing her helicopter forward.

'Like I said, it's too dense and—'

'There's a track at nine o'clock position,' Linc

interrupted Tom's caution as Piper brought the heli around.

'I have visual,' she confirmed, dropping slightly to get a better look. 'It's narrow, and the ground is bumpy.'

'But you can land it?' Linc urged.

Piper took another look. There looked to be a marginally wider section about fifty metres further up. The pylons were still there, but they dipped a little further into the tree line. It wouldn't be the easiest landing...but then again, it wouldn't be the hardest she'd ever managed either.

'I can land it,' she agreed. 'Probie, you're going to watch my tail. Tom, check the rotors on the right side. Linc...'

'I've got the left,' he said immediately, reading her thoughts. 'You just focus on the wires and the landing.'

Edging forward, angling her heli as they went, Piper dropped lower. Lower.

'Tail might be a bit low,' Probie's nervous voice suddenly piped up. 'I'm not sure... I can't...'

'Can you go forward another metre?' Linc asked, his calm voice taking over.

Piper eyed the track ahead of her. Another metre forward could be too close on the nose. But perhaps she could land on the hump a little further again, clearing both the nose and tail. She cast a critical eye over the power lines. Further forward would be moving out of the widest part, but she was fairly sure there could be enough room if she angled the heli a little more.

'How are the rotors looking on the left if I move forward about ten metres, Linc?'

He craned his neck for a better view. Tom and Probie were silent, clearly out of their depths. But she could deal with that. She absolutely trusted Linc's assessment anyway.

How unexpectedly easy it was to fall back into being a team with him. As it once was.

'Yeah,' he answered after a moment. 'It'll be tight but there's room.'

'Keep visual.'

'Understood.'

Carefully, she edged forward, constantly reassessing the wires, the rotors, the tail, confident that Linc was doing the same on the left side. And then, finally, they were down safely. Less than eight minutes since the emergency call had first come in.

'Nice flying.'

And it was ridiculous how good the compliment—however gruffly uttered—made her feel. But Linc was straight back onto the task.

'Okay, Probie.' He leapt out of the aircraft and grabbed his bags, with Tom following suit. 'Stay with Piper to help shut the heli down, then bring bloods and additional kit as fast as you can.'

And the next moment he was gone, racing along the track towards the waiting rider. Disappearing over a ridge exactly the way he'd done the last time she'd seen him, five years ago almost to the week.

'All right, fella, I'm Linc. I'm the air ambulance doctor. I'm here to help. Can I get in there, lads?'

Slipping through the cluster of dirt-bike riders—their bikes strewn around the area like machines at an abandoned scrapyard—Linc crouched down next to a couple of lads as they pressed some sort of coat to the fallen rider's wound.

By the lad's pallid countenance and the amount of blood on the ground around him, the injury was going to be severe, but the kid was alive.

'Well done, lads,' he praised. 'You've done a good job here, a really good job. Can you talk us through what happened whilst I take a look at your buddy? What's his name?'

'Kev,' one of them choked out, dazedly wiping his bloodstained hands on his padded trousers. 'He was near the front of the pack when he came off going over the mound. I don't know if he landed on the bike or the bike landed on him, but by the time the rest of us came up the rise, the bike was there, and there was blood, like, pouring out of him. We didn't know what to do except try to stop it somehow.'

'You did really well,' Linc reassured him. 'Did Kev lose consciousness at any time that you know of?'

'Don't think so.' The other lad shook his head wildly. 'Don't know, but he was groaning and crying out by the time we got on scene.'

'Okay, great,' Linc assured again before turning to the kid lying on the ground in front of him. 'Okay, Kev, mate, I'm going to need to take a closer look.'

As Tom slipped the mask over the rider's face to help him breathe, Linc removed the coat and carefully inspected the wound, the young lad's groans getting louder.

'Punctured the femoral,' Linc murmured the confirmation to the paramedic before adopting a deliberately breezy tone as he addressed his patient, all the while packing stuff into the wound to try to staunch the flow. 'You've got good mates here, they've kept you going. I just need to get the bleeding stopped, and then we can give you some pain relief. Yeah, I know that hurts, mate, but you're doing great. Your mates did a really good job.'

More than that, if it hadn't been for the other riders applying pressure, the likelihood was that their friend would have bled to death before the air ambulance crew had arrived.

And even with everything those kids had managed, if it hadn't been for Piper's unparalleled flying skills, then his crew would have had to put down a mile up the track and by the time they'd raced to the scene, it could have already been too late.

Maybe having Piper around didn't need to be so...*unsettling*, after all. She was a great pilot, and hadn't they always agreed that their professional lives came first—above everything else? It was the way they'd managed to keep that distance between them during that last tour, anyway.

So why would that be any different now?

Thrusting the jumble of thoughts out of his mind, Linc focussed on his patient, packing the wound, and applying a tourniquet, all the while talking to the groaning lad. It was a good sign that Kev could answer some of his questions, even through the pain, and it made their job faster. Finally, Linc turned back to his paramedic.

'The kid's going to need a transfusion. Can you get more info out of the group, and find out where Probie is with the other kit?'

At least the aircraft carried some blood and they could give him a transfusion. In the meantime, now that the bleeding was stemmed properly he could offer Kev some pain relief. The kid might not be able to feel his lower leg, but he was clearly in pain.

Linc worked quickly and efficiently on his patient as Probie raced up within moments with the second kit bag. The sooner they could get him to hospital, and to the vascular surgeons whom he needed, the better.

Linc's primary concerns now were about stabilising his patient and dealing with haemorrhagic shock.

'Blood pressure is one-twenty over ninety,' Tom advised him after a moment.

'SATS?'

'Ninety-five.'

Linc nodded, running through a final head-to-toe examination.

'Okay, let's get him onto the scoop.'

Within minutes, the team—assisted by a couple of other riders recruited by Linc—were carrying the kit and the patient as quickly yet smoothly as they could over the undulating terrain, back to the helicopter. Time was still of the essence, of course.

Linc cast another glance at the monitors attached to his patient. The kid was a fighter, that was for sure, alert and responsive so far, and his blood pressure seemed to be holding fairly steady. Now Linc just needed to keep him that way right up to reaching the hospital.

And who better to get them there quickly than Piper?

As if to prove his point, by the time the stretcher reached the landing spot, Piper was out and opening up the door for them to load the patient, slotting into her role and working with them as quickly and harmoniously as if she'd been a part of the crew for decades, rather than not even a day.

*As if she fitted.*

So maybe he should just get over his own personal feelings and take comfort from the fact that, of all the pilots that Regional could have got to cover Albert's sick leave, Piper was one of the best.

And he'd just have to find some way to live with his own sense of guilt.

'Talk about a baptism of fire,' Tom was gushing as Linc sauntered into the Helimed's rec room, an hour or so later. 'That landing was the most awesome thing I've ever seen. I don't know if even Albert could have made it. And then whipping the heli around that fast for that second shout…? Man, you're one helluva pilot, Piper Green.'

'Thanks.' Piper smiled, but it wasn't the bright, life-loving smile Linc recognised from five years ago.

It was just a little bit dimmer. A little sadder.

'So, you were saying that you flew Apaches,' the paramedic pressed obliviously, the admiration unmistakeable in his tone. 'Aren't there, like, two or three female Apache pilots?'

And it didn't matter how many times Linc told himself that Piper was a crewmate and nothing more, he couldn't stop his gut from tightening at the dark cloud that skittered over her lovely features before she deftly concealed it.

What was she hiding?

'There are only a few of us, yes,' Piper admitted after a moment, before seemingly reluctantly correcting herself. 'A few of *them*.'

*Did she miss her Apache?* Linc couldn't help wondering. It wouldn't have surprised him. Piper had always seemed committed to her career in the military—surely something had to have happened to make her leave?

And then, in the next thought, he reminded himself it was none of his business. She didn't need anyone nosing into her life any more than he would want anyone looking into his life. Into his secrets.

'I've got paperwork to finish up,' he muttered, making his excuses and leaving the room.

Anything to get away from Piper, and questions about what she'd been up to in the five years since he'd last seen her.

Slamming the door to his room, he sank down in the tattered wingback that he'd salvaged from some skip a couple of years earlier, and propped his feet up on the battered coffee table opposite.

There was no paperwork to finish, he'd already completed that well before he'd headed for the rec room, but perhaps a quick nap might help him to catch up on the last couple of weeks' worth of broken sleep.

It was certainly easier to switch off here, with the lull of noise down the hallway, than it was back in the oppressive silence of his own apartment. Thrusting his hands behind his neck, Linc closed his eyes and tried to nod off.

The sharp rap on the door had him springing to his feet—all the evidence he needed of how wound up he clearly was.

'Yep?'

The door swung open, but he didn't need to see Piper step through to know it was her. Every fibre of his body already told him that.

'Is this a bad time?'

'No,' he ground out. 'It's fine. I was just finishing the case reports.'

She cast a glance at his desk, then at the wingback.

'Trouble sleeping?'

He frowned.

'Not at all.' He might have got away with it, had he left it at that. But curiosity got the better of him. 'What makes you ask?'

She blinked at him, then squared her shoulders. A gesture so Piper-like that he couldn't believe he'd forgotten it. Or her characteristic bluntness.

'I always have trouble sleeping this time of year. The anniversary of that day, you know?'

He folded his arms over his chest before he could stop himself. Even just her words made the ringing louder in his ears. They made the screams that much more real. And they made his guilt that much more unbearable.

'Yes,' he rasped. 'I know.'

She scuffed her boot against the worn carpet, then seemed to get a grip of herself again.

'It was a bad night.'

Which didn't come close to describing just what hell the fifteen-some hours of that firefight had been.

'It was,' he agreed simply.

Another moment of silence stretched, long and taut, between them.

She wrinkled her nose.

'Do you want me to go?'

He opened his mouth to tell her it would be for the best. But the truth was that her leaving was suddenly the last thing he wanted.

'Stay if you want,' he heard himself say carefully instead.

She eyed him for a moment, then nodded.

For a moment, they each edged around the room, yet always keeping a piece of furniture between them. First a chair, then his desk. Eventually, he settled into his office chair whilst she perched on the edge of his couch.

'You look…well, by the way,' he offered, after a moment.

'Thanks.' She raked her hand over her hair, even as it was tied up in its usual tight bun.

But he could remember exactly what it looked like when she released it from the confines of that net. How soft it had felt that one time, beneath his fingers. That pleasantly light, vaguely coconut scent.

Angry with himself for his sudden weakness, he slammed the memories away. And then she started to speak.

'I never feel particularly great at this time of year.' She bit each word out, as though she wasn't even sure she'd intended to say them. 'I find it hard to sleep. Hard to keep my mind straight, you know?'

He did know. All too well. But that sense of guilt was threatening to suffocate him.

'I like my own company a lot of the time,' she continued. 'But just around this week, I find the solitude a little too...'

'Claustrophobic?' he answered, before he even realised he meant to speak.

'Exactly.' She nodded, with evident relief. 'I just like the company. Even if it's inane chatter in the background, it's comforting to hear it there.'

'Maybe you should talk to someone,' he managed. 'Do you still see some of the other guys from that tour?'

'A few.' She shrugged. 'And we used to get together the first couple of years. But, you know how it is, people get posted off here and there, and we end up losing touch. What about you?'

'This place keeps me busy.' He deliberately sidestepped the question.

'Which isn't exactly an answer.' Piper eyed him

ruefully. And when she spoke after another silence, there was a new quiver to her voice.

'I always hoped I'd see you again. To apologise.'

'Apologise?' Linc frowned as he watched her suck in a lungful of air, as she clearly tried to steady herself.

But it didn't make her voice any less shaky. Nor did it clear that glassy look from her eyes.

'For not doing more. I should have caught those leakers before they got to their weapons stash.'

Linc stared at her for a moment, then, before he realised he was even moving, he found himself walking around the desk and crossing the floor, pushing any last obstacles between them out of the way.

Like the spell that only this woman had ever seemed to be able to cast over him.

He didn't know if that made it easier to accept, or harder to. And he had no idea what he'd intended to say to her. But before he could speak, the shrill alarm signalling a new shout blasted through the base.

Habit and training had them both on their feet and lunging for the door handle in an instant but, for a split second, they stopped and looked at each other.

'Perhaps we ought to talk,' he said gruffly, without knowing he'd intended to say anything at all. 'After this shift. And not here.'

Piper stared for a second, then jerked her head into a semblance of a nod.

'To clear the air?'

'In a manner of speaking,' he bit out.

The truth was, he didn't know what he thought it would do. He only knew that Piper was the last person who should feel they owed him any kind of apology, though he had no idea how he was supposed to articulate the guilt racing through his head at that moment.

'Are you heading back to barracks tonight?'

'No.' She shook her head. 'I'm booked into a hotel in town.'

Linc frowned.

'I thought they flew you here in a hurry this morning? You won't have a car.'

'No, but I can get a cab. In two days' time we have a couple of days' downtime, don't we? I'll head back to barracks and pick up my car then, depending on how Albert's doing.'

'Fine.' He gritted his teeth, his mind still galloping away without him. It wasn't the cool, collected self he was accustomed to. 'I've a spare helmet, I'll give you a ride to your hotel tonight, and maybe we can get a drink and talk?'

Amber eyes locked with his.

'I'd like that.' She pulled a face. 'But I don't particularly want to be the topic of gossip around here.'

'No one else needs to know anything,' he assured her. 'In fact, it's better that they don't. It's just one former colleague giving another a ride into town. Nothing more to read into it.'

Was he convincing her, or himself?

'Besides,' he pressed on firmly, 'no one is even likely to see that much. Albert and I were always the last to leave at the end of a shift anyway, by the time he'd put the heli away and I finished any paperwork.'

It was odd, the way he could see the very moment when her last reservation fell away, and she nodded at him.

'That would be...great, then,' she confirmed. 'Thanks.'

And, just for a fraction of a beat, he paused a moment to nod at her, before pulling the door open and racing down the corridor to the air desk whilst she ran to start the heli.

'What have we got, Hugo?'

'A middle-aged female marathon runner has collapsed whilst training. Husband says she usually trains around fifty miles per week. Suspected cardiac arrest.'

'Send the details through,' Linc shouted, hurrying back into the corridor just as his paramedics were dashing past him. 'We'll get air-bound.'

Because, knowing Piper, she was already ahead of them and had called it in to the local air traffic control. Just another reason why she was the perfect fit for this team in Albert's absence.

# CHAPTER THREE

*THIS IS A MISTAKE*, Linc told himself some nine hours later as he sat in the hotel bar opposite the unsettling Piper, and tried not to stare broodingly at the drinks that stood, both still untouched, between them.

He certainly shouldn't have offered her that lift on his motorbike.

His body was still sizzling from the feel of Piper's arms wrapped so tightly around his waist as she'd pressed her body against his back—making him react as if he were a seventeen-year-old kid all over again, taking the devilish Missy Jackson out on his bike the very day he'd passed his test.

Only, to be fair, back then, having his bike had been more of a thrill than the feel of Missy hugging herself to him. The same could most definitely not be said of Piper, right now. He could still feel Piper's warmth, and smell that vague coconut scent of hers that he'd recognised in an instant. Like a long, slow lick down the length of his sex.

Thoughts that had no business invading his mind did so, all the same, whilst the secluded booth and atmospheric lighting weren't helping, either.

'I think perhaps I should leave you to it, after all,' he muttered. 'It must have been a long day for you.'

It was those amber depths that snared him. Keeping him rooted to his seat despite needling him to leave. Before he did something they might both regret.

'I thought you wanted to clear the air?'

He'd thought so too. Now, he wasn't so sure. He couldn't quite fathom what he thought he was doing here with Piper.

Was he here to clear the air? Or had a secret, traitorous part of his dark soul hoped that one night with this woman might finally slake this inconvenient attraction that had never quite abated between them?

Even now, seated across the low table from him in their quiet, tucked-away corner of the room, Piper was captivating. Simple jeans encased her long, elegant legs, which were stretched out in front of her in a way that exposed tantalising flashes of midriff.

His palms itched with the effort of not reaching out to see if her tanned skin was even half as smooth as he remembered it to be. No other woman had ever made him feel so out of control. Not before Piper, and certainly not since.

'Perhaps I should go first,' she rasped suddenly, snagging him back to the present. 'That apology I owe you—'

'You don't owe me any apology.' He cut her off far more abruptly than he'd intended. 'If anyone owes an apology right here, it's me. I let those leakers get out of the hospital. I afforded them the opportunity to get to their weapons cache.'

'And how were you to have stopped them?' she demanded softly. Too softly. It slid under his skin and he couldn't do a thing to stop it. 'You were the one trapped inside that hospital, Linc, trying to save all those women and kids. I was the one safe up in the skies.'

Linc shook his head incredulously. He thought of the surface-to-air missile that had blasted past her cockpit, leaving her Apache reeling in the air. Another metre and she wouldn't be here now.

Whether he'd realised it or not, it was yet another fact that had haunted him the past five years. Yet another reason why he couldn't seem to find peace.

'You can't seriously think you owe me anything,' he growled. 'If you hadn't stayed—if you'd done as ordered and returned to base—all those innocent people would have died. You saved a hundred or so lives that day.'

She eyed him intently. Too intently.

'Is that what your nightmares are about?' she challenged him, in that same soft, all too perceptive tone. 'Some misplaced sense of guilt?'

'It isn't misplaced. You can't have forgotten

how many lives were lost that day. Our guys, and all those innocent civilians besides.'

'Of course I haven't,' Piper choked out. 'You think you're the only one tormented some nights? I wake up hearing those screams, so vividly. Especially at this time of year...around the anniversary. You're not the only one who feels guilty, Linc.'

'What do you have to feel guilty about?' Each word punched its way out of him. The black truth that he hated to recall, let alone voice. 'You stayed, and went on to do more tours, protect more people. You did everything you could. I was the one who quit the military after that tour.'

She didn't answer immediately, watching him, instead. With anyone else, he would have changed the subject instantly—with anybody else, the subject would never have got this far. But he didn't. He simply waited for her to say whatever it was that was clearly racing around her mind.

As though he *needed* to know what she thought of him, after all that had happened.

'I guess, if I'm to be honest, that's the bit I never really understood. I watched you run into burning, bombed-out hospital buildings—quite literally, Patch—and emerge with a woman or a kid over your shoulders. You never seemed afraid of what might happen. In fact, a few times during that last tour, I thought you were almost daring anyone to shoot you. Like you wouldn't have cared if they had.'

Linc couldn't breathe. It was as if all the air had been sucked instantly from his lungs. Her assessment of him was so spot on, and so damning, that he wasn't sure he could even think.

Abruptly, he lifted his tumbler and downed it in one—something he never did. He didn't even taste it. Still, he stood up and walked to the bar, ordered another and returned to Piper.

It had been three years since he'd drunk enough so that his skull hurt, so that he'd forget everything, but tonight, he thought he might just sink back into that old self. It was that, or grab the woman sitting in front of him, and let them both make the mistake that their bodies clearly still wanted to make.

Drinking the memories away seemed like the lesser of the two evils—even if it was the one his body screamed against the most. At least his penthouse was within walking distance of this place so he didn't have to worry about getting caught on his motorbike and dragging the family name into his night of self-indulgence.

'Talk to me, Linc,' Piper pressed, by the looks of it taking herself by surprise as much as him. 'Why did you leave? It wasn't because of us… was it?'

'No, Legs, it wasn't because of us.' He laughed—a low, hollow sound. But still, he wasn't prepared for the admission that dropped, unbidden, from his lips. 'It was because of my father.'

Or, more accurately, the man he'd believed to be his father...right up until that deliberately cruel bombshell from his mother years earlier again.

But Piper certainly didn't need to know that. Any more than she needed to know that the man had been a duke, or that he himself was a lord.

'What happened to your father?' Piper asked, her tone instantly empathetic as she wrinkled her nose, clearly trying to remember things. 'Did something happen to him? I remember you saying that you and he had been incredibly close before you'd left to be a doctor in the army.'

'It was a long time ago since we were close,' Linc ground out, torn.

Half of him—the logical half—wanted to shut the conversation down the way that he would have done any other time, with any other person. But then there was an irrational part of his brain that seemed ready to spill any number of inconvenient truths to Piper, just because she was asking.

The way he never did.

It had to be the lack of sleep. And the alcohol.

He was terribly afraid it was neither. And then, as if to prove a point, his mouth started moving, apparently of its own volition.

'When I got back from that last tour my head was all over the place—just like everyone else who actually made it out of there, I guess,' he added hastily.

'That doesn't lessen the impact on any one of

us, trust me,' she assured him quietly. 'What happened, Linc?'

And even though every practical fibre of his body told him to shut the conversation down, he found himself not only continuing it, but actively answering Piper's question.

'My...father had been fighting Alzheimer's for years. But when I got home that last time, I got a call from my brother, Raf, to say that he'd really gone into decline during my last tour. My brother needed me to come home. The family business needed both of us.'

The family business, in point of fact, being the dukedom of Stoneywell, as well as Oakenfeld Industries—named after their Oakes family name. With their father mentally incapacitated but still alive, the position of CEO of the board hadn't passed automatically to Raf, and with Linc away with the military, it had seemed that various powerful members of the board, whose plans for Oakenfeld definitely didn't align with those of his family, were attempting a coup against Raf taking over as the interim CEO.

Another few points of detail that Linc didn't feel he could share with Piper. He had already blurted out too much.

'Basically, I didn't feel I had much choice but to leave,' he concluded tightly. 'Though, faced with the same set of circumstances, I'd make the same choice all over again. Raf needed me. So did our sister, Sara.'

'And that's what's driven the guilt,' Piper noted quietly. 'You aren't alone, Linc. I promise you. I stayed, but I feel just as guilty. So many buddies who didn't make it out of there because of that one night, yet I did. You did. There doesn't seem to be any rhyme or reason.'

'None,' he echoed, his voice too thick.

'So you put your family first. You had obligations to them. That's nothing to feel guilty about. In fact, it's admirable. And you and your brother managed to resolve things?'

'We did,' Linc confirmed. 'In time.'

Though it had taken a lot of blood, and sweat from them all, and a few private tears from their usually stoic sister.

'And your father is still...'

'He died.' Linc shook his head. 'Last month, in fact.'

'Oh, Linc, I... I'm so sorry.'

'Thank you,' he bit out automatically. Perfunctorily. 'But the truth is that, in many ways, he was gone a decade and a half ago.'

'It doesn't mean you don't feel the loss.'

And there was something so profoundly sad about her in that instance—a shadow that he thought he'd seen only once before, years ago—that reached inside Linc and tugged—implausibly—at his hardened heart. The one he'd thought he'd locked away years ago.

'You sound as though you're speaking from experience,' he rasped out, suddenly finding he wanted to know more about the enigmatic woman sitting across from him.

He wanted to finally hear some of those secrets he'd always felt she'd held so close—the secrets he'd always made himself respect when they had been serving together.

But they weren't serving together any more—working on the same Helimed team wasn't the same, and, anyway, it was temporary. And tonight had been a first in so many ways, not least the fact that he'd told Piper things he'd never voiced to anyone else—not even Raf or Sara.

What was it about Piper that made it so easy for him to talk to her? What was it that made their connection so...real?

Well, whatever it was, he needed to get a grip, Linc decided firmly, or else he might find himself unburdening himself to her with everything.

And nobody wanted that.

'So, *are* you speaking from experience?' Linc asked again, as though Piper hadn't noted the exact moment that he'd started shuttering himself down to her.

She tried not to lament the loss—in some ways,

she was surprised it had taken him so long and that he'd already shared so much with her.

It was more than he'd ever told her back in the army. More than he'd ever told anyone, as far as she was aware. She'd always found him something of a closed book, guarding his personal life as if it was nobody else's business—exactly the way she'd always done.

In a theatre of war, like they'd been in, it had felt like the safest thing to do. *Compartmentalising*, some of the guys called it. It probably explained how they'd kept each other at arm's length despite the attraction that crackled and fizzed inside her every time she was with Linc. Zipping through her body, straight to that ache in her chest. And, if she was going to be absolutely honest, at the apex of her legs.

She'd never been in any doubt that it was something Linc felt too, even if rules and regulations—and their own ranks—had helped them keep things strictly professional, at least for the most part.

But they weren't out there any more. They weren't even in the military any more—or she wouldn't be in a matter of weeks. There was no safety net. Now, here they were, in her hotel bar, with him sharing secrets that she suspected he'd never told anyone else before.

And she found she suddenly wanted to do the same.

It was a terrifying, heady realisation.

'My father died when I was seventeen,' she confessed, before she thought she'd even meant to. 'I found his death...confusing.'

'How so?'

A hundred things rattled through Piper's brain. Though none of them anything she wanted to say—least of all the way he'd died, or the fact that he'd gone from being a kind, loving father and husband to a violent alcoholic, in those final years. That wasn't just her secret, that was her mother's secret, too, and one Piper didn't feel she had a right to share.

'I was conflicted. He was also...ill in the years before he died,' she settled on at last—because, to her mind, alcoholism was a form of illness. At least, thinking that way made it easier to deal with what had happened. 'He hadn't exactly been the greatest father before his death.'

'That must have been hard,' Linc murmured, and she was grateful that he didn't point out how she'd always told everyone in the army that she'd come from a close, loving family.

'It wasn't pleasant,' she admitted. 'Part of me was glad he was gone. Another part of me felt guilty about not feeling sad enough.'

Linc dipped his head, and even though it was just a gesture, she felt as though he really understood. It was strange, how they hadn't seen each other for five years, yet one night had almost restored that closeness they'd once shared.

She'd missed it—*him*—more than she'd realised.

'Is that why you joined the army?' he pressed.

She hesitated. He'd asked her that once before, way back when. She hadn't answered then. She'd been afraid it would lead to more questions that she hadn't been ready to face.

She still wasn't sure she was ready to face them, even now.

'Sort of…it's complicated.'

'That's a cop-out,' he replied. But the faint tug of his lips assured her he wasn't about to press her further on the matter.

She offered a rueful smile of her own.

'My point was simply that I understand how difficult it can be when someone you love dies, even though a part of you feels as though you lost them years ago.'

'Something like that,' he muttered almost to himself, before turning his attention back on her. 'So, why are you leaving? I thought you were a lifer.'

Another question she wasn't ready to answer. Another situation over which she felt she had no control. Her mother and brother needed her. What more was there to it than that?

'Family obligations,' she said eventually. 'Like you said before, I guess.'

'Right.' He raked his hand through his hair

in a gesture that was heart-wrenchingly familiar to her.

'At least you have more hair now.' She made herself tease him instead. 'Not so regulation short.'

It was still short, but thicker somehow, and soft-looking.

Without warning, an X-rated image slipped into her mind, and even as Piper tried to slam it away she found herself shifting in her chair. The air between them as taut as ever, an almost delicious friction sliding between them, as though Linc could read her racy thoughts.

'I didn't mean...' She shifted again, trying to get comfortable. A feat that was impossible when the jostling feeling was coming from within. 'I just—'

'It's fine.' He cut her off in a tone that made it seem as if it was anything but fine.

A tone that was too heavy, and loaded, and full of all the things they always avoided saying.

'Linc...'

She wanted too much, that was her problem. She might have fought it five years ago, but it had been there, all the same. And now, she was here and the lines that they'd drawn were faded, and weak.

And this week, of all weeks, she hated being alone. Hated being trapped with memories of that night.

'What are we doing here, Linc?' she whispered, her throat scratchy and dry.

'We're…talking,' he ground out. 'Just like we used to do.'

And never mind if keeping himself from crossing that short space from his chair, to where Piper sat, cost him far more than it had any right to.

'Just talking?' she pressed, and he thought the naked desire in her tone might be his undoing.

'Just talking.' He barely recognised his own voice. 'Easy, and comfortable, the way it always was.'

'Except it isn't like that, is it?' rasped Piper. 'Things are different. It's…fraught.'

She paused, but he didn't trust himself to answer.

'Or are you going to tell me that I'm reading something into it?' she asked, eventually. 'Are things just simply awkward between us because I'm about the last person you would want to work with?'

'Piper,' he growled.

And he didn't know when he'd closed that gap, or when he'd taken her shoulders in his hands. But he couldn't bring himself to say anything more, and no more than he could bring himself to drop the contact.

He was trapped—in some kind of painfully exquisite limbo.

'Is it the memories of that day?' She swallowed. 'Only we used to get along well, the two of us, and...oh, I don't know.'

And he could have said it was that—the memories. He could have left it at something they both would have accepted. But he couldn't. He had to push that little bit further.

'It isn't the memories of that day,' he rasped.

*At least, not entirely.*

And he wasn't sure when he'd inched closer to her. Lowered his head a fraction to hers.

He told himself to back away. That he didn't need the ghosts of their attraction spiralling through him on top of everything else. But he couldn't seem to move.

'Linc...' She barely whispered his name, but it was enough. That longing he recalled all too vividly from that night in his tent. The one where he'd almost kissed her, before they'd remembered where they were, and the job they'd each had to do.

But hell, the need to kiss her again, *now*, was burning through him; so brightly that he thought it might sear him from the inside out.

Her mouth was scant millimetres away, and the closer he dipped his head, the more her eyes seemed to flutter closed. And when his lips finally brushed hers, it was like a kind of song that poured through him.

A celebration.

A symphony.

A glorious sound that he'd heard once before, but then had been forced to shut out for good.

And now, he could hear it again. He could revel in it. As her lips moved slickly with his, and her tongue moved to dance with his, it felt to Linc as though he'd been waiting for this for a whole lifetime. Maybe longer.

Hauling her to him, he revelled in the feel of her arms looping around his neck, the feel of her breasts pressed to his chest. He let his hand caress her cheek, indulging in the feel of her silken-soft skin under his fingers, he raked a thumb over her plump, lower lip, feeling her sharp sigh roll through him, right to his sex.

And he wanted more. So much more, that he was beginning to lose all sense of where he was, and what they were supposed to be doing.

It was only the background hub of the rest of the hotel bar that finally pierced through the fog in his brain and yanked him unceremoniously back to reality.

He pulled his head from Piper, and eyed her for a long moment as he struggled to refocus.

'We can't do this,' he managed.

By the expression on her face, she was fighting the same battle.

'No,' she breathed raggedly. 'We can't. This is...a distraction. Nothing more.'

She didn't sound remotely convincing, but he grasped at it all the same.

'A distraction, yes,' he agreed. 'It's the shock of seeing each other again.'

'The stress of the anniversary.' Piper nodded, too quickly. Too fervently.

As if she was trying to make herself believe it.

'It would be a pleasant diversion, but we still have to work together so ultimately it would be unprofessional.'

'Unacceptable,' she offered with a hollow laugh.

The sound echoed everything he felt himself. Desperately, Linc pretended the tightening around his ribcage wasn't so painful. Walking away from her—again—was the right decision, but that didn't mean he had to like it.

'So this never happened?' she whispered.

And it told him all he needed to know, that he hated the sound of it so very much.

'This never happened,' he rasped. 'We go back to normal.'

Whatever their version of normal had ever been.

# CHAPTER FOUR

FROM HER VANTAGE point at the top of the hill, Piper peered down into the valley and wondered how the team were faring.

Another shout, this time a road traffic collision involving a car and a pick-up truck allegedly overtaking vehicles when oncoming traffic had appeared around a bend.

From the information patched through by Hugo, the main casualty for the air ambulance was the fifty-year-old male of the oncoming car, who'd had nowhere to go when he'd seen the pick-up hurtling towards him.

The man's wife had been in a more stable condition, and had already been taken to the local hospital by road ambulance, but Piper could see the fire crews working to release the husband from his crushed vehicle.

It looked less than hopeful, but she'd seen Linc perform enough near miracles out in hellish war zones to know that if anybody was going to achieve it, then it was likely to be Linc. However, getting the patient up the hill to her location could well be an issue.

Checking out the scene as best she could without leaving her machine, Piper looked for a suitable site to land in the event that they needed her closer. Her radio crackled but she wasn't about to disturb her team whilst they were working, as long as she could be ready to move once they called for her.

By the looks of the terrain, the most feasible site was going to be the tarmac of the country lane itself, but the trees lining either side weren't going to make it easy.

Still, she was determined to spot a good LZ if it meant shaving a precious few minutes off her team getting their patient to hospital. Minutes that could, as both she and Linc knew from personal experience, save lives.

'Who pinched the last jam doughnut?' Linc demanded in good-natured disgust a couple of days later, as he crossed the rec room to find an empty pastries box. 'Was it you, Legs?'

It hadn't surprised him how well Piper had slotted into the team so easily—years of being an army pilot in a similarly close-knit team meant that she'd slipped seamlessly into the role of Helimed pilot.

However, it had surprised him that the two of them had somehow managed to fall back into their old roles of pretending the chemistry between them didn't exist. As if the other night in the hotel hadn't happened—another *almost-kiss* to add to the one from five years ago.

His libido could do without making a habit of not quite kissing Piper Green—not to mention that insistent thrumming in his soul, whenever she was around.

He ought to be elated it had been so easy to relegate their attraction to the outer limits of his consciousness. So why wasn't he?

Tearing his thoughts back to the present, Linc watched as their air desk operator poured out five steaming mugs from the coffee machine. He reached for one gratefully before turning to face the room to fully take in the sight of three shattered crew members sprawled over the various pieces of battered furniture.

'You snooze, you lose, Patch. You know the rules.'

In the corner, Piper threw her legs over the arm of her raggedy easy chair and licked her fingers unapologetically—not helping his wayward libido one bit. The thrumming in his ribcage shifted decidedly lower.

He fought to ignore that, too.

It was remarkable how a morning of intense shouts—one of the most demanding mornings Linc thought he'd experienced in the four years since he'd been with Helimed—bonded a new team. Even given the circumstances of Albert's absence. And if his libido didn't kick up into overdrive every time he spoke to Piper, Linc thought he might actually start to enjoy having her stand in.

As it was, pretending that he wasn't acutely aware of the damnable woman every time she entered a room, or left the room, or even shifted position in said room, was becoming exhausting.

Almost as exhausting as having to fight off some irrational urge to cross the floor, sweep her into one of the bunk rooms, and do devastatingly naughty things with her in the way he was certain they both should have done years ago.

It took an absurd amount of effort to eject the thoughts—and the deliciously erotic accompanying images—from his brain.

'I wasn't snoozing.' One-handedly, Linc balled up the empty doughnut box and launched it expertly across the room to the rubbish net—an old kids' basketball hoop—above the bin. 'I was restocking the medical supplies after the last shout. It's part of my job, go figure.'

As if that could convince anyone who might be watching closely enough that he wasn't remotely affected by this particular woman's presence.

'Whilst we were in here with the doughnuts.' Piper laughed, and the sound rippled through him far too easily. 'So I refer you to my earlier comment. You snooze, you lose.'

'Isn't there another box in the kitchen?' ventured the probationary paramedic as Piper rolled her eyes comically.

Sexily.

'Ugh, Probie. Don't tell him yet.'

'Thank you, Probie.' Linc forced himself to laugh before striding to the hatch and reaching right across for the other glossy white box.

Anything to occupy his hands. And his mind.

'Muppet,' he heard Hugo say. 'You should have let them squabble it out for a little longer before you reveal that. It's better than a TV soap.'

'Oh. Sorry.'

'You'll learn.' Hugo laughed. 'I reckon you're best off staying out of it where these two are concerned. I've a feeling they're going to be like an old married couple.'

'You two are married?' Probie gaped, eyes wide as Piper spluttered into her coffee. 'Aw, man, how come I didn't realise that before now?'

Linc grinned again, taking advantage of Piper's coughing fit to enlighten the poor kid.

'Yeah, happily married. Ten years now. We've got five kids and Legs is a complete slob. Our house is a tip.'

'You're kidding?' breathed Probie, his eyes flickering from one to the other.

'We are *not* married,' countered Piper, still spluttering. 'I wouldn't go near Patch if he was the last man on earth. And I'm not a slob.'

'Sure you are.' Linc was thoroughly enjoying himself as she narrowed her eyes at him.

And, just for a fraction of a heartbeat, their

gazes held. That split-second memory of the one time when something almost had happened between them. The kiss that still haunted his deepest dreams to this day. And as Piper half lifted her hands, as though she'd been about to brush her fingers over her lips, he knew that she too was thinking of that night.

But then, abruptly, she gave a toss of her head as if to shake the unwanted memory aside, and offered a snort of derision.

'My tent was always tidy, even out in Camp Harton. But anyone would look messy next to neat-freak Patch here. Or so the colonel said. Even the battlefield hospital area seemed that bit more ordered when Linc was around.'

'Wait.' The young paramedic looked from one to the other. 'So, you aren't really married?'

'We aren't really married, Probie,' Linc managed, determined not to let anyone see his internal struggle to regroup.

'But Hugo said...?'

'I simply meant that I reckoned, since they'd served together, that they were going to *act* like an old married couple.' The air desk operator chuckled.

'Is that why he's called Patch?' Probie asked suddenly. 'Because he has OCD and likes a clean patch.'

'Nope.' Swinging around, Piper brushed the

sugary crumbs off her cargo trousers. 'He's called Patch because he used to patch soldiers up.'

'Oh, I get it. And you're called Legs because you flew a helicopter instead of marching?'

'Nope.' Linc snorted. 'She's called Legs because she ran like a gazelle every time the alarms went off. She was always the first to her heli in a shout.'

Although, privately, he could think of other reasons why her nickname was so damned fitting for her.

'Yeah, I get it.' Probie nodded eagerly. 'Patch and Legs.'

'For the record, Probie,' added Hugo kindly, 'I don't recommend you call either of them by those names. I've a feeling those are nicknames the pair of them earned serving together out in some war zone. We didn't earn that right.'

'It's cool.' Piper shrugged, but her smile was overbright.

Linc said nothing. Hugo was right, it would be anything but *cool* if anyone who hadn't been on that tour of duty with them used those nicknames. And by the way Piper was carefully avoiding meeting the new kid's eye, Linc knew she felt the same, however welcoming she was trying to act.

'Oh.' Probie sniffed. ''Cause I was gonna say that I couldn't understand why you were complaining the other day about bridezilla, if you already had a wife.'

'Say again?' Piper's voice cut in a little too quickly, and a little too sharply, at least to Linc's trained ears. 'Patch is getting married?'

As though maybe she was...jealous?

No, not *jealous* exactly, he corrected hastily. But...*something*. It mattered to her more than it ought to. Enough to make something pull tight in him.

He eyed her with amusement.

'My sister is getting married,' he clarified.

'Oh.' She squirmed under his direct stare, but to her credit, she didn't back down. 'Sara? Hmm, she's your younger sister, isn't she?'

'Good memory.' Was it arrogant of him to think it proved how interested she still was in him? 'She keeps trying to pair me off for the wedding.'

'Why?'

It was Piper's characteristic bluntness that made him grin the most.

'Optics,' he lied. 'Long story.'

'Ah.'

It was one simple word, one tiny syllable, but it was loaded with so much meaning, and Linc hated that the very sound of it made it feel as though he'd just pushed her away again.

Then again, wasn't that what he did?

As tightly knit as he liked to think the crew

was, he didn't want to share his biggest secrets with them any more than he'd wanted to share them with his buddies back in the army. The men and women in whom he entrusted his life.

He found he couldn't tear his eyes from Piper's as they watched each other without saying another word. If there was ever anyone he would trust with his secrets, then it would probably be this woman.

But not the fact that he was a lord. Or, more to the point, that he wasn't really a lord at all; at least, not by blood—his mother had made that clear, in her own gleefully cruel way. And perhaps it was that which hurt the most. He'd not only lost the decent, moral old duke as his 'father', but the man had also been his compass. And his anchor. Without the duke claiming him as his son, by blood or not, was he really part of the Oakes family anymore?

And Raf and Sara could claim that it didn't matter to them one bit, and that he was their brother no matter what—but he didn't feel the same. He felt like more of an imposter than ever. Was it any wonder he'd joined the army the week his mother had so gleefully dropped her bombshell on the family—in all its brazen ugliness?

And was it any wonder that even now, over a decade later, he still couldn't bring himself to go…*home*?

'So just take someone with you to keep your sister happy, if it's just optics,' Probie interjected suddenly, causing Piper to finally break eye contact and look at the young lad.

Linc felt the loss far too acutely.

'He can't do that,' Tom scoffed. 'You don't take a casual date to a wedding and not expect them to read too much into it.'

'Humble as ever, Tom?' Hugo laughed, as he prepared to head back out to man the phones.

'You can mock, but you know I'm right. Linc knows it, too.' The paramedic grinned, calling after him. 'That's why he keeps refusing dates, even if it risks incurring the wrath of a kid sister. Which, trust me, isn't something you want to take lightly.'

'You have to have some female friends who don't want to sleep with you, don't you?' Probie turned to Linc.

'Men and women can't be platonic friends,' countered Tom before Linc could answer. 'Not really. At least one of them wants more. Possibly both.'

'I'm sure they can.' Probie frowned. 'Look at Linc and Piper.'

And suddenly, both pairs of eyes swivelled to consider the pair speculatively, and Linc didn't need to see Piper's reaction to know that she would be tensing up.

'Well, they're just odd,' Tom snorted.

'I know,' the young Probie exhaled abruptly. 'Since you're just good friends, maybe you ought to go to the wedding together.'

'I think not,' Piper objected, her voice tight.

And even though the logical part of Linc agreed, it didn't stop another part of him—a decidedly more primitive part—from wishing that maybe that could have been an option.

'Probie, I'm looking to convince my sister to stop setting me up with dates, not encourage her. All Piper and I do is quibble.'

'Yeah, like an old married couple.' Probie frowned, clearly not following. 'Just like Hugo said.'

'No,' Piper managed, just as the air desk jockey sauntered back in.

'Forgot my favourite pen.' Hugo paused mid-reach. 'Wait, what did I say before?'

Before Linc could change the subject, Probie had set it all out. But that didn't explain why Linc paused long enough for his old crewmate to answer, instead of shutting it down there and then.

'Might be a plan,' Hugo offered thoughtfully, before grabbing his pen and hurrying back out.

'No,' Piper repeated. *Stiffly,* Linc thought.

'I mean, you want your sister to back right off, don't you?' the crewman continued. 'And you two *do* act like you've got that something-something going on.'

'We most certainly do not.'

'Maybe not consciously.' Probie shrugged, refusing to back down. 'But it's there, all the same.'

'We've worked together before,' Piper repeated. 'Nothing more.'

And even though he knew the truth, Linc found he didn't want to actually hear her denying there had ever been anything between them.

'Enough, guys.' He thumped a coin onto the worktop as a distraction. 'Pool tournament. Who's taking me on first? Only ten pence a wager.'

'No chance. I lost a fiver to you last week, and we were only betting ten pence then,' Hugo scoffed. 'Besides, I have to get back to the phones.'

'I'll give you a game.' Tom stood with a dramatic sigh. 'If only to shut the pair of you up.'

'Suits me.' Throwing the rest of his coffee down his neck and snagging a second doughnut, Linc strode over to the pool table. Racking the balls, he shook his head as though to empty it of thoughts of Piper, and picked up a coin. He definitely needed the distraction.

'Call it,' he told Tom.

'Heads.'

Linc dutifully tossed the coin up and caught it.

'Heads it is. Your break.'

'No one's break, sorry, guys.' The door swung

back open as Hugo hurried in. 'A man's fallen off a ladder whilst trimming a hedge. The electric trimmers have made a partial cut through his upper arm. He's conscious but losing a fair amount of blood.'

# CHAPTER FIVE

LINC THRUST OPEN the door of the heli HQ with a sharp kick; the darned thing was sticking again. He made a mental note to repair it at some point in the day, but deep down he knew his sour mood was more to do with the text he'd just received than the door itself.

What was it about his usually fair-minded kid sister that was really pushing his buttons these days? That mile-wide obstinate streak that both amused and infuriated him, though not in equal measure. If he weren't so fond of her, he might have warned her fiancé that Sara was turning into the ultimate bridezilla, and to run for the proverbial hills.

But, for all her faults, he loved his sister to distraction. And his older brother for that matter. And if they were more concerned than he himself was with matters of appearance, and stature, then they were entitled to be. All he'd ever wanted in life was to be in the army, and to be a doctor, and he'd done both.

Ranulph—Raf—had been the one lumbered with the responsibility of primogeniture, as well as all the crushing responsibilities of their father whilst the old duke had been losing his mind to the cruel disease that was Alzheimer's.

Even Sara had played her part as the obedient daughter of a duke and duchess—despite the way their mother had undermined her own daughter, and scorned Sara's every choice her entire life. All because their mother had been jealous of her daughter's youth, and sharp intellect.

And none of that even came close to the horribly cruel bombshell their mother had dropped on Linc himself—from practically her death bed, as if she couldn't have been more dramatic. Finding out that his father was not the loving, kind-but-firm duke, but some playboy jockey who was as notorious for his women as he was for his racing wins, hadn't been the most grounding moment of Linc's life.

It had sent him hurtling from the family seat at Stoneywell for a start, joining the army and throwing himself into tours of duty as if he didn't care if he lived or died.

Back then, he *hadn't* cared.

But things were different now. His life felt more stable in the air ambulance. Still, returning to Oakenfeld for his sister's wedding wasn't something he was looking forward to.

Linc drew in a deep breath. Being the second male heir—if he could legitimately call himself that—unquestionably had its advantages, like ditching his title as Lord Lincoln Oakes, for a start. No one here knew who he really was, just as no one in the military ever had.

Not even Piper.

He was so caught up in his thoughts that the sound of a thump in the rec room caught him off guard.

'Who's there?' he barked out instantly, dropping his bag where he stood and striding down the hall, fists at the ready. 'You'd better give yourself up. I'll give you one chance.'

'Linc?'

The familiar, feminine voice punched straight through Linc. He lowered his fists and turned to retrieve his bag, and to catch his breath. It was one thing to act normally around Piper when the rest of the crew were there as a safety net...but the knowledge that it was just the two of them here now made things shift. Even the air seemed to grow thicker.

He pushed the thought away and strode into the room, frowning.

'You're here early. How did you get in? The door was still sticking when I unlocked it just now.'

'I came through the hangar.' She shrugged—slightly awkwardly, he thought. Or was that just his imagination? 'I wanted to just check on the heli. So, are you putting the coffee machine on?'

He eyed her briefly, but whatever he thought he'd seen was gone. It was definitely his imagination. He needed to get a grip. Piper had a way of slipping all too easily under his skin. He gritted his teeth and held up the shopping bag.

'I picked up a few ingredients from the local store on the way in.'

'Breakfast?'

And again, he wondered if he was reading things that weren't there when he thought that she perked up a little too much at the idea of food. As if she hadn't eaten recently... He knew the signs from the army—those lads who hadn't had a decent meal for days.

'Next time, it's your turn,' he said with a laugh, even as he watched her closely.

'Of course.' She dipped her head but though she did a good job of disguising it, there was something she was hiding.

'You want to start the mushrooms if I start the bacon?'

'Actually, I can't really...cook.' She wrinkled her nose.

'I didn't know that.' He eyed her in surprise. 'Then no time like the present to learn.'

And, under the threat of another wave of that thing he kept pretending didn't exist between them, Linc ducked into the kitchen just as there was another slam against the wall, signalling the arrival of more of their crew arriving early.

He really needed to remember to sort that door

out, too. Something about Piper's appearance this morning still bugged him.

'We've got an eighteen-year-old who has taken a tumble from height unknown at one of the waterfalls near Heathston Heights. He's responsive and breathing, but nothing else known for now. We need to get airborne now,' Linc declared, reaching for his helmet along with the rest of his team. 'We can be on our way to the grid until the exact location details come through.'

Racing out onto the tarmac, he wasn't surprised to see Piper already in the heli and starting her up.

'Strong winds today, guys,' Piper announced as she prepped to get the all-clear from the region's air traffic control. 'Good chance we'll be taking off sideways, so just keep alert for me, okay?'

Waiting long enough to ensure she was airborne and happy, Linc patched through to their HQ's air desk.

'Helimed hotel zero seven, any updates, over?'

'Negative, Helimed hotel one-niner, there are no land crews on scene yet, and the initial caller doesn't have much info, over.'

'We're going to need a better location,' Tom grumbled over the headset. 'Or we aren't going to know where to head to.'

'I could take a pass over the most popular waterfalls,' Piper suggested.

'Nothing to lose,' Linc agreed. 'I take it the

original caller is a kid who doesn't know which one they're at? Time's trauma and all that, so has to be worth a try.'

He peered out of the window as Piper dutifully took her first pass over.

'Anyone got visual?' she asked.

'Nothing yet,' Hugo denied.

'Nor here,' noted Linc. 'Wait, about two o'clock? Looks like something down there.'

Piper duly nosed the heli in the direction.

'Yeah, that looks like it. Nice spot.'

'A couple of kids are waving us down,' Tom added.

'There are power lines running just up from the river,' Piper noted grimly. 'But I can land in that field to the other side. Looks like a low wall for you to hop over, then a bit of a sprint, but nothing more.'

'Good call,' Linc agreed as Piper was already circling the heli around.

Quickly, smoothly, she landed it.

'Clear to go,' she confirmed as Linc and his two paramedics grabbed their gear and started moving.

It was a good call by Piper to try the pass over, Linc considered. He really ought to tell her that when they got back to base.

'All right, lads.' He turned his attention to the kids as they moved to greet the crew. 'I take it this is Bobbi? Can you tell me what happened, son?'

Squatting down next to the casualty, Linc began his preliminary observations. Although the lad was moving and making sound in response to Linc's questions, he wasn't making coherent replies.

It was going to be down to the kid's friends to piece together what they'd seen.

'He was climbing on that ridge.'

'No, he wasn't, he hadn't reached that ridge.'

'Wait, which ridge are we talking about?

Quickly, methodically, Linc worked with the group, until the land ambulance crew arrived on foot—their vehicle stuck a few hundred metres away in the car park.

'This is Bobbi, seventeen. About twenty-five minutes ago he took a tumble whilst climbing around the waterfall. He lost his grip and fell around twelve feet onto these jagged rocks down here.

'According to one of his mates, Bobbi was unconscious for around a minute, but he was awake and responsive by the time we arrived. He cites general pain around his lower back, towards his right-hand side, and some pins and needles in his right hand. Suspect spinal injuries, possibly T-Twelve fracture, and ideally I want to evacuate with the assistance of mountain rescue, using an inflatable mattress scoop. Bobbi's initially had morphine, but is still complaining of significant pain. We're about to administer ketamine.'

'You got here fast.' One of the land crew paramedics smiled grimly as she cast her eye over Linc's team. 'We couldn't even be sure which waterfall it was.'

'Yeah, it's definitely not easily accessible by road. You did well to get here,' Linc noted. 'We were lucky we got in scene within ten minutes of the call. Our pilot took a fly-by, and we happened to spot him.'

Linc thought of Piper and was surprised at the sensation that punched through him.

'You're taking him back with you guys?' the paramedic surmised.

Linc nodded at her.

'Affirmative. Once we get him on the scoop and into the heli, we'll alert the hospital that we're a few minutes out, and they can have a spinal team on standby. The sooner we get him into their hands, the better chance they've got of mending his broken back. But getting him out of here smoothly is going to be the biggest hurdle.'

The paramedic nodded. 'Should be easier with the six of us. You just tell us where you want us, and we'll do it.'

'That's the idea,' Linc agreed, returning to his patient for the last checks. 'Right, let's get things moving.'

Piper took her time last parading the heli, giving everyone time to leave. Almost getting caught by

Linc that morning had been too close; she needed to find somewhere else to stay. Time for another Internet search tonight.

If it hadn't been for Linc, she might have confided in the rest of crew hoping that one of them might know somewhere. But she didn't want to look weak...vulnerable in front of Linc. She wanted him to be as impressed with her as a Helimed pilot as he had been when she'd been an Apache pilot.

And it didn't matter how much she pretended not to know the reason for her pride, she was terribly afraid she knew precisely why it mattered to her.

Despite her bravado that it would be easy to set their attraction aside again, it was still there, sizzling between them. Only this time, now that they didn't have the rules and regulations of the army to shore up their defences, the pull was stronger than ever, and she had no idea how to snuff it out. She wasn't sure she even wanted to.

But she had to—there was nothing else for it.

Finally thinking she'd waited long enough, Piper poked her head through the door that connected the hangar with the crew area.

Blissful silence, and dark but for a small light someone had left on in one of the side rooms, spilling enough warm light into the corridor that she wouldn't stub her toe in the darkness, the way that she had done the night before.

Padding quietly down the hall, she slipped into the kitchen and flicked the radio on—the place was too deadly silent otherwise. Then she pulled the pot of ready-to-boil noodles from her bag. Hardly the most nourishing dinner, but it would have to do. It was better than the last couple of nights anyway, when she hadn't had anything. Reaching out, she flipped the switch on the boiling water tap.

'What exactly are you doing?'

Piper was fairly sure she leapt several feet into the air. She spun around, careful to stay in front of the offending pot of noodles, and her hand pressed to her chest as though that could somehow slow her racing heart.

Worse, she wasn't entirely sure it was purely down to the shock.

'Linc? I thought everyone had gone home.'

'Everyone else has,' he drawled. 'I had the last case report to complete. What's your excuse?'

She should have realised he was still here when she saw that light on down the hall.

'I was last parading the heli.'

Not entirely untrue, though she wasn't surprised when his eyebrows twitched sceptically.

'Just like you were checking it over before I arrived this morning?'

'You aren't the only one to take their job seriously.' She jutted her chin out defiantly.

His eyes narrowed.

'Are you sleeping here?'

'Of course not,' she blustered.

'You can't stay here overnight, Piper. This place isn't insured for that.'

'Good job I'm not, then.' She hadn't realised that. Oh, Lord, what was she to do now? Well, whatever it was, there was no need for Linc to know her predicament. 'Like I said, I was last parading the heli. Now I'm leaving.'

He leaned slightly to the side.

'So what are you trying to hide?'

'Not sure I'm following?'

'You've never been a great liar, Legs.'

Funny, but coming from Linc it sounded more like a criticism than a compliment. She frowned but suddenly, he was right in front of her, reaching around her for the packet. But she couldn't breathe, she certainly couldn't think. But then they were kissing, and she had no idea who had moved first but she was terribly afraid it had been her.

And he tasted every bit as magic as he had the last time. Every bit as addictive. Every bit as thrilling.

It was more than a shock when he tore his mouth from hers and set her away from him.

'Is this your idea of distracting me?' he growled. 'I must say, it's quite effective, you almost had me. Almost.'

She could admit that it wasn't a distraction at

all, and that the kiss had caught her off guard just as it had done with him.

Somehow, she didn't think Linc would believe her.

'Can't blame a girl for trying,' she made herself quip instead.

But it only earned her a narrowed gaze.

'You're eating here, and you're sleeping here,' he bit out. 'Why? What happened to the hotel?'

Piper dug her fingernails into her palm, silently praying for one last distraction to save her from having to admit her failings to Lincoln Oakes, of all people.

'Turns out it was just for those first few days,' she ground out eventually, 'because of the lack of notice. But once they flew me back to barracks for those couple of days' downtime, they expected me to drive down from there.'

'Every day?' he scoffed. 'It's a one-hundred-and-sixty-mile round trip.'

'It's just over an hour each way on the motorway at that time of day.' She shrugged. 'Plenty of people have to do that kind of commute in the non-army world, so I understand.'

'That's ridiculous. You couldn't just stay in the hotel?'

'Did you see the rates of that place?' She forced a laugh, hating the way he was looking at her.

As if she couldn't organise herself.

Or perhaps she was just projecting.

'Somewhere else, then?' he demanded. 'It might not be the biggest town but there are at least a couple of other places I can think of that are still decent.'

'I tried them both,' she admitted. 'Apparently there's some kind of expo going on at the moment and they're both booked out. So are the affordable but decent places further afield.'

'Oh, right.' He thought for a moment. 'Local B & Bs? There are some good ones.'

'Again, booked out, or astronomically priced.'

'There have to be some inexpensive but decent places a little further afield.'

'Only if I go about an hour out, and if I'm doing that then I might as well drive back to barracks. Otherwise, just whilst the expo is on, they're all outside my budget.'

'Your budget? You're a pilot, you can't exactly be hard up for cash.'

Piper fought down a rumble of emotion. Frustration, guilt, and a couple of others that she didn't care to admit.

'The Air Corps don't exactly pay commercial pilot rates. You know that.'

'Still, it's good pay.'

It was, she had to admit that. Reluctantly, Piper nodded.

'Yeah, okay, it's good enough. But it…isn't all mine.'

He narrowed his eyes at her again.

'You send it home, don't you? To your mother? That's why you joined the army when your father died, so that you could look after her?'

How could he possibly read her so easily? She hated it.

And, at the same time, it was something of a relief.

'My brother was a baby at the time,' she blurted out. 'Mum couldn't possibly cover the mortgage, and the household bills, and the cost of a baby on her own, though she'd always worked.'

'I'm not criticising her, Piper,' Linc said quietly. 'Or you.'

She swallowed. No, he hadn't been criticising anyone. And yet she'd taken it as such all the same—which probably revealed a good deal too much about her more than it did about Linc.

'Right. I know that.'

His expression shifted.

'Your brother was about seven when we last served together, right? He'd be about twelve now?'

'Yes, twelve,' she confirmed, marvelling that he'd remembered such a small detail. 'He's at secondary school.'

'And your mum doesn't work?'

'She does,' Piper countered. 'She took a job years ago as a dinner lady in his old primary school so that she could be there for him before and after school, but it doesn't pay that much and there's no work in the holidays.'

If it weren't for the fact that they needed to protect the young kid from the truth about his dad's death for as long as possible, maybe her mother could have got a better job and paid for afterschool care. He might only have been a baby when his father had attacked their mother, but who knew what a baby remembered, or later tried to process?

Little wonder that her mother had always wanted to be there for her brother, to make sure he stayed on the right path, and didn't fall in with a poor crowd. The kid was completely innocent and he deserved a normal childhood—and that was what she and her mother had always tried to give him.

Besides, none of that was what took the bulk of her money. But there was absolutely no way that she was going to tell the former Major Lincoln Oakes that in those final months before his death, her father had managed to rack up over-six-figure debt—borrowing more and more each month from a loan shark, just so that he didn't have to admit to anyone that he'd lost his job and couldn't get another one.

She and her mother had been paying him back for over a decade now, and they were almost clear. Almost free. She could practically taste it.

The moment they were released from that dark cloud would be the moment her entire family could finally start afresh.

But every penny she had to pay for some overpriced hotel was a penny they didn't have for the debt collectors. And that was something she couldn't just accept.

'So you're sleeping here because the journey back to barracks is ridiculously long, and you can't afford a hotel,' he summarised.

Her cheeks burned hotter, but what other option was there than to tell the truth? It wasn't as though she could bluff it—he was too sharp to believe any excuses. She splayed her hands out in front of her.

'Only because prices are high whilst this conference is on. I can't eat into what little they have. My brother's a nearly teenager, and aside from the household bills, there are all kinds of school bills now. Uniform, sports kit, field trips. Not to mention the fact that, as a boy, he could easily eat us out of house and home. He eats more than I've ever eaten—by a mile.'

'Yeah.' Linc grinned abruptly. 'I remember what my brother and I were like at that age. Still are now, to be fair. We'd inhale in one day what Sara would have eaten in a week. I remember after one full-on rugby tournament, we came home and ate a box of cereal each, and each with a litre of milk. Then a roast chicken and a loaf of bread between the two of us. Then we started on the cake that the cook had been baking for our father's birthday.'

'You had a cook?' Piper's eyebrows shot up to her hairline, and Linc could have kicked himself.

'My mother was terrible in the kitchen,' he covered as smoothly as he could.

It wasn't a complete lie, but it wasn't exactly the truth, either. Oakenfeld Hall had three cooks—the formidable Mrs Marlston, and her two very capable assistant cooks. But the woman had been more of a mother figure to him and to Raf, especially, than their own mother ever had.

Still, Linc kept all that information firmly to himself.

'So what are you going to do now you're leaving the Air Corps?'

'Hopefully I can get a steady gig. Otherwise I'll be a freelance pilot.'

'Meaning if you don't fly then you don't earn,' he noted.

She didn't answer.

'So are you going for Albert's job permanently? You know he's leaving, don't you?'

Linc wasn't sure what he thought about that. The idea of Piper being around permanently wasn't exactly an unpleasant one—far from it. But it would mean that those lines they'd drawn would have to stay in place for good.

Which, he told himself firmly, was absolutely fine by him.

'Actually, I was going for the position of pilot

for the Helimed across the border in the county over.'

'Which one?' he asked, curious despite himself.

She wrinkled her nose at him, as though weighing up whether to answer. It was almost comical. *Almost*.

'West Nessleton Helimed,' she admitted at last. 'It's closer to my mum, and my brother. This temporary placement here kind of fell into my lap. A good hearts and minds role between the AAC and the community, plus it's hardly worth sending me on a training exercise when I'm leaving.'

'And you still need to keep your flying hours up,' Linc realised. 'I fully empathise, truly. But you can't stay here, Piper. Like I said, the insurance simply doesn't cover it and I can't risk this entire base just for one person. Even for you.'

'I know.' She nodded furiously. 'I'll pack my things.'

There was a beat of hesitation.

'Where will you go?'

She squeezed her eyes closed, trying not to think of her mother or her brother. Or the fact that the boiler still needed replacing before winter set in. And of course the newer models meant that it couldn't be swapped like for like, so it would need to be sited somewhere else in the house; which meant floors lifted, new piping laid, and ceilings torn down.

It never seemed to be an easy job, and it always seemed to cost far more than it should.

Carefully, determinedly, she schooled her features so that none of this showed, and instead shot Linc her breeziest smile.

'Like you said, there are some inexpensive B & Bs a little further afield. I'll try them.'

For all his sternness, he looked back at her with concern.

'And your mother?'

'She'll understand.'

And she would. Her mother was always worrying whether she could afford to be sending them so much, as well as paying the mortgage, and most of the bills. It was one of the main reasons why Piper wished she didn't have to worry her at all.

Hastily, she began stuffing all her belongings back into her rucksack. Maybe she could sleep in her car instead. At least that way, she wouldn't have to let her family down. Shrugging her leather jacket on and throwing her bag over her shoulder, Piper headed out to look for Linc.

'Okay, I'm going.' She ducked her head around the door to the office, but he wasn't there.

He probably didn't want to hear anything more from her tonight anyway. She'd be better slipping out quietly, and in the morning they didn't have to discuss it at all.

She was halfway along the corridor when Linc appeared at the door of the kitchen, her noodles dinner in his hand and a distinctly unimpressed expression tugging at his features.

'Are you forgetting something? This was what you were going to eat?'

'Oh, thanks,' she muttered, not bothering to answer the question itself—what would be the point?

She stretched out her hand to take it, but he dropped it unceremoniously in the bin beside him.

'You aren't serious? You can't live on that.'

'Don't...' Piper gaped at the bin in dismay. 'That's all I've got. And I don't live on it. You made a full breakfast this morning, for a start.'

She hesitated, torn between needing the unopened pot, and not wanted to let him see her take it out of the bin. He skewered her with a look.

'You aren't honestly debating whether or not to go dumpster-diving, are you?'

Heat bloomed in her cheeks anew.

'Of course not.'

'And you're still a bad liar.'

'Fine.' She snorted. 'But it's hardly a dumpster. It's the kitchen bin, and I know for a fact that it was cleaned out at the end of the shift so there'll be nothing in there but my unopened pot.'

'Stop.' He shook his head, slamming the light off and stepping out in the hall so decisively that she almost stumbled in her effort to back up. 'I don't need to hear any more. You can come home with me.'

'What?' It felt as if all the air had been sucked

out of her lungs in a single instant. 'No. That's ridiculous.'

'No more ridiculous than what I've heard tonight,' Linc growled. 'You're camping on the couch and living off packet noodles, meanwhile I have a two-bed apartment, and a fridge full of fresh food.'

'I'm not staying with you.' She shook her head, horrified. 'I can't.'

Though whether at the idea of it, or at the way her body was reacting so entirely inappropriately, she couldn't be sure.

'Don't be a martyr, Piper,' he rasped. 'You can't stay here, and you clearly don't have much money if you're trying to support your mother and brother. The bedrooms at my place are opposite ends of the apartment, and we'll be here much of the time. You can stay just until the landlord has sorted your own place.'

She wanted to object, to politely decline. The idea of being in such close proximity to Linc seemed like a terrible one. Not to mention the wound it inflicted on her pride, having to rely on him like this.

But pride was no match for the crushing weight of responsibility. There was no doubt that even if she paid Linc something towards her stay, a week with him would be a lot cheaper than a week in a hotel. Especially around here.

Without doubt, her mother could use that money a handful of times over.

'Okay.' She nodded at last, stuffing back her unwanted sense of pride. 'Thank you. It would really help my family.'

And she pretended to herself that there wasn't a single part of her that was being tempted by entirely un-practical motives.

Not one single part of her, at all.

# CHAPTER SIX

LINC HAD NO idea what he was doing. He'd invited her to his apartment…to *live* with him. Temporary or not, it had to be the most insane suggestion he'd ever made. The veneer of professionalism had well and truly slipped.

He could dress it up in the excuse that he was doing a good turn for a colleague in need, but the reality was that he found the idea of her actually being here…*thrilling*.

And wasn't that a concern all in itself?

He watched from the kitchen as she made her way around the living area, taking in his apartment's open-plan layout, double-height ceilings, and full-height windows on three sides, and he found he actually cared what she thought of it.

Not that he was going to tell her that he'd designed it himself—or that his family business had built several of the striking, sleek, glass and steel tower blocks in this area of the city. Yet still, he couldn't help wondering whether it was something that she liked.

He couldn't explain why her opinion mattered.

'When you said apartment, you didn't say it was a penthouse that covered the entire floor,' she muttered, after a long moment.

'Does it matter?'

She turned to look at him, wrinkling her nose, but she didn't answer.

'Some warning might have been nice.'

'Why? What would it have changed?' he asked easily. 'You needed a place to stay, and I have a spare room.'

She glowered at him but still didn't answer. It was crazy how much of a kick her little show of defiance caused in him. A return to the confident, fiery Piper he'd once known, instead of this smaller version of herself that he'd been beginning to see around the heli base.

'Why does it bother you so much, Legs?' he asked her, without warning. As if the nickname could ground them again.

She cast him a dark look.

'It doesn't.'

'That's clearly a lie.'

Piper chewed on the inside of her lip for a moment. Then shrugged.

'Do any of the crew know you live like some kind of millionaire?'

'Hardly,' he replied tightly. 'But no, the subject has never come up.'

'Just as it never did in the army?' she challenged. 'I think you deliberately hide this side of your life.'

'Like you hiding the fact that you've been supporting your family all this time?' He tried turning the tables, but all she did was lift one delicate shoulder.

'Something like that.'

A simple admission that reminded him there was more to Piper that he didn't know—and that roused his curiosity far more than it had any right to. They eyed each other, almost warily.

Still, now wasn't the time.

'Perhaps I should show you to your room?' he suggested instead.

She spun around a little too quickly, a telltale ragged pulse beating at her throat. He tried not to notice the way her pupils dilated, turning her amber eyes a much darker shade, or the slight flaring of her nostrils that betrayed her.

Responses that were all so deliciously…base—despite all their drawing lines in the sand. And Linc knew he shouldn't feel that punch of triumph—but it reverberated through him all the same.

But that didn't mean he was about to give in to such temptation.

Without waiting for her to catch up to him, he stepped from the open area to the hallway and strode along the plush corridor to the left. Dutifully, Piper followed him.

'Guest suite is down that way.'

'And…your master suite.'

'Back up on the other side of the living area,' he assured her. 'Just like I promised.'

'Right,' she managed, clearly a little shocked. 'This place is incredible.'

Something pulled in his chest at the unexpected note of self-censure in her voice. As though she felt she'd failed in some way.

'I've been here a while.'

'Whilst I can't even afford a hotel room right now.' She shook her head.

Guilt stabbed through him. Clearly their very different circumstances were some sort of deep-seated issue for Piper that he'd never quite appreciated before now.

'It's no failing, Piper. For a start, doctors get paid more than pilots in the military, we both know that,' he noted. 'At least at our respective levels.'

'I understand that...' She bit her lip again. And he hated that she somehow thought less of herself.

But he could hardly tell her who he really was. Linc cleared his throat, searching for an easy way to explain it away.

'I've also made money by dabbling in the stock markets. It's a bit of a hobby.'

Which was true enough. He was good at it too; it was a hobby the duke had taught him as a child on his knee.

'I wouldn't even know where to start with stock markets.' She shook her head. 'I never realised how very...different we are.'

And he knew as soon as she said it that she

hadn't meant for that to come out, even if he couldn't fathom why this all seemed to matter so much to her. Why, at least in her mind, she was drawing a division between them. Why she was highlighting the differences between them, and using that as an excuse to keep their distance from each other.

He found that it was his *not understanding* that rankled so much, and it occurred to him that distance was the last thing he wanted from this woman.

What the hell was wrong with him?

'Not so different.' Linc shrugged, deliberately playing it down. 'You learned to fly helis as a seventeen-year-old, around your family estate, did you not?' Although come to think of it, if that was the case, what had happened to that estate?

She eyed him oddly, and he had the distinct impression that there was a war going on in her head.

'No, I didn't, actually.'

'Oh?' He frowned. 'I thought I heard it mentioned back on that last tour of duty.'

'The two other female pilots on that tour had learned that way. And, given how every other pilot in the entire corps were men, they assumed I'd learned that way too. I stood out enough without telling them I wasn't a product of boarding school or super-rich parents, so it was easier just to let them think that I was like the other two females.'

'It was about fitting in?'

Even as he said it, a few other pieces of the puzzle he hadn't realised he'd started began to fall into place.

The way she'd always kept herself to herself; the way she'd never quite looked comfortable socialising with some of her peer group.

Had the military been an escape for Piper the way it had been for him—albeit for different reasons? She'd been running away from who she was, whilst he'd been running away from who he wasn't. As ironic as that was.

After his mother had pulled the proverbial rug from under him, he'd lost his identity. Joining the military as a doctor had given him back a sense of purpose, and a sense of worth. If it had somehow done the same for Piper, then no wonder they'd always felt that pull towards each other.

But wasn't that all the more reason to keep that proverbial line between them?

'Go and settle in,' he advised, not quite recognising the rasp in his own voice. 'Freshen up, get some sleep, whatever you need. Help yourself to anything in the kitchen. Tomorrow night I'll cook for us.'

And maybe they could finally find a way to be more comfortable around each other. Before the entire crew began to think there was more going on than there actually was.

\* \* \*

Piper closed the door behind her and leaned against it, her hand moving instinctively to her ribcage as though she could slow down her racing heart. It felt as though it was going at about Mach 10, and she knew it couldn't handle the G-forces.

She'd never been able to handle her attraction to Linc; it was one of the reasons she'd been so firm about drawing that professional line between them, five years ago.

Yet it had been easier to do back then, on a tour of duty, with all the military rules and protocols. Now, by contrast, the only rules, the only boundaries, were self-imposed. And it was getting harder and harder to enforce them. She was terribly afraid that here, in such close proximity with no colleagues as buffers, that invisible line was going to disappear altogether.

Worse, she wanted it to.

Pushing back off the door, Piper took a step into the space. Belatedly, she realised that she wasn't standing in a bedroom, she was standing in a private living room. A generous space with a couch, and an antique study desk, and a breathtaking view of the city below occupying one wall. Solid doors occupied the other three walls, the double set she'd entered through, and opposite was another double set. Carefully—as if she were afraid she might intrude on a stranger in the space—she padded around.

The two single doors opened up on a bathroom and a dressing room that were each probably the size of the main bedroom in the terraced house she'd bought for her mother. She doubted her entire wardrobe would have filled even one of the bespoke cabinets in the dressing room, whilst the travertine-tiled bathroom was like something out of a high-end, glossy hotel brochure.

She eyed the enormous bathtub—clearly designed for couples—and wondered whoever had the time for a bath. Growing up in her childhood home, and then in the military, showers had been de rigueur, and she'd never really missed the long soak that so many other women seemed to enjoy.

Now, however, the bath seemed to call to her. Piper moved falteringly forward, flipping the taps and watching a stream of hot, inviting water flow out. A peek into a small basket on the honed, polished counter top revealed a selection of spa products, and she selected one at random and dropped it almost nervously into the bath. The scent was instantly relaxing.

Feeling a little more confident, she made her way back through the room, piling her hair onto her head and snagging it into place. And then she allowed herself a little flourish as she pushed open the set of double doors that surely had to lead to the bedroom.

Her breath actually caught in her throat.

The room itself was the size of an entire floor

of her house. It had walls, a floor and a ceiling, but the similarities ended there. A huge bank of windows flooded the room with light, making it feel even more spacious and inviting. It took her a moment to realise that a set of patio doors led onto a wide balcony with gleaming oak wood decking, and a sleek metal and glass balustrade that offered tantalising views of the city beyond.

Piper stepped outside on autopilot, drawn to the spectacular sight. Like a carpet of land right at her feet. It made her feel free and powerful being up here and looking down on the city. As if she could do anything, conquer anything.

No wonder Linc loved it up here.

More than that, it allowed her to feel so far removed from her ordinary life that she could almost imagine she was a different person. Not herself. Without thinking, she followed the balustrade as it ran around the outside, lured by the sights as well as by the warm afternoon sun.

Then, tilting her face up towards it, the brightness making up for the lack of summer heat, Piper spread her hands out on the smooth wooden balcony rail and inhaled deeply.

*Perfect relaxation.*

'I assume you do know that you're outside my bedroom?'

The dry voice had her spinning around in an instant, fumbling for her words.

'What? Oh...no.'

Piper stopped dead. Linc was wearing nothing more than a pristine white towel around his waist, and his hair was slick, evidently from a shower. And everything become a hundred times worse. That hypersonic boom in her chest reverberating loudly—too loudly—in her head.

She couldn't seem to peel her eyes from the solid wall of his body, no matter how fiercely her brain screamed at her that she should. She'd always known he was muscled, the way his clothes had always clung so lovingly to him—from his army combats to his flight suit—had made that clear, but to see him in the flesh, naked, was a whole different ball game.

Like staring at the model for one of the great classical sculptures. A study in sheer masculinity.

Piper swallowed hard, desperately scrambling for something, anything, to say.

'You got a shower,' she managed to choke out at length.

Well, *accuse*, really. As though he didn't have the right to do what he liked in his own home.

'I did,' Linc agreed. 'I'd imagine you'd want to do the same, after a day like today.'

'I do.' She nodded, a little emphatically. 'That is, I usually do. But I saw that bath and I thought… I mean, it's clearly a bath for two.'

If the balcony had crashed under her feet and plummeted her down to ground level, she didn't think she'd have minded. In fact, she would probably have welcomed it. Wincing, she chanced a glance at Linc. Sure enough, he looked stony-faced.

'I mean... I didn't...' She felt more flustered than she thought she'd ever felt in her life. 'That wasn't supposed to sound like...'

'An invitation for me to join you?' he finished for her—grimly, she thought. 'No, I didn't imagine that it was.'

'Of course not,' she managed.

*Liar,* whispered that traitorous part of her body that was already starting to go molten at the mere suggestion.

'I don't normally indulge in baths, you understand.' Her mouth kept talking and she couldn't seem to stop it. 'I know it's probably not environmentally friendly...and sharing a bath is probably better in that sense...'

She tailed off awkwardly as Linc looked all the more pained.

'I think...perhaps...' She struggled to work her jaw. 'I think I should go to bed. It has been a long day, and the past few nights haven't been the most restful.'

'Then I hope you enjoy a relaxing bath,' he managed tightly. Gruffly.

'Yes. I...ought to get back to it.'

Evidently, this proximity to a practically naked Linc was frying her brain in a way that was more than a little embarrassing.

'I think that's for the best,' he rumbled as Piper grasped at the excuse to leave.

It was crazy how out of control she felt here, alone with him. With no military and no Helimed to act as a buffer, she felt fairly certain she was perilously close to losing her mind.

Either that, or she would lose every shred of her dignity, throwing herself at Linc the way she didn't seem to be able to stop herself.

Even as she scurried along the balcony, his low, rumbling voice seemed to chase her all the way back into her suite. And it didn't matter how firmly she slid the glass doors closed, it couldn't keep out that heavy ache in her chest. And lower, if she was going to be honest.

Swinging the bathroom door closed, then locking it, Piper hauled off her clothes and proceeded to drop them unceremoniously into the woven basket she always used as a laundry bag. The one that her mother had made for her before her first ever tour of duty. The one that, no matter where Piper was, always made her feel like home. Then, at last, she turned off the taps, stepped into the oversized tub and slid blissfully beneath the water, lying back and finally closing her eyes.

Slowly, slowly, the water lapped soothingly over her skin as the heat eased away the tensions of the day. Without warning, images of Linc exploring her body flew into her brain.

With a start, she lurched forward in the bath,

making the water slosh precariously up the sloped sides. She ought to be embarrassed, having such sinful thoughts about the man.

Instead, she couldn't seem to stop them.

Reaching for the loofah she'd already set out on the side, she began to scrub crossly at her skin.

Linc was spoiling everything. Being alone with him was definitely very different from working with him, and coming here had been a mistake, she told herself furiously.

So why didn't the rest of her body seem to believe that one bit?

# CHAPTER SEVEN

Piper was running through her pre-flight checklist the next morning and flushing the engine compressor section with de-ionised water, when Linc entered the hangar. And before she could stop it, her chest leapt in some kind of misplaced anticipation.

'I feel perhaps that I owe you an apology,' he declared without preamble. 'For last night.'

'Shh.' Automatically she glanced around the empty space before taking a step towards him.

*A mistake*, she realised instantly.

That stony look threatened his face again, and she tried not to take it as a kind of unspoken rejection.

'There's no one here, Piper. They're all in the crew room, or rec room, I checked.'

'Of course you did.' She scrunched up her nose.

'Listen, I offered you a place to stay because I wanted to help. I apologise if I made you feel awkward, or uncomfortable in any way.'

'You didn't,' she replied quickly.

She'd done that all by herself—by having such wholly inappropriate thoughts about him.

'Well, I hope that's true.' He inclined his head.

'I want you to feel you can relax. And stay as long as you need to.'

'Thank you,' Piper managed, fighting the urge to run her tongue all over her suddenly parched mouth.

No doubt Linc intended to be kind. Chivalrous. But, crazily, that only made him all the more appealing to her. Somehow it was easier to resist Linc when he was being a devilish playboy, rather than this solicitous, softer man.

*Easier to resist?* a voice mocked in her head. And that fraught knot in her stomach pulled tighter.

'I also wanted you to know that I'm going out tonight. So you'll have the place to yourself, just in case that makes things easier.'

It didn't. Not at all. Something sliced through Piper and she told herself it couldn't possibly be jealousy.

Definitely not.

'Thank you for letting me know,' she managed stiffly, instead. 'Should I…?'

She stopped abruptly, hating herself for caring where he was going. Or who with.

Linc frowned at her.

'Should you…?'

It would be better to shake it off and make some kind of joke. But Piper found she couldn't. She needed to know.

'Should I make myself scarce? In the morning? In case they think we're...'

He eyed her incredulously.

'I'm not going on a date, if that's what you think.'

'Oh.' She forced herself to sound casual. 'Well, okay, but, for the record, I don't expect you to curtail your private life. It isn't any of my business, and I don't care either way.'

He skewered her with the intensity of his gaze, and she forgot how to breathe.

And then, without warning, he took a step towards her.

'Do you really not care?' he murmured, moving his face closer to hers.

So close that she could feel his warm breath caressing her cheek, and it was all she could do to fight some ridiculous impulse to lean forwards and press her lips to his.

'Not at all.'

Maybe she would have sounded more convincing if her voice hadn't cracked, right at that moment. Fire burned in her cheeks, then spread over every inch of her skin. And still, she couldn't move.

'You lie like a cheap NAAFI watch,' he muttered suddenly.

'I'm not lying,' she croaked before snapping her mouth shut.

She feared she revealed more and more of herself with every unguarded thing she uttered.

'For what it's worth,' Linc drawled slowly, 'I'm meeting my sister. She's flying in tonight and we're having dinner to talk about what she expects of me for her wedding. So, no date. Not that that matters to you, I know.'

'I see,' she managed, and she hated herself for the way her heart soared at his words. 'But it still isn't my business.'

'True, but still, now you know,' he murmured before turning to head for the doors. 'I'll get back before anyone comes looking for me and finds me here.'

'Thank you,' she gritted out.

'Unless you want me to be your second for the two-person checks?'

There was another kick in her ribcage.

As the critical care doctor, Linc wasn't the designated data pilot, and therefore no one could reasonably expect him to run through the checks with her. Offering to be the stand-in now would certainly give them a legitimate excuse to be in here together for a little longer. But she really shouldn't read into the fact that he was offering to do so.

Was it a test? If she really didn't care where he went or who he dated, should she say she'd wait for the data pilot and tell him to leave?

'Well, you do happen to be here now,' she heard herself reply instead. 'And the sooner this thing is first paraded, the sooner she's ready for any shout.'

She could pretend it was about practicality all she liked, she suspected they both knew the truth. Still, picking up the digital notepad, Piper cast her eye over the stats for the heli.

'It won't hurt to just give a final check to the bowsers outside, either,' she told him. 'With the charity day coming up, and several longer-distance flights to get to events, we should ensure they have enough fuel of their own if we can't access the airport's main supply for any reason.'

'Good plan,' he agreed. 'Then we should probably also check the medical supplies, since we're both here.'

'Probably.'

And what did it say that the idea of being alone with Linc, with the safety net of work, seemed more than a little appealing?

For the next half-hour or so, they worked quickly and efficiently together, prepping the supplies and kit for the shift ahead. The easy banter between them seeping back in as the work tasks diluted the tension that had been building around them. It was a welcome breather.

They were about five minutes from the official shift start, and about to head over for a mug of tea, when the red phone sounded across the base. Hugo raced over a few moments later to pass on the details.

A twelve-year-old who had been thrown from her horse on a stretch of narrow country lane.

'We're good to go,' Piper acknowledged, grabbing her helmet and heading out onto the tarmac to get her heli started.

Within moments Tom had joined her, pulling up the map and punching in the grid reference, passing on the location details that had initially been transmitted.

'You're all clear for lift, Helimed hotel one-niner,' the ATC voice crackled over the headset.

'Thanks,' Piper acknowledged as she got her bird into the sky before banking sharply.

'I'd suggest following the main A road up to the supermarket roundabout, then follow the country land from there,' Linc's voice came over through her headset. 'This is the third accident in the same location this year—usually the drivers were morning commuters taking a short cut to bypass traffic on the motorway. They hurtle along the country road, don't observe the speed limit drop from sixty to twenty on this particular section where there are several sets of stables and a dairy farm, and end up screeching their tyres trying to stop when they round the bend to find a herd of cows crossing the road, or horses just coming off the end of the bridleway.'

'That's going to spook the animals,' Piper noted grimly, duly turning the nose to follow the A road. 'You know the best place to land, too?'

'Yeah, there's a field just to the left as we head to location. Albert usually lands there, and there's a decent gap in the wall, so it's easy enough to get out, as well as bring the patient back through.'

'Sold,' she confirmed, concentrating on getting them there quickly as the radio crackled again.

'This is hotel zero seven, we have an update on the casualty,' Hugo's voice told them. 'Twelve-year-old female was thrown from her horse. Landed on the undergrowth and was unconscious for about a minute. She has been confused ever since. No other injuries reported.'

'Update received, out,' Linc acknowledged, addressing his team as Hugo ended the update. 'We'll check her over head-to-toe anyway, of course, but it seems we're looking at assessing whether she's suffering from simple concussion or extradural haematoma.'

'I'll get the heli as close as possible,' Piper assured him. 'In case you need to get the casualty to a major trauma unit as quickly as possible. We're coming up on the location now.'

Bringing the heli around, she looked for the field Linc had mentioned.

*Damn.*

'It's a no-go for the landing,' she told him. 'There are livestock in the field.'

'Hell. They're usually in the area on the other side of the road.'

Piper cast her eye over in that direction.

'Well, one of those fields is clear, but the overhead wires on that side of the road are going to push us to the back corner.'

'Anyone see an exit point?' Linc asked quickly.

'Nothing on the left,' Tom advised after a moment. 'What about you, Probie?'

'I think there's a gate at the bottom corner of the field,' Probie advised carefully. 'Yes... I'm sure there is.'

'Good eye, Probie,' Linc's voice agreed after a moment. 'There's a gate leading to a dirt track which joins the country lane itself. Wait a moment...yeah, there's someone running over that way now, waving. Land here, Piper. You're clear on the tail.'

'Left is good,' Tom agreed, as Probie chimed in that the right side was also clear.

Slowly bringing the heli down, Piper nosed down the field before finally letting the skids touch the ground.

'You're as close as I can get,' she told them, as the team all started to move. 'But if you need me to move, just let me know.'

Then they were gone, and all she could do was sit. And wait.

Linc's mind was still on that last shout as he pulled on his shirt later that evening.

By the nature of what the air ambulance did, they were usually only called to serious cases, and his time with the army had exposed him to any number of horrific injuries. But cases involving kids were always worse.

Seeing such young patients—whose whole lives should be ahead of them—suffering life-changing injuries could be almost unbearable sometimes. Especially when, like that last shout, there had actually been nothing more for his team to do than to load the girl onto the heli and get her to hospital for the right scans.

The kid might not have had any external injuries that he and his team could patch up and help to heal, but it had been clear from her constant confusion that she'd suffered some kind of brain injury despite her riding helmet. And his team could do nothing about a head injury except get her to a major trauma unit as quickly as they could.

He hated that sense of helplessness. That feeling of not being able to *do* something to change the situation.

And now he was supposed to go out and enjoy an evening with his sister, albeit also endure her inevitable reprimands, as though everything were fine. Yet tonight was one of those nights when all he really wanted to do was stay here and maybe hit his home gym. Anything to expend the fraught feeling—the sense of frustration—that was slamming around inside him like a ball on a squash court.

But he had to go. He'd already delayed it to try to get his head back to reality, but he had to go. It was part of his responsibility to his family, to his sister. Hauling open his door, he stalked down the hall, picking up his mobile from the hall stand where he'd dropped it, and had his hand on the penthouse door when Piper emerged from her end of the hallway.

Linc dropped his hand without even meaning to.

Clad only in a short dressing gown that revealed acres of mouthwatering skin and offered yet more proof of why the nickname *Legs* was perfect for her, she sauntered up the corridor, her nose so buried in a book that she hadn't even noticed him.

His body reacted instantly. Viscerally.

As though it were traitorously exempt from whatever practical, cerebral agreement he and Piper had come to concerning not crossing any professional boundaries. Surely no red-blooded male could have failed to respond to the glorious sight of Piper? Though perhaps he would have fought his body's instinct a little harder had a part of him not welcomed the fact that it distracted from the sense of frustration he'd been feeling after the shout.

Piper was closer now, and still she hadn't noticed him. Dimly, he thought he ought to say something, or make a noise to alert her to his presence. But when he did, he barely recognised his own voice.

'Piper?'

She stopped short, the shock evident in her expression.

Her hair still wet and slick from the shower, her bare feet with the delicately painted pink toenails that he would never have believed if he weren't seeing them now.

The last thing Piper had ever seemed to him was soft, or pink—he found he rather liked seeing this unexpected softer side of her.

'I thought you were out,' she accused tightly, visibly swallowing.

He moved and her eyes dropped instantly to the small open V at the top of his shirt, and her tongue flicked out wickedly over her plump lips.

Rather as if she couldn't stop herself.

He felt a kick somewhere in his gut, revelling in the way she seemed to have to fight herself to lift her gaze back to his face.

'You're supposed to be at dinner by now,' she continued, in a strangled voice.

And he revelled in that, too.

'Not for about an hour. After the last shout, I called Sara and pushed the time back.'

Her expression grew pained, but her darkening pupils betrayed her. He knew women well enough to know that look. Moreover, he knew Piper well enough to know that look.

'You didn't tell me,' she accused. But hoarsely.

He couldn't help teasing her.

'And miss the show?' he rasped, his eyes sweeping slowly over her before he could stop himself.

He was rewarded instantly when her nipples tightened visibly beneath the soft fabric of the dressing gown, like a scorching lick of heat over the hardest part of himself. Even as his brain bellowed at him to back away—to maintain that divide between them—a far more base, more carnal sound roared through his body. And the longer he sinfully indulged in her, the more that fraught knot in his gut began to slip undone.

The devil on his shoulder whispered how easy it would be to call his sister and cancel their meeting altogether just to stay here with Piper so they could make their own entertainment.

His head filled all too easily with images of her wrapped around his body. Not to mention those tantalising glimpses of soft skin that kept peeking out from beneath the collar of her silky dressing gown.

As if reading his mind, she clutched it a little closer to preserve her modesty. But those darkening eyes, that ragged breathing, told a different story.

'I was planning on getting something to eat and going to bed early.' She managed to sound prim yet sexy all at the same time.

A true skill, Linc rather thought. He took a step towards her, and watched that pulse flutter manically at the base of her neck.

Crying out to him.

'That sounds like a wise idea,' he ground out. 'I would do the same if I could.'

'You're going out.' Piper's voice was hoarse.

'I am,' he acknowledged, battling the urge to take another step towards her.

He succeeded. But that didn't mean he was ready to take a step towards the door.

'It was a difficult day,' she murmured, after a moment.

'It was.'

'Do you think the kid will be okay?'

'I hope so,' he muttered. 'I hope she regains her memory quickly.'

'Sometimes, it's easy to forget how short life can be.'

'And get caught up in the rules?' His gaze held hers. 'The idea of what's right, or what's appropriate?'

'I guess…that's what I'm saying.' She hesitated, and he tried to quash the sense of victory that rolled towards him.

'Do you want me to stay?' he demanded, the rasp in his tone seeming to echo around the room.

Her eyes darkened and she moved one single step in his direction before seeming to stop herself.

'I…your sister is waiting.'

And he tried to cling onto the logical, practical argument that said they should keep their distance, but there was no quashing his triumph this time. It punched through him. Loud, and vibrant.

'How tempted are you?' he heard himself demand.

'Who says I'm tempted?' she replied on a choppy whisper—wholly undermined by the way her body leaned towards him.

'That isn't precisely an answer,' he managed, his voice raw, his body jolting at the way her breath caught audibly. 'Are you as tempted as I am? More?'

Linc couldn't have said who moved first, but abruptly the gap between them closed, and her body was against his, and fighting temptation was no longer a question. Something else was in control of them now: the attraction, the lust, that they'd been staving off for weeks—for years, if they included back in the army.

Finally, *finally*, he slid his fingers through her damp hair and set his mouth to hers, glorying in the way she lifted her hands and seemed to simply…cling on, and the fire licked at him in an instant.

It moved through him, getting higher and hotter as she let him angle her head for a better fit, testing first this way and then that way, seeming to melt against him that little bit more with every delicious slide of his tongue against hers.

Dully, he was aware of a mobile phone ringing in the background, but he didn't care. Scooping her up, his hands cupping that perfectly toned backside, he carried her over to the kitchen countertop and sat her down. Was it him, or her, who wrapped her legs around his waist to pull him in, just a few layers of fabric separating her soft, wet heat from the very hardest part of his body, just like in every dirty dream he'd ever had about her?

And he liked that carnal sound she made, low in her throat, when he told her as much.

And still, he wasn't even sure she meant to move and yet her hands lifted up between them until her palms were spread gloriously over his chest. So that the pulse in her thumb was right over the drumming of his heart.

He shifted and she moaned against his mouth, pressing her breasts to him, so tightly that he could feel how proud and pert her nipples were. His mouth watered. The need to take her, to claim her, was almost painful. This thing they'd shared had been arcing between them for so long. But he was determined not to rush. To take it slow.

Slowly, with painstaking deliberation, he slid his hand down to cup the base of her head, tipping it back so that he could feast on the long, elegant line of her neck, relishing the way she shivered in response and leaned back further to grant him better access.

He couldn't have said what it was about the scrabbling outside—perhaps the unusualness of the sound, perhaps his subconscious had been expecting something the moment his phone had started its incessant ringing—that alerted him something was wrong moments before the door to his apartment swung open.

And all he could do was shove Piper behind him, his first thought preserving whatever he could of her modesty.

# CHAPTER EIGHT

PIPER HAD BARELY registered what was going on as Linc pulled her down from the countertop and set her firmly behind him just as a woman—a stunning woman, to be precise—strode into the room.

Linc's sister, presumably.

The woman stopped abruptly when she saw them. But rather than looking embarrassed or shocked, she looked angry. With an odd undercurrent of…curiosity.

By contrast, Piper found all the self-confidence she'd had to finally kiss Linc seeped out of her in an instant. She wasn't even certain she could remember how to breathe.

'What the hell do you think you're doing, Sara?' Linc growled, clearly not suffering from the same lack of confidence.

Any other woman—any other person—would have cowed at the unmistakeably dangerous edge to his tone. Even Piper found herself desperate to move, but unable to budge. Embarrassment and anger were waging their own little war inside her head, and she wasn't yet certain which was going to win.

Sara, however, barely even flinched.

'You weren't answering your phone,' she continued, her focus on Linc. 'I didn't think you were home.'

'So you just let yourself in?'

He advanced on her, clearly furious, but the woman just jerked her chin up at him as only a sister could.

'You gave me a key.' She lifted her immaculately tailored shoulders in a gesture too elegant to be considered as unsophisticated as a shrug.

'For emergencies,' Linc growled, but his sister seemed to ignore that, too.

'We were supposed to be meeting for dinner earlier.'

'I called you to tell you I was running late from our last shout.'

'By which time I was already in the air,' his sister noted disdainfully. 'Coming here seemed like the logical solution. Was I supposed to divine the fact that the reason you pushed our meal back an hour was because you're…otherwise engaged.'

Sara scrunched up her nose, evidently unimpressed, and despite her best efforts Piper couldn't stop the heat from flooding her cheeks at the loaded accusation. But in the war between shame and anger, the latter was beginning to win out.

'We didn't…that is… I'm not the reason…' Piper began in a clipped voice before Linc took over for her.

'Piper had nothing to do with me pushing the meeting time back tonight.'

And Piper wondered if she was the only one to notice that slightly thicker note to his tone. Whether she was the only one who understood the reason behind it, that sense of helplessness as they'd flown that confused twelve-year-old kid—who couldn't even remember her name, or that it was her birthday that very day—to the hospital.

'I think I ought to leave,' Piper managed.

'Good idea,' Linc's sister agreed coldly.

But as Piper began to move out from around Linc—her state of undress be damned—Linc snaked his hand around to protect her.

'I'll walk with you,' he murmured reassuringly, before turning his attention back to his sister. 'This is my home, Sara, you don't speak to my guests like that. And you certainly don't send her scuttling back to her bedroom like some chastened child.'

'Her bedroom?' his sister echoed in disbelief. 'She's living here?'

'Staying temporarily.' There was no hint of apology in Linc's voice. 'Not that it's your business, but for Piper's sake I'm telling you that she's our emergency pilot since our usual one was in an accident. Since she's from out of the area, she found herself without accommodation.'

'Of course she did.' The sarcasm was unmistakeable. 'And I can see the attraction, I can, Lincoln. But moving her in with you? You aren't pregnant, are you?'

This last bit was patently directed at her, but Piper didn't get chance to respond before Linc had dropped his arm from around her waist, and advanced on his sister.

This time, he didn't think there was any way he was reining in his anger.

'Too far, Sara,' he growled, as he took his sister firmly, though not harshly, by the shoulders, and began to propel her swiftly to the exit. And Piper thought the woman must have realised she'd overstepped because, this time, she didn't argue.

But, at the last moment, another man appeared in the doorway.

'Is there a problem?'

His low voice rumbled through the penthouse, sounding so achingly familiar that Piper had to twist her head around to check that it hadn't come from Linc himself.

In an instant, every line of Linc's body changed. He stopped ejecting his sister as she thrust out her hand to the door jamb and spun herself around, whilst Linc folded his arms over his body.

'I didn't know you were coming,' he told the other man, and Piper thought it was interesting how his attitude had changed.

Clearly this was someone who mattered to Linc, who he cared about—his older brother, Raf, perhaps? The man certainly had an air of quiet authority about him that was so similar to Linc. Plus, even though she'd never met him, the way Linc had always talked about him, it had been clear that he respected and loved his brother. She'd always known when he'd managed a video call with his brother from out there, in that theatre of war. Linc had always seemed to be much more settled and grounded for weeks afterwards.

Though she'd never really bothered to ask herself why Linc's state of mind had always been so important to her.

'I told you what I need to discuss with you is important,' Sara announced now, triumphant as her glance encompassed the other man. 'Why else would Raf have come?'

So it *was* Linc's brother, Raf.

At least her own presence here had been apparently forgotten, for the moment. Piper wondered if she could slip away unnoticed.

'About the optics of your wedding,' Linc was saying to his sister as Piper inched towards the hallway to her suite—not that she dared break cover from behind the countertop. 'Isn't it always, these days?'

Despite the circumstances, Piper winced on Sara's behalf at the evident disdain in Linc's voice. Linc didn't mean to, that much was clear, but his dismissal of his sister's wedding clearly hurt her, though she rallied impressively. And even though Piper knew it probably wasn't her place to comment, nonetheless, she made a mental note to mention it to him when they were alone again.

'It's about more than just me, Linc,' Sara pleaded.

'I know what it's about,' he scoffed. 'It's always the same.'

And this time, when Sara bit back, Piper could almost understand it.

'No, you don't, because you never listen, and you never bother to come home. Tonight is a prime example. Apparently, Raf—' she spun again, this time to look at her other brother '—the reason Linc decided to make us wait this evening is because he was otherwise occupied with his new... houseguest. *Piper.*'

And as easy as that, the woman was back to a barely concealed contempt that cut right through Piper.

'That's enough, Sara,' Linc bit out, with audible fury in his tone. 'That's your last warning.'

And though she appreciated him defending her, Piper could only wish the ground would open up and swallow her whole. Anything to get away from the scrutiny—and the disdain.

For all the confidence she had in her career, and on the battlefield, she'd never found it easy to deal with strangers. Especially those who were clearly monied, and accustomed to throwing their wealth around. Like this woman.

Now, as much as it galled Piper to admit it, Linc's siblings were making her feel smaller and smaller with each passing moment. She certainly wasn't prepared for the brother's reaction.

'Wait... Piper?' he mused, as though the name meant something to him.

A dull drumbeat started up in Piper's chest, though she told herself that she shouldn't read too much into it. She mustn't.

'You served with Lincoln, didn't you?' the brother pondered. 'A few years ago?'

'Just around five years,' Piper forced herself to answer.

'Is that right?' Sara interjected. 'And now you're here and living with my brother, though we've never been formally introduced.'

Her tone was pointed, but Linc wasn't having any of it.

'Nor will you be now,' he gritted out, moving back to be closer to Piper. Half shielding her, half lending her strength.

'It would be good to remedy it, though,' his brother stated evenly. 'Perhaps Piper would like to get changed and accompany us to dinner.'

'I don't think so.' Linc didn't even hesitate, meanwhile Sara was gasping with obvious dismay.

'Raf...this is family business.'

'Sara, you've been rude enough already,' her older brother chastised. 'Linc and Piper have both been more than patient and I think we can all agree that these aren't the circumstances under which any of us would have chosen to meet. I think going for a meal together would help to remedy that. Would you not agree?'

And even though Raf was looking at both of them, Piper could tell that his focus was on his brother.

This was a test. Raf was using the invitation to gauge his brother's feelings towards her.

And even though a part of her wanted to jump in and tell both siblings that she and Linc were just friends, she found herself waiting for Linc to speak. Steeling herself—though she didn't care to examine why—for the moment he told them that she had no place joining them.

Slowly, she dragged her eyes from Raf, and Sara, to rest on Linc. Preparing herself for the inevitable. And, at last, he responded.

'The choice is yours, Piper,' he told her slowly. Thoughtfully. 'Would you care to join us?'

Shock walloped into her. She didn't need to look at Linc's brother to know what he was reading into the moment—not that she could have dragged her gaze from Linc even if she'd tried—and she could certainly hear the sharp intake of breath from his sister.

What was Linc even playing at? He might as well have announced some intention to commit himself to her. It was certainly what it sounded like. She couldn't explain it. Certainly couldn't understand it.

She opened her mouth to tell him that she would

be spending the night here, with her bath and early night as planned.

'Give me a few minutes to change,' she heard herself say instead.

And then, with a confidence that she hadn't known she'd had before—at least outside a helicopter cockpit, she stepped out from behind the counter, and strode as casually as she could across the hallway and down to her guest suite.

Let them make of that whatever they would.

It only took her a few moments to push herself off the closed door, where she'd been leaning and trying to catch her breath. She didn't have long to get ready if she didn't want to irk Linc's siblings—notably his sister—any more than she already had.

There was no pretending that she hadn't noticed the critical way that Sara had eyed her up and down, leaving her feeling as if she were a dog, or a horse, rather than a human. Only Sara probably would have shown more interest and care if she *were* of the four-legged variety.

She still didn't know what had possessed Linc to invite her; less still why she'd accepted, but at least she was grateful that she'd already showered. There might not be enough to time to blow-dry her hair the way she might have preferred, but she was accustomed to deftly twisting it up into an elegant chignon, and brushing on a quick hint of make-up.

As for her clothes, she didn't have much choice.

Her go-to evening wear was a pair of flowing black trousers—her only non-work pair, in fact, but she liked that they seemed to make her more glamorous, less gangly—and a pretty top that she'd brought on the off-chance of going out for an evening.

And she told herself that Linc definitely hadn't been in her mind when she'd been standing in front of her locker in barracks, taking that particular top off its hanger.

It would have to do. Nothing that she had would come anywhere close to the exquisite creation that Linc's sister had appeared to be wearing, but at least she would feel sufficiently dressed-up to hold her own at whatever restaurant they seemed to be booked into.

Linc was still trying to work out why the heck he hadn't shut his brother down when he'd invited Piper to join them for the evening.

He'd known it had been a test. Clearly, he'd failed it. By allowing the situation to play out he'd left his siblings with the impression that there was something going on between him and Piper.

*Isn't there?* a voice taunted in his head, before he could shut it down.

The fact remained that he'd needlessly opened Piper up to more scrutiny, and he only had himself to blame.

'I still don't understand what she's even doing

here.' Sara flounced across the room and threw herself into one of the pristine dove-grey leather chairs in the living area.

'I told you, it's about practicality,' he repeated, though he was beginning to doubt that, even of himself. 'We're old friends, so when she needed somewhere to stay for a week or two, I was happy to oblige.'

'Yes, I can see how happy you are.'

If it hadn't been for Raf's presence, he wasn't sure he would have continued to indulge his sister. For all her prickliness he loved her intently but, had his brother not shown up, he would have happily ejected her from his penthouse the first time she'd been rude to Piper.

Even now, her snort of derision wound him up even tighter than before.

'You looked like a pair of guilty, libido-ridden teenagers standing there when I walked in. And, frankly, you were never that guilty as a teenager, Lincoln.'

'You're sailing close to the wind, Sara,' Linc growled.

A wiser person would have heeded the warning. His sister, however, actually waved her hand in the air even more derisively.

'You might not be a monk, dear brother, but I can count the number of dates you've had with the same woman on one hand. Now you're telling me that you've actually moved this *Piper* into your apartment?'

'I told you out of courtesy,' Linc replied coldly, 'but ultimately it isn't really any of your concern. Yours or Raf's.'

'It's entirely of our concern. Which you'd know if you'd take your head out of your backside long enough to listen to us. To come back and be the part of the family you've always been—'

'That will do, Sara,' Linc ground out, just as Raf uttered something along similar lines.

Sara spun around instantly.

'The point of this evening is to talk family matters with Linc. *Private* family matters. How can we do that with his "houseguest" in there?'

'Sara.' This time it was Raf who cut her off first. 'I know you're worried about the family company, but I've never known you to be so catty before. I can't say I care for it.'

Raf's tone was the perfect balance between commanding and caring. It was a skill that his brother had always known just how to execute, and one that Linc had long envied.

'I'm also worried about you,' she added stubbornly, before swinging back around to Linc, her eyes flashing. 'You do realise that two of the board members have been trying to topple Raf by secretly buying up shares and now have forty per cent. They're weeks away from organising a coup.'

'What does it matter?' Linc growled, his eye on the door to Piper's suite, beginning to regret his earlier decision. This was definitely not a conversation he wanted her to overhear. It would mean having to explain too much. 'So long as you, Raf and I stick together, they can never outvote us; we still hold the controlling interest.'

'Except that the devious bastards have managed to dig up some of the truth about you. About Mum. They've got a whiff of the fact that...well, you know...and he's going to use that against Raf.'

It was as if the world froze—his siblings, his penthouse, time itself.

'This isn't the place, Sara.' Linc was aware of Raf's censure, but it was too late.

It was said. The box was open. The thing the three of them never, *never* discussed swirled around the room.

'They know that the old duke isn't my father.' Linc wasn't sure how he managed to sound so calm. So in control. He felt anything but. 'Say the words, Sara.'

'They know,' she choked out. 'And they're using that to claim that your shares were never yours to inherit. They're trying to have you thrown off the board. The board votes next week.'

His tongue felt too big for his mouth. Too unwieldy. Yet somehow, he didn't know how, he spoke.

'Then let them. If that's the weapon he's using

to unseat Raf, let him use it. If the board votes me out, and claims I'm not a proper Oakes, then let them. They aren't wrong. The duke wasn't my biological father. I'm just your half-brother.'

It was as if every fear he'd ever had—the very reason for him leaving Stoneywell and not returning—was suddenly coming to pass. His past was rushing up on him, threatening to swallow him whole, and there was nothing he could do to hold it back.

'You *are* our brother.' Sara pushed herself up from her seat and flung herself at him furiously for a moment. 'I don't care what anyone else says or thinks.'

And it was ridiculous how touched he was at her unfailing love. The way she'd always been, even that first night their mother had so gleefully announced the truth about her infidelity. As loving and supportive as Raf, as their father, had been—even when she'd produced a DNA test to prove it, driven by some vicious compulsion to hurt the old duke that little bit more.

But somehow, that had only made it all the harder to accept. Because the more they had closed around him, the three of them in a protective ring around him—the more he'd felt as if he wasn't one of them. Like a cuckoo in their nest.

Ultimately, it had been their love that had pushed him to join the army to get away from them. Irony at its worst.

'He was our father. To all three of us,' Raf rasped out as Sara moved back to her own seat. 'I will not hear otherwise.'

'But if the argument is accepted, it will make things easier for you. My shares would just revert to you two. Those old cronies win nothing by getting rid of me, so let them do it.'

'That isn't the point,' Sara cried.

'I think it is,' argued Linc, as though his heart weren't cracking, right there in his soul.

'No,' Raf disagreed quietly. 'Besides, even if it were the point, there's more to it.'

'Meaning?'

'Meaning that they also know Daddy knew about the infidelity,' Sara revealed. 'And that you couldn't be his…biological son. So they're contesting his state of mind at the time his will was drawn up.'

'Say again?' Linc thundered, his head swirling with the revelations.

'They're saying that the Alzheimer's started earlier, and that decisions he made during the later years—the direction that the company took—might not have been taken had he been in his right mind.'

'He was in his right mind.' Linc frowned. 'He knew exactly what he was doing with the company, right up until those last few years. It's the same direction Raf has been taking the company—'

He stopped abruptly, his mind beginning to work through the noise.

'Which is precisely why they're using it as a means to get Raf out, too,' Sara bit out.

Linc turned to his brother.

'You can't let them get away with it.'

'I'm dealing with it,' Raf rumbled softly. Steadfastly.

Looking from one brother to the other, Sara threw her hands up in frustration.

'But it would be a whole lot easier if you came home and helped. Raf, will you please tell him that he needs to come home?'

Linc didn't know why he looked at his brother. Raf couldn't possibly need his help. His older brother was always so in control, so strong. And still, he watched, certainty turning to shock when Raf didn't instantly refute Sara's claim.

'It would…help,' his brother acknowledged after a moment.

There was little need to say anything more. For Raf to even say that much meant that they were in trouble. It was almost unconscionable.

'Most of the board members don't want a coup,' Sara pressed after a moment. 'They want the problem to just go away. And maybe it would, if you were home. If you were part of the business, just like you were always meant to be. Like we were all always meant to be.'

'I don't see what my presence would change,'

Linc growled, feeling even more of an imposter than ever.

'It would show your commitment to Stoneywell. To the family name, and the family business, just as Daddy always believed we would be.' His sister's voice trembled, somewhere between grief and ferocity.

Still, Linc shook his head.

'That won't change the facts. I'm still...who I am.'

*Not his father's biological son.*

'It would change things if you came back home and settled down. Maybe took on the role as Chief of the Stoneywell Medical Centre,' Sara pointed out. 'There are plenty of old-guard board members who supported Daddy, and who would like nothing better than for him to be proved right by the three of us running Oakenfeld Industries together, the way he had always envisaged.'

'I'm not a private practice doctor.' Linc hated that she was suggesting such a move. And hating himself even more for refusing to help. 'I'm a former army doctor. I'm an air ambulance doctor. I go where I'm needed, not where cash-splashing celebrities want me to be.'

'Then reconsider,' Sara snapped. 'For Raf, if not for yourself.'

'Raf doesn't need me. He can resolve this issue without my help,' Linc argued, even as several pieces began to topple into place. 'Is that what all your phone calls have been about? All this pressure to bring a plus one to your wedding rehearsal next week? To your wedding? You want me to pretend to the board that I'm finally settling down and thinking of coming back to the fold, a changed man?'

'It couldn't hurt,' his sister blasted.

He begged to differ. He'd never known a problem his older brother couldn't fix.

'It's fine, Linc.' His brother dipped his head, as though reading his mind. As in control as ever. 'I'll think of something. I still have a few plays in motion before next week.'

'Right,' Linc agreed.

But guilt still moved through him. If it was that easy, then Raf wouldn't be here in the first instance.

The glittering, shimmering tears in his sister's eyes didn't help, either.

'Since when did you get so selfish, Lincoln Oakes?' she choked out. 'All these years we've supported your choices, from the army to the air ambulance. But now we need you and...'

The click of the door down the hallway silenced whatever else his sister had been going to say, and he and his brother stood automatically as the surprising sound of high heels clicked down the marble flooring towards them.

And then it was his turn for the words to pile up

in his chest. Caught in the vacuum, every breath in him was sucked out.

Piper looked stunning. No, more than that, she looked positively majestic, standing in front of them like some kind of goddess, with the most dazzling smile falling from her lovely face.

And he thought only he could read the tiniest of tension marks around the normally smooth edges.

*Mine,* the shockingly primitive thought bellowed in his head. In his soul. *All mine.*

Then his remarkable Piper stepped towards his sister, her arm outstretched.

'Shall we try this again?' she asked lightly, almost breezily. 'I'm Piper. It's lovely to meet you, Sara. I've heard so much about you over the years, it's great to finally put a face to—'

'Lady Sara,' his sister cut across her with a smile of her own that was bright but sharp.

Instinct made him step forward.

'For God's sake, Sara,' he growled, moving to stand next to Piper, but it was too late. His gut pulled taut as Piper twisted to him, blinking in shock.

'Lady Sara?' she asked tightly.

'Just as my brother here is Lord Lincoln.' Sara's voice sounded muffled as he held Piper's gaze. 'Surely you understand that's how titles work?'

Tearing himself from Piper, he moved to his penthouse door and yanked it back open.

'Leave now, Sara,' Linc gritted out.

How had he not realised that his secret would be revealed if Piper spent any time with his siblings? Had he been so caught up with what had happened between them in the moments before his sister had walked in?

Regrettably, he realised the answer was *yes*.

'Titles?' Piper was still echoing, evidently stunned.

'Of course.' Sara was eyeing her curiously now. 'You'll understand my surprise that you're apparently living with my brother but claim not to even know that.'

'She didn't know.' Linc stepped in. 'And it really is time you left.'

'What about dinner?' Sara demanded.

'Goodbye, Sara,' Linc managed icily, his eyes on a reeling Piper. 'Go home. Go to dinner. But you will leave my home.'

'I have a better idea.' Raf stepped in calmly. 'Linc, you and Piper go to the restaurant, and talk on neutral ground. Clearly we've overstepped the mark here. I apologise. Sara, you and I are leaving.'

'No, but—'

'Now, Sara.' Raf ushered her to the door in much the way that Linc himself had before.

Linc was grateful. For all his own usual self-control, looking at Piper's ashen face at this moment, he could happily have kicked his sister out on her designer-clad backside.

'I'm glad to have met you.' Raf shook Piper's hand smoothly, even as he kept propelling Sara towards the door. 'I regret that it wasn't under better circumstances. Perhaps next time.'

And with those words hanging in the air like some kind of simultaneously unspoken criticism and assurance, Raf removed the two of them from the penthouse leaving Linc to finally be alone with the only woman he realised he could ever have imagined knowing his most guarded secret.

# CHAPTER NINE

PIPER WAS STILL processing the revelations of the previous evening as she first paraded the helicopter the following morning. Hardly surprising, since she'd also been thinking about it all night; barely able to sleep.

They'd eaten at the finest restaurant Piper thought she'd ever been to. A ten-course tasting menu fit for the lords and lady that Linc and his siblings were.

But between the glazed scallop with salt-baked parsnips, nasturtium, and crisp pork belly starter, and the rich, mirror-glazed cocoa delight with edible gold leaf flecks for dessert, they'd also talked.

Linc, the man she'd known for years—the army doctor she'd served alongside on multiple tours—was a lord? It still seemed too crazy to be true.

He'd talked to her about his family's Oakenfeld Industries, and shared inheritances, he'd explained to her about Raf being the new Duke of Stoneywell, and given her a brief outline of the board members who were trying to topple his brother, but she still wasn't entirely sure that she understood all the facts, even now.

She hated his guilt that his abandonment of the family business had led to such instability, and a part of her could now begin to understand what his sister meant by using the optics of her wedding to make it appear that Linc was finally ready to settle down and return to the family fold.

But Piper couldn't shake the feeling that he was leaving out something more to the story. She couldn't escape the idea that there was a vital piece that he wasn't sharing.

Perhaps it was to do with the way his siblings had seemed much more open and receptive towards Linc than he had to them. As though there were a sheet of one-way glass between them, and Linc were on the protected side of it.

Five years ago, he'd given her the impression he would have moved heaven and earth for his brother and his sister. Now, she wasn't so sure. Part of her felt as though he wanted to…it was simply as though there was a wall stopping him. A wall that only Linc himself had built. She wished she understood it.

It all made her wonder if she'd ever really known him at all.

She'd been about to sleep with him—well, perhaps not *sleep,* precisely—and she hadn't even known the truth. Worse, she wasn't even sure a part of her cared. She, who had always told herself that she would never give herself to a man she couldn't be completely honest with.

Yet here she was, still wondering whether she was imagining something between herself and

Linc, or whether it really existed. Even lying in that luxurious guest bed last night, still reeling from the revelations, it had been like some form of exquisite torture—knowing that Linc had been only metres away, at the other end of the penthouse.

How could it be that he was sending her out of her mind on so many different levels?

It felt as though the more time she spent at his home, the more she wasn't sure she understood herself at all.

How was it he could leave her feeling so gloriously desirable, yet at the same time so damned easy to resist? No wonder the more time she spent in his penthouse, the more sexually frustrated she seemed to be feeling. She, who had never really considered herself to have a particularly high libido in general.

Which was surely why spending time with Linc intimately, even for pretend, was the last thing she should do?

'Hey, Piper, grub's up. My famous chilli.' Linc interrupted her thoughts, appearing at the door of the base just as she was finishing pulling the trailer back to the hangar. 'You okay?'

'Sure.' She regrouped quickly. 'I didn't know you were cooking.'

Because if he could pretend that everything was normal between them, then so could she.

No matter that it cost her dearly to do so.

But then he stayed by the door, as if there was something else on his mind.

'Something else you wanted to say?' she managed, impressing herself with how nonchalant she actually sounded.

Surely he couldn't hear that slight quiver in her voice?

'Have you heard the news about Albert?' he asked abruptly.

And there was no reason for her heart to plummet, but it did.

'What news?'

'Albert and Jenny are being discharged tomorrow. Jenny suffered a couple of fractured ribs from the steering wheel but nothing critical so she'll be laid up for a little while, but Albert got off with only a few minor injuries so he should be back within a fortnight.'

'That's great.' Guilt sliced through Piper at how hard it was to keep her smile bright.

'You could be back at barracks, away from here before you know it.'

'Even better,' she acknowledged, her smile so wide she feared her face might actually fracture.

She was pleased for the crew, obviously. The idea of any of them being injured wasn't one she would wish on anyone. At the same time, a part of her would have welcomed a little more time with Heathston Helimed.

*With Helimed, or with Linc?* that insidious little voice challenged. And even as she told herself the idea of leaving was only hard because the steady income was just what she needed to help her family—not any other reason, of course—she knew she didn't believe it.

For a moment, they seemed caught in time. Watching each other without a word. And then Linc spoke. Quietly, catching them both off guard.

'Is it, though?' he asked, making a move to close the gap between them.

She held her hands out palms up. Neither trying to stop him, nor caution him.

'Isn't it?'

Before he could answer, the alarm sounded for another shout. Wordlessly, they each sprang into action, as if the moment had never happened. But even as she leapt into the cockpit, she couldn't quite evict the thick feeling that squatted heavily on her chest.

By the sounds of it, she had a handful of shifts left here and then she would be gone. From Heathston Helimed…and from Linc's life.

'What's the call?' Piper demanded as the crew raced over the tarmac and to her heli.

'Road traffic collision on the main A road, up near Farm Mere. High-impact collision between bus and motorcycle; potential head injury. Police are already on scene controlling the site.'

If the police had cleared the area, she might

even be able to land on the road. Running through her checks, Piper started the heli up.

'Everybody ready?'

Quickly, the crew ran through their own checks before Piper adjusted her headset and contacted the local air traffic control.

'Heathston Tower, this is Helimed hotel one-niner,' she identified herself. 'We have four on board and we're ready for lift. We're heading about thirty miles north to Farm Mere, following the line of main A road, over.'

And it was strange how, if these were to be her last two weeks for shouts with this crew, she already felt as though she was going to miss it.

'I think the best bet is going to be to RSI him,' Linc decided, less than twenty minutes later as he and his team finished their assessment of the casualty.

It had turned out to be a twenty-five-year-old male who had been heading down the main road when the bus driver, blinded by the sun at the rider's back, had pulled out in front of him.

The young man's body seemed to have borne the brunt of impact, with a broken rib and an open fracture to his lower limb, but it was the potential head injury that was concerning Linc the most.

'Gary was heading to his girlfriend's to propose,' the young man's mother sobbed, having arrived on scene a few minutes earlier, along with the land ambulance crew. 'He said when you know, you know, right?'

'Of course.' Linc nodded empathetically, not prepared for the image of Piper that flashed, unbidden, in his brain.

He thrust it aside.

'So, we've carried out a physical examination, and, along with Gary's agitation and lack of awareness, we're concerned he may have a brain bleed,' Linc informed her, as simply as he could. 'We want to put him into an induced coma to help protect his brain until we can get him to hospital, okay?'

He didn't add that the decision to RSI the woman's son hadn't been taken lightly. His crew knew that timings would be critical, first administering a strong induction agent to sedate him, and swiftly following it up with a rapid-acting paralytic agent in order to both induce unconsciousness and allow them to intubate.

'What do you think he weighs?' Linc asked Tom. 'About eighty kilos?'

'Yeah, I'd say eighty, maybe eighty-five,' Tom agreed as they considered the levels of drugs they needed to administer.

'Okay, Probie, let's run through the checklist,' Linc instructed. 'Then, Tom, you sedate, and we'll bag him for a minute to let that take effect, before administering the next.'

The team worked systematically, running through

the list, and taking advantage of the road ambulance crew who were now also on the ground.

Ten minutes later the team were loading the patient into the heli, with Tom calling it in to the hospital before they set off on the flight. They'd dealt with the lad's other injuries as quickly as they could, but the main focus was still on the brain bleed and trying to stop Gary's brain from swelling.

For the duration of the flight, Linc knew he was going to have to focus primarily on keeping his patient's oxygen and carbon dioxide levels stable.

And still, the mother's comment was floating around Linc's head. *When you know, you know, right?*

Linc wondered if that was true.

Then he wondered why he cared if it was or wasn't.

He was still wondering about it several hours later as his own motorbike hugged the lanes, taking him home after the shift. And most of the evening, as he paced his unexpectedly quiet penthouse. Which felt ridiculously quiet and empty, without Piper's soft voice, or her laugh, which reminded him of a hundred twinkling Christmas lights.

Before Linc realised what he was doing, he picked up his phone and flicked the screen to her number, his thumb hovering over the call button before reason got control of him.

*What was he even doing?* Had he really been about to call her to find out where she was and if she was okay? Like the kind of boyfriend he definitely wasn't, had *never* been. What had got into him?

It had to be the unexpected news that Albert was on the mend and would be returning sooner, rather than later. News that should delight him. In one way, it did. He was unquestionably relieved for his old buddy that the accident had turned out to be less serious than first imagined, and pleased for Albert that he would be ready to return to the field so relatively quickly.

But at the same time, his thoughts had leapt straight to Piper, and something in his ribcage kicked hard at the idea of her leaving. At never seeing her again. It didn't seem to matter how many times he told himself that she was simply an old friend, or that her leaving his life again had been inevitable.

Even welcome.

It didn't feel very welcome now, knowing that once she returned to barracks, it could be another five years—another fifteen—before he saw her again.

Most likely, it would be a lifetime. And he ought to be fine with that. So why wasn't he?

Why did his body feel as though it were going to implode with the things he was keeping inside?

Piper had been the only person outside his siblings who he'd ever told so much about himself. And even then, it was all he could do not to share the darkest, most damaging secrets of all.

If he wasn't careful, this pent-up sensation was going to swallow him whole. He needed to expend it in some way—he didn't care how.

Stalking down the hallway to his home gym, and hauling off his T-shirt as he went, Linc flicked on the music, letting the low reverb of the bass fill his head. Maybe it could drown out any unwanted voices, needling otherwise.

He had no idea how long he stayed. At least long enough until his hand ached despite the gloves, the sweat was running rivers down his back, and his lungs burned with the effort of breathing.

He was nearing the end of the boxing session when Piper walked in unexpectedly, and, though there was nothing overtly sexual in her attire, his gaze went almost of its own volition to admire the way her jeans clung so lovingly to her backside. He promptly felt like a jerk as she launched into conversation without preamble.

With a low growl of frustration, he turned his attention fully back to the leather bag that had already been bearing the brunt of his confusion— and imagined himself. As though he thought he could wallop some sense into his own head.

'I didn't realise you were home already.' Piper faltered. 'I've been waiting for you in the living room ever since I got back.'

*Jab.*

'I came straight here.'

*Jab, hook.*

'I wanted to talk about Albert's return,' she began, before adding hastily, 'Which is great news, of course.'

Abandoning the punchbag, Linc moved quickly to the speed ball. Anything to distract his head and his heart. The rhythm was almost hypnotic, the familiar *thwack-thunk* quickly gathering pace and helping to keep some distance between him and Piper.

His personal best had long been about three hundred and five hits in a minute, but right now he was fairly sure he could easily smash that.

It wasn't something he thought he ought to feel proud about.

'Linc, please,' she blurted out abruptly. 'Stop. Just talk to me.'

The worst of it was that he simply obeyed. Catching the ball with one hand, he turned slowly to face her.

'What do you want to hear, Legs?' he ground out. 'That's it's okay to be upset about your job without anyone accusing you of not being happy Albert's recovering well?'

And he hated himself for the guilt that skittered over her face.

'Of course I'm happy for Albert.'

'As am I.'

*When you know, you know, right?*

He shook his head free of the echoes.

'I...have a proposal for you,' Piper bit out, on an awkward breath.

And Linc told himself there was no reason that his body should react to that, at all.

'I'm listening,' he told her solemnly instead.

'You remember that I told you I was going for a role at the air ambulance over the border in the next county?'

'West Nessleton Helimed,' he agreed. 'I remember.'

'I understand they already have their go-to list for pilots but what if I agreed to play the part of your date, in exchange for you putting in a good word up there for me? Just to get me an interview, nothing more.'

'You're negotiating with me?' Linc asked, and it was on the tip of his tongue to tell her that he'd already mentioned her name when the regional coordinator had called him a couple of weekends earlier—but something stopped him.

He suspected he knew exactly what that *something* was.

'Yes.' She bobbed her head. 'You need someone

for your sister's wedding, and I need someone to give me a recommendation.'

He ought to say *no*. He ought to walk away. But he found that he couldn't. Faking a date might have seemed like a bad idea when his sister had suggested it but now that Piper was offering to be that date, he found he was suddenly considering it. As insane as it was.

'It isn't a game, Piper,' he growled. 'We'd be staging a relationship, a new side of me.'

'Which you told me last night would buy your brother enough time to convince the wavering board members that the direction he wanted to take the company in is the right one.'

'It would,' Linc confirmed. 'He has several lucrative contracts lined up—they're with the solicitors now but Raf won't rush them. He wants to dot the proverbial "i"s and cross the "t"s. He's thorough—it's what makes him so good at what he does.'

'But the board votes before that, yes?' she pressed. 'So you give the board something to think about and that buys him enough time.'

'In a nutshell,' Linc agreed. 'But using you to convince them I'm ready to change my life? Do I need to remind you of what happened between us the other night?'

Piper twisted her hands in front of her body.

'That was the other night. We were caught off guard and we let things get away from us,' she muttered. And he wondered which of them she was trying to convince more. 'But we've dealt with that now. It's no longer an issue.'

'Isn't it?' he muttered, fighting the pressing urge to take a step forward and reach out his hand to roll a lock of her hair between his fingers.

And when that delicious heat bloomed across her silken skin, he actually *ached* to press his mouth to it.

'It isn't. Like you said, this is a negotiation, nothing more. We both have something the other needs and if we handle it right, then we can both win. West Nessleton is near my family, I couldn't land a better role. But that job opportunity won't be out there for me for ever. So please think about it, Linc. Just don't think too long.'

And then she disappeared through the door and down the hall to her suite. But only because she didn't trust herself with him if she'd stayed in the gym.

He knew, because he didn't trust himself with her either. Not when he suspected that he only had to pull her to him and begin kissing her again for them both to go up in flames.

And *that*, he told himself firmly, would not be a good idea for anyone.

# CHAPTER TEN

WHEN HE'D SAID the family home, Piper realised a few days later as they were flown over the countryside in the family's private helicopter, what he'd really meant was *ancestral* home.

With hindsight, she shouldn't have expected anything less than the vast, sprawling country pile with land surrounding it in all directions.

'This is where you grew up?' Piper couldn't help but gape as she shifted in one of the oversized, butter-soft seats. 'How far does it extend?'

Without warning, Linc leaned closer to her, to place his eyeline approximately around hers. The effect on Piper was instantaneous, making her hot and jittery. And her skin seemed to pull so tight, almost as if it were suddenly too small for her own body.

'See that treeline over there, by the stone church?'

She wasn't sure how long it took her to remember to breathe.

'I...yes.'

'To the shoreline down there?' He swept his arm across the other way, where Piper could see the sea in the near distance.

'Right.' She swallowed. Hard.

'And then from that winding country lane that bisects the county up there, down to the golf course over there.'

'I guess it's some people's dream to live next to a golf course,' she managed, her voice sounding thicker than usual.

'In the interests of full disclosure, the golf course belongs to us. Stoneywell Golf Course— it hosts some of the top annual gold tournaments.'

'Of course,' she choked out, but that could hardly be helped.

Just another thing to add to the fact that the area he'd indicated had to be hundreds upon hundreds of hectares. The entire housing estate where she'd grown up could have fitted into his mere back garden, several times over. Linc came from an entirely different world from the one she'd come from, and that gap between the two of them couldn't have been more striking.

Or humiliating.

For the first time, something slid down her back. Perhaps it was apprehension, more likely it was resignation. Just another place she didn't really fit in—no matter how much she might try to tell herself otherwise. Pretending to be Linc's fiancé in exchange for his good word was one thing. But what if someone got curious about her? Or worse, recognised her?

'It is,' Linc's voice came back over the headset as he dipped his head in acknowledgement. It left her scrambling to remember what her question had even been.

And still, she couldn't seem to stop her tongue from moving.

'Say again?'

'You asked if this was where I grew up,' he reminded her. 'And it is. It's where Raf and I climbed trees and built forest dens. It's where we learned to shoot clay pigeons, and fish, and ride.'

'You ride?'

Of course he would do, coming from a place like this, she realised belatedly.

'Not as much as I'd like to, any more. Though I used to love it. Raf and I often took our horses down to the beach and then galloped on the sand. You've never ridden?'

'Never.' She shook her head.

'Not even on holiday?'

'Not even donkey rides on the beach.' Her smile was rueful.

A part of her had dreamed of it, as a kid. But when she was growing up, her family had never had that kind of money. Not even before all the financial worries.

'I'll teach you. It's easy enough.'

She seriously doubted that, though she didn't say as much. What was Linc doing anyway, suggesting things like that? They both knew she was only here for the wedding rehearsal dinner, definitely not long enough for her to do anything like learning to ride a horse.

For the next few moments, she sat in silence, drinking it all in as the pilot brought their luxury heli down onto the estate's bespoke helipad. Just like another parking bay, to a place like this.

What she wasn't particularly expecting was the welcoming party that appeared to be waiting for them near what had to be an imposing eight-foot-high wooden front door. Linc's sister, of course, along with who was likely her fiancé. And Raf—as tall, dark, and brooding as before. Today the fraternal resemblance seemed all the more striking.

Then, before she knew what was happening, the heli was down, the engine off and the blades stopped, and Linc was out of the aircraft and reaching back to help her down. Under other circumstances, she felt she would have brushed away his unnecessarily chivalrous offer, but now it was all Piper could do to release his hand once her feet were firmly on land.

The welcoming party swept forward, and she noted that Sara's fiancé appeared to have slipped away as they'd landed.

'Lincoln.' Sara smiled, hugging him quickly before turning to her. 'And... Piper. It's nice to meet you again.'

The steely smile was still there...just decidedly more polished. Presumably under threat from either Linc, or Raf. Possibly both. Even so, Piper felt her mind go blank and just as she was about to wish she'd never agreed to do this she felt Linc's warm hand brush the small of her back, silently lending her strength.

She discreetly drew in as steadying a breath as she could and turned to Linc's sister.

'Lady Sara,' she managed politely, before turning to Linc's brother. 'Lord Ranulph.'

'Sara and Raf will be fine,' Linc stopped her tightly. 'Isn't that right, Sara?'

'As you're our brother's guest, we don't stand on formality,' Raf's rich, deep, familiar-sounding voice agreed smoothly. 'It's very good to meet you again, Piper. We're grateful to you for persuading my brother here to finally return home.'

Raf held out his hand to shake hers, and the severe expression on his face gave way to that surprisingly warm, equally familiar smile. And once again Piper was struck by the connection between the two brothers. That kind of easiness; a bond. A trust.

It made Piper want to trust Raf, too.

'Isn't that so, Sara?'

'Raf...' This time the interjection earned her a withering look from her older brother.

'Would you care to address Linc's guest as Captain Green for the duration of her stay?' the older brother asked quietly. Firmly.

'She isn't serving any more,' Linc's sister objected for a moment, before appearing to bite her tongue. 'Fine.' She flashed a tight smile, though it was clear she didn't like it.

'Piper acting as my fiancée was your idea, after all.' Linc finally deigned to speak but made no attempt to conceal the amusement in his tone.

'You having a date was my idea,' his sister snapped. 'This engagement twist was all your idea. Be it on your heads when people ask you all about your relationship and you can't answer.'

'And therein lies the fun.'

Sara cast him a withering glower.

'That's always been your problem, Lincoln, you treat everything like a game.'

Linc slung his bag over his shoulder, his hand returning to the small of Piper's back. 'Shall we find our rooms?'

Strong, comforting, and more than a little welcome.

'Linc, if you have a moment.' His brother moved to walk beside them, his hands clasped behind his back, back to serious mode again. 'There have been a couple of recent developments with the board.'

'You want to talk about them now?' Linc asked, his deep voice matching the calm gravity of his brother's.

'Not this moment, but as soon as you get chance.'

'You ought to know about them,' Sara noted

pointedly. 'The sooner the better. I can show your guest to the suite.'

'I think not,' he declined, moving to walk with her.

And she could accept it gratefully or do what she was supposed to be here to do.

'I'll be fine,' Piper told him quickly, before she could bottle out.

'I thought we could take a walk together.' He leaned in so that only she could hear, the soft sweep of his breath at her neck making her shiver with delight before she could stop herself. 'Perhaps escape this place.'

'I'd like that,' she murmured back. 'As soon as you're finished with Raf and Sara.'

'Piper...'

'Truly,' she managed firmly.

Linc eyed her wordlessly, then he looked at his brother. Finally he dipped his head and fell in beside his brother, the two of them walking with their heads bowed together. And Piper couldn't help but notice Sara staring wistfully after them as they went. The younger sister who might have spent her whole life racing to catch up with her two, bigger brothers.

Piper couldn't explain why she had to fight back the wealth of emotions rioting through her at that moment. Perhaps because it made her think of her own family—her own sister—and the ugliness that had marred their relationship ever since before their father had died.

Seeing Linc's interplay with his family—both the other night, and now—had been unexpected... and unsettling. In an instant, she'd been able to imagine exactly what the trio must have been like as kids. A tight little band of three, growing up in a place like Oakenfeld Hall.

It had her revisiting all her military memories of Linc, seeing them in a new light. Raf the older one, always trying to be responsible and keep the peace. Sara was the baby of the group, the daughter torn between living up to her title as a lady, and wanting to tomboy it around with big brothers who she clearly idolised.

As for Linc, he was the middle kid. The second brother who would neither be the heir to the dukedom, nor the much-vaunted daughter. No wonder he'd carved out his own place in the world by joining the army, and becoming a doctor.

Could it be that his enigmatic personality was less about keeping others out, and more about protecting himself? Piper stared at Linc for a moment, her mind reeling.

'Can I ask you something?'

Piper swivelled around in surprise as Sara fell in beside her. And even though it was phrased as a question, there was a peremptory tone to Sara's voice that brooked little argument. The customs of being a lady who commanded attention, Piper presumed.

Still, she forced another smile, for Linc's sake.

'Of course. I'll try to answer if I can.'

'Why are you doing this?'

She didn't need to elaborate for Piper to know what she meant. For a moment, she wondered whether she should stick with the old army buddies connection, but there was something too practical about Sara for that to satisfy her. In the end, Piper plumped for the truth.

Or a part-truth, at least.

'I'm leaving the Army Air Corps. We agreed that if I attend this weekend's rehearsal dinner and next week's wedding as his fiancée, then he'll recommend me as pilot for one of the other air ambulance bases.'

'One of the other air ambulance bases?'

'In the next county.'

Sara cast her an assessing glance.

'Why not the one where you both are now?'

'Heathston already has Albert.' No need to tell Sara that he was retiring. 'Besides, my mother and brother live a county over. The other base will let me be nearer to them.'

'You're moving to be closer to your family?' Sara eyed her even more intently. 'How old is your brother?'

'He's twelve,' Piper couldn't help but smile.

'Sometimes twelve going on forty, other times twelve going on about seven.'

'So family is important to you?' Linc's sister didn't even crack a smile, but there was an earnest note to her voice that hadn't been there before.

'It is,' Piper answered after a moment. 'Even when I was away, I used to speak to them as often as I could. They're all I have.'

'Just like Raf and Linc are all I have now. And my future husband, of course.'

'Of course.' Piper kept her voice light.

'It's why I want Linc to come home. We need him here. He belongs back here.'

'He doesn't belong in a clinic.' The words tumbled softly from Piper's lips before she could stop herself. Before her brain could engage. 'He's an army doctor, or an air ambulance doctor, getting out there to the patient and saving lives in the field. I don't think Linc would ever be a good wait-for-them-to-come-to-him kind of doctor.'

Instantly, she realised her mistake. She braced herself, waiting for some cold dismissal from Linc's fierce sister. Sara might have engaged in this conversation with her, but, for Linc's sake, she should have thought twice about saying something that would agitate the bride-to-be.

'That's pretty much what Linc said the other night.' The sad admission shocked Piper.

And even though she knew she shouldn't press her luck, she heard herself speaking again.

'For what it's worth, it's always been evident that Linc loves you and your brother very much. I think a part of him would even want to return home. I just think...there's a barrier there, and I don't know why but he can't seem to overcome it.'

Slamming her mouth shut, Piper braced again. There was no question this time that Sara would think she had overstepped her boundaries.

Yet, once again, Linc's sister shocked her.

'Do you...?' She tailed off, shaking her head. And then, 'Do you think he wants to, though? Overcome that barrier, I mean?'

'I don't know,' Piper told her truthfully. 'I don't know the full story, clearly—Linc has never shared that. But... I think so.'

Sara nodded. And then, as if she hadn't shocked Piper enough already, she drew in a deep breath.

'I think, perhaps, I have misjudged you,' she managed, awkwardly. As if she wasn't accustomed to having to make such admissions. 'Perhaps you're not such a poor decision by my brother, after all. We shall see.'

Then, as though putting an end to the exchange, Sara lifted her head and picked up the pace as they hurried to the great staircase. All Piper could do was follow.

'Is this walk so that I can escape this place?' Piper asked wryly as she followed him through a door off the long, elegant hallway. 'Or so that you can?'

'Perhaps a little of both,' he admitted grudgingly, leading her down a tight, winding staircase, and through a low door. 'I have a confession to make, Piper. You don't need to be here.'

'I don't?'

'I talked to Regional about you weeks ago—the moment I heard about the pilot opening at West Nessleton. So you don't need to be here.'

'I don't understand.' Her brow furrowed in confusion. 'You don't *want* me here?'

'I'm saying you don't *have* to be. I know how overbearing Sara can be, not to mention the people who'll be watching us this weekend, scrutinising us, and looking for any weakness.'

'Did your brother say something?' she asked, without thinking.

Still, she wasn't prepared for Linc to look so sheepish.

'He may have reminded me what I was about to subject you to between extended family and the board. I wanted to give you one last chance to back out.'

And Piper thought it was that moment that made her all the more determined to stay and help him out. Smiling to herself, she glanced around at the scenery, then pulled up short.

'Wait, are these the kitchen gardens? They're beautiful.'

She stopped to take a better look around, pleased when Linc moved to stand next to her.

'They were designed by my great-great-great-grandmother in eighteen seventy, and re-imagined by my father and grandfather before Raf was even born. Over there, you can see fig trees and apple trees, and over that way are grapevines.'

She followed his hand, taking in the rich display.

'And if you look this way—' he placed his hands on her shoulders to turn her as she pretended not to notice the shiver of pleasure that danced along her spine '—you can find prickly cucumbers and even liquorice.'

'Is this where you spent time with your father?'

He turned back sharply.

'What made you ask that?'

Piper shrugged. The question had been out before she'd even realised she'd intended to ask it.

'I don't know, you just love cooking and you're so passionate about the ingredients you use...' She tailed off.

But just as she thought Linc was going to ignore her and start walking again, he surprised her.

'Yeah, I guess it is where my father and I bonded most. Here, pottering around the gardens in the precious little time he got to spend here, or riding across the fields.'

'But here was more special?' she guessed. 'Because riding was with your siblings, and the garden was just you and him?'

Another pause.

'The garden was just for the two of us,' Linc agreed at length. 'And a couple of gardeners, of course. Now it's just the gardeners, and we run culinary courses from the estate; the guests get to choose their ingredients from everything that we grow.'

They stood, quietly watching, for a few more moments before Linc seemed to take in a deep breath, and strode forward.

'Come on, there's plenty more to show you.'

For the next couple of hours, Piper let Linc take her around his childhood home, showing her everywhere from the formal gardens where the public were allowed to admire the house, to the private grove of trees where he and his siblings first learned to climb.

She walked the light trail with him, imagining how pretty the stone bridge must look at night, strewn with colourful lights that twinkled and shimmered in the reflection of the water beneath.

And then, suddenly, they were down by the sea; on the private stretch of beach that belonged to the family.

'I don't understand why Sara doesn't just get married in some private ceremony here on the beach, instead of some spectacle with a couple of hundred guests we barely even know, let alone like.'

Piper blinked, and she despaired of herself for

the butterflies that were now fluttering madly—unfittingly—around her stomach.

Grimly, she attempted to quash them.

'Is that why you're so against your brother-in-law? Because he's agreeing to what you'd call a *spectacle* of a wedding?'

'I'd rather he asked her to scale everything back. I think that might take some of this unnecessary pressure off her. Duke's daughter or not, there's no need for all the fanfare. I can't help wondering if he's encouraging Sara because of how good it could make *him* look.'

'Have you asked your sister?'

Linc didn't answer immediately, instead choosing to glower out to sea—and at the bright sunlight as it glanced off the cold waves.

Piper wrinkled her nose and tried again.

'Sara doesn't seem the type to let herself get pushed into something she doesn't want.'

'You'd be surprised,' Linc replied darkly. 'She has always demanded more of herself than anyone else ever did. I suspect she might think a lavish wedding is her way of supporting Raf.'

'Why?'

'I don't know. As a reminder of how much weight the Stoneywell name holds?'

It was so far removed from Piper's own reality that she was almost frightened to answer and show herself up.

'The point is,' he continued, when she didn't answer, 'that it isn't just about me not seeing why she needs all this fuss or fanfare. It's more that I don't even understand why she's getting married at all.'

'Perhaps because she loves her fiancé?'

Piper tried to keep her voice upbeat but there was no mistaking the strain in her voice. After the way her father had treated her mother, she wasn't sure she believed in love either.

Wasn't it just a way to get away with treating another person as if they were dirt?

'You don't believe in real love any more than I do, Legs.' Linc snorted humourlessly, as if reading her mind. 'You act happy for couples, but I know how much we both wonder what the hell they're thinking of, tying themselves to another person for life.'

'I don't think that,' Piper objected. Weakly.

He shook his head.

'You might fool others, but you forget how long we've known each other. I've seen your expression when buddies gave up their military careers for their new spouse, the disbelief. Something you couldn't quite understand because you never would have done that. Neither would I. You and I are the same.'

'I gave up flying army helicopters for the love of my family,' she pointed out, but the nose wrinkle gave her away.

'Did you?' he challenged. 'Or was your reason

more practical? Did you actually have much of a choice?'

She didn't answer him. She didn't need to.

'The same as I did,' he carried on after a moment. 'The only reason I gave up my army medical career was because of that final ambush. Because I have responsibilities within this family, and because my father's ill health meant that Raf was fighting avaricious board members. At that time, he couldn't have held them off whilst Sara and I were living the lives we were living.

'You were an army doctor.' Piper frowned. 'What's so damaging about that?'

'Nothing, in itself.'

But the dark look that stole across his taut expression told a different story. Furious yet lost, all at the same time. The two emotions seemed to war across his features, then stole inside her ribcage like a fist, and squeezed. And then squeezed some more.

'Linc?' she prompted, unable to help herself.

'It's a story you don't want to hear, Piper.'

She didn't understand what made her close the gap between them. Or what made her reach up and place her palms to his chest. But suddenly, there she was. More than that, he wasn't pulling away.

'Try me,' she whispered. 'Why do you seem to be carrying such guilt around with you, Linc? What is it that you feel you owe your siblings?'

And she wasn't sure how long they stood there—perhaps whole lifetimes—and Piper pulled her lips into a tight, nervous line as she tried to will him not to shut her out, the way he always seemed to shut everyone out.

But even as she knew that was exactly what he was doing, preparing to push her away, a movement across the landscape caught her attention. A figure swaying oddly.

She watched in horror as the man suddenly buckled, then collapsed to the floor.

'Linc...' she cried instinctively. 'Over there.'

# CHAPTER ELEVEN

VAULTING THE WALL, not needing to look to know that Piper would be following, Linc raced across the fairway and to the men.

He was almost grateful for the distraction. There was no way he had been prepared to answer Piper's questions.

Even as he ran he noted the two figures hunched over a third. It certainly looked as if they were attempting chest compressions but the rhythm was wrong. Too slow. And the closer he got, the more he could see it looked like two guys in their twenties over a likely fifty-something bloke.

'Is he okay? Can I help?'

The two men cranked their heads to him in evident relief.

'It's our dad. We think he's had a heart attack,' one of them—the older-looking one who was attempting chest compressions—managed in a strangled voice.

'Can you do that CPR thing?' The other looked up at them helplessly.

'I can. I'm a doctor,' Linc assured them as he dropped beside the collapsed man and checked for breathing or a pulse. The man had neither. 'Can you tell me what happened?'

The two sons eyed him, somewhat stunned, before the older one spoke again.

'He said he was feeling a little bit faint, and then he just...collapsed.'

'Any history of illness?' Linc pressed.

'No.' The two men looked at each other before shaking their heads. 'Nothing.'

'Have you called emergency services?'

Again the two men looked blankly at each other.

'We were more concerned with doing CPR. I mean, that was the right thing to do, wasn't it?'

'Exactly right,' Linc assured them. 'You did well, and now we're here to help. Piper, can you—?'

'Already on it,' she confirmed as her mobile connected to the emergency services, stepping to one side to deal with them whilst Linc continued the chest compressions.

They both knew the odds on a person surviving a heart attack outside a hospital were low—around ten per cent, according to heart charity figures. But it didn't mean he wasn't about to do his damnedest to make this the *one*. It was what he was programmed to do.

'Right, I'll do the compressions.' He looked at the calmer of the two brothers, then indicated to the ground on the other side of their father. 'You can kneel here and ensure his airway remains clear.'

'The clubhouse has a defib,' the other brother remembered suddenly. 'Should I call them?'

Linc nodded.

'Yes, call them. Tell them that your father is in cardiac arrest, and to bring any other kit they have.'

'I'll help.' Piper stepped back to the group. 'The land ambulance is on its way.'

'Acknowledged.'

With one ear to the boys, and the rest of his focus on the man on the ground in front of him, Linc realised it was good to realise that one person he wasn't worried about was Piper. If anything, her presence could only make the entire scenario that much easier.

It was more than he could say for any other date he might have chosen to bring to this damned wedding.

For the next few minutes Linc worked with one of the sons to keep the blood and oxygen flowing around their father's body, surprised when Piper returned so quickly with the medical kit.

'They were already on their way,' Piper told him quickly. 'Another player had seen him collapse and alerted the clubhouse.'

'Right, can you take over chest compressions whilst I set it out?'

She hurried around to drop by his side, already in place to minimise time off the chest, as Linc made way for her, counting out her rhythm before he'd even got to his feet.

Quickly, he took a pair of scissors from the kit and cut the man's clothing away to give them better access.

'Okay, machine is charging.' He announced his warning a minute or so later, having set everything up. 'And stand clear.'

As the machine gave its warning sounds, Piper lifted her hands off the man's chest, moving backwards.

'Rhythm check,' Linc announced, bending down to check for a pulse. There was nothing.

'No.' Piper shook her head, also checking the femoral, as the defib machine reported its own automatic results.

'No output PEA,' Linc confirmed. 'Continue CPR.'

Wordlessly, Piper resumed compressions. Another couple of minutes and they could try shocking the patient again. The bleeping and automatic instruction from the defib machine rolled around them, but it was Linc's presence that was giving her the most confidence.

'Machine charging,' he warned again, a few moments later as the defib bleeped. 'Off the chest, and clear.'

Another shock. Another check.

'Rhythm check?' He had nothing.

Piper began to shake her head, then hesitated.

'I think they can feel a beat.'

Linc moved to her position and made a check of his own. It was faint, but there was something there.

'Let's continue CPR,' he said. 'Do you want a break?'

'Okay for now,' she confirmed, bracing her arms and beginning another strong set, leaving him free to carry out his other checks.

By the time the land ambulance turned up about five minutes later, the man's heart was beating again.

'He's making some respiratory effort,' Linc told them as he handed over. 'You'll want to intubate to minimise damage to the brain, as well as give him some medication to help blow off the carbon dioxide build-up.'

With both teams working together, it wasn't too long before the man was on a scoop and in the ambulance, his chances looking far more promising than they had done less than half an hour earlier.

And as they watched the ambulance roll off the fairway and back to the main road, Linc couldn't help thinking how easy everything was with Piper around. Not just the way she had slotted in to help, even though she was usually the pilot, not the paramedic, but the way she'd slotted in here with his family. Into his life.

It was the same way she'd been out on tour all

those years ago. That same quiet confidence that had attracted him to her back then.

But that still didn't explain why he'd almost decided to open himself up to her the way he had done, down on the beach earlier. Why he was ready to reveal secrets to her that he had never even shared with his sister. Or fully explored with Raf.

What was it about Piper Green that had him turning inside out? Worse, he wasn't even sure that he minded.

Piper watched the land ambulance roll carefully off the fairway, hoping that everything they'd just done would be enough to save their impromptu patient's life.

But her mind was already shifting back to the man beside her. The man who, if she wasn't very much mistaken, had been about to shut her down the way she was beginning to realise he always did. Only now, he was looking at her with a different expression on his face. One that was familiar, and unfamiliar, all at the same time.

'You asked me what is it that I feel I owe my siblings,' he repeated without warning, and when his gaze slid to hers she refused to look away.

'I did,' she agreed softly. 'Anyone who watches the three of you together can see the love and respect you all share, so why have you built this wall between them and you? Do you begrudge your sister's wedding so much?'

It wasn't even a guess. It was more words that flitted through her head and out of her mouth, trying to find some button, some trigger, that might help him to talk to her.

'I don't begrudge my sister anything,' he bit out defensively.

It wasn't the button she'd been looking for, but it was something. The tiniest wedge, a fraction of a millimetre in an almost non-existent gap. All she had to do was nudge it in that little bit further.

'Then what is it, Linc? Because there's something going on here, and if I'm going to play this part for you all this weekend, then I ought to understand it, at least.'

'There is no *ought* about it,' Linc clipped out. 'But since you're suddenly so damned interested, I'll tell you. My parents never had what you might call a good marriage—no great shock there, plenty of couples don't—but as the Duke and Duchess of Stoneywell, divorce was never on the cards. Lady Oakes, the Duchess of Stoneywell, you surely know the name, Piper?'

Even as she shook her head to deny it, something shifted in the recesses of her brain. An old story she hadn't heard since she was a kid.

'The Duchess of Stoneywell… Lady Oakes.' Piper's brow furrowed deeply. 'I think I know those names.'

'I imagine you do.' It was all he could do to keep his mouth from twisting up in disgust. 'She was nothing if not attention-hungry, our mother. If she wasn't centre of attention then she wasn't happy, and if she wasn't happy then no one else could be, either.'

Piper wanted to answer. She wanted to say something to help, but nothing would. So she stayed silent, and simply listened.

'No matter that our father was trying to be the duke and run a demanding estate, and keep a business afloat in a harsh economic climate so that hundreds of employees didn't lose their jobs—my mother wanted more of his time. His attention. Not because she loved him, you understand, but because she was a narcissist and couldn't stand the idea that not everything revolved around her.

'And when she didn't get the duke's attention—she looked elsewhere for her fun. Worse, she made sure everyone knew how overlooked and unappreciated she was, and how her husband didn't make time for her. She told anyone who would listen how unkind he was to her. Emotional cruelty, I believe she told one paper.'

So that was why Linc had never courted attention, Piper realised suddenly. It was why he didn't want publicity, and had never told anyone in the army, or in the air ambulance, who he really was. It was beginning to make sense now.

And crazily—dangerously—it made Piper feel special that she was the one he was confiding in.

'My father was always blinded by my mother. She was his downfall from the start. She wanted money, and to live the life of a duchess, but she didn't want any of the responsibility. She hated my father for being so upright, and moral, and boring.'

'I don't understand.'

'My mother brought scandal after scandal to the family—in fact, she was a scandal all to herself. The revelation that I was a bastard son was just her final coup de grâce. Raf and I only realised recently how much our father protected our family from her indiscretions—even up until her death. The papers had run stories about her from time to time, over the years—from deeply unflattering stories, to downright disgusting rumours. I'm surprised you didn't read any of them. She certainly did her best to get them into every media outlet going if it increased her exposure—in more ways than one.'

Piper squinted, fervently trying to recollect vague memories. She'd never really been one for gossip columns, or glossy mag tell-alls. Now that Linc had put it into her head, she did think she recalled a few less than pleasant things.

'That was her?'

'That was her.' Linc dipped his head curtly. 'You understand now why I never wanted to bring anyone back here. I didn't want to subject them to this, but also, I didn't want the gossip or the attention. Raf can do well without my name being associated with his.'

She shook her head vehemently.

'You didn't give them anything. Your father knew the truth and he didn't care.'

'Our mother did our best to drag our family through the mud, whilst our father was fierce about protecting the three of us from all of it.'

'Your father sounds like a decent, upstanding gentleman.'

'He was,' Linc managed fiercely. 'He stood up for what he believed in, and what he thought was right, and damn the rest of it. I'll never match him. Not like Raf does. I'm my mother's son, but I'm not his son.'

The roaring started in her brain in an instant, at the mention of scandal. As though she feared her own life might seep into his. She thrust it aside. That wasn't going to happen. Here she was telling Linc not to let his past and his mother's sins ruin his relationship with his siblings, and she was about to let her own past, and her father's sins, ruin this moment with Linc.

It was too much for either of them to have to bear.

'These aren't your sins to bear, Linc,' Piper said softly, realising that her words were as much for herself as for him. 'Your father never thought they were, and your siblings certainly don't. Raf and

Sara are asking for your help because it's their excuse to get you back home. They aren't holding you accountable, you must see that.'

'They don't need to hold me accountable, Legs. I hold myself accountable.'

'Is that why you've built this invisible wall between them and you? Is that why you keep them at arm's length? Why you joined the army? The only reason your sister keeps pushing you towards the Stoneywell Medical Centre is because it's the only thing she can think of to bring you back home.'

'It isn't for me,' Linc growled, but it wasn't as fierce as before.

She was getting through to him, and for some reason that made her feel good. More than good.

'And she knows that, but she tries anyway because she wants her brother back in her life. They both do.'

'Our lives aren't compatible.' Linc refused to agree, as Piper splayed her hand over his ribcage as though that could help her to reach him faster.

'Only if you don't want them to be. There are a hundred things you could do back here, with your medical skill, and as Lord Lincoln, if you wanted to. Like setting up a Stoneywell air ambulance for a start—look at what might have happened today if you and I hadn't been passing that golf course right at that moment.'

'You can pretend scandal goes away all you want to, Piper. But take it from someone who knows, the truth is that it never does. It follows a person, and rears its head at the worst times. No one can escape it. No one ever will.

And later, much later, when the roar had died down in her brain and her heart had stopped hammering around her ribcage, Piper would think it was that precise moment—those precise words—that had felled her at the knees.

Because he'd brought her to the table as a way to help douse any vicious rumours. But if anyone decided to look into her, and expose her own set of sordid truths, then she could do Linc and his family far, far more harm than good.

Her stomach heaved, and lurched. She'd spent so many years trying to bury this truth, from herself as much as anyone else. But now, there was nothing else for it; she needed to tell him the truth. Not now. Not when the rehearsal dinner was this evening.

But after that, perhaps when they left Oakenfeld Hall and went back to his penthouse. Certainly before the wedding next week.

Before someone else lit the match and it all went up in flames.

Taking both of them with it.

# CHAPTER TWELVE

*THE WOMAN WAS a damned enchantress.*

Linc watched Piper shimmer and charm her way around the room—just as he'd known that she would. Just as she'd always been able to handle herself around brigadiers and generals, and charm their respective spouses.

Just as she'd always charmed him.

It ought to concern him just how easily he felt she slotted into the role as his fiancée—*pretend* fiancée—but he found he was more spellbound than disquieted. And didn't that say something in itself?

Even Raf had remarked how happy he looked, earlier that evening when his brother had walked in to find him retrieving his grandmother's jewels from the study safe to lend to Piper. And when he'd pre-empted Raf's objection to lending out their grandmother's ruby necklace, reminding his brother—and possibly himself—that it was all just a ploy, he thought it was telling that Raf's only response had been, 'At least one of us should be happy.'

As though it were real.

It didn't help that Piper's words were still stalking around his brain. Could she be right about why he'd stayed away all this time—with the army, and now as a Helimed doctor? She made him question whether he had really been helping his family the way he'd once told himself he was doing.

Not that he was about to give up being a doctor. But perhaps moving a little closer to home might not be the worst idea, after all.

*And Piper?*

Ignoring the question, Linc set down his brandy tumbler onto the bar top, so loudly that the ice cubes rattled, and swung around so that his back was completely to the woman who seemed to occupy more of his thoughts than ever.

It didn't work.

Moments later, Linc found himself striding across the floor and towards her, before he even realised what he intended.

'Dance?' he bit out, less a suggestion and more an order, as he held his hand out.

And he had to fight to pretend not to notice the current of electricity that jolted through him, when she reached out obligingly, and slipped her smaller hand into his.

Without a word, he led her to the floor, before sweeping her into his arms for a simple waltz. And, just like that, the rest of the room—the rest of the world—fell away, and Piper was all he could see. All he could smell—from the pleasant citrus notes of her shampoo to that delicate note of her perfume.

His entire body prickled with awareness—and not just the more obvious, baser parts of his anatomy. Had any woman before ever affected him the way that Piper did? Pretend relationship or not, he was terribly afraid he knew the answer to that.

'Was my role not to mingle whilst you talked to board members and let them think you were ready to return home to the family fold?' she murmured up at him.

Though he noticed even as they danced that she seemed as incapable of tearing her gaze from him as he was of looking away from her. Linc took that as a positive.

'It was indeed.' He lowered his mouth closer to her ear, telling himself it was so that no one could possibly overhear their conversation. 'I understand we've already given them a great deal to mull over.'

'Oh?'

'I'm told that those who were arguing for my shares to be stripped from me, and who were using this evening as an opportunity to put forward their case, are now beginning to lose their collective voice.'

'That's good news, isn't it?'

Was he only fooling himself to think that the faint quiver in her voice intensified the closer his lips came to her skin?

'It's very good news,' he agreed. 'What's more, Raf tells me that he has already been approached by several board members who had been wavering before, but who are now ready to throw their full weight behind him. And I'm beginning to wonder if returning home might be a good idea, after all.'

She stiffened in his arms, her feet momentarily faltering. But he held her to him and kept them moving gracefully around the dance floor.

'You're thinking about really leaving Heathston? Not to run a medical centre, surely?'

This time, he knew he didn't imagine the shiver that rippled through Piper.

'And what happens when you don't have a fiancée after all? When you don't get married, or have kids, or all those things they believe a true Oakes lord should do?'

And the odd thing was that Linc couldn't explain why. He had never, not once, imagined himself getting married and having a family. Now, suddenly, he could. The image was distant, and somewhat hazy, but for the first time in his life, it was actually there. The only thing he could make out clearly was Oakenfeld Hall in the background.

Had Piper been right, that being an army doc had been his way of escaping the life to which he'd never quite reconciled himself? And had she also had a point that the day he would find peace would be the day he accepted that he was part of this family whether the duke was his biological father or not?

'What you said today about it being time this

region had a Helimed to service it, that made sense to me.'

Piper blinked at him.

'Well, yes. It would certainly have helped that man today.'

'Perhaps Oakenfeld Hall could sponsor a Helimed team up here. It would be something that would fit with my father's vision for Oakenfeld Industries—giving back to the community.'

'It makes sense,' she agreed, though her unexpectedly taut body was at odds with the sentiment.

'It does. That way I could also attend board meetings. Perhaps it's time I actually supported Raf and Sara and be present at these things.'

What made it so strange was the fact that he actually wanted to. Ten years ago, being back here he'd felt like a cuckoo in the nest. Even five years ago, he hadn't quite...*fitted*. But now, with Piper by his side, it felt somehow...*right*.

Except that Piper wasn't part of the equation. He shouldn't have to keep reminding himself of that fact.

Whatever the hell that was supposed to mean.

'That's great,' she managed, forcing a bright smile that was entirely at odds with the way her body was tensing so strangely in his arms.

Though he told himself he had no intention of saying anything, Linc heard the next suggestion slipping out of his mouth.

'The place would need a pilot. Should you decide West Nessleton Helimed isn't for you.'

'I can't move anywhere.' Piper laughed, though it sounded hollow to his ears. Or perhaps he was merely imagining it. 'My mother and my brother need me.'

He wanted to ask what it was that Piper herself needed. But he stopped himself.

'Of course.' He nodded curtly.

'If it wasn't for them, then maybe...' Her voice sounded thick. Unfamiliar.

But he could hardly process it for the racket going on in his head.

'You don't need to explain yourself,' he growled.

And he assured himself that the uninvited feeling in his chest—which felt altogether too much like regret—was purely because it would be a shame for his new Helimed operation to lose out on a pilot of Piper's calibre.

'Linc, there's something...' The tortured words caught in her throat as she stared at him miserably. A haunted note that reached inside his chest and squeezed. 'There's something I need to tell you.'

'You don't need to say a thing,' he made himself bite back, telling himself he was grateful for the reality check.

He even thought he might believe it himself.

'I do need to.'

And he couldn't tell whether it was the most honest truth she'd ever told him, or a complete lie. Before he realised what he was doing, Linc lowered his head to Piper's ear.

'You should never feel as though you have to do anything.'

'Right,' she muttered, turning her head.

And as their lips brushed each other's, the contact shot through him, demanding more, and making him greedy.

'I think we can do better than that,' he murmured.

Wordlessly, Piper pressed her body tighter against his, and perhaps it was the way her body seemed to mould itself to his, or maybe it was the incredible soft, sweet groan of pleasure she made as he fitted his lips to hers, but an intense heat seared through Linc.

White-hot and gloriously electric—unlike anything he had ever known before.

*Because Piper's unlike any woman you've ever known before.*

He beat the voice back, but there was no denying the truth in the words.

Piper was perfection. She tasted of longing, and need, and all manner of sinful things that he'd spent the better part of a decade telling himself he didn't imagine every time he'd looked at this woman. From the swell of her breasts pressing against his chest, to the scrape of her tongue against his.

As if they'd both been waiting for this moment

for a lifetime. Even two. Linc forgot that this was all meant to be a show, pretend. He only knew that he didn't want to stop. Didn't think he *could* stop.

He found himself pouring himself into the kiss. Confessing a thousand truths to her that he couldn't say with words—not even in the privacy of his own head.

But they were in that kiss, and he couldn't seem to stem them.

This was the excuse he'd been looking for. The moment to allow them both to cross that invisible line they'd drawn between them in the desert sand, all those years ago. And her presence at this dinner no longer felt pretend, or staged, perhaps it never really had done. It felt right, as though she belonged here, by his side, every bit as much as he did.

The kiss stretched on for ever, glorious and exultant. But when they finally pulled apart, coming up for air and remembering where they were, he knew he wasn't ready to let the evening end with just that.

By the glazed expression in Piper's stunning eyes, and her telltale rapid pulse at her throat—the one that begged him to cover it with his mouth—she felt exactly the same way.

Suddenly the ballroom felt too crowded. Too suffocating. Abruptly, he dropped his arms from around his fake fiancée's luscious body while keeping hold of her hand, then turned her round and ushered them both off the dance floor.

'Where are we going?' she asked breathlessly as they weaved their way through the crowd.

Linc couldn't bring himself to answer. He couldn't bring himself to do anything to break the moment; to give him pause to rethink what he was about to do. What he'd wanted to do with this one woman from the first time he'd ever laid eyes on her, before they'd thrown up obstacles such as *professional behaviour*, and *duty*.

But now none of those obstacles existed any more and finally, *finally*, they could be honest with each other about who they really were. And what they wanted from the other.

Piper allowed Linc to guide her out of the ballroom without another word.

After that earth-shattering kiss, she was finding it hard enough to remember to breathe, let alone talk.

*That kiss...*

It took everything she had not to lift her fingers to her lips in wonder—just to check that she hadn't been dreaming it.

He'd turned her inside out. In one single kiss, he'd wiped away all the fears that had been racing around her head that evening. Even now, her mind grappled for them but came up empty-handed.

All she could think about was Linc. The kiss

had erased every apprehensive notion she'd ever felt. It had been perfect. They'd fitted together perfectly.

*As if they'd been hand-crafted for each other,* something inside her whispered.

If he could do that with just one simple kiss, what could he do to her with something more intimate? If she continued walking with him along that corridor and upstairs to the bedroom—where he was patently taking them—then she was certainly about to find out.

Piper told herself to stop. Instead, she kept walking—and she didn't falter for even a step. As if she'd been waiting for the moment her entire life.

*Aching* for this moment.

Right up to the moment when her heel snapped off the high heels she'd never quite got used to wearing, and would have sent her tumbling to the ground, if not for Linc catching her fall.

'I can't walk like this,' she muttered, not sure if it was embarrassment or frustration that she felt the most potently.

'Hold on,' he gritted, and placed her arms around his neck.

And then, before she could ask him what he was doing, he simply lifted her up as if she were as light as air to him. Any thoughts began to seep out of Piper's brain. All she could think about were his strong arms around her; and how solid, how unyielding, his chest felt against her body.

She ran her tongue around her suddenly parched mouth. Not that it made it any easier to speak in anything approaching her usual voice.

'What...do you think you're doing, Patch?'

As if using his nickname could shift this...*thing* vibrating inside her. As if it could remind her of that nagging voice that was now shoved to the back of her brain; and she couldn't quite hear what it was trying to say, even if she'd wanted to.

But all Linc did was offer a wordless smile—a dark, utterly masculine curve of his mouth—before striding across the room to shoulder open a discreet door that she hadn't even noticed existed.

Craning her neck, she peered down the long, quiet, spine of a corridor that was presumably the servants' route through the house. A way of getting around quicky and easily, without cluttering up the main hallways where the gentry would be.

As if proving her theory, Linc made straight for a narrow, spiral staircase, and there was something so thrilling about the focussed look in his gaze, and the effortless way that he was carrying her, that made her feel ridiculously feminine, and...obedient. And made her forget everything else.

And then, finally, they were back in their suite. Alone.

'Should we really be doing this, Linc?' she whispered.

'I want you,' he answered simply, his deep voice grazing deliciously over her as surely as if he'd used his teeth.

'Here?' she whispered. 'Now?'

'Here,' he growled in confirmation. 'Now.'

He unzipped her dress, the deliciously naughty sound of it filling the room. Then he slid her dress off her shoulders, stripping her. But it wasn't a race—oh, no—instead, Linc worked painstakingly carefully, pressing his mouth to taste each newly exposed part of her, lavishing attention on every single inch of her bare skin, and taking his time as if he could have feasted on her for ever.

It was a dizzying, glorious notion.

Piper gave herself up to the feel of his lips, his mouth, his tongue inching his way over her flesh as though they had a lifetime to indulge. Maybe two. He tasted her and teased her, tracing exquisite patterns down the long line of her neck, and over her shoulders, his fingers brushing up and down her arms, and she gave herself up to the dazzling sensations that were ricocheting around her body.

It was as though he intended to learn every bit of her, from her forehead to her chin, and from her jawline to her collarbone, he kissed her. Soft, hot brushes of his mouth that sent shock waves through her every single time. And if a century or more had passed them by, then Piper wouldn't have cared.

Then, at last, he turned her round. Inch by stirring inch whilst he slid her dress lower to expose her spine, and then spent perhaps another entire century pressing his lips to the skin there and lavishing attention as he made his way carefully down.

And all she could do was obey. And feel. And marvel.

Never in her life had she known that the mere act of undressing a person could be so electrifying. So indulgent. This bit was the means to the end. The rushed bit of foreplay that was over and gone before she could even blink.

But Linc made it an art form all on its own.

A teasing, thrilling, stirring show that stoked the already smouldering fires in her higher and higher. She wanted more. So much more, and so very badly, that as his mouth moved lower, her dress pooling at her feet as he turned her back around to face him, she feared she would start shaking with desire.

She was sure that she shook with need, and still Linc took his sweet time, giving the removal of those lacy scraps of underwear as much painstaking time as when he removed her gown.

And then, when she was finally naked in front of him, he lifted one leg, kissing down her thigh, and her shin, before moving his mouth to inside and making his way back up again. Closer and closer to where she was aching, *actually aching*, for him the most. But he skimmed past it and when Piper heard a muffled sound, it took her a moment to realise that it was her own voice.

As he repeated the exploration down her other leg, all she could do was grip her shoulders with her hands and wait, just wait, for him to make his way back up again. And if she'd stopped breathing somewhere along the line, then there was nothing she could do about that.

Then, at long last, he was there. His lips inching their way up the inside of her thigh. Higher. Higher. And suddenly, his mouth was right there, at the apex of her legs, where she was molten, and sweet, and yearning for him—and finally, he slid her leg over his shoulder, pressed his mouth to her core, and he feasted on her.

Piper wasn't sure how she stayed standing. She heard her own rasped breathing as his wicked tongue did things to her that she had only ever dreamed of. And not even in such incredible detail. He was toying with her body in ways she hadn't even known were possible, and she wasn't sure she would ever be the same again.

She didn't want to be.

She only wanted this. *Him*. And if everything else simply faded out of existence, then Piper couldn't have cared less. And still, he played with her, driving her on faster, harder.

Her raspy breaths turned to gasps, and cries. At some point she must have slid her fingers into his hair as if that could somehow offer her purchase, as he finally toppled her, high and fast, into blissful oblivion.

By the time Piper came back to herself, she realised he must have carried her across the room to the bed, and he'd laid her down, and rid himself of his suit.

She watched, almost hungrily, as he moved to the end of the bed. Naked, and proud, and every bit as magnificent as she'd pretended not to imagine him to be.

'Are you ready for this, Piper?' he gritted out, and it occurred to her that he was only just managing to control himself.

The realisation was a liberating one. Pushing herself up onto her elbows, Piper reached out with one arm and hooked him around the neck to pull him down onto the bed.

He was all hers, if only for this one night; she would never get this chance again.

She might as well make the most of it.

# CHAPTER THIRTEEN

'Come back to bed.'

Piper jumped guiltily as Linc's hoarse voice floated through the dark. Still, she didn't move, keeping her eyes trained on the blackness of the gardens beyond the window, and her arms wrapped tightly around her body.

As if she could somehow ward off the cold guilt that crept through her.

'That should never have happened,' she muttered quietly.

There was no need to say anything more than that; they both knew she was referring to the fact they'd just slept together. Well, not so much *slept*… But the truth was that she wouldn't have changed it even if she could have gone back in time. Just to have that one, perfect night with Linc had to be worth it.

So what did that say about her moral fibre?

Piper heard the rustle of bedsheets, and the soft padding of his feet as Linc crossed the room to her. She still didn't turn around, but then she didn't try to stop him either.

'What's going on, Piper?'

She shook her head, searching for the right words.

'I just...' She steeled her shoulders, hating herself more than ever. 'I haven't been honest with you. I never thought things would get this far. I should never have let them get this far.'

'So be honest with me now.'

His easy tone took her breath away. As if he thought that whatever it was, they could get through it together.

More likely she was just projecting.

'I lied to you about my family,' she blurted out, hating herself. 'That is, not lied exactly; more, omitted.'

He didn't answer, but his hands moved to her shoulders. As though *he* wanted to soothe *her*. It was an odd notion, though not an unpleasant one, though she was too accustomed to being the one taking care of others to really appreciate someone else taking care of her.

Or give herself up to the temptation.

Carefully, she moved to the side and away, trying to put a little distance between them. All the same, when he didn't close the gap again, she felt strangely...bereft.

'I'm all wrong for you. We come from different worlds.'

Linc shook his head.

'No, we come from the same world, you and I. First the military world, now the Helimed world.'

'You're the son of a duke, Lincoln,' she burst out.

'Accepting that I'm his son and not just my

mother's unwanted kid, then I'm the second son of a duke, which, to all intents and purposes, means very little. I'll never become the duke—that's my brother's role, not that he wants it either. But he has no choice.'

'You're still a lord. And I'm...'

'You're what? A bright, intelligent woman? A skilled pilot? A beautiful human being, inside and out? Take your pick, Piper; just don't start any nonsense about not being good enough for a lord because, trust me, titles don't mean anything.'

'Nonetheless...' Her teeth were worrying at her lower lip so hard it was beginning to chafe. She forced herself to stop. 'I'm not the person you think I am.'

'That doesn't even make sense, Legs. You're overthinking things.'

'No, I'm not.' She shook her head, trying to stop the shaking from overtaking her entire body.

She had to do this, no matter how unpalatable it was.

'I once told you that my father died.'

'You did,' he agreed after a moment's thought.

'What I didn't mention was that my mother was accused of killing him,' she confessed heavily, resenting every word that was coming out of her mouth.

'Say that again?'

She found the barely concealed horror in his tone disheartening. Or was she just imagining it would be there? And then, as suddenly as her moment of boldness had come, it disappeared again. Without warning, she swayed, and stumbled, and just as she felt herself about to crash to the floor she felt two strong arms catch her and carry her to the wingback chairs that overlooked the expansive gardens.

It was surely the height of irony that staring at them through the bars of the lead-paned windows was as though she were staring at them from behind the bars of her very own prison.

Piper gritted her teeth and forced herself to speak.

'It wasn't true, of course,' she managed. 'It didn't take much for the police to realise that my mother would never have hurt my father. Though I wouldn't have blamed her if she had.'

'You're going too fast, Piper,' Linc rumbled. 'Back up a few steps and tell me from the start.'

But she couldn't. Her mind was spiralling and her mouth seemed hell-bent on blurting out whichever details popped into her head first.

'The point is that I should never have come here and pretended to be your fiancée,' she rushed on. 'And when we were on the beach and you told me about your mother and how bad a scandal would be for your family, I should have told you then. At the very least, I should never have slept with you. That was wrong and I'm…sorry.'

Or at least, she really ought to be. She shouldn't

be neatly wrapping up what had just happened between them into some perfect memory she could open up in the future and replay. Relive.

'Piper, stop. Breathe.'

Linc's voice cut into her thoughts and she realised she'd been speaking faster and faster, as though putting it all out there as fast as possible could get this whole ordeal over with sooner.

As if Linc wouldn't have a mine of questions.

'Sorry,' she muttered, struggling to catch her breath.

'Just take your time, Piper. Start from the beginning and explain it to me. All of it.'

And it was the quiet empathy in his tone that struck her more than anything. Very much as though he cared.

*Ridiculous notion.*

'I don't know where to start,' she admitted, after a moment, splaying out her hands helplessly. 'I'm sorry, I just…'

'It's fine, let me help,' he soothed, and she wondered how he could be so calm after what she'd just said. 'You once told me that you had a good childhood. You said that there was a lot of love, if not a lot of money.'

'I did,' Piper managed miserably, though the words felt strange in her mouth. Thick, and heavy, and gloopy. 'And that was true, for the most part.'

She lifted her shoulders helplessly. It wasn't that she didn't *want* to tell him the truth—for the first time in her life she'd found someone she actually felt she could explain it to—it was more that she had no idea *how* she was supposed to tell him. How she was even to begin to explain. Words swirled around her head, but she couldn't seem to make any of them come out of her mouth.

'I actually have a sister as well as my brother. She's three years older than me but we don't get on any longer. She and I grew up with my parents in a small terraced house on a housing estate. My sister was the pretty one, the bold one, the funny one, she charmed everyone she met within moments, and I adored her. Everyone adored her. But my father was the one she loved most—a daddy's girl from the start—whilst I was closer to my mother. I was quieter, more reserved, like my mother. He loved us all, of course, but not the same way.'

She paused, trying to slow her racing pulse and order her thoughts. All the while, Linc knelt quietly opposite her, his hands at her elbows as though he wasn't appalled by the very sight of her. She wondered what must be going through his head.

'I was fifteen when my father was in an industrial accident. He lost part of his right hand and his job. He'd been a manual labourer all his life, and without his hand, he'd now lost his job, and couldn't provide for his family.'

'What about compensation?' Linc asked. 'If it

was an industrial accident, surely he should have got a payout?'

'The company couldn't afford it and so they declared bankruptcy. There was nothing my father could do. He'd always been a proud man, but then he found himself thirty-eight, unable to work.'

'What happened, Piper?'

She took a breath, beating back the memories that she'd pushed away for so long. Carefully locked behind a thick door in her mind, where they couldn't get to her. Couldn't hurt her.

'We didn't have much money. My brother hadn't even been born but my mum worked a waitressing job already, and she got a second one cleaning an office block in the evenings. I got a job in a local corner shop.'

'And your sister?'

'She'd moved out when she was eighteen, just before Dad's accident. She'd met a boy, fallen for him, got pregnant, and got married. He'd landed a job at an oil refinery across the country, so they'd moved away.'

'So she couldn't help,' Linc noted.

'No, but I don't think anyone could have given that he didn't tell them. He didn't even tell my mum. He pretended that he'd got a job but borrowed money from a loan shark,' she bit out. 'I can only imagine that he thought it would tide him over until he really did find something. But then the next month came and he borrowed more.

And the month after that. I think that was when he started drinking.'

'Your father became an alcoholic,' Linc guessed.

Piper jerked her head stiffly, hating that she had to confirm it.

'He'd never really been a drinker, but I guess he found it numbed his brain and helped him to forget his situation. But he was a mean drunk.'

'By *mean*, I'm guessing you mean violent? Abusive?' Linc gritted his teeth, as though he was angry on her behalf.

It was…unexpectedly endearing, Piper thought dimly.

'Not to my brother or to me, but to Mum.' She didn't care to go into too much detail, but that didn't mean the memories weren't there. The screams, the sight of him, the fear for her mother. 'It didn't help that she just kept making excuses for him, and practically killed herself doing everything he demanded to keep him happy. She fell pregnant at the age of forty-two with my younger brother.'

Piper didn't elaborate, the look on Linc's face—reflected in the moonlight—assured her that he understood.

'I tried to get her to leave so many times, but she just kept saying she'd taken a marriage vow with him. *In sickness and in health*, and that he was sick. Even when he broke her arm, she just said that he was sick and that it was her role to take care of him.'

'I'm so sorry, Legs,' Linc growled. And she found herself smiling—albeit weakly—at the nickname, just as she suspected he'd intended that she would.

It was a moment of levity that she'd needed. Sucking in a deep breath, she pressed on.

'I think it would have been different if he'd ever tried to hurt me, or my brother,' Piper mused. 'I think she'd have left straight away. I'd like to think so, anyway.'

'So he never touched either of you kids?'

'Never.' Not that it lessened what he'd done to her mother. 'One night when he had put her in the hospital for the umpteenth time, I decided enough was enough. The hospital recognised the type of injury and they sent in a social worker as they always did, but this time I refused to cover for him. I told them what was happening, then I contacted our sister and I told her too.'

There was no way that Piper could keep the sorrow out of her voice, nor the tinge of anger, no matter how she tried.

'She said I was lying. That I was mistaken. She argued that if Dad was going through a hard time, then it was because he'd been through such a traumatic accident, and Mum ought to take better care of him and have more empathy.'

'She can't have really believed that.'

'I don't know.' Piper shrugged. 'Maybe she did. She never personally saw that side of him. To her, he was a quiet, gentle man who wouldn't even kill a spider in the bathtub. He used to take them outside and release them into the garden.'

'Events can change people, Piper. Not always for the better.'

Piper pulled her lips into a tight line, as though that could somehow ward off the sadness of the memories.

'I know that. I suppose my sister simply didn't want to see the truth. So she said it wasn't possible.'

'Your mum didn't collaborate your story to the social worker either,' he growled. 'Did she?'

Slowly, Piper moved her head from side to side.

'No, she refused to back me up. She claimed she'd been in the house alone, vacuuming the stairs, when she'd tangled her feet up in the hose and fallen. We all knew she was lying, but without her speaking out against my father, no one could do anything about it.'

'So you all went back home together.'

'We did. Mum didn't talk to me, except to say that she would never forgive me. She could barely even look at me. But, for a while, it was okay. I think maybe me telling the truth had scared him. Even if no one could act without my mum admitting it, he knew I wasn't going to be complicit.'

'It didn't last though, did it?' Linc demanded. 'It couldn't. He wasn't going to change.'

And the bleak expression on his face reminded her that, in her own way, Linc's mother had been just as cruel and abusive. It was just that hers was mental abuse rather than physical.

They each had their demons, her and Linc. How had it taken all these years to realise that?

'Eventually, he couldn't keep it up and the cycle started again. I was seventeen and desperate to join the army as soon as I could, but I was afraid what he'd do if I left him alone with her. Or with my baby brother. I tried to get her to leave again. To say something. To do something, but she wouldn't. Then, one night, when I was out at work, he came in steaming drunk as usual, but he'd run out of money.'

She squeezed her eyes shut as the memory slammed into her, and a wave of nausea threatened to overwhelm her.

'It was bad, wasn't it?' Linc growled, though his hand didn't stop caressing hers.

It was an unexpected comfort.

'The worst it had ever been,' she admitted, swallowing hard. 'I…'

'You don't need to go into details if you aren't ready.'

She nodded, grateful.

'I threw the money I'd earned that day at him, and grabbed the baby, then I got Mum out of there.

I didn't really have a plan, I just thought we could go to a halfway house or a shelter, or something. We were just leaving the front gate when we heard the smash. I don't know what possessed me to go back inside. I think it was the eeriness of the silence that followed. Just...nothing. But when I peered around the doorway, I saw he'd fallen into the coffee table and as it had smashed, a shard of glass penetrated his femoral, a little like that motocross kid on the first shout we did, really.'

'He bled out?'

'We tried to stem it. We got some tea towels and tried to apply pressure, but neither of us really knew what to do back then. By the time the police and ambulance arrived, he was dead.'

'There was nothing more you could have done with that kind of injury,' Linc managed gruffly.

Piper didn't answer. Logically, she knew that was true, but it didn't always help.

'How could they possibly have accused your mother of killing him, though?' Linc frowned.

And perhaps this was the worst of it all. Piper inhaled deeply.

'They didn't. My sister did.'

'Your sister wasn't even there.' Linc sounded infuriated.

'No, but she couldn't accept it had been an accident. She insisted we must have done something to him. Even when two different neighbours concurred that they'd heard him still shouting in the house when we were on the driveway, and then the crash, she refused to let it go. She has always blamed my mother for living when my father died, and she has never accepted the truth.'

She'd even tried to win custody of their baby brother, claiming that their mother was unfit for the role. But Linc didn't need to know that additional sordid secret. He already had enough gory truths to disgust him about her family.

'I'm only telling you all of this so that you understand why I should go. Why I have to leave now. Before any of this comes to bite your family.' She shifted on her chair, but Linc didn't move. He caged her, without even touching it.

Or perhaps it was simply that a traitorous part of her wanted to pretend that he was stopping her from going.

Oh, she never should have come.

'I'm so sorry that happened to you.' Linc lifted his hand to her chin, cupping it.

Piper twisted her mouth awkwardly and stayed silent.

What else was there to say?

He dropped his hand. 'I promise you, as soon as we get back to Heathston, I'll help you find a place for your mother and your brother to move to, so they can be closer to you now.'

'No,' she bit out. Loudly. 'I don't need your help. I can look after my family myself. If this job in West Nessleton comes through, we'll be fine.'

'You don't need to leave,' he argued softly.

And dammit if all she wanted to do was believe him.

She stamped the urge out viciously.

'Of course I do. I'm a landmine in your family just waiting for someone to detonate it. And you said it yourself today. The last thing your family needs right now is more scandals to make the board topple Raf. I'll head back to Heathston tonight and I'll find somewhere else to live. You need to stay here and come up with some plausible reason as to why I can't come to the wedding next week.'

*'Legs...'*

She shook her head, refusing to listen.

'The sooner we go our own ways, the better. And I think your plan of moving back here to be closer to your family and set up a new Helimed for the region is a great idea.'

'Piper.' His voice was still quiet, but this time it was firmer.

Enough to silence her.

But she still didn't look at him until he hooked his fingers under her chin and lifted it up.

'I don't care about your past,' he told her. 'I certainly don't care about dragging up a horrid past that no one should ever have had to go through, least of all a mother you've always said was kind, and generous, and good.'

'That's admirable.' She tried to pull her face

away but found she couldn't. For all her attempt to resist him, she couldn't bring herself to break that contact. 'But you know what they say: mud sticks, and all that.'

'Then turn it into a cleansing mud treatment.' Linc shrugged. 'My sister claims they're all the rage.'

'It isn't a joke.' Piper blinked at him.

'Perhaps not. But nor is it the end of the world, the way you're telling yourself it is. I want you. I like you. And you like me, too.'

'But you said it yourself, your family have endured enough scandal with everything your mother did. If they should dig up my past, then everything we did here to try to help your brother will have been for nothing.'

'I highly doubt anyone will delve into your past, Piper.'

'They might.' She jutted out her chin. 'You can't risk it. You said it yourself, there are people looking to discredit you just so they can get your shares.'

'And Raf and I have talked and come up with a way to deal with them. Me being here with you has gone a long way to helping that. So come back to bed, Piper. No one will care about me by tomorrow, or who I date. And no one will care about your secret. You're safe with me.'

And it was tempting, oh, so tempting, to just obey. To put the ugliness behind her and simply be with Linc. Be herself. Because it was true, she did feel safe with Linc.

She just wasn't sure he was entirely safe with her.

'I can't…' she forced herself to say.

He slid his hands down her legs, straightening them out so that he could help her to her feet. As though he could help her to move on.

God, she should have told him the whole truth. Everything. Even that last part about her sister. If she ever discovered that Piper was dating someone like Linc—that she was happy—Piper didn't think there was anything her sister wouldn't stoop to in order to take away that happiness.

It had never before occurred to her that her sister was acting out of her own sense of guilt.

'Linc, wait.' She faltered, hating this bit more than anything. 'There's something else.'

'I don't want to hear more.' He stopped her with his mouth. His tongue dipping so enticingly into her mouth. 'It's your past, Piper. Let it stay there.'

'But…'

'Just enjoy this for what it is,' he growled, dropping kisses from her mouth to move lower, to that sweet spot just on the column of her neck. 'For however long it lasts.'

And later she would think it was that last remark that convinced her to stay quiet. Even though a part of her wanted to tell him the truth, he was making her brain go fuzzy. Her thoughts dissolving into sheer sensation.

And, as he said, there was no need for everything to be laid out there. They were having fun for now. It wasn't as if this relationship could ever really go anywhere.

She ought to be grateful to him for reminding her of that fact.

And even though she wasn't convinced Linc was entirely thinking things through—even though she knew the moral thing to do would be to walk away, the way she should have done two weeks ago—she let him lower his mouth down to hers.

She let him, and she surrendered to him.

Because she might have wanted to listen to her head…but right now, her traitorous heart was the one in control.

# CHAPTER FOURTEEN

'Anyone see anything?'

Piper brought the heli around as all four members of the team scanned the ground below them for signs of their new patient. Not helped by the hazy mist that was beginning to roll in over these mountains.

'Nothing this side,' Probie answered over the headset.

'Nor this side,' added Tom.

'Can you take us back up a little higher?' Linc's voice rumbled. 'I might have something, though it's a little further south-east than the caller said it was.'

Piper duly took the bird up, her eyes still expertly scanning the ground even as she considered how well they were working together these days. Better than ever, she might even say.

It had been almost a week since she and Linc had returned from Oakenfeld Hall, and neither of them had raised the subject of her family since then. Instead, they'd spent their days pretending to their colleagues they were still nothing more than friends, but their nights exploring every inch of each other.

Piper thought that Linc had probably learned

every line and every contour of her body, first with his wicked hands, then with his even more wicked tongue. Not that it made each night any less of a revelation. Another journey of exploration. And she couldn't imagine ever tiring of such adventures.

Still, she didn't know what it meant. Linc hadn't mentioned his idea of him returning to his home since the evening of the wedding rehearsal. Had he changed his mind since things between the two of them had shifted? Or was he simply waiting for whatever this...*thing* was between them to peter out?

Sometimes Piper thought she didn't want to know. Other times, she thought the uncertainty could drive her insane.

Or perhaps that was just the guilt, eating away at her no matter how many times she tried to stuff it back down. Ultimately, it would ruin everything, she knew that. And still, she couldn't bring herself to do anything about it. As if gorging on her time with Linc could somehow save her from when it all fell apart.

And it would.

'See better now?' Piper asked, having taken the heli up to a better height. Not so high that it made things too small to see, but enough to give them a clearer, longer view. 'The caller said she wasn't familiar with this range. If her walking partner fell the opposite side to the one she thought, she could have given us the wrong info.'

Linc leaned forward, peering closer.

'Yeah, pretty sure I saw a flash of blue over there, two o'clock position.'

Piper followed his direction. It certainly looked as if someone might be down there, behind a mid-sized outcrop. Probably hoping to take shelter from the downdraught of the rotors, without realising they didn't actually know where their casualty was.

'Can you take a fly around?' Linc asked. 'Or is it too close to that rock face?'

'I wouldn't like to go all the way around. There might be loose rocks. But I can certainly bring her round a little more.'

'It isn't the best place to land down here,' noted Linc. 'If that blue *is* them, we might have a bit of a trek in.'

She'd been thinking the same thing. Down at this level the ground was too uneven for the heli. The only flat area she'd seen was too close to the sharp mountain face, which meant there was a good chance she would have to take the heli back to the top and let the crew either make their way down the long, winding path, or abseil.

Usually, it was mountain rescue heli that operated in these parts, but they'd been called to a shout just out to sea with a man overboard.

'Let's see if we've got the right people.' Piper

grimaced as she manoeuvred her heli into a better position. 'Anyone got a clear view?'

'Yeah, that's our guy,' Linc confirmed after a moment as he called it in, whilst Piper backed the heli away and looked more earnestly for somewhere to land. 'Hotel zero seven, this is Helimed hotel one-niner, over, ready with an update, over.'

'Go ahead, hotel one-niner.'

'We've located the casualty but the ground is too rocky to land close by. Confirm a land mountain rescue crew is on their way, over?'

'Yeah, that's confirmed, Helimed hotel one-niner, they should be with you within the next fifteen to twenty minutes, over.'

Piper waited for Linc to conclude the call.

'I want to head down this valley a way,' she told him. 'I think I saw a flatter area on the way in, which wouldn't make it any faster for you guys to get to the casualty, but it would make evacuation a lot easier if you don't have to get them back up the mountainside.'

'How long?'

'Not long,' she assured him. 'I know time is of the essence.'

Turning the nose in the direction she wanted, Piper flew as efficiently as she could. Sure enough, the flat area she hoped for came into view quickly.

'Here okay?'

'Yeah, great. Well spotted,' Linc agreed. 'Take us down.'

She didn't need to be told twice. Quickly, skilfully, she turned her heli until it was on the granite plateau.

'You make that look a damned sight easier than it is,' Linc complimented as he opened the door and bundled out with his bag.

And Piper tried not to flush like the kind of giggly schoolgirl she couldn't remember ever having been, as he cast her a wink that only the two of them shared.

She might have known it couldn't last.

It was late by the time Linc arrived home—and wasn't the truth of it now that it really did feel like a home, not just a penthouse, since Piper had moved in?

But his anticipation was short-lived when he walked through the door to see Piper looking ashen, and Sara glaring at her as if she were something not even the stable cat would deign to drag in. He had a feeling it was only Raf's presence that was keeping things from degenerating further.

And it should have concerned him—that dark sensation that pierced straight through his body at the thought that someone had hurt Piper.

He wanted to wring them out for their audacity, no matter who they were. Even his sister.

'Care to tell me what's going on?'

His voice might be silky smooth, but surely

no one could have missed the warning note that threaded through it. Not even bull-headed Sara.

'This...woman—' Sara spat the word out as though it were poison in her mouth '—could destroy our family.'

'I suggest you're a little more careful concerning what you say about my guests in my home,' he managed, the warning note even clearer.

But it seemed that his sister was even more obstinate than he'd anticipated.

'You should steer clear, Linc. She isn't who she pretends to be. Her name isn't even Piper Green. Did you know that?'

'I did not,' Linc acknowledged as casually as he could whilst he turned to Piper. 'You took your mother's name after his death, presumably?'

She blinked at him, and he realised she'd been expecting accusations.

'I did.' Her voice cracked.

He took a step closer as if to lend her his support, but she refused to even look his way. It didn't matter, he could read the shame in every line of her body, and he balled his fists into his pockets as though that could somehow contain his anger.

He loathed the sight of the scarlet stain that stole cruelly over Piper's cheeks. He knew how it felt. He'd felt the same way when his mother had announced with such delight that he wasn't even his father's biological son.

'So that explains the name,' he turned to his

sister coolly. 'And I'm also aware of her father's death. After all, that was going to be your next question, was it not?'

'What do you mean, you're aware?' Sara's voice pitched higher.

'I already know what you're going to say,' Linc clipped out. 'Piper told me herself. The question is why were you nosing in her private business?'

'Because unlike you, I believe it's prudent to know about the people trying to insinuate themselves into our lives. And if you know, then you should have told me. And Raf.'

'I wholly disagree.' He forced a casual note into his voice, knowing it would lodge itself under his sister's skin with far more effect than raising his voice to her. 'I know Piper's past because she chose to tell me herself. And I didn't choose to share it because I determined that it wasn't our business. Though I'm surprised at you, Raf.'

'No.' Raf shook his head, taking a step away. 'Not me. I just wanted to be sure you knew about it. If you do, and you're happy you know the truth, then I am too. I trust you.'

Any remaining words Linc had for his brother died on his lips as Raf turned to Piper and offered her an equally dignified apology before turning to Sara.

'We should leave now. Linc knows, we have our answer. Piper, you have my apologies.'

'Well, you don't have mine,' Sara snapped. 'I'm

not going anywhere until Lincoln realises exactly how this…phony has played him.'

'Then you're doing it alone,' Raf growled, taking his leave with only a final nod of his head to Piper, causing Sara to turn back on her.

'I trusted you. I told you that I was *happy* you were in my brother's life.'

Linc blinked in surprise.

'Did she really say that to you?'

And, finally, his beautiful Piper lifted her head and met his sister's glower head-on.

'You told me that maybe you had misjudged me, and that perhaps I wasn't such a poor decision for your brother, after all,' Piper managed, every word like glass in her mouth. 'And I didn't have the decency to tell you that you hadn't misjudged me at all. I should never have gone to your wedding rehearsal, and for that, I truly am sorry.'

'You don't owe anyone an apology,' Linc growled, his ribcage tightening at the misery in her expressive eyes.

'I do. I told you my past could damage your family, and I was right.'

'It hasn't damaged anything. What was it you told me, Piper—that I didn't carry anyone else's sins but my own?'

'It isn't the same thing,' Sara blasted out furiously. 'She helped to kill her own father.'

Beside him, he heard Piper's sharp intake of breath, her anguished gurgle. He wasn't sure how he manged not to bodily eject his sister from his penthouse, there and then.

They both knew there was only one person Sara could have got that information from. But surely even his sister wouldn't have gone that far.

'You have no idea what you're talking about,' he ground out coldly.

'I know she and her excuse of a mother covered up what they did.'

'Since when do we blame victims of abuse, Sara?' he managed icily. 'And, for the record, Piper wasn't even there when it all happened.'

And right now, he could only imagine what had to be going through Piper's head.

*His* Piper.

The realisation walloped through him, leaving him almost light-headed. He needed to talk to Piper alone. Sara needed to go. Striding across the room, he flung open his penthouse door.

He was throwing his sister out twice in as many weeks, but there was nothing else for it.

'I also suggest you follow Raf's lead, and leave.'

It was the most controlled thing he could think of to say. Moving back across the room, he put his arms around Piper, his entire body feeling it when she stiffened against his touch, as though she was barely stopping herself from ducking away.

And all he wanted was his sister gone so that he could make Piper talk to him. Make him understand that his sister had no right to do what she was doing.

'You're choosing her over us?' Sara pulled a disgusted face. 'You can't do that.'

'Then I suggest you don't make me,' he warned her. 'Get out, before either of us say or do something which we might regret.'

'You can't do this, Linc, I won't let you.'

'Leave. Now.'

She opened her mouth as though ready to respond, before appearing to think better of it. And then, at length, she snatched up her bag and stormed to the door.

'You'll regret choosing her over family.'

'I think not.'

'I don't want her at my wedding.'

'That is regrettable, but it's your wedding. But know that if Piper isn't welcome, then neither am I.'

'Of course you are. You have to be there, you're my brother.'

'If Piper isn't welcome, then neither am I,' he repeated. 'Your choice.'

And he waited, his chest pounding, as his sister finally got the message and left, leaving him and Piper alone.

'You shouldn't have done that,' Piper managed as aftershock wave after aftershock wave slammed through her.

It twisted her tongue, preventing her from answering. She wasn't even sure she could still breathe.

'I had to,' Linc bit out after what felt like an age. 'You were letting her talk to you as if she had a right to say those things.'

'I can't stop her.' Piper pressed her hand to her forehead as if trying to stave off a headache.

Hardly surprising.

'You could have told her the truth. Everything you told me.'

'You aren't serious?' Piper breathed incredulously. 'I told you because I trust you, Linc. I don't want to talk to Sara. It's humiliating enough without having to tell everyone.'

'Sara should never have spoken to you that way, but you could have told her what really happened. Not let your sister keep spreading lies about you and your mother, going unchecked every time.'

Did he know how much he was asking of her? He couldn't possibly. And what did it matter, anyway? What had just happened had been avoidable, if only she'd stayed away from Linc the way that every fibre of her had screamed to do from the start.

Even before he'd told her how far from scandal his family needed to be. Even before he'd told her about his fame-hungry mother.

A bomb like this had always been inevitable, the fallout predictable. And still she'd gone ahead and let herself be with him.

She'd brought it on herself. And she told him as much.

'You did not bring anything on yourself,' Linc declared instantly. 'If anything, my sister brought it on herself. But you should have trusted me to have your back.'

'Why, Linc? Why should I ever have trusted you?'

He stared at her as though she had two heads.

'We're supposed to be a couple.'

Piper snorted derisively, if shakily.

'Fake couple, Linc,' she managed—giving the impression that the words tasted acrid in her mouth. 'There's nothing real about what's between us.'

'I disagree.'

So simple. So certain. It caught her off guard, and for a moment she only stared at him.

Then she offered the faintest shake of her head.

'You're confusing love, and lust, and yearning, I fear,' she managed, with a coldness of her own.

And if he didn't know her as well as he did then he wouldn't have realised that her heart was being ripped out, just as his was.

'Whatever has been between us was sexual attraction, Linc. That was *all* it was. Sex. There was nothing real—nothing substantial. We don't even really know each other.'

'I think we both know that's a lie.' His tone changed.

And as easily as that, all the heat slid out of the situation. Piper stared at him miserably.

'Maybe it was,' she admitted, so quietly that he almost missed it. 'Maybe we did have a chance at something more than just *pretend*. But that's gone now. This was meant to be Sara's wedding week, from her rehearsal last weekend to her wedding this weekend. Now it will be tainted with my squalid past for ever.'

'Trust me.' Linc moved towards her. 'There's nothing my sister will relish more than a meaty story to make her wedding more memorable than any of her friends'.'

'You're wrong.' Piper shook her head. 'We were meant to be a couple to make things go more smoothly, now it will only cause more gossip and upset. If the board members use this to help their coup, do you really think either Sara or Raf will ever relish such a *meaty story*?'

And he hated that she had a point.

'I'll deal with it,' he promised her grimly. 'I think it's clear to her that if you aren't welcome, then neither am I.'

'So you're issuing ultimatums?' Piper challenged sadly. 'That's how you want to handle the wedding of your only sister? By backing her into a corner?'

A dull bellow started in his chest. Was that how it would look to his sister?

'I'm not backing her into any corner.'

'We both know that isn't how Sara will see it.' Piper shook her head. 'And for what it's worth, I think I'd feel the same, in her position.'

The bellowing got louder.

Piper was right, he couldn't force Sara to accept Piper at her wedding. But if he attended alone, then he might as well be giving Sara licence to investigate anyone he ever chose to date.

*Can there be anyone else after Piper?*

He stuffed the thought away quickly.

But still, she deserved better than this. Better than accusations that neither she nor her mother—both victims in different ways—would ever deserve. And Piper was right, now wasn't the time to punish his sister for trying to look out for him in her own, slightly twisted way. But given the way their mother had always treated her—jealous of her daughter's youth, and acuity, and looks—was it any wonder that Sara had never known quite how to communicate with other women?

Still, right now, his main concern was Piper. If he wanted his family to accept her at all—though if it came down to a choice between the two of them, he knew now that there would only ever be one winner—then he needed to wait until after Sara's honeymoon.

He would attend the wedding alone, avoiding a scene, because it was what Piper wanted. And because he had long since known how to pick his battles.

'This isn't about anyone else,' he ground out. 'This is about you, and it's about me.'

'We both know things aren't that simple,' Piper denied, as the resignation in her tone made his very soul ache.

'Nonetheless, I'll go to the wedding,' he confirmed after a moment, watching the relief chase across Piper's face. 'But only because I won't allow your name to ever become the reason for any distance between my siblings and me.'

'Linc…'

'However, this isn't the end of our conversation, Piper.' He gently lifted her chin so that she could see the promise in his eyes. 'We'll talk when I get back.'

'Yes,' she whispered.

And later, much later, he would wonder if she'd really meant it, or if he'd abjectly failed to read the lie behind that one, simple word that had fallen so easily from her lips.

# CHAPTER FIFTEEN

'LET'S GET TO our patient.' Linc leapt out of the heli as soon as Albert landed at the new shout.

Without waiting for a response, he raced across the field and vaulted the drystone wall at the end, and into the residential street, following the direction pointed out by various bystanders.

It had been just over two weeks since his sister's wedding. Over two weeks since he'd returned home to find that his penthouse was empty and Piper had left. The place hadn't felt like home ever since.

Even now, he didn't know whether she'd gone the moment he'd walked out of the door, or whether she'd left the next day, when the story her sister had sold to the press about the undeserving Piper bagging herself a lord had hit the gutter press.

But the question that really ate away at him was why she hadn't taken any of his calls, even when she'd realised that the story hadn't gone anywhere—especially when the few desperate journalists who *had* tried to follow up on the piece had realised that both he and Piper had served together in theatres of war.

The potentially 'juicy scandal' had faded into

obscurity as quickly as it had appeared. No one had cared, least of all his brother, or the Oakenfeld board. In fact, if anything, it had made the old cronies review him in a different light—a military hero who could be an asset to Oakenfeld Industries. Linc couldn't say he cared for the image change but if it meant Piper would be free of any hounding—and Raf would be given a boost—then he was prepared not to argue.

But what had really come home to Linc was that he wouldn't have cared what anyone had said. The only person he'd realised he truly cared about was Piper. She had gazed into that dark void in his soul, but instead of fearing it she had flooded it with light, with warmth, with *Piper*. Without her, he wasn't even sure he felt whole.

So tonight, at last, he was determined to find her in person—no more unanswered phone calls—and tell her. He'd given Piper long enough to come around to his way of thinking, to come back to him on her own. Now it was finally time to go out and bring her home. It was likely the only thing that would make him feel he could breathe again.

Even the return of Albert had only just taken the edge off his sense of disquiet—the old pilot slipping back into his role with obvious relief.

Rounding the corner, Linc hurried to where a paramedic—one of the land crew already on scene—was signalling to him. He could already see the patient over her shoulder as the man lay groaning on the ground.

'This is Jez?' Linc surmised.

'Yes,' the paramedic confirmed as she led Linc over. 'Jez is a normally fit and well forty-year-old male. Approximately thirty minutes ago he was on the roof of his home repairing the mortar around the chimney stack when he slipped and fell around ten metres onto the flower bed below.'

'Loss of consciousness?'

'None reported.' The paramedic shook her head. 'He's talked us through events and there doesn't appear to be any loss of memory. He's complaining of mild back pain. He is able to breathe deeply and there is good bilateral air flow. I'm concerned about a laceration to the back of his head, but he isn't complaining of any head pain.'

Linc glanced over to the patient, who was still lying on his side.

'No collar?'

'I didn't want to move him until you got here, in case he had a spinal injury.'

'Okay, thanks.' Linc nodded, indicating to Tom and Probie to approach the patient. 'Hello, Jez, I'm Linc, the air ambulance doctor. Mind if we take a quick look at you?'

He crouched down on the opposite side of the patient to Tom, and the two of them began their assessment.

'Can you tell me what happened, Jez?'

The man talked them through the accident with surprising accuracy and calmness.

'And on a scale of one to ten, Jez, if one is mild, and ten is the worst pain you can imagine, can you tell me what your pain level is?'

'I dunno, Doc,' the man pondered slowly. 'It isn't bad actually. It's more of a dull ache around my back. About one. Not much more.'

Linc and Tom exchanged a glance but didn't speak. Given the height of his fall, and the way the man had landed, if his pain wasn't acute then he was either miraculously lucky, or he'd done some serious damage that was preventing him from feeling the pain.

'I'd like to get him out of this narrow passageway so that we can examine him more easily,' Linc told the crew. 'Best thing is going to be to get him on a scoop and to a level part of the garden. Tom, can you hold the neck whilst we turn him and then we'll get a collar on as soon as we can?'

The team worked quickly and efficiently, working together to get the patient onto the scoop without causing any further injury to what was potentially a serious neck problem. Soon, they had Jez on the flatter part of the lawn with better access around him, and began a more thorough examination. The most concerning discovery was that the man seemed to have damaged his C-Four and C-Five neck vertebrae, which was impairing his body's ability to transmit the pain.

A false move, and there was a chance their patient could end up being paralysed.

'Okay, Jez.' Linc moved over his patient until the man could see him. 'We're concerned you may have injured your neck, so we're going to keep your head stable with some tape, as well as the collar.'

'Okay, Doc.'

'We're going to get you in the air ambulance now, and get you straight to Heathston Royal Infirmary, okay?'

For the moment, despite the laceration on the back of Jez's head, the man's good cognitive function didn't suggest any major head injury. But without full scans and X-rays at the major trauma unit, Linc couldn't rule out the possibility of a brain bleed.

The sooner they got their patient to hospital, the better.

Piper huddled down in the seat of her car as she watched Linc and Albert in the distance, whilst they pulled the helicopter back in after their shift.

It had been a little over a fortnight since she'd last seen him—as if she didn't know it right down to the days and hours. Possibly the worst time of her life, if she was going to be honest—which was saying something. And every day she'd had a moment of weakness when she'd almost, *almost*, taken his phone calls, or picked up the phone herself.

Somehow she'd resisted. Until now. Until the letter—the job offer—that had arrived in her barracks' post box this morning. Not just any offer, but the offer of a job at Stoneywell air ambulance—with Linc as the critical care doctor, just as he'd once suggested.

Her heart rattled against her ribs with nervous anticipation. She needed to know if he just wanted a pilot, or if he wanted something more from her as well.

Piper shifted again in her seat, and eyed the car clock as Linc dropped the handle to the trailer and headed inside to complete his paperwork whilst the old pilot completed the last of the post-shift checks.

The rest of the crew would be leaving within the next half-hour or so, leaving Linc alone in the base. And then she was determined to go and speak to him—despite her jangling nerves.

Because the truth was that she'd had plenty of time to think these past couple of weeks. Plenty of time to realise that sneaking out of Linc's penthouse the day after his sister's wedding—the day that first venomous piece from her sister had come out—hadn't been her finest hour.

In truth, she felt it had been the biggest mistake of her life, not least because every inch of her had missed that maddening, thrilling, gorgeous man, every second since she'd done it. It had taken her more steel than she'd ever known—even flying her Apaches in war zones—to ignore her phone every time his ringtone had shattered the semblance of peace that she'd pulled around herself.

Only, perhaps he hadn't missed her the same way. Perhaps he'd been calling to detail exactly the damage that her sister's story had done to him. And to his family's name. Little wonder that she was ashamed at herself for lacking the moral fibre to take his calls and find out, and even less surprise that, after a while, he'd stopped calling altogether.

Clearly he must have realised that his life was far less complicated—far less messy—without her in it.

At least, if there was such a thing as a silver lining, the press didn't seem to have published anything more than that one single story. She'd scoured the newspapers every day since yet, to her shock, nothing new seemed to have been written.

And finally, *finally*, Piper had started to try to breathe once again. Enough to regret running from the man who had stood by her even against his own family that last night. But the more time had passed, the more it had felt as if it was too late to change it.

*Until now.*

Instinctively, Piper's fingers felt for the letter in her pocket. Linc might not have sent it personally but it felt like an olive branch, all the same. A last chance. And what did it say about her feelings for Linc that she had jumped into her car and travelled all the way back to Heathston to speak to him, instead of simply picking up a phone?

Piper started as the door to the base burst open and Probie sauntered out, followed by Hugo. She hunkered down in her seat hoping they wouldn't spot her car, nestled as it was between an old airport minivan and the fence line. But they were too caught up in their own conversations to look her way, and within minutes they were gone.

A short while later, both Tom and then Albert followed.

Which only left Linc.

Her heart lodged somewhere between her chest and her throat, Piper folded her legs out of her car and hurried towards the base door. She was halfway across the tarmac when she spotted him. Lolling on his muscular motorbike and waiting as though he had all the time in the world.

*For her.*

The others might not have spotted her, but Linc hadn't missed her.

A part of her wanted to turn around and run in the opposite direction. Another part of her wanted to run to him. In the end, she merely hesitated and then walked slowly over, pretending that her entire body didn't notice when he stood up, feet apart and arms folded over a simple black tee that only served to enhance that utterly male body and remind her of the last time she'd explored every inch of it.

But her palms didn't itch—she wouldn't allow them to. She refused to remember just how it had felt, running her hands all over this man's body, again and again, as though she had a thirst that only he could sate.

And she told herself that, for all her apprehension, she hadn't imagined this moment—seeing him again—a hundred times. A thousand.

He looked so casual, so easy, standing there. But she knew only too well the dangerous edge which lay, barely concealed, beneath the surface. The one that judged her and made her feel lacking.

'You changed crews,' he stated simply. Evenly. That low voice doing things to her insides even now. Even under the cloud she could feel hanging above her, pressing in on her. 'Even before Albert returned to Heathston.'

'The schedule suited me better,' she lied.

She should have known better. Linc quirked one eyebrow upwards, though there was no amusement in it.

'Let us be honest, shall we? You wanted to avoid me.'

'No... I...okay, yes.' Her eyes slipped away from his in shame. 'I did. But can you blame me? After what that tabloid story said about you?'

'This is your apology?' He arched his eyebrows even as the corners of his mouth quirked up.

Remorse flooded instantly through her.

'You're right. I'm sorry. My sister had no right to sell such a story to a paper. It was filled with lies and vitriol—'

'I don't care about your sister, Piper,' he cut her off easily. 'And I certainly don't expect you to have to apologise for the choices *she* made. If anything, she couldn't have sold any story had Sara not alerted her to the fact that you and I were together. So let us not waste our time with any pointless blame game, shall we?'

She frowned at him.

'You understand that Sara was just trying to protect you all.' Piper lifted her shoulders defeatedly. The action revealed far too much of how she really felt, but she couldn't stop herself. 'I know how your sister feels about the importance of family.'

'Then it is unfortunate that she chose to go about it in a way that resulted in more negative attention for us all. But that isn't the apology I am looking for, Piper.'

'It isn't?' She eyed him incredulously as dark things began to fill her up inside.

Could it be the hint of possibility?

'I'm talking about an apology from you,' he clarified, as if he could read every one of the questions that had been flying around her brain up until a few minutes ago. 'For simply leaving like that. For not waiting for me.'

It hit her squarely in the chest. She opened her mouth, closed it again, then drew in a breath.

'You're right. The way I left was cowardly but I couldn't bear the idea of hearing you say to my face how disgusted you were...*are* with me. How I'm the reason for a scandal that you all wanted so badly to avoid. I don't think I want to even imagine the things your sister is calling me right now.'

'I can deal with my sister,' Linc told her ominously. 'Just like I told you I could do that night.'

She wasn't sure it made her feel any better. It was all she could do not to let her shoulders sag suddenly, in defeat. And still that steady gaze held hers, threading through and making her feel hot yet unsettled, all at the same time.

'Why are you here, Piper?'

And this was it. She could bottle it, or she could do what she came here to do.

'I came to talk to you,' she told him simply. 'To ask you a question.'

'Fire away,' he invited.

Reaching into her pocket, she retrieved the letter but, though she held it out towards him, he made no move to take it. Clearly, he was expecting her to talk instead.

'Did you send me a job offer to join you at Stoneywell air ambulance when it's up and running next month?'

And she found she was actually holding her breath, waiting for him to answer.

'I did not.'

It took her a moment to realise that the crashing sound was only in her head.

She should have realised that it had only been her imagination that Linc would still want her. Miss her.

Regret sliced through her.

'Of course you didn't,' she stumbled on, wishing she were anywhere but here, making an even bigger spectacle of herself.

But at least she knew now. She could put that ghost to rest.

'I should... I'll go now.'

'But I knew it about it,' he announced, halting her in her retreat. 'And you aren't asking the right question.'

'The right question?'

He pushed himself off the motorbike and sauntered, too casually, towards her. She could only watch, paralysed. Her throat feeling suddenly parched.

'How does a letter like that get sent out without board approval? Without every member of the board knowing about it?'

Hope jolted in her chest. Kickstarting like an old engine with a faltering battery, but starting all the same.

'How does a job offer like that get sent out without board approval?' she rasped.

'It doesn't.' Linc shrugged.

The silence was almost crushing as it wound around Piper's brain.

'It doesn't? So, you knew? And your brother knew? And...'

'And Sara knew. She sends her apologies, by the way. Grudging and sheepish though they may be, she has finally accepted that her meddling caused this latest debacle.'

'I can't see your sister apologising for anything.' Piper shook her head. 'If anyone knows her own mind, it's Lady Sara—'

'Sara is acutely aware that we all have our secrets,' Linc cut her off, and there was something in the way he said it that made Piper stop. 'She just forgot that salient fact for a while. Call it the noise of her impending nuptials, but she is far more herself now it's all over. She will tell you that in person, if and when you decide you're ready to meet her again.'

'Right.' Piper pursed her lips, not sure she could quite believe that. 'Nevertheless, I know you don't want to hear it again, but I really am sorry about what my sister did.'

'You should have stuck around to tell me that at the time.'

'I was going to,' she admitted, before she could

censure herself. Another detail she hadn't intended to just blurt out.

But the intent look that overtook his angular features stole any other words from her mouth.

'Were you, Piper? You didn't leave the moment I walked out of the door to the wedding?'

'Of course not,' she cried, though perhaps she should have, had she been a more honourable woman. 'I wanted to stay and talk to you. But then the newspapers came out the next morning, and my sister's story splashed all over them...'

'I would hardly call a half-story buried in a middle page *splashed all over them*.'

'No.' She flicked her tongue out over her suddenly dry lips. 'Right. But still, I was ashamed. I didn't think you'd believe I had nothing to do with the piece.'

'Is that really how little you think of me?' he challenged her, a dark frown clouding his maddening, beautiful face.

Something—she didn't care to name what it was—sloshed around inside her.

Had she really thought he wouldn't even hear her out? Or was that just the excuse she'd told herself? The only thing that helped her to push away from her true feelings—the fact that she was in love with Linc.

After all, the only reason she had even been at the wedding rehearsal dinner had been to play at being his fake girlfriend because settling down was the last thing Linc wanted to do.

'I was supposed to be there to make people think you were ready to settle down and return to Oakenfeld. The idea was to get the board members on side. I knew that story could only hurt and there would be no coming back from it.'

'Do you really think Raf and I didn't have a back-up plan?' Linc stepped forward abruptly.

Before she could react, or step back, his palm was cupping her cheek, and moving away wasn't an option. If the entire world had just rocked on its foundations, she wouldn't have been more shocked.

'Linc...'

'You were there because I wanted you there.' His husky voice scraped over her. 'I wanted them to meet you, whatever excuses I may have told you—told myself—at the beginning.'

'You don't mean that,' she managed, but she wasn't sure how.

'I know what I mean, Legs.'

It wasn't just his words that swirled within her chest, making her feel...lighter, and more hopeful, than she thought she'd felt in a long time—perhaps ever. No, more than what he was saying, it was the way that he was looking at her. The intensity of the expression in his gunmetal-grey eyes.

The same expression he'd worn that last night they'd shared, when he'd lifted himself wordlessly above her in bed, their gazes locked as though nothing could tear them apart, and then he'd buried himself so deep inside her that she hadn't known where she'd ended and he'd begun.

Her heart slammed into her chest wall as every fibre of her screamed out to listen. To stop being so hell-bent on protecting herself that she turned her back on something this incredible.

But it wasn't that easy.

'You can't,' she rasped out, finally finding the strength to step back. Away.

But the space didn't make Piper feel better. It just left her feeling empty. Bereft.

'Why can't I?'

And he actually sounded…amused. But how could that be right?

'We're from two entirely different worlds. It wouldn't work. *We* wouldn't work.'

'We're from the same world, you and I.'

'Hardly.' She snorted. 'You're the son of a duke, and I'm the daughter of a woman who was once accused of killing her husband. No matter how false it is, it's one of those things that I don't think will ever go away. You said it yourself.'

'Then we'll find a way to turn it around to our advantage.'

'You can't. Your family don't need the scandal. You told me that, too.'

'My family can handle it. Or *would have* had it been necessary. As it was, the couple of journalists who visited Oakenfeld looking to follow up on your sister's story ended up digging up the fact that you and I used to serve together.'

'Oh.'

'Indeed.' Linc pulled a grim expression. 'They started talking about us as war heroes, which made the board prick up its collective ears. Apparently, they'd never considered using me in that way to enhance the Oakenfeld name.'

'I see,' she managed, not sure whether she really saw at all.

'But even if they hadn't felt that way, it would have been a sorry state if standing up for an abuse survivor like your mother—like you—brought my family scandal,' Linc growled. 'And if it had done, it wouldn't matter because it's the right thing to do.'

'Actually, I spoke to my mother after that newspaper story came out.' Piper almost giggled at the shock of what she was about to say. 'She told me that she was tired of hiding away. Sick of still feeling like she was my father's victim after all these years.'

'Is that so?' Linc arched an eyebrow.

'She said it was almost a relief that my sister had finally done something. That she'd been waiting for some kind of attack all these years and now it had finally come, but no one who knows her seems to care. Some don't even realise it's our family, and those who do have told her how brave and inspirational they think she is.'

'So your mother is happy?' Linc pressed. 'I ask because there's one of the old estate keeper's cottages available, which Sara said she would be more than happy to renovate for your mother and brother. Her way of trying to prove she's sorry.'

'That's...surprisingly sweet of her,' Piper managed. 'Thank you. But my mother is happy where she is. She feels she has people around her who genuinely care for her, and for my brother. She told me that if the story has done anything, it has shown her the kind of good people her friends are—and that she hoped I have the same.'

'So your sister's plan has backfired on all fronts,' Linc mused.

Piper nodded jerkily.

'So it would seem.'

'Yet, even if it hadn't, I would have still been there for you, Piper. I would have stood side by side with you, because I care about you.'

'You care about me.' She heard the torture in her own voice, but that couldn't be helped.

She wanted to hear more. *Needed to.*

'I...care for you, too, Linc.'

Except that wasn't the word she meant to use. Not at all.

'Linc...'

'As for our different backgrounds, which you seem so hung up about, it doesn't matter. You and

I are more alike than you seem to want to admit; we both chose an army life because we thought we could make a difference. We each chose Helimed for the same reason. We're more right for each other than anyone else I know—our different backgrounds don't change that fact.'

'I know,' she muttered, not sure what else to say.

'I hope you do.'

Without warning, he smoothly closed the remainder of the gap between them again. Piper held her breath, waiting for him to reach his palm out to her cheek as before but he didn't. Instead, she found her own hands had crept up and were lying on his chest, though she didn't recall moving.

Clearly her body knew things her head was still denying.

'I love you, Piper Green,' he told her soberly. 'I think I've loved you from the first moment I met you.'

'That was lust,' she croaked, but he shook his head.

'It was love. You were strong, and fearless, and I loved your dry sense of humour from the get-go. Though I'm not denying there was a healthy dose of lust in there, too. Denying it these past few years hasn't helped.'

'You're mistaken,' Piper whispered. But it was crazy how badly she wanted to believe him. 'It was just some silly attraction fuelled by that interrupted kiss. If we'd slept together that night, then it would have all fizzled away years ago and last week would never have happened.'

'You and I both know that's a lie. Nothing would have fizzled away, no matter how many times we slept with each other. Though we weren't the same people back then that we are now. We each had our pasts to deal with, and we needed to come to terms with that in our own time.'

And, for some reason, it was that that made Piper smile the most.

'You're saying we were too immature back then, *Patch*?'

'I would never say that out loud,' he replied dryly.

'I love you, Linc.'

The words were out before she could stop them. But then she repeated them because it felt better than she could ever have imagined to finally be able to admit it. To him, to herself, out loud.

'I love you, too,' he growled, cupping her face in his hands. 'You make me a better man. The man I think I always thought I couldn't be. You make me want the life I have tried to shun, because, with you at my side, I know I can still make a difference.'

He lowered his mouth to hers and finally, *finally*, as he kissed her for what felt like entire, glorious lifetimes, they found their way back to each other.

And when they surfaced at last, with Piper clinging to her lord as they stared at each other in wonder, he reached out and took something from the rucksack at his feet.

'Marry me, Piper.'

She wasn't sure she kept breathing.

For a long moment, she gazed at the stunning ring that seemed to wink at her from its antique box.

'You had that in your bag?'

'I was coming on my way to see you tonight, when I spotted your car hiding over in that corner.'

It took everything she had to try to think straight.

'It's too soon...your family,' she murmured. 'We should wait to see if everything dies down for your brother.'

'Raf can handle himself,' Linc growled. 'He told me so himself. As for waiting, you and I have waited for years.'

It was as if he was echoing the thoughts in her head.

'I want you now, Piper. As my wife, my partner, the mother of my children.'

'I want that too,' she breathed.

'Then marry me.'

'Yes.' She nodded. 'Yes, of course I'll marry you.'

And she watched wordlessly as he slipped the magnificent ring out of the box and onto her finger.

'We can have it resized if it doesn't fit.'

'It fits perfectly,' Piper whispered. 'Like it was meant to be. It's stunning.'

'It's a three-and-a-half-carat marquise-cut diamond that belonged to my great-grandmother. Now it's yours.'

'And now you're mine.' She laughed, as a sort of frothy, fizzy happiness seemed to bubble up inside her, filling her with joy.

It was a revelation. It made her feel as if she was finally home.

\* \* \* \* \*

# Her Secret Rio Baby
Luana DaRosa

MILLS & BOON

Once at home in sunny Brazil, **Luana DaRosa** has since lived on three different continents, though her favourite romantic location remains the tropical places of Latin America. When she's not typing away at her latest romance novel or reading about love, Luana is either crocheting, buying yarn she doesn't need or chasing her bunnies around her house. She lives with her partner in a cozy town in the south of England. Find her on Twitter under the handle @ludarosabooks.

Visit the Author Profile page
at millsandboon.com.au.

Dear Reader,

Thank you for choosing to read *Her Secret Rio Baby*. I'm excited I get to share Eliana and Diego's story, which is close to my heart because it's set in Brazil and celebrates and highlights Latin characters and their lives.

The first version of this story was fuelled by coffee and cake as I sat in my kitchen with the real Ana. I was stuck, you see. I knew who Diego and Eliana were, but I didn't know how to get from where they are to where I envisioned them to be. A lot of obscure and outrageous ideas later and their story and journey started to take shape.

Eliana struggled with her sense of belonging her entire life, not knowing who to call her people or where to find them. She returns to Rio de Janeiro to deal with her father's estate.

And runs straight into Diego, who knows exactly who his people are and goes to great lengths to do right by his community.

It's that sense of community I'm so excited for you to read about.

*Luana <3*

# DEDICATION

For the real Ana, thank you
for being an amazing friend.

# CHAPTER ONE

WHEN ELIANA CAME down to the hotel bar she hadn't planned on meeting anyone. Especially not the out-of-this-world-handsome man sitting on the barstool one over from her. While catching up on the *futebol* game she hadn't noticed him sit down, until he struck up a conversation about the new manager of one of the teams. Something that threw her off. Men usually assumed she knew nothing about the sport.

At first glance he seemed no more than a well-dressed businessman finding refuge at the bar after a long day. But the longer she kept looking at him, the more her skin tingled below the surface as the extent of his devastating handsomeness coalesced in her mind.

His suit was tailored to perfection, clinging to his body as if he had been born in it. The fabric was the kind of black that swallowed a man not confident enough to wear it. Not him. He dominated every fibre with a quiet but electric sensuality.

The only thing that seemed out of place in this vision was the charcoal-black shoulder-length hair that had been carelessly ruffled on one side to keep it out of his face. Eliana wanted to dig her fingers through the strands of that hair and tug him closer to her.

The fantasy came over her unbidden, intruding on her already exposed nerves, and she shook her head. It must be her tired brain, she told herself as she bit the inside of her cheek to stop herself from licking her lips as she noticed his eyes dart to them for a fraction of a second.

Eliana had spent the better part of her day travelling from Belo Horizonte to Rio de Janeiro. A bereavement had brought her here. Her father Marco, along with her half-brother Vanderson, had died in an accident a couple of days ago. A fact that had left her numb on the inside.

She had never been close to either of them—hadn't even attended their funeral. A part of her had wanted to…to take that final opportunity to say goodbye to the only family she'd had left. But when it had come to it she'd backed out, staying locked in her hotel room as she got to grips with the new reality she now lived in.

She was now the heiress to her father's hospital and fortune, and that was a twist of fate no one had seen coming—Eliana least of all.

'May I?' the man asked, pointing at the empty barstool between them.

Eliana nodded, taking a big sip of her wine as he slipped into the seat. She could almost feel the heat of his body radiating towards her. They were discussing last night's *futebol* match, yet her body was reacting as if he had whispered tantalising words into her ear.

She glanced at her wristwatch. It was late enough not to seem impolite if she left. Her flight was early the next day, and today had already been long and tedious. Going now would save her a lot of energy she didn't have.

Except Eliana didn't want to leave. Not really. The man's casual banter had made her forget about her heavy heart for a moment, and the way his dark eyes looked her over ignited small fires all over her skin.

It was a reaction she didn't expect, but one that also wasn't entirely unwelcome. This was what people did, right? They met in bars, decided to have some fun.

'I'm Diego,' he said, and it was only then she realised she had been staring at him.

His name sent a cascade of heat down her spine. He had only introduced himself. Why did it feel as if he just said something dirty to her?

'Ana,' she replied and took his outstretched hand. His grip was firm, and his fingers grazed her skin for just a moment as he held onto her hand a flash longer than was necessary.

A spark appeared at the spot where he'd broken their physical connection, travelling down her arm before settling in the pit of her stomach.

'What brings you to Rio?'

A smile curled the full lips, highlighting the distinguished features of his face even more. He wore his jacket open, the linen shirt visible beneath giving her an idea of the pure masculine fantasy hidden underneath the fabric. A thought that dominated her to the point where she had to remind herself that they were in the middle of a conversation.

She'd been a woman at a bar before, talking to men like Diego. But she couldn't remember ever having such an instant and visceral reaction to anyone's proximity.

'The funeral of my father.'

She didn't want to discuss her father with anyone, but she needed something to distract herself from the fire eating her insides. He didn't need to know she hadn't gone.

'I'm sorry to hear that.' Diego's face softened.

'Don't be. We weren't close.' Eliana tried to keep the bitter edge out of her voice as much as she could. But the words tumbled out of her mouth before she could think better of it.

To her surprise, Diego scoffed and took a sip of his drink. 'I know what that's like.'

'Ah, we have father problems in common?'

His eyes darted to hers, darkening as their gazes meshed. A shiver crawled through her as she glimpsed a hint of the vulnerability he must keep hidden away behind his detached facade. The moment only lasted a second, before shutters fell over his eyes, cutting her off from anything that lay beyond the surface.

Which was just as well. Eliana wasn't looking for any attachment here in Rio. The complexity of her father's estate meant she'd need to briefly come back in a month, to claim the hospital and wrap up anything else that needed to be done to have Marco Costa out of her life for ever. She hoped to see as little of Rio de Janeiro as possible. The city bore nothing but nightmares for her.

Diego shrugged her question off, shifting his attention from his own contemplations to her. His pupils were dilated as his eyes darted back to her mouth. A signal that sent fire licking across her skin.

She wasn't imagining the crackling air between them. At least not if she trusted the signs she'd noticed.

'I see how it is. It's fine for me to reveal my secrets, but you won't tell me any of yours.' She took a sip of her drink. Her gaze locked into his. 'I'm always going to be a stranger you met at a bar. What do you have to lose?'

Eliana wasn't sure why she was prying. Under normal circumstances she never would. But Diego intrigued her. Their conversation so far had already differed from the usual bar flirting she knew. Instead of asking about her life or her job, he'd found a common interest to talk about.

Did that mean he wanted to get to know her better?

The thought gave her pause. Hotel bar flirtations weren't the romances one read about in novels. Besides, such a concept had no place in her life right now.

'Why spoil the evening?' He smiled—only half sincere—but even that was enough to bring heat to her cheeks.

In a defeated gesture, Eliana raised her hands. 'Have it your way, *senhor*, but then I get to know something else. Tell me what brought *you* to Rio instead.'

He relaxed against the bar, with one arm resting on top of it while the other hand came up to his face, scrubbing over the light stubble covering his gorgeous high cheekbones.

'Would you believe me if I said the funeral of my brother?'

He wasn't *really* his brother. There had been no blood relation between him and Vanderson. But, despite Diego having ten siblings, he'd felt closer to that man than to any of his actual relatives.

He'd met Vanderson Costa when they were both eighteen and starting their mandatory military service in the Brazilian army. They'd both signed up for the medical training, their eyes set on med school after their service concluded.

Under normal circumstances the two would never have met. Vanderson had lived in a mansion in Ipanema, Rio's most luxurious neighbourhood, while Diego himself had grown up on the outskirts of Complexo do Alemão, one of the largest slums north of the city centre. But during their service they'd all been recruits, brothers-in-arms going through it all together. Their friendship had bridged the gap in wealth and privilege, teaching Diego so much about himself and his path in life.

And now Vanderson was dead.

Losing his chosen brother clung to his heart as if someone had tied heavy weights to his chest when the news had reached him. To his surprise, he realised that this moment was the first during which he felt he could breathe easier again.

Somehow, this woman sitting in front of him was part of that process.

Diego had lived in Rio de Janeiro his entire life, and the only reason he found himself in a hotel was Vanderson's funeral. He'd attended a small dinner with the surviving family—Vanderson's husband and daughter.

He'd been about to leave when the woman sitting alone at the bar had caught his attention. Red undertones wove themselves through her dark brown hair, which flowed in lavish curls over her shoulders and looked silken to the touch. But what had drawn him in more than her hair, and the sensual curves visible even while she was sitting down, was what she'd been doing. She'd been looking at a nearby TV, watching the sports pundits who were discussing last night's *futebol* game.

Being a *futebol* enthusiast himself, he had felt his interest piqued enough for him to walk over and see what she was doing.

Though Diego hadn't been as subtle as he'd thought, and a few moments after he'd sat down she'd turned her head to look at him. Time had stopped for several heartbeats when their gazes collided, and he'd experienced an unusual twinge in his chest. He'd tried to look nonchalant—as if he hadn't checked her out—but his body had refused to take any orders.

The light brown hue of her eyes was mesmerising. Every now and again the light hit her irises just right, giving them the appearance of pure gold.

She clearly didn't understand the beauty she possessed. He could see that in the way she held herself. More than that, though, her analytical mind and quick wit had jumped out at him when they'd discussed the game. It spoke of passion, and he wanted to get to know her better, to understand what other areas of her life this passion unfolded into.

Which was a strange thought in itself. Diego never got to know the women who entered his life. It wasn't anything personal, and he was upfront about it. He had watched his parents destroy themselves in the name of love, and knew the path of a romantic relationship only led to pain and forced sacrifices.

Diego made sure he got out before things got too emotional and involved. And one way to avoid all that was by not asking too many questions before moving on to the key event of the evening.

So why was he sitting here, asking about her relationship with her father? Or even telling her why he had come here?

Ana's eyes narrowed as she looked him over, a slight frown pulling the corners of her mouth downwards. 'Interesting how this bar is collecting the bereaved.' She paused for a moment. 'I'm sorry to hear about your brother.'

He smiled, feeling the sincerity of her sympathy radiate a gentle warmth through his skin. 'Life is going to suck without him.'

Diego allowed himself to feel the truth of his

words with this virtual stranger he found himself drawn to.

He watched as her eyes drifted to the watch on her delicate wrist and saw the signs that she was thinking about leaving. Something he knew he didn't want her to do.

Her lips parted, no doubt to bid him farewell. Not wanting the evening to end just yet, Diego reached out, placing his hand over hers while obscuring the watch. Her skin was soft under his hand, radiating more heat into him that turned into a fiery spark as it penetrated his skin.

'How long are you staying in Rio?' he asked, and noticed a strange huskiness coating his voice. As if he wanted her to stay. Which was ridiculous. Because one night was all anyone ever got with him, so it didn't matter how long she planned on staying.

Ana looked at him with wide eyes. Was she feeling the same intense spark jumping between them when he touched her? She twisted her hand so that their palms were touching, the tips of her fingers grazing over the inside of his hand.

'Only tonight.'

She hesitated for a moment, and Diego saw the wheels behind her eyes turning. There was something she wanted to tell him. For a moment he held his breath in anticipation, but then the light in her eyes dimmed and she remained quiet.

Ana didn't know her assumption about him being from out of town was wrong. He hadn't corrected her. The information was irrelevant. Tomorrow she would be back wherever she came from, while he would be left alone to contemplate a new reality where his best friend was no more.

He hadn't been able to stop himself when he'd seen Ana. Her presence seemed soothing, and it had required only one bat of her long lashes to awaken a roaring fire in his chest. He knew this reaction was different...unlike the usual flings he satisfied himself with. But he didn't care in this moment. His pain faded when that flame spread through his body. He planned on feeding it until exhaustion took him.

'Then I'm glad I spotted you when I did, or I might have missed the opportunity of a lifetime, Donna Ana.'

'You sat down at the bar because you saw me?'

Scepticism laced her voice, and Diego almost laughed at that. There was no way a gorgeous woman like her didn't have men approaching her in bars all the time. Yet she seemed surprised.

'Couldn't help it,' he replied, his voice dropping low as he wove his fingers through hers.

While his mind was still trying to decide his body had taken control, reacting to the attraction arcing between them.

Eliana's heart slammed against her ribcage as Diego's fingers wrapped around her hand, giving it a gentle squeeze. The brown-green hue of his eyes darkened as the attraction that had been whirring around them for the last hour became almost tangible. Their hands touching had created a rapturous reaction within her, and her breath had caught in her throat. How was this even possible?

'An unlikely story,' she said, not able to keep her scepticism at bay.

She knew he was using honeyed words to flirt with her, and yet she couldn't stop the chemicals firing in her brain. Their connection was an intense physical sensation, clawing its way throughout her body.

'You don't believe that I had no choice once I saw you?'

His voice vibrated low, seeping through her pores and into her body, settling behind her belly button with an uncomfortable pinch.

'I think that's a phrase you came up with and that it has proved most successful with all the different women you meet at bars.'

The words rang with the sound of an accusation although she hadn't meant it.

Diego had clearly picked up on the subtle nuance as well, for he arched one of his eyebrows. 'What do you think I'm after?'

His fingers were still entwined with hers, and the tips of them were rubbing against the back of her hand, sending sparkling showers across her arm. Heat rose through her body, entangling itself with the knot his touch had tied in her stomach and colliding with the sparks that were descending through her arm.

Everything about him made her react. He was like a potent magnet drawing at the fibres of her body. Control had slipped from her hands, and Eliana needed to regain it. She wasn't the type of person to let it go that easily. But Diego was shrouding her thoughts in the thick mists of an instant attraction that was unlike any she had ever experienced before.

'You want to sleep with me.' No use beating around the bush.

'Ah, straight to the point. Do you really want to skip the witty back-and-forth?'

His lips parted in a devastating grin, and Eliana caught her breath for a moment.

'I've been told I'm a pretty good flirt,' he said.

She chuckled at the aura of confidence he exuded, not wanting to let him know how deeply it impacted on her. 'I'm sure that's what they've all told you.'

Her words had the desired effect, for Diego took his free hand to clasp his chest with an indignant expression on his face. 'You wound me, Donna Ana. You're not wrong with your assessment, but I make sure a woman feels worshipped and cherished above anything else.'

Eliana raised a delicate eyebrow, thrown off guard by his bluntness. It matched hers, so she shouldn't be surprised the way she was. His fingers wrapped around hers were creating a luscious fog around her, draping her in a cloud charged with desire and passion.

It made her wonder what else he could do with his fingers if this innocent touch had already raised all the hair along her arms. The soft curve of his lips begged to be kissed... She wanted to lose herself in the delicious promise they wrote on his face.

'What is your usual plan of seduction?'

Maybe she didn't want to skip all the foreplay. Eliana was still telling herself that she wasn't in his thrall, that she could step back at any moment. But the flames of desire uncoiling themselves in her chest had already surrendered to his charms. She wanted *all* of him.

'Normally I would buy you some drinks, and show my appreciation for your taste in alcohol. We'd discuss some unimportant things about our lives, and I would grab at every opportunity to flatter you. Touch you here and there as you tell me about yourself…'

Diego got up and stepped closer to her, forcing her to tilt her head up so she could look at him. His hand wandered up to her exposed arm, touching her shoulder before slipping down, leaving a series of fires under her skin.

'I don't like to talk about myself that much,' she told him. Her voice sounded husky, and she was enthralled by the pure masculine magnetism he exuded. He could have her right this second if he asked.

He dipped his head, his face so close to hers now that the smell of his aftershave drifted up her nose. The scent of moss and earth shrouded her thoughts in an even more alluring mist, and without giving it a second thought she leaned in closer, wanting to close the gap between them.

'Well, it's a good thing you've already figured me out, so we can skip that part, can't we?' Diego whispered in a deep voice filled with promises of desire.

He shifted his head further, his lips grazing her ear and sending a sensual shiver down her spine.

*No,* would be the correct answer. But why? After the stress of this day, a bit of comfort in the arms of an otherworldly handsome man would be a soothing balm for her battered nerves. He'd made it clear that this was what he did, so there wouldn't be any feelings hurt. And from the way he'd wrapped her around his little finger from the very beginning, she knew it would be *good*. What harm could one night do?

Eliana grabbed her bag before getting off the stool and stepping closer. Her hand trailed down his arm as she leaned in, so her lips brushed against his skin in a small suggestion of a kiss as she whispered, 'I'm in Room 901. Finish your drink and meet me upstairs in fifteen minutes.'

# CHAPTER TWO

Diego's night had been restless. He'd thought sleep would come easier now, more than a month after Vanderson's funeral, but rest still eluded him now and then. Sometimes it was due to grief, but more often than not worry kept him awake at night. Worry about the future and the low hum of an unmet need stirring in his chest.

*Ana.*

The beautiful stranger he'd met at a bar.

He had followed her to her room that night four weeks ago, where he'd had the best sex of his entire life. So good he still remembered how her body had felt on top of him. They had fitted together as if they were made for each other.

That thought kept crawling back into his mind, and Diego had to shake it. They were most definitely *not* made for each other. What had possessed him even to think that? They'd spent the night together and enjoyed an explosive connection. There was no need to attach more meaning to it.

But he wanted more. More of someone he couldn't have. Diego didn't know how to *give* more. His parents had made sure of that. Their constant betrayal of one another had taught him that love only made people do foolish things. He would rather stay single for ever than risk doing to a woman what his father had done to his mother.

His eyelids still heavy with the lack of sleep, Diego threw on some grey scrubs and flipped the switch on the coffee machine in the kitchen. He left the room through the glass door leading outside, crossing a small patch of grass and entering the garage next to his house. He squinted when he flipped on the light, his senses still awakening after his poor sleep.

Instead of a car and other household items, the garage was filled with medical and sports equipment. A big workbench stood on the far side of the room, with a prosthetic limb on top of it.

With a heavy sigh falling from his lips, Diego approached the bench to look at the small leg he had spent most of his free time on in the last week. He was supposed to be fitting it to its owner, a young boy who had visited him last month with a request for a new leg as he had outgrown his old one.

It wasn't often that Diego found patients who needed prosthetics visiting him in the free clinic he ran in Complexo do Alemão. The average person sought him out for the kind of maladies any general practitioner could take care of, as well as wounds that needed stitching. His expertise as an orthopaedic surgeon wasn't called upon very often.

Diego never refused a patient—sometimes at significant personal cost. But he remembered all too well what it had been like growing up in that area, devoid of any kind of hope for a better future. He had escaped his life of poverty, relying on tenacity and just the right amount of luck. And that last thing—along with his memories of his time in the slums—inspired him to work hard and give back to his community.

'Is this the leg for Miguel? I've just seen his mother at your sister's shop, and she told me about it.'

Diego jumped at the sudden voice behind him and spun around. His grandmother, Márcia, had come into the garage with a small tray that held a cup of coffee and some pieces of toast.

'Avozinha, what are you doing here so early?' he asked as he approached her, taking the tray out of her hands and kissing her on the cheek in greeting.

'Pelé likes to be out in the morning, so we took a walk here to check in on you.'

Diego looked past his grandma and into the garden. A large greyhound was sniffing around the grass, lifting his long snout when Diego whistled and bolting towards him with an excited yelp.

Diego went down on one knee and scratched Pelé's throat. The tags around his collar gave a soft jingle as he rubbed his hands up and down the neck of the animal.

'Wait, you went all the way to Aline's shop? You shouldn't walk in that neighbourhood on your own.'

He looked up at Márcia, who frowned, flipping her hand in a throwaway gesture. 'I'm not alone. Pelé looks after me.'

'This little coward? Remember when you had a trespasser in your garden and he hid under the coffee table when he noticed a stranger? He is cute, but that won't save you.'

Diego smoothed the light brown fur flat with one last pat and then rubbed the greyhound between his large, trusting eyes before he lifted himself off the ground to face his grandmother.

'Don't you lecture me on where I can and cannot go, young man. I've looked out for you since you were knee-high and see what you've become.'

Diego tried his best not to roll his eyes as Márcia went for her favourite topic: her surgeon grandson and how she had saved him from ending up on the street mixed up with the wrong crowd. If he was honest with himself, she did deserve all the credit. She had taken it upon herself to raise him when his parents had been too busy sorting themselves out.

'*Sim,* Vovo. You know I worry about you,' he said and raised his hands in defeat. He could never defeat her in a duel of words.

'You'd better worry about Miguel. He needs a new leg.'

Diego turned around with a frustrated grunt, looking back at his workbench and the prosthetic limb that was giving him such a hard time. 'I didn't expect to be doing it on my own. Vanderson had agreed to let me borrow some time from the paediatric specialist on my team.'

'What about Marco's daughter? She will be the new owner, yes? Maybe she won't be against you helping Miguel.'

He turned around to look at his grandmother, a sceptical eyebrow raised. 'I don't know what to expect from her. She and the Costas weren't even on speaking terms for the last seventeen years. Vanderson told me she's a doctor, too. But his father wouldn't let him have any contact with her.'

Diego shook his head. This wasn't just about him needing hospital resources to help one patient. The free clinic he ran whenever time permitted required more support than he could provide on his own. Even if he could hire just one nurse to work there during the daytime, he would be able to help so many more people. But to do that he needed the help of the chief of medicine at Santa Valeria Hospital. A role that had belonged to Marco Costa until his recent death.

*Eliana Oliveira.* That was her name. The word in the corridors of Santa Valeria was that she would arrive any day now, to assume the position as chief of medicine.

Outside of the scandal surrounding her birth, no one knew much about her. She was a complete unknown to Diego, who had a lot more than just his staff at the hospital to worry about. He planned on getting the leg sorted out for the little boy Miguel with or without approval from the new chief. Though he'd prefer to do it with her blessing.

'I'm sure she'll be reasonable,' Márcia said, and patted his arm with a reassuring smile.

He wished he could share her optimism about the new chief, but he'd rather prepare for the worst and be surprised.

With a sigh, Diego glanced at his phone's display to check the time, grabbing the toast his *avozinha* had made for him.

'I'd better go. I don't want to be late if today is the day she actually bothers to show up.'

Eliana sat behind the opulent desk that stood in the chief's office—formerly inhabited by her estranged father—and her stomach roiled again, making her hand fly to her mouth. The stress of being back in Rio de Janeiro to deal with the administration of the Santa Valeria General Hospital was taking a lot more out of her than she had expected. She had woken up from an uneasy slumber with nausea cascading through her in violent waves as she'd tried her best to look presentable for the day.

Suelen, the assistant to the chief of medicine, had given her a diary with all her appointments for the day. Ten people wanted to speak to her today, all of them about an important matter—according to them. Eliana doubted any of them were as urgent as they made them out to be.

Leaning back in the chair, she let her head fall back and closed her eyes for a moment, willing the next wave of nausea away.

She was nervous, and her body was reacting to the tension. She was meant to be a consultant—not the chief. Her training as a general surgeon had not prepared her for all the administrative work she was now expected to do. All the different reports on financial matters only worsened her already troubled stomach.

It was only going to be for a couple of weeks, she told herself as she scrubbed her hands over her face. She would pick a new chief of medicine to do the job for her and go back to Belo Horizonte. Rio held nothing but old pain for her, and she didn't want to be here. Hell, she didn't even want to be the owner of this hospital.

People who had known her father might think she had followed in his footsteps going into the medical field. He had been the prestigious hospital's owner, after all. But he'd only played a small part in her motivation.

Her mother was the one she wanted to be like. She had been a nurse at Santa Valeria when she'd got pregnant. Her parents had been having an affair, and instead of stepping up and assuming responsibility her father had driven her mother out of town so no one would learn about his infidelity.

Time and again Marco Costa had shown himself to be a dishonourable man, and Eliana wanted nothing to do with anything that had once belonged to the man. Not when he had broken her mother so wholly that she hadn't been able to hang on to life. She could almost hear the whispers of the older staff—the ones who had known her mother and what Marco Costa had done to her.

But life rarely considered what someone wanted, so despite her quite visceral opposition in this matter she now had to deal with the inheritance her father had left her. The day she heard his name for the last time couldn't come soon enough.

'Excuse me, Dr Oliveira?'

Her head snapped back to its original position when she heard the knock, followed by the soft voice of her assistant.

Eliana cleared her throat, swallowing the bile she felt rising in it. 'Is it already time for my first appointment?' she asked, glancing at her schedule.

'Ah, no...' Suelen hesitated for a fraction before speaking again. 'A registrar in general surgery has called for help. There are some complications with a surgery, and none of the other consultants seem to be available.'

Her words made Eliana blink slowly for a couple of seconds, unable to comprehend what she had just said. 'There are no consultants to help the junior surgeons? Where are they?'

Suelen looked down at her notepad, a faint blush streaking over her cheeks. She was clearly uncomfortable with the answer. 'It seems one of them called in sick, three are stuck in their own surgeries, and another two are...' she looked down to check her notes again '...playing golf.'

'What?' Eliana got up from her chair and waved the assistant to come with her. 'Move my meetings around. I'll take care of it myself. Just show me to the OR.'

Despite the nerves flipping her stomach inside out, Eliana felt an odd excitement rise within her at the thought of stepping into the

OR. That, at least, was a world she understood and felt comfortable in.

They rushed to the general surgery wing, where Suelen pointed her towards OR Three. Eliana wasted no time scrubbing in as fast as she could, and thanked the OR nurse when she stepped out into the scrub room to greet her.

'Do you have a pair of spare shoes around?' she asked the nurse, glancing down at the high heels she was wearing. 'Anything will be a vast improvement.'

'I think we have some *chinelas* for such cases here.' The woman bent down, opening a small cupboard and rummaging around before pulling out a pair of neon green slippers.

Eliana stared at them for a moment, as if she was facing off a venomous snake. They really couldn't have been less flattering if they'd tried. 'Well, I did say anything would be better,' she said with a laugh as she kicked her heels off and stowed them in the cupboard the nurse had just pulled the slippers from.

She received a gown and gloves with a smile, tying a mask around the back of her head as she readied herself to help the surgeon. The doors to the operations room opened with a familiar sound, and a sense of control enveloped her, calming her rioting stomach.

Eliana stepped up to the patient and watched

as the registrar struggled to keep the surgical field clear.

'What happened?' she asked, her voice calm. For the first time today, she felt as if she knew exactly what was happening.

'Blunt force trauma caused a tear in the diaphragm. When we went in we found unexpected damage to the kidneys as well. There was a lot more blood than we had expected.' The panicked registrar looked around at her colleague. 'The consultant was supposed to be with us, but we had no time to wait.'

'It's all right. I'm here to help.' Eliana stepped closer to the patient. 'First we want to isolate the bleeding. Clamp, please.' Eliana stretched out her hand and a moment later the cold steel of the instrument hit her gloved palm.

'I think there must be a rupture on one kidney.'

Hesitation was mixed with despair in the doctor's voice and it made Eliana frown behind her mask. They must have spent a lot of time looking for a superior while the situation was unfolding.

She nodded to reassure her. There was no room for panic in the operating room. 'Yes, blunt force trauma strong enough to hurt the diaphragm like that can cause damage to the kidneys as well. Let's clamp the renal artery to see if the bleeding subsides.'

Looking down at the patient, Eliana pointed out the artery in question and placed a clamp there.

'Suction here so we can see better,' she instructed the other junior surgeon, who moved the instrument to where she had indicated.

The visibility on the kidneys soon cleared and a lot less blood was replacing the stuff they suctioned away.

'Good. Always isolate the source of bleeding by clamping the right artery. Now we can work on the repair unobstructed.'

With the blood flow stemmed, they could focus on repairing the damage.

'I think this should be familiar territory for you. What are the next steps?'

The junior surgeon looked at her before dropping her eyes back to the patient.

Eliana listened to her instructions, nodding as the surgeon explained the next steps.

Her hands were itching to grab the scalpel herself. It had been some time since she'd performed any kind of surgery. After earning her general surgeon's classification she'd been asked by her teaching hospital to stay on as a consultant—which she'd agreed to do, with a request for a sabbatical so she could have a break after studying for her board certification.

A break that she had only been able to enjoy

for a few days before the news of her father's accident had reached her.

But even with her desire to work on the patient herself Eliana took the opportunity to talk the two junior surgeons through the procedure rather than do it. If these junior staff had been empowered to make their own decisions to begin with, maybe they wouldn't have been so lost in what she considered a rather common complication in a case such as this one.

Eliana repressed a sigh behind her mask, pushing the thought away and focusing on the task in front of her. This was only her first day, and she was already uncovering things that would threaten to extend her stay in Rio de Janeiro when she wanted nothing else but to leave this place behind.

Diego had just left a patient's room when his phone vibrated with a page. The nurses' station in the general surgery wing were asking him to report to their department on an urgent matter. He furrowed his brow, unsure what that meant. As the head of the orthopaedics department, he rarely dealt with anyone outside of his own staff.

He hesitated, staring at the screen of his phone. Something wasn't right. His staff had told him that the new chief of medicine had arrived today. Did it have something to do with her? The orthopaedics head nurse had told him Chief Oliveira had requested a meeting with him next week.

Putting his phone back into his pocket, he hurried towards the general surgery wing and stopped at the nurses' station, looking at the man standing behind it. 'What happened? I got an urgent page to come here.'

The nurse nodded with a heavy sigh. 'Thank you, Dr Ferrari. I didn't know who else to page in this situation. None of the consultants answered my call, and I have two very nervous junior surgeons freaking out in OR Three.'

Diego glanced at the whiteboard with the surgical schedule written on it. There were four surgeries scheduled for right now, with two additional consultants on floor duties.

'Where are those two?' He nodded towards the whiteboard.

This time the nurse rolled his eyes. 'You know them… They were Dr Costa's lackeys and they won't lift a single finger if no one makes them. They made themselves such a cosy nest over the years, they don't know how to do actual work any more.'

Diego had to suppress a sigh at that. Unfortunately for him, and the entire hospital, not every doctor in the building had the work ethic he considered essential. In fact, quite a few of the higher-ranking doctors were friends and associates of the former chief of medicine, and that was exactly the way they acted around the hospital. As if they were untouchable and not bound by the rules everyone else was following.

But now was not the time to think about that. 'You said OR Three?' he asked.

The nurse nodded, but his gaze shifted slightly, as if he was trying to decide whether he should say something more.

Diego arched his brow in a silent question.

'We paged you ten minutes ago. The registrars were freaked out. We weren't sure whether you were coming, so we had to page someone else.' There was mild apprehension in his voice.

'Who did you page?'

'The chief. She came down straight away, so I think they should be done by now. Though I haven't seen them leave the OR yet...'

Diego couldn't keep the surprise out of his expression. It seemed Marco Costa's estranged daughter was not just a doctor but a surgeon. 'I'll go and have a look anyway. Maybe she needs more help.'

He glanced at the whiteboard once more, looking for the procedure that was happening in OR Three. The letters MVA were written on the schedule.

Diego frowned. Junior surgeons shouldn't be operating on a car crash victim unsupervised. With cases like that there was no telling what might await them once they opened up the patient.

He left the nurses' station with a nod towards the nurse who had paged him and arrived at the OR just in time to see the team wrapping up the surgery.

Through the thick glass of the scrub room it was hard to read their mood. One of the junior surgeons was dressing the wound while the other one was talking to the woman he presumed was the new chief of medicine. His eyes glided over her. He appreciated the fact that he had a moment to check her out before she knew he was there.

Her hair was hidden underneath a generic grey surgical cap and her face remained behind the mask. She looked pale under the surgical lights, almost unwell, with a soft sheen of sweat covering her forehead. Was she nervous?

Diego was about to enter the OR when the new chief lifted her head and looked directly at him. Her forehead furrowed for a moment, and he felt an unexpected flash of passion uncoil itself in his chest when their gazes collided. Her golden-brown eyes widened in recognition and he knew it was her. He would have recognised those eyes anywhere.

The woman who had been stuck in his head for the last four weeks.

*Ana.*

Diego struggled to comprehend this revelation. For a few heartbeats they stared at each other. His thoughts were racing. Ana was Eliana Oliveira. Vanderson's sister. The second the thought manifested itself in his head the puzzle pieces fell into place and he couldn't believe he hadn't seen it the night they met.

They had the same colour hair, that dark brown shade with just a hint of red, and even without seeing the rest of her face he noticed the similarities in their eyes. This was Vanderson's sister. The woman he had spent one incredible night with.

How was this possible? They had spoken about their lives, had they not?

He tried hard to remember what they had spoken about, but the only part of that night remaining vivid in his memories were the hours they'd spent together in bed. He remembered the feel of her skin on his, his tongue trailing down her sternum, her cries of pleasure when his mouth found her essence...

The last memory made Diego shiver with renewed desire and anticipation.

How could he not have seen that she was Vanderson's sister? Now that he knew it seemed so obvious. She had even said that she'd just come from her father's funeral. Though he now knew that to be a lie. He had been at the funeral, and had kept an eye out for the unexpected heiress of the Costa fortune.

But what were they supposed to do now?

He could see the flame in her own eyes, mirroring the instant desire that flashed through him. It seemed their night together had done little to satisfy her hunger, either. Or was he reading too much into one brief glimpse?

Eliana was rooted to the spot. She blinked once to shake away the shock, and then her eyes found their way back to the surgeon standing in front of her.

From the corner of her eye she saw Diego following every movement she made. Tiny flames were igniting across her skin. For a second, the sight of him even drowned out the renewed nausea that had started up at the end of the surgery. Eliana was glad she hadn't had to operate herself after all. She could feel trembles going through her body. This wasn't just nerves, she thought. She must have caught a stomach bug.

'Make sure you page me if there are any changes in the patient's vital signs,' she said to the junior surgeon, who nodded and left as the patient was wheeled out on a gurney.

She peeled herself out of the surgical gown, pulled both gloves and mask off before removing the cap, closing her eyes for a moment and taking a few deep breaths to compose herself.

The last person she had expected to see here—the last person she'd *wanted* to see—had just shown up in the OR.

Diego stood in front of her, tall and handsomely dark. His appearance came with so many questions Eliana didn't even know where to start. He was a doctor. Not only that, he must also be a surgeon if he felt comfortable coming into an operating room just like that. And, even worse, by the looks of it he was a surgeon at *her* hospital.

If he lived here in Rio, what had he been doing at the hotel last month? Eliana had thought she would never see him again.

How to start such a conversation? She didn't even know where to begin.

She opened her mouth and immediately closed it again as another wave of nausea churned her stomach. Her hand flew to her mouth, covering it on the off-chance that something might escape. Standing still, she took another deep breath to steady herself.

'Are you okay?' Diego asked, his voice sounding distant and yet strained with concern.

Eliana tried to speak again, but she only moved her hand away from her mouth a couple of millimetres before feeling ill again. Keeping her palm pressed against her lips, she shook her head, and a second later Diego's muscular arm wrapped itself around her waist as he guided her towards a small stool at the far side of the operating room.

He popped up in her field of vision when he crouched down in front of her, a concerned expression on his face. The warmth she saw in his eyes would have sent her heart rate through the roof in any other circumstances, but the way she was feeling right now she was thankful to have someone there who wasn't a complete stranger.

That thought caused a slight twinge in her chest—something she couldn't focus on. Her mind was too absorbed with whatever illness it was that was making her stomach perform loops within her.

Diego's hand pressed against her forehead for a moment. 'You don't feel warm,' he said. 'But you are sweaty and, from the looks of it, nauseated. Could be a stomach bug. Did you eat anything this morning?'

Deep breaths had calmed her stomach just a bit, and Eliana dared once more to move her hand away from her mouth to answer his question. 'No, just coffee. I woke up feeling like this already, and one glance at food made my stomach turn.'

Diego frowned at her. 'You should know that coffee isn't a substitute for a proper breakfast.'

Under any other circumstances she would not have let him lecture her, but she was feeling increasingly lightheaded. The room around her darkened and turned, giving her a sense of vertigo that worsened the nausea.

'I think I'm going to pass out…' she whispered, sensing her impending doom.

She felt his hands grab her shoulders as her eyes closed. He mumbled something to her in a distorted voice, but the meaning of his words didn't reach her mind as she slipped into unconsciousness.

# CHAPTER THREE

A BRIGHT LIGHT was trying its best to find a path underneath her closed eyelids. Eliana moved her head to one side to escape the glare. Her temples were throbbing, and her tongue clung to the roof of her mouth as if she hadn't had any water in days. Her lips felt dry as she opened her mouth slightly.

She heard a soft rustling above her, then hushed whispers of conversation, and it was only then that her confused mind realised that she did not know where she was. The thought penetrated the thick fog around her, and she slowly opened her eyes.

An older woman was looking at her with a friendly sparkle in her eyes. She wore a white coat and was putting on some disposable gloves. Squinting at her, Eliana read her name tag: *Dr Sophia Salvador, Accident and Emergency Services.*

'Welcome back, Chief. You gave us all quite a scare when we saw Dr Ferrari carrying your limp body.' Dr Salvador smiled at her before turning to the tray next to her. 'I'll take some blood for a test, to make sure you're okay. But your pulse ox is normal, and pupillary response is also fine. Probably thanks to Dr Ferrari, here, who cushioned your fall.'

Eliana nodded her silent consent, trying to remember what had happened as the woman drew her blood. She'd woken up this morning feeling rotten, as if she had come down with the flu. She had put it down to nerves about her new job. It wasn't the first time she had felt sick to her stomach because of nerves.

Eliana groaned as she understood what had just happened. Despite her best efforts to look as if she knew what she was doing—as if she belonged here—she had managed to faint. On her first day at work. In front of the incredibly hot almost-stranger she had met at a bar a month ago.

Memories of Diego came rushing back into her consciousness, worsening her headache as a cascade of hot sparks rampaged through her body, igniting her already frayed nerves. 'Wait…where…?'

She looked to where Dr Salvador had nodded, and winced when she tilted her head to the side too fast, causing pain to spear through her throbbing head. Diego was sitting on a chair a few paces away from the bed she lay in.

He got up when she looked at him, his expression still a lot more worried than she'd thought it would be. Snippets of what had happened in the operating room drifted back to her. He'd been holding her when she'd regained consciousness, lifting her off her seat.

Dim memories of him examining her while she was lying down on a gurney came to life in her head. Had it only been a couple of minutes ago? Her sense of time was off kilter. Had he been waiting here this entire time, watching over her?

The thought drove a different heat through her body. Not once in her life had someone watched over her. Being raised by nannies and teachers had taught her early that she was the only person in her life she could count on. Everyone else had their own agenda and she would only ever be an instrument in their achieving it.

What were his reasons for staying with her? What did Diego want? Those intrusive thoughts crawled into her head before Eliana could stop them. They had only spent one night together. There was nothing more to it.

'Let me expedite your lab results so we can release you as soon as possible,' Sophia said as she picked up the phial with her blood sample. 'From the symptoms Dr Ferrari described, and my own examination, I think a stomach bug is likely.'

The woman left, and when the door behind her fell shut silence enveloped the room for a few heartbeats as she searched for the right thing to say. It seemed it was true. Diego had not only brought her here, he'd stayed to watch over her.

She almost laughed at that thought—at how foreign and unbelievable it felt in her mind. This must be some kind of professional scheming. She was the new chief of medicine, after all.

Yet she could see a hint of concern still etched into his expression as she turned her head to look around her. She paused to look at him for a heartbeat. She opened her mouth, ready to say something, but words wouldn't form in her brain, so she looked back down to her hands, her heart suddenly pounding against her chest at the sight of the worried spark in his eyes.

It was only then that she noticed her surroundings. It was a private room, the interior much more luxurious than she had expected any hospital room to be. The sheets were soft against her skin, the mattress comfortable beneath her. The door to an en-suite bathroom stood ajar, giving her a view of the room which had a large rain shower.

'This is not the emergency department. What is this room?' she asked, forgetting about Diego's dark gaze for a second. How could this be a room in a hospital?

Diego looked around himself, and she saw an expression of contempt fluttering over his face before he regained full composure.

'This is one of the rooms Marco had designed for his various VIP patients. When I arrived with you at A&E they insisted on moving you here once they'd assessed you. They thought you had passed out from exhaustion. Do you remember?' He furrowed his brow.

'Vaguely... The whole thing is just a blur of light and headaches right now.' Eliana looked at the opulence of this place. It was fancier than her hotel room. 'This seems...excessive. I don't want to know what budgets got cut to make this happen.'

She wanted her patients to convalesce in peace and comfort, but this looked more like a room in a spa than a hospital.

Her train of thought stopped mid-track when she looked up at Diego, who had a thoughtful smile on his face as he regarded her. The gentleness in his expression sent sparks flying all over her body.

'I said the same thing when Marco started working on these rooms. Turns out he cut each department's pro bono fund to basically nothing.'

The thought seemed to fill him with renewed resentment for her father.

'You didn't get along with my father?'

As her father had hired all the department heads at the hospital, Eliana had assumed they were his minions. The people he had hired would no doubt also think it acceptable to banish a pregnant woman from the only place she had ever called home. Like Marco had done with her mother.

But it seemed she had found another person who shared her opinion about her father. How odd to think the stranger she'd had a one-night stand with four weeks ago was now her potential ally in this hospital...

Diego snorted a derisive laugh. 'Marco Costa would have fired me ages ago if he could, and over the years I gave him enough reasons to try. But he only ever caught me with my little toe over the line and nothing else,' he said, and shrugged. 'By the time he realised I would be more trouble than my talent was worth it was already too late. If he'd let me go half of his staff would have walked out with me.'

He said it so matter-of-factly Eliana had no choice but to admire his confidence. It took a lot to know one's worth. But there was something else hidden in his words, too. A sense of accountability and belonging. And from those words alone she knew exactly who Diego considered his people.

It was a thought that made envy needle at her heart. Belonging was a foreign concept to

Eliana. She'd grown up isolated from the only family she had ever known—which hadn't been much to begin with—and her experience at boarding school had been little better.

'Sorry, I know he was your father—' he started, but she interrupted him with a shake of her head.

'You might remember me saying how I wasn't close to my father back at that hotel bar. Your words are docile compared to what I have to say about him on any given day.'

Understanding rushed over his expression, but it only remained there for a moment before his face slackened again. He was clearly not letting her see his thoughts.

But he must know about her. Everyone in this hospital did. In the thirty-five years since her birth—since her mother had fallen for a guy she never should have—the staff of Santa Valeria had not forgotten the scandal surrounding her conception. From the moment Eliana had set foot in the foyer of the hospital she'd been able to sense the eyes on her, the whispers following her around as she was introduced to different staff members.

Even Diego, who of course hadn't worked here when her mother had got pregnant, must know about her—how she had grown up as the black sheep of the Costa family, escaping her abusive home the moment she'd turned eighteen.

'I'm sorry,' he said, and somehow she knew they both understood in that moment what he was apologising for. Not for something that he'd done, but for the circumstances that had led to him knowing so much about her.

'So, you think Santa Valeria should do more pro bono surgeries?' Eliana asked, going back to what he had said about the budget cut.

'Among other things, yes,' he said, crossing his arms in front of his chest and giving her a view she didn't want to dwell on. She knew the strength those arms possessed. She had found pleasure in them throughout their entire night together.

'What else do you suggest?'

It was a genuine question for the man she'd thought she would never meet again, only to find out that they would now be working together—at least until she went back home in a couple of weeks.

Diego tilted his head to one side, his eyes narrowing as he looked at her with such intensity that her breath caught in her throat. His hand wandered up to his face, stroking over the light stubble covering his cheeks.

'Community outreach. We have some high-calibre donors supporting us. Instead of building private suites and taking those donors on lavish cruises, we could take Santa Valeria's facilities and help the poorer communities in this city when they are most in need of care. God knows there are enough people requiring help right now.'

His words seemed to her to come from a place of experience, with a small nugget of truth shining through.

'Why is that important to you?' she asked, and almost flinched when his eyes grew darker, narrowing on her. Her question seemed to have crossed an invisible boundary.

His jaw tightened for a moment as he stared her down, but Eliana forced herself to meet his gaze straight on, despite the defences she spotted going up all around him.

'It's the right thing to do. I might have got out, but they are still my people.'

'Your—?'

The door opened, interrupting their conversation, and Dr Salvador strode back into the room. The fierce protectiveness in Diego's eyes vanished, leaving his face unreadable.

Eliana's eyes were drawn to the emergency doctor, who stepped closer. She was wearing an expression of medical professionalism on her face that quickened her pulse. She knew that look. She had given it to patients herself.

She whipped her head around, looking at Diego, and whatever he saw written in her face was enough to make him get off his chair and step closer to her side. A similar look of protectiveness to the one he'd had a few moments ago was etched into his features.

'Would you mind giving us some privacy?' Sophia asked him, and a tremble shook Eliana's body.

The nausea came rushing back, her head suddenly felt light, and Eliana reacted before she could think, her hand reaching for Diego's and crushing it in a vice-like grip.

'It's okay if he stays,' she said, in a voice that sounded so unlike her own.

Something deep within her told her she needed him to stay. Whether it was premonition or just a primal fear gripping at her heart, she didn't know.

Diego stopped, giving her a questioning look, but he stayed, and his hand did not fight her touch.

'Well, it looks like it's not a stomach bug, but morning sickness. Or, in your case, late-afternoon sickness.' She paused for a moment, before confirming the absurd thought that was rattling around in Eliana's head. 'You're pregnant.'

Eliana opened her mouth to speak, but no words crossed the threshold of her lips. Pregnant? How was she pregnant? Her head snapped around to Diego, and whatever expression she was wearing on her face seemed to convey to him all the words she didn't want to say in front of the doctor.

The baby was his. *They* were pregnant.

His hand slipped from her grasp as he took a step back. The shock she felt at the revelation was written on his face.

'How long?' she asked, even though she knew it didn't matter.

Eliana had only slept with one person in the last six months, and that was the man standing here in the room with her.

'I can't say without an ultrasound. Do you remember the date of your last period?' Dr Salvador paused for a moment, to give her time to digest the information, before she continued, 'Normally I would get someone from OBGYN down here to talk to you, but since this is your hospital, and you're a doctor yourself, I'll discharge you. But make sure you start your prenatal care straight away.'

Her last period? She had no idea. Her periods were always irregular and hard to track—something she'd made peace with a long time ago. When she didn't have one, she didn't believe anything amiss.

Four weeks. That was when she'd fallen pregnant. Because that was when she had met Diego.

Eliana didn't register Dr Salvador's words, her mind too busy trying to understand the new and unexpected reality she found herself in. As if her life hadn't been complicated enough, with her father's death. Now she could add an unplanned pregnancy to the pile.

A baby growing right below her heart.

Her hand darted to her still flat stomach.

'All right, I'll leave you to digest this information. But medically you're good to go about your day.'

Sophia Salvador left them, closing the door behind her.

Every muscle in his body was tense with anticipation in a strange fight-or-flight response to the situation. His mind was reeling from the explosive information Sophia had just shared with them, and he was struggling to make any sense of it.

He'd had about a million questions floating around in his mind, but he didn't know how to verbalise any of them now he'd heard her say those words, acknowledging out loud what Eliana's eyes had already told him. How was he supposed to start this conversation?

Diego grabbed a chair from the far side of the room and brought it closer to the bed, sitting down and looking at her. 'Am I—?'

Eliana nodded before he'd finished his sentence. 'It's yours. There's no doubt about it. I've not slept with anyone else.'

There it was.

A large boulder dropped into his stomach as she said those words. Their one night of searing passion had resulted in a child.

'That's not what I expected to hear when I saw you again today,' was all he managed to say, his mind going blank. All he could think of was that life-altering revelation.

Eliana gave a short laugh, and Diego wasn't sure whether it was genuine. He barely knew the woman lying on the bed in front of him. It was a thought that made him laugh in return. The mother of his child was nothing more than a stranger to him.

'I don't even know how it happened,' she said in a quiet voice, more as if she was talking to herself than to him. 'I'm on the pill…'

Her voice trailed off, and there was a thoughtful expression on her face. Then her eyes went wide with shock and her hand darted up to her mouth, clasping it with a gasp.

Diego stiffened in his chair, reaching out to her. 'What is it?'

'It's my fault. When I came here last month it was after the news of my father and brother's accident. I was nervous and felt ill. I went through my morning routine, including taking the pill, and then…' She stopped and looked at him. 'I threw up. I threw up the medication. But I didn't even think about it because I didn't think I was going to meet someone.'

That explained it. On the night in question they'd had that conversation every responsible adult should have about avoiding unwanted consequences of their consensual encounter. Diego had even worn a condom that first time. Maybe even the second time.

His memories became blurry around the third time, with the night growing longer and the passion hotter, each union burning more intensely than the one before. Her touch had been intoxicating—to the point where he could remember little else about that night.

He couldn't say it was her fault. It might just as well be his. *Theirs*. But the fact was they were now bound to each other through the life they'd created.

'It's not anyone's fault. These things happen—you know that as well as I do.'

He knew that wasn't reassuring, but in this moment—with the shock of discovery still sitting deep in his bones—he didn't know what else to tell her. Or how to ask the question burning on his lips. This was her choice, after all.

Whether it was his expression or the unexpected connection they suddenly shared he didn't know, but Eliana seemed to have read his thoughts, for a moment later she said, 'I don't have a plan, but I'm not abandoning this child the way I was disregarded. The rest I can figure out.'

Something strange bubbled up within his chest at her words. A feeling of heavy responsibility, but with something lurking underneath it as well. A protectiveness unlike anything he had experienced before.

'The rest *we* can figure out,' he said.

Her eyes narrowed as she looked at him. 'Are you up to the task of being a father?' she asked rather bluntly, zeroing in on a vulnerability that he hadn't shared with her yet.

His mind had always struggled to comprehend the enormity of what fatherhood meant. His father had been such an abject failure in teaching him what it meant to be a decent person. Instead of raising him, Ignacio Ferrari had given the young Diego to his mother—*avozinha*—to raise while he went sleeping around all of Rio.

How could he be a proud Latin father in a world where the odds had been stacked against him from the very beginning and his own father had been the worst possible role model? There were things he would have to teach his child, weren't there?

'That's going to be one of those things we'll have to figure out,' he said with a wry smile.

He rested his face in his hands for a moment, pressing his fingers against his temples in a reminder to himself to stay collected. The tension was gone, but it had been replaced by a reality they were both starting to understand.

'Diego, this is a lot to consider. I need some time to think about your...' Eliana didn't finish her sentence, prompting him to raise an eyebrow at her.

Diego straightened his back to look at her. 'My what? This is my child, too. Whatever you may have heard about me from gossiping staff, I don't shy away from my responsibilities.'

He'd made up his mind. For better or for worse, they were in it for the long run. He didn't know how to be a father, but at least he knew how to be around children. His father had created so many offspring, all of them sooner or later arriving at his grandmother's house to get to know their family, that he had experience with all the different stages of childhood.

'What do you want us to do?' he asked, and watched as she shook her head.

'I don't know, Diego. Right now, I can't handle any thought of *us* in this context. I came here to find someone to lead this hospital—not *this*.'

The silence between them grew tense as he watched different emotions flutter over her face, as if she was chasing her own thoughts in her head. He reached his hand out to her—only to stop when a soft buzzing interrupted him.

Diego frowned as he checked his phone. 'They're paging me for a Code Blue. I have to go.'

Eliana nodded, her face blank except for her golden-brown eyes, which were still wide in shock.

'Can we talk about this later?' He didn't want to leave. He wanted to stay and for them to work through this life-altering news together. Especially when she was still so fragile from earlier.

'Go and attend to your patient. I need some time to think. I...' She hesitated for a moment, finally looking at him, and he could see the doubt swirling in her eyes. 'I need some space to work through this. I'll let you know when I'm ready to talk.'

His phone kept on vibrating, and Diego hissed a low curse as he turned around to rush to his patient, his mind still reeling at the way his life had changed for ever in the last two hours.

He was going to be a father.

# CHAPTER FOUR

ELIANA SPENT THE better part of two weeks looking for her replacement. The news about her unexpected pregnancy still sat deep in her bones, and she had yet to make a plan. Or talk to Diego about it. Staying locked up in her office interviewing people had made it easy to avoid him, as she didn't know what to tell him. Planning had never been her strength.

*'Everything else we can figure out.'*

That was what Diego had said. As if they were a team now. Fused together by their one night of passion.

She would have to make a plan with him. Whether or not she wanted Diego in her life didn't matter any more. Eliana had grown up deprived of both parents, so if Diego was willing to be a father she would make sure he could be a part of their child's life. Regardless of how she felt about him.

'Good morning, Suelen,' Eliana said as she passed the desk of her assistant and waited for her to hand her the usual diary full of appointments and a list of important queries she had to attend to as the interim chief of medicine.

But her assistant had only one item on her agenda. 'You asked me to schedule you some time in the emergency department today. Dr Salvador is expecting you.'

'That's right. I almost forgot about that.' She'd asked Suelen to block off some time with each department head so she could observe different procedures. Diego had already alluded to the changes he would like to see at Santa Valeria, and he wasn't the only department head with a wish list.

Even though Eliana yearned for some OR time, her first stop had to be the emergency department under Sophia Salvador. It was the beating heart of their entire trauma centre, and deserved a lot more attention than it seemed it had previously received.

Eliana went inside her office to put down her jacket and bag, and then came out and stopped in front of her assistant's desk again, when a thought dawned on her. There was something she needed to do and had been avoiding for the last couple of days.

'Can you get the obstetrics head up here for a meeting as soon as they have time? I have some matters to discuss.'

Those 'matters' being her child.

She balled her hand into a fist to stop herself from reaching for her stomach. That instinctual protectiveness emerged every time she thought of the tiny being inside her, but she wasn't ready to reveal anything to the world just yet.

Eliana was aware of the looks and whispers following her around, reviving the rumours around her mother's affair with the old chief. Who knew how the conversations would turn when they found out that she was in a similar position—pregnant with the baby of a high-ranking doctor in this hospital? She was still a stranger to everyone here, and didn't dare risk showing any kind of vulnerability. Things had got so bad for her own mother she'd ended up fleeing this place.

An old pain clawed at her heart, and not for the first time she wished her mother were still alive to give her some advice. Had she ever regretted what had happened with her father? Would Diego turn out to be a similar man?

*One day at a time*, she told herself as she walked to the emergency department. Only time would tell what kind of parents she and Diego would be together.

The second Eliana stepped through the doors to A&E noise erupted around her as nurses and doctors saw to their patients, with ailments of varying degrees of seriousness. She tried her best not to stand in anyone's way as she walked to the far end of the room, looking at a large screen on the wall that held all the information on their current intakes.

'Who are you?' the nurse behind the counter asked her, tearing her gaze away from the screen.

'I'm—'

She was interrupted by Sophia walking into sight. 'Chief Oliveira, I was wondering when you would show up. Our admissions board is already full, so you won't mind getting to work straight away?'

'Work?' Eliana raised her eyebrows.

When she'd scheduled this time she hadn't expected any of the department heads to put her to work. Though she was quite excited at the idea of practising medicine. Being the chief of medicine involved a lot more paperwork than patients—a fact she lamented.

'You wanted to get to know my department. There is no better way than to work here for a day—and we can always use a hand.' Sophia turned around and looked over at the screen. 'Why don't you look at Bed Four? One of our regulars is back, and she'll have lots to say about her time at your hospital.'

'All right.'

Eliana smiled, liking this idea more by the minute. She'd thought she would have to wait until she was back in Belo Horizonte to see patients again. This was an exciting change of pace from her usual chief's duties.

Stepping up to Bed Four, Eliana grabbed the patient chart attached to the end of the bed and scanned it. The intake nurse had scribbled *'shortness of breath and palpitations'* on the form, at which Eliana raised an eyebrow. Why had they left a patient with these symptoms unattended?

The older woman was lying down, giving the impression of sleeping at first glance, but she was actually reading a somewhat tattered-looking book as she lay on her side. Her chest was heaving with laboured breaths, but other than that she seemed unperturbed by her struggle to breathe.

'*Olá, senhora*, I'm Dr Oliveira. Do you mind if I have a listen to your breathing?'

The woman turned her head as if she had only just noticed her. 'I haven't seen you around. Are you new?'

Not a question she had expected. 'That I am,' she answered after a short silence. 'And Dr Salvador has already told me this isn't your first visit.'

Eliana looked at the chart again, but the only part filled out on the admission form was the first name: Selma.

'I'm here more often than I would like, and it takes me a whole day to get here. I usually go to the clinic close to home, but the doctor hasn't been there in a while.' An expression of concern fluttered over her face. 'He said I should come here whenever I need help managing my condition.'

'Condition?' Eliana arched her brows.

Selma put her book down on her lap and grabbed her bag, digging through it to produce a small notebook with torn edges and crinkled paper. She licked her finger to help her turn the pages as she searched for the right one.

'He's such a helpful and kind man, so he wrote it down for me...along with everything the other doctors will need to know. It's called...' She paused, squinting at the words scrawled on the paper. 'Pulmonary hyper...'

'Hypertension?' Eliana asked when Selma struggled with reading the next word. 'Can I see the doctor's notes?'

Someone with such a serious condition should be under the continuous care of a physician. Why had this doctor told her to come to *this* hospital?

If the clinic is closed, go to the Santa Valeria General Hospital. If they refuse to treat you, ask to page Dr V. Costa.

Eliana's heart stuttered in her chest when she read the words written on the piece of paper.

She stared at the ink in disbelief. Her *brother* had told this woman to come here.

Selma had said the doctor hadn't been at the clinic for a while. Was Vanderson the physician in question? Her eyes went back to the woman, scrutinising her. She clearly didn't know about his death.

'Have you stopped taking your medication?'

Among the scribbles describing Selma's condition, she could see that she had been prescribed benazepril, a type of medication to treat high blood pressure in older patients.

'Well, yes, I go by the clinic to get my medication from the doctor. But since he hasn't been there for a while I had no choice but to stop.'

'You don't have a GP who can fill your prescription for you?'

Eliana was confident she knew the answer to that question, but she wanted to ask anyway.

They could only be one reason why her brother had instructed this woman to come to his father's hospital's emergency department. Because she had nowhere else to go and she needed to be treated.

Selma's expression faltered for a brief moment. She glanced around, as if uncertain what to say.

Noticing the hesitation, Eliana quickly shook her head. 'Never mind about that. There's probably some built-up fluid in your lungs. We'll treat you for that, and I will stock up your supply of medication. No questions asked.'

She smiled to reassure the patient, before moving away to get a portable ultrasound machine as well as a set of hypodermic needles and syringes to drain the excess fluid compressing Selma's lungs.

Still new to the hospital—and to the emergency department in particular—it took her a couple of minutes to find the right closet and the materials necessary to do the procedure.

The newfound knowledge about the steps her brother had taken to help this patient had unleashed a torrent of different emotions in her chest, mingling with the still-fresh news of her unexpected pregnancy. It was becoming harder for her to focus on just one thing when every day came with a new revelation about herself, her family, or the hospital she now owned.

The thoughts swirling in her head came to an abrupt halt when she spotted someone next to Selma's bed. Diego stood beside the woman, holding his stethoscope to her chest as he examined her.

Eliana froze in place, her senses overwhelmed by Diego's sudden appearance. Her flight reaction kicked in, urging her to turn around and run—as she had been doing for the last two weeks whenever she saw him. But this time her feet didn't heed the command, staying rooted to the spot as an instant and visceral awareness of him thundered through her. The new information about her brother was forgotten as longing gripped her, unexpected in its intensity.

They hadn't spoken since they'd received the news about her unexpected pregnancy, and Eliana knew that was her doing. Diego had tried to reach out, asking for time to talk. Time she had yet to grant him. Because she didn't know what he was going to say as much as she didn't know what *she* would say.

After all, making plans had always been her greatest weakness. And the decisions they were supposed to make together required a lot of coordination and planning.

Eliana forced herself to take a deep breath, shaking away the shock of seeing him. There was still a patient who needed her help, and she couldn't get distracted by her personal issues.

She stepped up to the bed, clearing her throat to gain their attention. 'I didn't expect to see you here, Dr Ferrari,' she said as she passed him.

'I can say the same thing about you, Chief,' he replied, and Eliana could swear she heard a hint of reproach in his voice.

Sparks filled the air the second they were close enough to touch, igniting a longing heat just behind her belly button. It was a reaction completely inappropriate, and so out of control it almost made her flinch. The second he came too close to her all her inhibitions seemed to melt away, and she just wanted to be a part of him again.

With his own wing being as busy as it was, Diego didn't have the freedom to answer pages that weren't work-related as fast as he would like to. So when the admissions nurse in the emergency department had paged him about a patient from the free clinic it had taken him almost an hour to get there and check for himself.

What he hadn't expected was to see Eliana taking care of his patient.

A thrill of excitement mixed with dread in his stomach. While the need to see her pulled at his chest, he didn't want to do it in front of Selma, because he might have to explain some things he didn't know how to.

The new chief didn't know about the free clinic he was running—sometimes using hospital resources like medicine, or time from him and his colleagues. Everyone he'd ever involved in helping out had done so voluntarily, and with the understanding that they might be in a grey zone where the hospital policies were concerned. They were helping people who needed assistance—even if Diego had to beg, borrow and steal from Santa Valeria.

What he hadn't decided was if he wanted to tell Eliana about his side project or if he should lie low until a new chief was appointed and deal with them.

Oblivious to the tension zipping like electricity between them, Selma beamed at Eliana. 'You didn't mention that you knew Dr Ferrari. Does that mean we'll see *you* at the clinic as well?'

A boulder dropped into Diego's stomach. So much for finding his own way of broaching the subject with Eliana.

'I was paged here for a consult when I saw you, Selma,' he lied, and in an almost automated gesture he took the instruments Eliana was carrying into his own hands to start the procedure.

'Do you tend to take a lot of the consultations registrars should be doing?' she asked.

Her voice had an edge to it, but not one of hostility. Was she amused by his attempt to cover up the true reason he was down here? What had Selma already told her?

Unwilling to drop the charade, Diego shrugged. 'They're better off studying procedures in the OR rather than looking at every sprained ankle that comes into this place.' He paused for a moment and couldn't help but flash a grin at Eliana. 'I'm that good.'

The surprise his shameless innuendo brought to her face caused the heat of desire to flash through his body. He knew better than to indulge those feelings by flirting with her, no matter how subtly. But whenever he got close enough to her, control slipped through his fingers and he was seduced into forgetting why he couldn't be with anyone. *Ever.*

Especially not the woman carrying his child.

It had been two weeks since the news broke, and yet those two words together still sounded strange in his ears. *His child.* Diego was going to be a father when he didn't know the first thing about doing it.

He would never be with someone just for the sake of a child. Diego would be there for his kid—sure. But that was as much as he could give.

Eliana was now ignoring his flirtatious attempts at conversation and was focusing on the patient instead. 'Your pulmonary hypertension has caused fluid to build up in what's called the pleural space. May I move your gown down a bit to access your chest?'

Selma nodded and sat up, pushing her feet past the edge of the bed, while Eliana wheeled a small tray table around for the patient to lean on so she would have access to her back. Diego had already performed a thoracentesis on her, with the help of a cardiologist. The thorax wasn't an anatomical space he was familiar with, but in his efforts to providing healthcare to the disadvantaged people of the city he'd had to learn a lot of procedures that lay outside his expertise.

'To drain the fluid we'll use a needle to get to the space between your lungs and your chest wall. That should allow you to breathe easier. This will be cold for a bit.'

She dabbed some cool gel onto the patient's skin and then surprised Diego when she handed him the transducer.

'I will do the procedure—you can assist,' she said, in a voice that didn't leave any room for negotiation, which made it that much harder for him not to argue.

'I'm familiar with the steps of a thoracentesis,' he said, and watched as her eyes narrowed on him, the golden sparks losing their warm light right in front of him.

'Is it a common procedure in your orthopaedic cases?'

Diego had seen the trap he'd laid for himself before she had even opened her mouth, and he cursed himself silently. Some primal force in his chest had urged him to prove himself to her in any way possible. Show her that he could provide for her and their child. Look after them the way his father had never looked after him.

The blood froze in his veins as the jumble of thoughts caught up with him, rendering him mute for a couple of heartbeats. Where had *that* come from? Their night together had altered his life for ever, but that didn't mean they were meant to be anything more than co-parents.

'You know it's not,' he answered in a low growl when he found his voice again. The unexpected depth and chaos of his feelings towards Eliana had thrown him so much he had to remind himself where he was.

'Then you can take the ultrasound while I perform the thoracentesis.'

Eliana prepared the needle and syringe while he sat down on a small stool next to the bed. He made eye contact with Selma as he placed the transducer on her sternum to show Eliana what she needed to see.

'The pressure will be uncomfortable. I'm sorry. I'll try to be as fast as possible,' she said as she looked at the screen of the ultrasound machine for a moment, surveying the field.

Diego watched Eliana's hands as they probed the patient's ribs for a moment before she picked up the needle with her right hand and inserted it in the ninth intercostal space—quick, but precise—her eyes only occasionally leaving the ultrasound screen to look at Selma over her shoulder.

'You're doing great. I've positioned the needle, so we can begin the drain.'

Even though Selma was staring ahead, Eliana kept a gentle and reassuring smile on her face, making him wonder about the work she had been doing before she came to Santa Valeria. The way she'd handled the patient so far was unlike anything he'd ever seen from Marco. He would never have spent his time in any department helping out. He'd valued his own time above patient care.

Diego was relieved to see this wasn't the case for his daughter. Eliana clearly knew how to explain every step of the procedure so her patient knew throughout what was happening. After Marco Costa and his 'money first' attitude towards healthcare, she was exactly the kind of chief of medicine Santa Valeria needed.

Selma winced, and Diego grabbed her hand with his free one, keeping the other steady so that Eliana could do her work.

'Remember to take slow breaths, just like last time. Once we're done, you can rest, and I'll ask the nurse to bring you some books from the library.'

He knew Selma well. Her high blood pressure needed to be controlled with medication, but without medical insurance she could only ever get help from the emergency department when things got as bad as they were now.

'I'll be fine. I need to get back home and pick up my grandson before my daughter has to go to work, so I can't stay too long.'

Diego saw a frown appear on Eliana's face as she listened to their conversation, and he could almost hear the thoughts in her head. She'd want Selma to stay for observation—a wish he shared. But he knew that Selma had no option to stay. Her daughter's work was keeping all of them fed.

He had seen the same thing in his grandmother as well. She had worked herself to the bone to help her grandchildren achieve a better life, to escape the *favelas*, and Diego counted himself fortunate in being able to repay her for her efforts. She had been the only consistent parental figure in his life, raising him after his father had dumped him at her house when he had been busy cheating on his mother. Only to retrieve him again once his parents had 'fixed' their marriage and wanted to pretend they were a family again.

'And we are done,' Eliana said after a couple more minutes had passed, and put her instruments down. She pulled the gloves off her hands. 'I'll ask a nurse to give you the medication as well. Please get as much rest as you can and come back before you run out of medicine.'

She took the notebook that was lying on Selma's lap and stuck her hand in her pocket, retrieving a pen from it. Diego stood up from his seat, leaning to look over her shoulder. The handwriting on the page was his friend's—instructions he had written down when Selma had first sought him out for help.

He watched as Eliana struck out Vanderson's name and wrote a note beneath it, before handing it back to the patient.

'Tell them I have authorised all your treatments already, so they can give you your new medication along with a physical, okay?'

Selma nodded, and a moment later Diego felt Eliana's deep brown eyes were on him, peering so deeply he thought she was staring straight inside him, past all the locked barriers he had put up.

But she didn't say anything. Instead, she turned around on her heel and hurried off.

*'Ana, esperar!'* This was the first time they had spoken to each other since the bombshell announcement of her pregnancy. 'Where are you going?'

He caught up to her in three big strides, taking her by the elbow and leading her into a free exam room at the far end of the emergency department. Closing the door behind him, he flipped the lock so they wouldn't be interrupted.

Hot sparks travelled up and down her arm where Diego had just touched her. Despite his insistence, his fingers had been gentle as he'd guided her to this empty room so they could talk.

A talk Eliana knew had been coming—and yet she didn't feel the least bit prepared. They needed to talk about their child and what their lives would look like as co-parents. The strong surges of desire infusing the fibres of her body didn't help in untangling the mess she found herself in.

She couldn't trust her feelings. Not when everything was so foggy and tangled up.

Diego stood in front of her, his corded arms crossed in front of his impressive chest as he heaved a long sigh. The lines around his eyes told her he had been struggling just as much as she had in the last two weeks. Was he struggling to cope? Or was he trying to find the best way out of the situation?

A sudden fear gripped at her chest when she thought about him running away. Would he really do that?

'What are you doing down here? Shouldn't you be...?' His voice trailed off.

'Shouldn't I be what? Resting?' Eliana scoffed, hoping he had stopped himself from completing his sentence because he'd realised how ridiculous he sounded. Though the protectiveness in his voice had kicked something loose within her that made her heart stutter in her chest.

He was worried about her.

'I'm sorry. I know I'm not handling this situation very well.'

He looked at her, and the spark in his dark brown eyes was so disarming that her breath caught in her throat. She thought she could forgive him anything as long as he promised to look at her like that for ever.

Eliana hesitated for a moment before extending an olive branch. 'I've scheduled some time with each of the department heads so I can get to know their service. The emergency department seemed a good place to start, since I spend a lot of time there at my own hospital.'

Diego dropped his arms to his sides as he relaxed a bit. 'Where is your hospital?'

'In Belo Horizonte. I did my training there, and they asked me to stay on after I got my general surgeon certification. I took a short break between my certification and starting my new role and then...well, you know what happened.'

Diego nodded.

A frown was pulling on his lips and it made her chest contract. She wanted to reach out and smooth the corners of his mouth up into the self-assured smile she preferred. He looked genuinely sad, which didn't match the conversation they'd had on her first day. Back then he had complained about how her father had cut spending on pro bono surgeries to build lavish rooms for his VIP patients. Why did he now seem sad at the mention of his death? Or was something else troubling him?

Her hand went to her stomach in what now felt like an automated gesture. Even though there was hardly anything to see or feel at the moment, the presence of her child comforted her more than anything else had in the last couple of weeks. Their bond was already forming, giving her strength for the challenges ahead of her.

'I want to go back to Belo Horizonte. With him. Or her. Which might make things a bit harder if you're planning on being around.'

'If?'

Something in his face contorted—a look of pain she hadn't expected. Her doubt had hurt his feelings, and she struggled to understand that for a moment. They were still hardly more than strangers who were finding themselves in a position where they had to raise a child together.

He seemed genuine in his intentions, really wanting to do what was right. It had been him, after all, chasing her around the hospital to talk about their child while she'd been avoiding him. Would he have done that if he meant to be an absentee father?

'We've never spoken about it, so I wasn't sure how you feel about your involvement,' she said, and felt his answer coming even before he spoke.

'We haven't spoken because every time I tried to approach you, you ran for the hills as if I had some contagious disease,' he retorted, with an edge of bitterness in his voice.

She deserved that, yet it still made her flinch. She hadn't been thinking about his feelings. The news had sent her into preservation mode for several days as she'd gathered her thoughts.

Because there was more than just the matter of their child to discuss. There was the attraction humming in her blood, flooding her with a sharp awareness every time she so much as glimpsed Diego somewhere in the hospital. It stood in stark contrast to her rational side, which wanted to retreat far away from this way too sexy man and let their lawyers do all the talking.

She wondered what it had been like for her mother to fall pregnant by a man she wasn't in a serious relationship with. If she had lived would she be urging Eliana to find a way to be together, even if it was just for their child?

No, her mother had been stronger than that—even if she hadn't been able to hang on to life at the end. She would have wanted her to forge her own path. It might intersect with Diego's—and she found that she really wanted him to remain in her life in one form or another—but they didn't need to be in a romantic relationship to be good parents. Even though the look he was giving her in this moment was ratcheting up a tightness in her core that she had to will away with a few breaths.

'I'm sorry.' She cast her eyes down, her hands

crossed over her still flat stomach. 'I needed some space to think, to figure out what I want to do. I think it's great that you want to be involved. In fact, I was hoping you would.'

Eliana sighed. Her limbs felt heavy all of a sudden as the day caught up to her. Selma's procedure had taken a lot more energy out of her than she had expected.

Diego must have seen her falter, for he stepped up to her, wrapping his hand around her arm. With ease, as if he was picking up a child, he grabbed her hips with his other arm and placed her on the exam room table. Her feet dangled above the floor, grazing along his thighs every now and then, and each contact created a trail of sparks that went shooting across her skin.

The attraction between them was palpable, and the glances they exchanged were heated with desire but underpinned by the gravity of their situation.

'Are you ready to talk now?' he asked her.

Regret tied a knot in her stomach when he took a step back. Even though it had been only a slight brush of her feet against his legs, she didn't want it to stop.

'I still don't have a plan. But, yes, I'm ready to talk about things.'

Only she didn't know what. If it wasn't about her plans for their child, what was there left to talk about? The way every time she closed her eyes she could smell the scent of earth and petrichor as his tongue and teeth had grazed over her neck?

'Have you already had your first prenatal appointment?'

She blinked, finding her way out of the unbidden fantasy. 'I'm actually going to speak to someone today. I asked Suelen to tell them to come see me.'

Diego's lips curled upwards in a grin that made her heart stop for a second before it continued beating twice as fast.

'Two weeks on the job and you're already making people come to you. That's a boss move, Dr Oliveira.'

She laughed, feeling some of the tension draining out of her. 'I had to learn to stand up for myself early on. That habit dies hard, no matter what job I'm in.'

'I know what you mean.'

Eliana looked at him, her head tilted to one side in a gesture of curiosity. She wanted him to elaborate but he remained silent, his face not revealing the thoughts in his mind.

'Do you want to come to the scan in a couple of weeks?' she asked.

This time his expression shifted, and she could see the beginnings of panic bubbling up in the corners of his eyes. A sentiment she understood well. Appointments, scans…those things rooted their surprise baby in reality when they were still coming to terms with the change in their lives.

Her mother had been forced to do it all by herself. Marco hadn't wanted anything to do with his affair or their child. But Diego was already showing himself to be different, wanting to be a part of the whole journey. The thought of going it alone sent terror thrumming through her body, and she wanted to trust him—trust that he would support her throughout the journey. That she could let him be a part of it without her attraction to him burning her alive.

'Yes, I would like that.'

He lifted his hands, and for a second she thought he was going to reach out to her—a thought that thundered excitement and terror through her in equal measures. But he quickly dropped them back to his sides again.

Whatever it was floating between them was affecting him too.

Their one night together had already given her all the comfort she'd get from him. Anything beyond that was never going to happen. A baby didn't change the fact that she didn't want to pursue a relationship—especially not in Rio de Janeiro, when she already had one foot out of the city.

In fact the baby just reaffirmed her feelings

about a relationship. Staying together for the sake of a child would only ever ensure that everyone involved grew resentful of one another. That kind of thing never worked out.

'When are you going back to Belo Horizonte?' he asked.

She tried to read his expression, but shutters had fallen over his eyes, revoking the access he had very briefly granted her.

'I don't know. Not for a month or two, it seems. It depends on how fast my father's estate can be wrapped up and how much work needs to be done here. This place is so different from the hospital in Belo Horizonte.'

Diego raised an eyebrow in question. 'How come?'

'Well, for starters the hospital there is part-owned by the local municipality, so the area we service is a lot more diverse than here. Though from our encounter some moments ago I can see you're trying to change that.'

Diego had the decency to look away as her words sank in. It had been obvious Selma knew him, and she had connected him to the free clinic she had mentioned during their initial chat.

'You held yourself well with her. I was glad to see the compassion in your treatment,' he said after a few moments, his lips curving in a small smile that sent her heart rate racing.

'Sounds like you didn't expect me to be a competent doctor,' she replied, willing the heat rising to her cheeks to go away.

'Not at all. I just liked seeing that we're now being led by someone who thinks of the patients first.' He stopped talking for a second. Then, 'I meant to pay you a compliment. I enjoyed watching you work.'

'Oh…' The heat within her flared out from her cheeks in every direction through her body, making it impossible for her to find the right words to reply.

Silence fell over them and grew more tense with each moment passing as neither of them spoke, each chasing their own thoughts. Eliana was bursting to say something—to set boundaries from the very beginning so things wouldn't get messy. But she didn't know how to start that conversation. Especially not if he was paying her compliments like that.

'I think we should be friends,' Diego said, throwing her completely off track with those six simple words. 'We both went into this thinking it would be a one-night stand. Neither of us wanted more than that. And I don't think either of us wants to get into a relationship just because there's a child. But if we're doing this together, we should be…friends.'

'Friends?' she repeated, as if she hadn't heard right. When she'd been thinking about boundaries, that hadn't been the approach she had thought about.

'Yes. Friends. We're going to be in each other's lives from now on, for better or for worse. Don't you think we should find a way we can be comfortable with each other without...?'

He let the pause speak for itself, but Eliana wasn't sure she understood what he meant. Without sleeping with each other again? Without acting on the intense attraction that wrapped itself around them every time they spoke?

'So, we're going from giving each other multiple orgasms as complete strangers who will never see each other again to being...friends?'

Diego cracked a smile at that, a soft chuckle escaping his gorgeous throat. 'Well, if you put it that way you make it sound like a terrible idea.'

'No, friends sounds good. I only ever had emotionally unavailable parents, so I imagine parents who are friends will be a big step up.'

*Friends sounds good.*

Doubt crept into her heart the second she said those words, and she fought hard not to let it be visible on her face. At several points during their conversation she had imagined running her mouth along his collarbones. Her desire for Diego was overpowering, firing a heat through her system that left the nerve-ends singed.

How was she supposed to be *friends* with

someone who stoked a fire of passion in her with mere glances?

But he was right. They were going to be in each other's lives one way or another.

Was that what her mother had been hoping for when she'd found out that she was pregnant? That she and Marco would find a way to co-exist? Would she still be alive today if Marco had made the same suggestion Diego had?

It was worth a try. She wanted her child to grow up knowing both of its parents' love and support. If that meant she needed to get over her attraction to Diego, she could do that. Right?

'So...how do we go from this...' she raised her hands, motioning around her '...to being friends?'

'Let's start by doing some activities that don't involve a sick patient. Or taking our clothes off. Something like lunch on a Saturday.'

He paused for a moment, the mischievous gleam in his eyes telling her that taking her clothes off was all he was thinking about.

Eliana took the pen out of her pocket again and pretended to take notes on her palm. 'No patients. No taking off clothes. Got it.' She paused for a moment, seemingly inspecting her invisible list. 'Can we talk about work, though? I have some questions about Selma.'

Diego let out a sigh, raking his hands through

his already unruly hair. 'I hoped you'd forget about that.'

The discussion about their child *had* made her forget for a moment. When they'd come in here she had planned on confronting him about the clinic, but their attention had quickly turned to other matters between them.

'Did you know my brother? Was he working at a free clinic somewhere in the city? Selma's notes—'

Diego raised his hands, interrupting her. 'Lunch on Saturday. I'll pick you up from your hotel. We can get to know each other. As friends.'

Eliana hesitated, suddenly not sure if meeting Diego outside of work was such a good idea. While they might both be sincere about being friends, their attraction was undeniable—and she could read it in his eyes as well. How were they supposed to dial this kind of visceral intensity back to friendship?

No matter how. They had to do it. Somehow Eliana had to learn to be around him without dissolving into a puddle of need and longing.

# CHAPTER FIVE

THE COOL AIR circulating through the hotel lobby did precious little to calm Diego's nerves as he sat in one of the armchairs, waiting for Eliana to meet him. Eliana. The mother of his child and now, apparently, his friend.

Their conversation from a few days ago replayed in his head. He was unsure what had driven him to say that when he didn't mean it. He wanted to run his hands all over her sensual body in various activities that required both of them to take their clothes off.

Except he had to mean it. On a different level of consciousness he realised they needed a tried-and-true framework for their relationship with each other, so they wouldn't be stumbling in the dark while they figured out how to be parents. If his parents had chosen to think about him rather than their own desire and chaotic relationship, maybe he would have had a more stable home.

Diego wanted to do what was best for his child.

The thought still felt foreign to him. Having lived through such a volatile childhood, he'd never thought he would have a child himself. A baby meant stability, a partnership, a family built on trust and love. Two essential qualities he didn't know if he even possessed.

*Time to find out*, Diego told himself as he watched her come down the stairs.

His reaction to her was instant. The blood in his veins hummed with awareness as he repressed the urge to pick her up and carry her back to her room for a repeat show of that night several weeks ago.

'Olá,' he greeted her, his eyes running all over her body as she approached him.

She wore a dark red dress that sat tight around her torso and flared out into a wide skirt that accentuated the supple curve of her hips. Diego had to swallow the dryness spreading through his mouth as he imagined what the dress would look like in a pool around her feet.

'Bom dia...amigo.' She said the word 'friend' slowly, as if she was trying it on to see if it would fit.

He prayed that it would. That was the only way he saw to keep on being a part of her life, not just that of his child. Because for reasons Diego didn't dare to examine too closely, for fear of what he might see, he wanted to be a part of her life, too.

'You ready?' he asked after clearing his throat.

Looking at her drove blood to places that needed to remain dormant if they were to become friends. It wasn't as if Diego was particularly rich in friends. Although with his father's innumerable affairs he'd grown up with many half-siblings—some of them a very similar age to him. Being the woman she was, his grandmother had insisted on meeting all of her grandchildren, regardless of her son's stance on the issue, and had always maintained an open-door policy for any Ferrari child. That meant his childhood home had never been empty, but he'd had to grow up seeing his half-siblings' mothers involved in their lives while he only got to watch from afar.

He loved his half-siblings, and was glad to have them in his life, but he still sometimes struggled to see them because their mothers had chosen them, while he had become collateral damage in his parents' disastrous marriage.

His child would have a different life—he would make sure of that.

'What's the plan? Do you just want to have a bite here?' Eliana looked around.

The current passing back and forth between them was almost visible, making him feel ill at ease with their plan to keep things platonic.

'No, you've been living off hotel food for too long. Let me show you a special place.'

'Special?' Eliana asked with a raised eyebrow, but he only winked before he laid his hand on the small of her back to guide her to his car.

The touch was minuscule, so small that it could barely be called a touch, but the heat of it seared the tips of his fingers nonetheless, shooting small fires up his arm and into his chest. He bit the inside of his cheek to suppress the surging desire.

This was not how friends thought about each other.

'It's a nice place by the beach, but hidden enough so the tourists can't find it. I like to go there whenever I have the time—which isn't as often as I would like.'

A brief fifteen minutes later they pulled into a parking garage and walked a short distance to the beach, where they sat down at a small table right at the beachfront.

The expression of wonderment on her face was one of the most marvellous things Diego had seen in a while, and he had to bury his face in the menu so she wouldn't catch him staring at her with unabashed desire.

'See anything you like?' he asked, to distract himself from the unbidden heat rising in his chest.

'I don't know...' Eliana looked over the menu, a slight frown drawing the corners of her lips downwards. 'I like the sound of the steak sandwich, but lately red meat doesn't really agree with me. Or maybe it's the baby who doesn't like it. It's silly, but I think it's already developing its own tastes. As a doctor, I know that's impossible, but... I like to think it doesn't like meat so much. Maybe we're having a vegetarian.'

She paused, looking down at her menu with an intensity that almost made him chuckle. The embarrassment in her voice was incredibly sweet and sexy, and not warranted in any way. Their child was becoming more tangible with every passing day—it was only natural she would associate it with some characteristics.

A smile he had no control over curled his lips, and a warm sensation took tentative root in his chest as he enjoyed the purity of the moment they had just shared. Her care for their unborn child was extraordinary. Already it was so unlike the way his own mother had treated him, ripping him from his home with his *avozinha* whenever it had suited her.

Diego cleared his throat as he felt his chest suddenly constrict. No matter how intense the longing got he would not act on it. Passion faded; it always did. Their co-parenting relationship needed to be built on something more substantial and solid.

'Don't be embarrassed,' he said now, his voice a lot huskier than he'd intended it to be. 'Of course you're putting a lot of thought into what it might like and dislike. One day soon our baby will appreciate that.'

Eliana lifted her eyes off her menu to look at him, and the sparkling intensity of her gaze robbed him of his breath. 'Our baby... It's so strange to hear it, even though I know it's true. When I came to Rio I wasn't expecting anything like this.'

He raised an eyebrow at that. 'What *was* your plan?'

They had never really talked about it. Other than her desire to get back to Belo Horizonte in a few weeks.

'I don't make plans. In the past they haven't worked out for me, so I've stopped putting energy into planning things.'

The warmth in her voice had almost completely faded. Whatever lay behind her aversion for plans was clearly still a painful memory to her.

As someone who carried quite a few of those around himself, he knew better than to probe. If anyone did that to him he would shut them down instantly. Some borders weren't meant to be crossed, and his past was definitely one of them.

'Why is that?' he asked anyway, unable to stop himself.

He wanted to know her—the good things as well as the things that pained her. She was the mother of his child...a baby they'd decided they would bring up together. Surely that meant he needed to know something about her other than whatever Vanderson had told him about his long-estranged half-sister.

Eliana remained quiet, staring down at the glass of pineapple juice the waitress had just put down in front of her. She grabbed the little umbrella sticking out at the side of the glass, stirring the drink as she thought about her answer. Or rather thought about how she could best *not* answer him, he thought with a wry smile.

'Is it safe to assume you've heard all the rumours about Marco Costa's illegitimate daughter?' she asked, without raising her eyes from the glass.

Diego sighed. He abhorred the gossip that was spread in the corridors of Santa Valeria, especially when it involved Eliana. Being from a dysfunctional family himself, he knew exactly what kind of damage it could do to one's psyche, and it could just as easily have been him they gossiped about.

'Yes, I have,' he confirmed, and nodded although she wasn't looking at him.

'Good, so I can skip some things.' She laughed, but it sounded so unlike the laughter they had shared during their night together that Diego almost flinched at the bitterness.

'After my mother died in childbirth, my father did the bare minimum to raise me, leaving it to the hired help. Once I was old enough, he shipped me off to boarding school. A good one—and that's the reason why I was able to get into university—but the spoiled children of Brazil's elite weren't interested in befriending society's latest scandal child.'

She stopped to take a sip of her drink. Her voice had been calm and steady, but when she raised the glass to her lips he saw it shake, the ice cubes softly clinking against the glass. Her visible distress struck at something deep within him, and he reached out underneath the table, laying a supportive hand on her thigh.

'School was awful, and whenever I was home during the school break that was awful as well. Marco had a guest house set up as my apartment, so he didn't have to invite me into the house with his wife and son. Being all by myself, I dreamed of a different life…of parents who actually wanted me. I made so many plans, thinking that one day my father would come around. That one day he would see me as more than just a stain on his legacy. And I watched all those plans crumble into dust.'

Eliana heaved a deep sigh as she took another sip of her drink, finally lifting her eyes away from the glass to look at him. Her expression was guarded, and he couldn't see in it any of the emotion he had heard in her voice just a few seconds ago.

'Sorry, you didn't come here to listen to my sad childhood stories.'

'I'm glad you've said something. Plus, having problems with Marco Costa is something we have in common. You would have had a friend in Vanderson as well. He fought my corner when it came to dealing with Marco.'

He shrugged, trying to lighten the mood that had grown increasingly tense between them. His problems with Marco Costa were dwarfed by the cold and loveless childhood she had gone through.

That was something else they had in common, but he wasn't ready to share that part of himself with her. He didn't know if he ever would be. Probably not. Even friends didn't tell each other everything...

She smiled, but it didn't quite reach her eyes. 'I never saw much of Vanderson. I think our father didn't allow him near me. It's odd to think he disagreed with my father later on, when he obeyed him like that in the past.'

Diego shrugged, trying to defuse the tension still growing between them. He knew how much his best friend had regretted making the choices he had. But was it really his place to tell her that?

'I know Vanderson had to play by your father's rules because he held the keys to everything...hoarding power like he hoarded his wealth. Santa Valeria is a prime example of that. Marco chased profit and prestige above anything else, compromising the ability of his staff to do the good work they tried to do. Building those extravagant rooms, for example, was just one of many decisions he made that showed he was never about helping people.'

Eliana tilted her head to one side in an inquisitive look that kicked his pulse into overdrive. One minute she was pouring her heart out... the next she was sending him looks that made him want to forget about decency so he could have his way with her right here on the beach.

When that was the last thing he should want.

Not with a child between them.

There was too much at stake for any rash decisions, no matter how much his blood was burning for him to touch her.

It wasn't going to happen, and he'd better get that into his head now.

\* \* \*

The words had tumbled out of her mouth as if she'd genuinely meant to say them—which she hadn't. Those memories—her father, the boarding school, the score of nannies—weren't meant to be brought to light and examined by anyone. Especially not by this man in front of her.

Eliana had enough problems resisting the fire of attraction sizzling between them without giving herself more reasons to like him. *Really* like him.

But something about Diego's compassionate eyes and the way he had laid his hand on her thigh as she poured her heart out had reassured her that she was in a safe space. That whatever she had to say he wouldn't judge her or make her feel silly for feeling like that. Not like the people she had grown up around, who had told her how lucky she was to be Marco Costa's daughter no matter how badly he treated her.

On the other hand, her half-brother had started to morph into a mystery in front of her eyes. He'd never been cruel to her when she was growing up, but he'd also never stood up for her, and he hadn't ever let on if he'd thought their father was mistreating her. She knew nothing about him as a person, and had always assumed that since he hadn't said anything to make her think otherwise he was one of his father's minions—

just like some of the other people she'd met at the hospital.

But Diego had started to paint a different picture of Vanderson. For the first time she began to wonder if he had been a victim of their father's manipulations just like her.

'You promised to tell me about Vanderson and how you two were involved. Did you know him well?' she asked, watching him with intent. She knew the two men were somehow connected.

A different kind of expression fluttered over Diego's face. Not contempt, but something else that hinted at a wealth of pain and complicated emotions.

'I knew him, yes. We both agreed that we couldn't let Marco run Santa Valeria the way he did, so we started working with each other.'

There had been a slight hesitancy in his voice as he spoke, as if he was choosing his words with deliberation.

'I noticed that Selma came in with instructions about her medical history written down,' she said. 'A note specifically asked her to come to Santa Valeria if she needed to, and to get them to page Vanderson if they had any questions.' She paused for a moment, tapping her finger against her chin as she followed her train of thought. 'I wondered if he was the one who initially treated her. She said she got her medicine from a free clinic, but that the doctor hadn't been there in a while. I think that might be because he died.'

'Not quite,' he said, and glanced away for a moment. 'Vanderson wasn't the one running the clinic, though he was involved. That note was from him. Your brother would help me with the free clinic in many different ways. One of them was covering patients if they came into A&E for treatments they normally received at the free clinic.'

Her heart stuttered in her chest as she processed his words. He had worked with her brother to bring free healthcare to people in need. A noble effort that was twisted by her unresolved feelings towards Vanderson. She had to admit that she didn't know what she had expected from him—only that what she had got wasn't enough. The picture she'd always had of him didn't quite fit in with caring about the disadvantaged people in the city.

'He helped you?'

Talking about her brother had unleashed a torrent of hurt inside her chest, but she wanted to know. What kind of man had he grown into? Had he regretted staying quiet?

Diego nodded, and she watched his expression as he scrubbed his hand over his clean-shaven face. He looked as if he was trying hard not to give anything away.

'He did, and I probably couldn't have done it without him. I bent a lot of rules so I was able to help people in my clinic, and Marco was suspicious when I...' He shook his head, his voice trailing off into a chuckle. 'I shouldn't be telling you this. You're still the new chief.'

'Oh? Why would you have reason to hide things? I already know you've convinced the emergency department staff to treat uninsured people.'

Her eyes narrowed on him as she thought about that. Was that what he'd been dancing around each time she'd felt him hesitate? How did his role at the Santa Valeria play into the free clinic?

Eliana's mouth fell open when she remembered their interaction with Selma. 'That's why you wanted to do the thoracentesis. Because you'd done it before.' She gasped, replaying the memory in her mind. 'Selma didn't let on a single thing!'

Diego had the decency to look somewhat embarrassed as a hesitant grin took over his face, robbing her of what little breath was left in her lungs.

'She's been coming to Santa Valeria long enough to know the drill whenever she meets a new doctor.'

'And Marco was riled up so much that he tried to fire you?'

Eliana remembered what Diego had told her. How good he had become at toeing the line to keep his job. Was that going to happen to them as well? Were they doomed to become antagonists at work while trying to figure out how to be good co-parents in private?

Was that something her mother had struggled with—co-parenting with a person who held all the power at work?

Diego hesitated, seeming to know what she was getting at. But she wanted to hear everything. A full confession.

'So we're doing it like this, huh?' he said.

She shrugged. 'I'm going to find out sooner or later, no? Might as well get it out there now, as we're clearing the air.'

'You wield a chief's power well, Ana,' Diego said as he leaned forward, resting his elbows on his thighs, giving her a view of the sculpted chest she remembered all too well.

A shiver ran from the top of her head all the way down to her toes, curling them inside her slingback sandals.

'From time to time I would spend some of my working hours in the free clinic rather than at the hospital. Only when there were other senior staff to help out in the orthopaedics department, and only when the patient load was manageable. Also, I would take the samples that pharmaceutical representatives brought and give them out at the clinic whenever someone needed something more than ibuprofen. That's how people like Selma keep their chronic conditions in check.'

He paused for a moment, his brow knit together.

'Most of the time we get general practice patients visiting the free clinic. Though the word has spread, and the lines outside get longer and the cases grow more desperate. Conditions that are very treatable under normal circumstances are exacerbated by the lack of healthcare available to the people living in the *favelas*.'

Diego leaned back in his chair, obscuring her enticing view down his button-up shirt again, and sighed.

'They're my people. I can't abandon them, no matter how difficult it is or how much trouble I might get into. Growing up, I watched people succumb to treatable diseases because families in the poorer parts of the city don't have adequate access to healthcare. So when I needed more hospital resources, I asked Vanderson for help.'

'You and Vanderson worked together to help the disadvantaged community?'

'We did. He would make sure that I got the time I needed with certain specialists. Marco didn't allow any kind of pro bono or community outreach work, but Vanderson was very good at packaging things in a way so that Marco could see a monetary benefit to it.'

Silence grew between them as Eliana took her time to process all the new things she had just learned about her brother, as well as Diego.

The waitress came by to ask about food, and Eliana realised that she hadn't even thought about it. She looked at Diego and he picked up on her silent plea, quickly glancing at the menu before ordering a variety of appetisers so they could have some bite-sized portions while they spoke to each other.

They were only just starting to get to know each other, and Eliana didn't want it to stop. The stranger she had met at a hotel bar on the day of her father's funeral was beginning to take shape right in front of her eyes. The more they spoke, the more she discovered about the compassion that drove him to be an excellent medical professional as well as a good man.

A *really* good man.

Their discussion had been so intense she hadn't noticed the low and persistent hum of awareness coursing through her body with every heartbeat. This was *not* good. She was supposed to find a healthy distance from him, so they could be co-parents without her head getting filled with mists of desire and longing every time she looked at him.

Maybe even friendship was a step too far.

What if being cordial acquaintances was all they could manage?

Eliana didn't know what she had hoped for today, but she knew that this strange closeness—the way her attraction was morphing into a deep longing in front of her eyes—wasn't it.

'So, what are you going to do now?'

Diego's low voice cut through her confusing contemplations and she looked at him with wide eyes.

'What do you mean?'

He chuckled. 'I've told you how I regularly misappropriate hospital resources to run my free clinic.'

'Oh, right...' That was the least of her concerns. Or else it was the root of her problem, depending on how she chose to look at it. It was his devotion to doing the right thing, helping the less fortunate, that turned the hot spear of desire piercing her chest into something larger and softer.

He was right. As the chief of medicine she should care about staff members disregarding the rules of the hospital. Whatever the reasons, his confession was a severe breach of protocol and should be met with some form of investigation.

Which was at direct odds with what she wanted to do. He was helping people...doing the right thing. Instead of investigating him and potentially reprimanding him, she wanted to help him. Make it official so he could stop sneaking around.

Was it that simple? Eliana wanted to believe so, although her feelings were getting entangled with business decisions. Did she like the idea because it was good for the hospital, or did she want to do it because she liked *him*?

'Will you show it to me?'

It was a terrible idea to get more involved with him than she already was. Their unplanned child was hard enough to deal with. If she dived further into personal things with him, it would take so much more effort to untangle herself.

Diego furrowed his brow, seemingly in agreement with her internal monologue. 'You want to visit the clinic?'

'Yes. Will you take me?'

He hesitated, his gaze shifting in and out of focus as he contemplated his answer.

'When do you want to go?'

'I'm not doing anything right now.'

# CHAPTER SIX

DIEGO TRIED HIS best to watch her without staring as they entered Complexo do Alemão. They had left his car in the parking garage and waved down one of the yellow and green taxis so prominent in the streets of Rio de Janeiro. While the people in the neighbourhood knew him, and his practice, he still didn't dare drive up in anything that looked too expensive. He remembered what it had been like to grow up in the *favela*, and knew he wouldn't be making any friends by flaunting his wealth.

And safety was his primary concern with Eliana—much more than when he was on his own. He knew how to deal with people from his old neighbourhood, but she hadn't grown up here. He doubted that she had ever seen one of Rio de Janeiro's slums.

Her wide eyes as they drove up to the inconspicuous building that housed the clinic confirmed his suspicion. He tried to read her emotions as her expression fluttered and changed, but it was hard to guess what was going through her head.

Diego barely had any clarity in what was going through his own mind. He had shared so much of himself with her that he hadn't planned to—the things he had been doing in the free clinic most of all. She was the chief of medicine—the person holding the reins at Santa Valeria. He definitely shouldn't have volunteered the fact that he played fast and loose with the rules and hospital resources.

But something within him felt he owed her the truth—about his clinic, and also about himself. He still struggled to talk about Vanderson. The pain of his loss was dulled with every passing day, but every now and then it came rushing back to him, reminding him. Especially when it came to the plans they'd made to expand the clinic.

Was that why he had decided to tell Eliana? Did he want to bring her on board with those plans? She had asked him about her brother, and while he'd felt safe to share what they were doing here, he hadn't said how much he'd meant to him, scared that it might alienate him from her. When she'd spoken about Vanderson he'd seen a myriad of feelings flutter over her expression, and he had known there were a lot of unresolved feelings. Feelings that would now stay that way for ever.

No, he hadn't shared the clinic information with her for his own gain. That wouldn't have rung true within him. He had told her because he wanted her to know him—really know him. Which was a thought so terrifying Diego pushed it away.

He never got to know the women in his life because he didn't ever plan to spend more than one pleasurable night with them. Though Eliana would be in his life always, as the mother of his child.

But he could feel it running deeper than that—further than anything he had felt before. The rising heat inside his chest was messing with his head to the point where he had to use every ounce of self-restraint he still possessed not to sweep her up in his arms and carry her back to his place.

They were not meant to be more than what they were right now, though. Regardless of how electric her presence felt in his blood.

Diego shook his head, willing himself back into the present as he unlocked the door and held it open for Eliana. She walked through with a small smile on her full lips that instantly reignited the fire within him that he had just stamped out. Her light floral perfume drifted up his nose, making him long to have that scent lingering in his bedroom, the way it had back in the hotel all those weeks ago.

A different lifetime ago, when they hadn't been having a child together.

'Here we go. It's not much, but we don't really need much here. It's rare that anything complicated comes in.'

Diego had been expecting a comment about the state of the place. While it was clean, and furnished to his best abilities, it didn't even begin to compare to any facility her father had built in his long career as a medical professional.

But Eliana didn't comment on the clinic's appearance, her expression veiled, as she pointed at a closed door. 'Is that the exam room?'

'Yes. We technically have one on each side. Though currently only one is in use.'

She opened the door and walked through with Diego following on her heels. The exam room didn't look much different from the reception area. A sturdy table dominated the room, with two chairs standing next to it. There was an old-looking ultrasound machine in one corner, its protective covers gathering a layer of dust.

Eliana looked around with curious eyes, taking everything in as if she was taking stock. She walked past the exam table and looked at the closed cabinets lining the wall. Finally she turned around and leaned her hip against the table.

'I really don't know what I was expecting when you told me about it.'

Her voice sounded thick, and Diego crossed his arms in front of his chest, ready to defend his clinic. 'Do you have anything to say?'

She shook her head, her lavish red-brown curls bouncing around her face and making her look irresistible even in the poor lighting of the room.

'No, I'm impressed with your dedication to this place. You made it sound a lot worse than it is. I thought I'd find an MRI machine you'd stolen from the basement.'

Despite himself, Diego chuckled. 'I think you'd find an ambulance gone missing rather than one of the machines, if I ever dared to go that far.'

While he did technically steal—both his own time and his colleagues', and any pharmaceutical samples the companies left with him—he didn't consider it theft in a moral sense, although he didn't want to seem too blasé about it. Vanderson had given him permission for these things, bringing him close to but never across the hard lines.

But, going by the curious expression on her face, Eliana didn't seem to mind his clandestine activities. Was there still hope for the plans he had for the clinic?

'And you get a lot of people asking for help?'

she asked as her eyes drifted around the room once more.

'Why do you think I didn't turn on the light in the reception area? If someone sees the light on there'll soon be a queue of people outside.'

He sighed as he imagined the number of people he would see in the short blocks of time he spent here. Sometimes his *avozinha* would help him triage patients, so that he could attend to the most severe cases first.

The concern sparking in her face kicked something loose within Diego and his pulse quickened. Her next words almost undid him.

'There are really so many people that need treatment? Maybe we should turn the light on since it's the two of us here? I can help.'

*Help.* That was where her first thought went—to help all the people who needed her to cure them. She didn't ask him about the hours he spent here when he should be in the hospital. Nor did she want to know about the medication he had admitted to misappropriating from Santa Valeria's pharmacy. No, Eliana wanted to know how she could help the underprivileged people in his community.

Diego was speechless, gaping at her as he tried to find words for the feeling erupting in his chest.

Eliana shifted under his stare, raising her

brows in a half worried, half questioning gesture. 'What's wrong?'

'You must have received your generous heart from your mother, because there is no way it could have come from Marco,' he said, before he could think better of it.

He reached his hand out, wanting to fix the hurt he saw in her face without knowing how to do it. From the gossip echoing through the corridors of Santa Valeria he knew that her mother had been a nurse there before Marco had pushed her to move. The scandal of her getting pregnant by a married man who was also her boss was still something people liked to talk about—especially now that the result of this particular scandal owned the hospital.

Her brows reached even higher, transforming her expression into a look of surprise. 'Unfortunately I don't know much about her at all. I wish I could have met her. I'm sure she would have some advice for me about having an unexpected baby with a man who was a fling.'

'It'll be different for us,' he said without thinking, reaching for the first words that manifested themselves in his mind. 'Our baby will have a loving home no matter where it is.'

'Thank you, Diego. That means a lot.'

Her smile for him made his heart stop dead in his chest for a couple of seconds before it kicked back in, driving his blood to all the wrong places.

If she kept up like that she would prove to be his undoing. He felt himself slipping, wanting her right now, but also imagining having her working by his side at the clinic. Eliana cared about the people—his community—and she didn't even know them.

He'd be lucky to have a woman like that on his side. He could learn how to be different from the kind of man his father had been. Was there a world where they could be a family?

The softness in her eyes as they looked at him sparked a longing that pumped through his body with every heartbeat, spreading a heat he didn't know how to process.

He couldn't let himself hope for that. They had agreed not to. He didn't even know how to deal with what he was desiring in this moment. He should step away.

The thought echoed in his head even as he took a step towards her, drawn in by the look on her face.

'So, are you going to turn a blind eye on my clinic dealings?' He wanted to talk about something safe—something to distract him from the longing mounting within his chest.

'I don't know what to do about it. About anything, really. I wasn't ever supposed to be the chief of medicine at a hospital where everyone knows my story.'

He saw a shudder trickle through her body, and pain glimmered beneath the surface of her face.

'It doesn't surprise me that you had to do this behind my father's back. I never saw much of him when I was growing up. He couldn't even take care of the child he'd accidentally created. Sure, I was fed and clothed, but that was the end of it.'

Diego shook his head at the awfulness of that thought. He tried to imagine his *avozinha* rejecting any of his half-siblings for whatever reason, but she would never have gone in that direction. Just as he could never turn his back on his child, no matter the nature of its conception.

'I was raised by my grandmother. My parents weren't around much either,' he said, his mouth moving in a strange urge to share this part of himself with her—so she would understand that she wasn't alone in her conviction to be a better parent than those she'd had.

'What did they do?' She tilted her head to one side, her brown curls sliding over her shoulder, creating a picture of such pure feminine sensuality that he forgot what they were talking about for a fraction of a second.

'They were—are still—very unhappy together. My father would cheat on her, she would kick him out, then he would eventually come back to beg for her forgiveness. Their separations weren't easy. Lots of shouting, breaking things, accusations... And more often than not they'd forget that they had a son to look after.'

He shrugged when he saw the horror on Eliana's face. These memories had stopped bothering him a long time ago. They had done their damage on him, teaching him only chaos and volatility, to the point where he didn't know how to accept calm and love in his life.

'Whenever my dad strayed he would dump me at my *avozinha's* place. That went on for a couple of years until my grandmother put her foot down and kept me with her.'

'I'm sorry that happened to you,' she said with a frown of genuine concern for him.

He shrugged again. 'That's why I want to be better with...'

His voice trailed off as he struggled to finish the sentence. The word *us* echoed in his mind, but it would be a ridiculous thing to say to her. They were not anything that could remotely be considered an *us*. As small as that word was, it carried a lot of emotional depth that Diego wasn't prepared for.

'With...our baby?' Eliana prompted him, and he was relieved and disappointed that she hadn't said the word either.

'Yes,' he said, to distract himself from the emotions rising in his chest. 'We should have at least some idea of what we're doing before you leave.'

They were going to be parents, but that would be the extent of their relationship. They would never be more. Couldn't be more than that. He didn't know how.

With the small frown on her face deepening, she wove her fingers through each other, clasping her hands together. 'I know I've been avoiding this conversation, and I'm sorry about that. It probably didn't feel very nice...'

Diego had to smile at that. At least she was aware of what she had been doing. 'It didn't feel great, no,' he replied, letting her know the truth.

But when she hung her head he stepped closer to her, reaching out. He stayed his hand just before he made contact with her and felt heat radiate from her skin.

'This came as such a surprise...' she said. 'I needed some time to process things and—'

Their skin connected when Diego finally laid his hand on her bare shoulder, interrupting her mid-sentence. He noticed the small shudder run through her body the moment he touched her.

'You will never have to justify your choices to me, Ana. You had your reasons. The important thing is that we're talking now.'

\* \* \*

Eliana's mouth fell open as she looked at Diego. The sincerity shining through his words sent hot sparks flying from behind her navel up her spine. Her cheeks flushed, and she could only imagine what kind of pink shade the fire rising inside her had chosen to show on her skin.

It wasn't his touch that sent a tremble through her extremities—though the memory of what his touch could do to her certainly contributed to the overall turmoil rising within her. It was the kindness in his eyes, the gentle understanding that lay underneath his words, that brought forth a whirlwind of emotion she wasn't prepared for.

This wasn't what friendship felt like. Her entire life Eliana had been short on friends, never really forming any kind of attachment to anyone. Yet she was still fairly certain that her feelings now ran a lot deeper than she wanted them to.

'Did you ever think about having a child?' Diego asked into the quiet.

Caught off guard, she gaped at him for a moment, her brain still busy with deflecting the feelings he was evoking in her. 'I… No, I didn't. My father not only drove my mother away from the one place she called home, he also failed to live up to his responsibilities after her death. I thought that once the right person showed up in my life I would tackle family planning with him…hope they would be able to teach me the qualities I lacked from growing up the way I did. But…'

Her voice faltered, and she looked up at Diego when his hand slid down her arm, his fingertips grazing her skin and raising the fine hair on it. His eyes were shining with sympathy, as if he knew the pain weaving itself through her words.

And today she had learned that he did know her pain. Hearing how his parents had dumped him, with no regard to what that might do to him, had broken her heart. He'd been through a lot more than he let on, but was shrugging it off as if it were not a big deal. No wonder he felt so strongly about his part in their child's life.

'What about you?' she asked. Growing up like that must have left a mark on him, too.

Diego stayed quiet for a moment, his eyes drifting away from her face and to his hand, which was still gently caressing the skin of her arm, sending small shivers down her body with every sweep of his fingers.

'I didn't ever think I had what it takes for fatherhood. Still don't—not with how much of a failure my own father has been. A happy family is a foreign concept to me. I don't know how to make one myself, so I never indulged in any thought of having a relationship or children.'

His voice took on a strange quality, as if all of

a sudden he had drifted miles away. He seemed to notice, for he cleared his throat.

'That doesn't mean I won't be there for my child every step of the way. I fully acknowledge my responsibility in all of this, and I'm not going to shy away from it.'

An unusual disappointment gripped Eliana. She tried to shove it away almost immediately. She shouldn't be disappointed that he wasn't interested in any kind of attachment—the opposite, really. While deep down inside she wanted to find a person to spend the rest of her life with, this wasn't how it was going to happen—just because he felt a sense of obligation towards her.

'Why do you say that?' she asked, though she wasn't sure what drove her to dig deeper. Somehow she simply wanted to know more about him for her own selfish reasons, if nothing else.

Diego seemed taken aback by her question. 'Do you not want me to be there every step of the way?'

'No, I meant… Why do you believe you don't know how to be happy with someone?'

A flash of something intangible streaked across his expression. An ancient pain and vulnerability. Eliana held in a breath at the sight, as if she was standing face to face with a precious creature that would skip away at any moment if she made a wrong move. If she remained still enough would he open up to her?

'That's a complicated question to answer,' he said after some deliberation.

Despite his words implying a need to distance himself, he stepped closer and leaned his hip against the exam table she now sat on. The increased proximity sparked a fire under her skin, raising the fine hair on her arms.

'Try me. I'm pretty smart,' she said. Her voice was a lot raspier than she'd intended it to be, and she resisted the urge to clear her throat. Maybe he hadn't noticed.

His eyes narrowed, and the gaze gliding down to her lips told her that he definitely had noticed the huskiness of her tone.

'My father took vast liberties with his wedding vows, and instead of seeing him for the man he was my mother kept returning to him every time he came crawling back. I grew up watching my half-siblings—the by-products of my father's countless affairs—have a relationship with their mothers. Those women had been betrayed—just like my mother. But they hadn't shifted the blame to their children. No, I was the only Ferrari child who'd ruined his mother's life just by being alive.'

He scoffed, turning his face away from her and staring at an undefined point at the wall. The pain resurfaced on his expression so slowly that Eliana was sure he was fighting himself on the inside. But he didn't have to hide—not from her. She knew that hurt...had experienced some of it herself. Her father had resented her for existing.

The moment she saw Diego's face contort again she felt her heart make a decision before her brain could caution her to think twice. She reached out to touch him, laying her hand on his cheek and drawing his eyes back to her.

Her thumb rested on his sculpted cheekbone, brushing against it with a slight hesitancy, testing the waters. His expression went blank the moment her hand connected with his skin, nothing but a subdued spark remaining in those dark brown eyes.

'You're too hard on yourself,' she said in a low voice. 'You aren't turning away from your responsibilities. That's something your father would do, right?'

Eliana wasn't sure why she was consoling him, or what had led her to ask such personal questions in the first place. Her upbringing had lacked any parental figure to learn from, making her believe she was missing the special 'something' children got from watching their parents. Why was she so adamant about Diego criticising himself unfairly when she thought the same thing about herself?

But despite her own doubts Eliana's words

seemed to reach him—for his eyes grew wide in bewilderment. It was as if he had never thought about his own actions, with his head too wrapped up in what he believed to be true about himself.

Eliana's heart stopped beating for a second when he moved his hand up to his face, placing it on top of hers. He leaned in, and the intensity in his eyes was reminiscent of the night they'd met. The night they had made their baby.

'I'm not the kind of man you think I am,' he whispered in a low voice as he got closer to her face.

He slid her hand off his cheek and over his mouth, brushing her palm with a soft kiss that shot a flare of flames through her system, to settle in the depths of her core.

She wanted to move, to escape this situation. She was getting dangerously close to making the same mistake again. Diego had an incredible talent whereby he could bypass her defences with little effort on his part. Make her feel she wanted him—which she definitely didn't. Shouldn't, really.

Not when there was a child in the middle of it all.

'What kind of man do I think you are?'

'A man who is capable of giving more than I've already shown you. A man who sticks around.' He paused for another moment, his face so close to hers that she felt his breath on her skin. 'I can tell you now that I'm not your happily-ever-after, so don't waste your feelings on me.'

His words hit her with an unexpected ferocity that created an uncomfortable pinch in the pit of her stomach. Was that what she was looking for? Someone who stuck around no matter what? Her father certainly hadn't, leaving her with the bare minimum of attention to survive and little else. Eliana had never been anyone's priority, which had led to her never feeling quite settled wherever she was—never feeling safe.

*Did* she want that from Diego? Permanence?

She swallowed her emerging feelings as he looked at her. 'We both agreed this would be for the best,' she said, 'so I'm not going to turn around and demand a romantic relationship from you. I want to know you because you're the father of my child, not because I'm pining for you.'

Her words stood as a stark contrast to their actions. Their faces were inching closer to one another as they seemed lulled into a sensual cloud of their explosive desire for one another.

'Good, I'm glad we settled that—so I can do this,' he said, with a grin that brought her blood to a boil inside her veins.

'Do wha—?'

The rest of the word didn't make it past her

lips, for Diego had closed the remaining distance between them and pressed his mouth against hers in a kiss she had been waiting for since the day they'd met again.

Her flight instinct melted away under his gentle yet probing touch as his hands wandered over her neck, his fingers creating hot fires underneath her skin as they moved.

This was not what she'd had in mind when they'd spoken about getting to know each other better. But this kind of getting to know him—despite the vagueness of his words—felt so right. She had glimpsed something of him beyond the detached surgeon he let the rest of the world see. It had awakened a need within her that reached far beyond the initial desire that had brought them together so many weeks ago. Could there be something more to their connection?

The thought barely took shape in her mind as Diego's hands slipped to the back of her head, his fingers weaving themselves through her hair and gently pulling her head back, deepening the kiss as her lips parted, receiving the warmth of his tongue that was sending a shudder through her body.

Her hands clutched at him, holding on to his strong shoulders and pulling him even closer into their sensual embrace. Whatever hesitation Eliana might have felt when she'd agreed to meet him this morning it had melted away now, under the power of his words and the desire his touch evoked in her.

They had both stated their boundaries. Neither of them was interested in a long-term commitment, and they didn't believe in staying together just for the sake of their child. So there was no danger in giving in to the flood of passion cascading through her body, right?

The stakes were clear. She would still walk away from here as soon as her business was done.

Why not enjoy the moment?

He knew he shouldn't give in to the boiling desire bubbling in his blood, but he could not resist the temptation that was Eliana. The second he had seen her in the hotel lobby Diego had known he was fighting a losing battle to keep his hands to himself. Though his intentions had been pure—and he really did want to ease into some sort of friendship with her that would help them raise their child together—he'd soon felt the pull of her unbelievable sensuality tugging at him whenever he'd been able to observe her with her guard down.

Her questions had caught him off guard. While he could acknowledge that closeness would come with getting to know the other person better, he still wasn't sure what had urged him to disclose as much as he had. Other than Vanderson, no one knew about his parents and what kind of damage they had left on him.

His confession about his past had broken the last barrier that had seemed to be keeping his mounting lust in check, and a few moments later he'd stopped resisting and let go of control, his body taking over while his mind was still busy catching up with what they had discussed.

Now Diego crushed her against him, his hands roaming over her back, dipping into every curve of her body and exploring each angle as they were locked in a kiss that spoke of the passion both of them felt simmering between them. Soft moans escaped from her throat, muffled by his own mouth. The vibration of the sound penetrated his skin and set his blood on fire, as if someone had swapped it with a flammable liquid. All his blood rushed to the lower half of his body, pooling in his groin as Eliana's hands slipped under the seam of his shirt, grazing over the skin of his stomach.

But they were still in the clinic—not the best place to do what they were both dying to do… again. It cost him a lot more effort than he'd thought possible to rip his mouth from hers.

A soft gasp escaped Eliana's lips when he drew away, her hands immediately going limp and letting go of the fabric of his shirt. She looked shocked, as if she had just caught up with reality.

'This might not be the right place,' he said when she remained quiet.

There was a small apartment above the clinic, where he sometimes stayed in a pinch, if he was too exhausted to drive. But the look on her face was changing between passion and confusion.

He didn't want to let the moment disappear like that—even though his rational side urged him to take a break and retreat. Their lives were already messy enough...maybe he shouldn't add more sex into the mix.

Yet the beast inside his chest still roared, demanding to fulfil the promise of passion hanging between them. Even now he could see her chest heaving, her flushed cheeks showing the heat coursing through her veins.

'This used to be my grandmother's house,' he said, to fill the silence between them. 'We bought it from her to have a place for our clinic.'

Eliana looked at him, with a sudden curiosity in her face that he hadn't expected. 'Who?' she asked.

Diego stared back with a blank expression, not comprehending the question. 'Who...?' he repeated with a puzzled inflexion.

'You said "we". You and who?'

And just like that the fire in his veins died as if someone had doused him with icy water.

He hadn't even realised that he still thought of the clinic as a shared effort between him and Vanderson until she had pointed it out. Even though it had been almost two months since the funeral, the unexpected loss of his friend kept creeping back into his consciousness at the oddest moments.

'Huh... I didn't even notice I'd said that,' he mumbled, and gave in to a sudden urge to share his thoughts. 'I initially started this clinic, but it didn't take long for Vanderson to get involved. He was the one to handle his father whenever we needed to bring one of our patients from here to Santa Valeria. You have your own opinion about him, and I'm not going to excuse anything he may have said or done. But your brother...' Diego hesitated for a moment, not sure how he wanted to end that sentence. 'He cared. And I know he struggled with how he had let things happen.'

'Were you close to him?' Her voice had adopted a strange quality, as if she was afraid of his answer.

What would be worse for her?

The tension of their desire for each other had left them with the mention of Vanderson, to be replaced by an unusual stillness. They were still somewhat intertwined, with her hands lying on his chest while he gripped her hips and held her close to him, their faces only inches from each other.

'Yes,' he said, watching her face for any kind of clue to how that answer would make her feel, waiting for a reaction from her.

She opened her mouth to speak, but a loud knock on the door interrupted her. A moment later the door opened, and female voices filtered through the air.

Eliana went stiff in his arms and immediately backed away from him, freeing herself from his grasp.

'Diego, *você está aqui*?' a familiar voice shouted from the reception area, and he got up with a sigh.

'Yes, I'm here, *Avozhinha*. But we're not open right now.' He glanced at Eliana with an apologetic look. 'Sorry, I'll deal with this real quick.'

He stood up to greet his grandmother. But as he moved towards the door she walked through it—and with her a tired-looking woman pushing a wheelchair with a young boy sitting in it.

'Oh, hey, Miguel. I wasn't expecting you here so soon,' Diego said when he recognised his patient. He went down into a squat to greet the boy, and in a gesture that was more habit than anything else started examining the stump where his left leg had used to be. 'Are you okay? What brings you here?'

'I was just in the area to bring Layla some

food,' his grandmother said. And then her eyes fell onto Eliana, who had got up from the table and moved closer with a curious expression. 'Oh, I didn't know you had company.'

'This is Eliana, the new chief of medicine at Santa Valeria,' Diego said as he checked on the boy's leg.

Miguel had outgrown his previous leg quite a while ago, and the ill-fitting prosthetic had caused some damage to his skin and muscle tissue. The scarring was not very visible, but Diego felt it under his fingers. They were lucky that Miguel was so young, or his scars might have prevented him from fitting a new prosthesis.

'How wonderful! Does that mean we can fit Miguel's leg soon?' Layla, Miguel's mother, looked hopeful at his grandmother's words, and both of them looked to Eliana for an answer.

Her eyes went wide with surprise, and she looked at him. 'What's the problem with the leg?'

Diego gestured her to move closer, and had to suppress a shudder when she knelt down next to him, as the floral scent of her perfume danced around his nose, robbing him of his concentration.

'He's outgrown his old prosthetic leg. We see that a lot with patients who lose a limb at a young age. Unfortunately, Miguel doesn't have the privilege of regular check-ups with an orthopaedic specialist, to see when the prosthetic leg has grown too small. The damage to his soft tissue is not too stark, but still noticeable.'

Eliana looked at the boy with a small smile on her face. '*Olá*, Miguel, I'm Eliana, and I'm a doctor, too. Are you okay with me examining your leg?'

He nodded, and a moment later she wrapped both of her hands around the small stump where his leg had used to be.

'Hmm, I see what you mean,' Eliana said as she withdrew her hands and looked at Diego, concern etched into her features. 'Can we bring him in? I don't think you have the right facilities here.'

'I...' He hesitated.

The last couple of days he had been making clandestine plans with the paediatric specialist on his team to get Miguel the help he needed. Something that wasn't exactly above board, as he would technically be misappropriating hospital resources to help a patient who couldn't afford treatment.

But Eliana's reaction to this moment was one he hadn't dared to hope for earlier, when he had asked her what she would do now that he'd shown her the clinic. She didn't care about the price tag—she just wanted to help. That fact made the beast roar inside his chest again. If this was her first reaction to seeing a patient in need maybe there were other things they could do together. Maybe even...

'Yes, with your permission I would like to get my team on this case. I've done what I can on my own, but I've reached a point where I need more help,' he said.

Eliana nodded. 'Good, let's get him admitted right now. The fitting will take a couple of days, and Miguel will probably also need some physical therapy before we can release him again.' She walked over to the examination table where she'd left her tote bag and retrieved her phone from it. 'I'll ask my assistant to send over an ambulance.'

'Wait, I can't leave. My work...' Layla looked at his grandmother and then at Eliana, lifting her hands in a helpless gesture. 'I can't miss work or I won't be able to afford any of this.'

Diego watched as Eliana walked over to the woman, laying a hand on her arm to pacify her.

'I don't want you to worry about money. Santa Valeria has a fund for cases like this, so you won't have to pay a single *real*. Miguel needs some special treatment before we can fit his new leg. It will take a few days, but I will ensure someone sends you regular updates. Diego will be supervising his case personally, so you have nothing to worry about while Miguel is away.'

She tilted her head to look at him, and he nodded. 'You know I'll take good care of him, Layla.'

The woman still looked frightened, but she agreed to their plan with a nod. When he had first seen Miguel he had made sure to let her know they were looking at quite a lot of work if they wanted him to regain full mobility with his prosthetic leg.

'It's so nice to meet you, Eliana. My grandson tells me you came to Rio on your own. Why don't you join us for the *churrasco* I'm hosting at my house next weekend? Diego's sister has just graduated, and we're celebrating.'

His *avozinha*'s words launched him back into reality, and his eyes went wide in surprise. What had she just said?

'Oh, thank you, but I couldn't possibly impose on you like that when I don't even know your granddaughter.'

Eliana smiled, but he could see the hint of hesitance bubbling in the corners of her mouth.

'Avozinha, *por favor*... This is my new chief you're talking to,' he said in a low voice. The warning in his words was clear, and he knew his grandmother would make him regret that tone later on.

'Even more important to make a good impression and invite her to dinner, then. I'm not having any arguments about this. With her helping my friend Layla the way she is, that is the least I can do, *querida*.'

Márcia waved her hand in a way he knew all too well. She had made up her mind, and it was going to happen. Which put Diego in a difficult situation. Despite their best intentions, they hadn't got any closer to making decisions about their child today. The only thing they'd managed to do was entangle themselves further into the mess they had started two months ago.

Diego knew better—knew that he shouldn't let his need overpower his rational side. Yet all he could think about was how fast he could get everyone out of here so they could pick up things right where they'd left off. Preferably upstairs in a comfortable bed.

'Well, if I'm not imposing...thank you, I would love to come.'

Eliana glanced at Diego with an expression he couldn't quite read. She looked apologetic, but there was something else mixed into it as well. Was she excited to be invited to his family's barbecue?

'Of course, dear. Vanderson used to come by all the time—everyone will be excited to meet his sister.'

The short howl of a siren interrupted his

*avozinha*, and a moment later the ambulance pulled up to the house.

'There's our ride,' Eliana said to Miguel, with a smile that looked plastered on.

The mention of her brother had made her freeze up, and Diego hissed internally at his grandmother's careless words. He had told her enough about Eliana that she should have known better than to mention Vanderson. Especially since they had only really started to speak about his relationship with her brother today, and hadn't got far into the conversation before they had been interrupted.

'Are you coming with us to the hospital?' she asked.

Diego stared at Eliana for a second, fighting the disappointment that was spreading through his chest. He had been hoping they would have a moment alone so they could talk. They had so much to talk about. His relationship with her brother... The child they had yet to tell anyone about... Their kiss...

But he understood this request was coming from the chief of medicine and not his...his *what*, exactly? She shouldn't be his anything, yet the ambiguity of it tightened his chest as if someone was wrapping a rope around it.

'Yes, of course.'

Miguel had been cleared for treatment, and that had to be his highest priority at that moment. No matter how much he wanted to revisit that moment from an hour ago, when they had been intertwined once more.

# CHAPTER SEVEN

ELIANA LOOKED AT herself in the floor-length mirror of the hotel room, turning to one side and scrutinising her profile. Her hand lay on her stomach, searching for an indicator of her baby, but everything remained flat and undetected. This wasn't surprising. She was only at the end of her second month, and most pregnancies didn't start to show until the second trimester.

By then, she hoped to be back in Belo Horizonte, far away from Diego and that fire in his eyes that she wanted to get lost in.

'I'm blaming you for this, little one,' Eliana mumbled at her stomach, even as she felt a prickle of arousal trickle down her spine, settling in her core in an uncomfortable pinch.

Her hormones made this whole friendship endeavour with the incredibly hot Dr Ferrari a lot harder than she wanted it to be. Or at least she used her hormones as a convenient excuse to cling to, because she could hardly believe that she would have been so careless of her own volition. To make out with Diego when they had both agreed to take a step back from the passion sizzling between them.

She let herself fall on the bed with a sigh and grabbed her phone to stare at the screen. She read the message she had typed out to Diego, giving her apologies and telling him that she couldn't attend the party after all.

That was what a smart person would do. Untangle herself from any more situations that weren't strictly necessary and keep any and all conversations centred around one of two things: their work or their child.

But the voice urging her to send the message was weak, drowned out by the mounting curiosity inside her. Despite things not going as planned, Eliana had glimpsed a part of Diego that lay beyond the thick wall he hid behind, and from his reaction she knew he rarely let anyone see that part of him—if ever.

Diego had suffered a lot more than he let on, and even more than that he seemed to think that he was damaged beyond repair. She wanted to know more about him—both about his family and his relationship with her late half-brother. He had hinted that they'd had a close relationship…something his grandmother Márcia had confirmed when she'd said that he would have been invited to the barbecue were he still alive.

Would she and Diego be able to get over their electrifying attraction and be the kind of friends they wanted to be? Diego had shown her a different side of himself—one she understood all too well. And even though she knew he was nothing like her father, the comparison kept creeping up into her brain, making her wonder.

Had her mother at some point believed Marco to be committed to raising their child together?

Even if Diego's commitment was solid, would he really make the time as he'd promised?

Losing her mother even before her own life had begun and being raised by a rotation of employees without ever knowing a loving touch, Eliana wanted more than anything else to be someone's priority. Wanted nothing to be more important than what they had together.

Diego had already picked what was most important to him—his community. She wouldn't change that, and didn't want to either. His commitment to helping the disadvantaged had opened her heart to him more than she cared to admit.

But they couldn't be together. Not when they wanted such vastly different things in life. Diego strived to be of service to his people—those who had brought him up when his parents had failed him. Eliana, on the other hand... For once, she wanted to matter. And if Diego had to split his attention it would be for the sake of their child, and not because of some misguided romantic feelings for her.

'Okay, we can go and meet your extended family. But only if you promise to behave, young one,' Eliana said to her unborn child. 'No mood swings, no hormones that make Mamãe feel things—are we clear?'

She waited in the quiet for a moment, feeling her connection to her child on such a deep level she was almost overwhelmed. It had been nothing more than an accident, and yet her chest was filled with love and affection for this tiny being already. She didn't know how she could have lived her life without that feeling.

'Good, then let's go and meet Papai.'

Diego had texted her the address of his grandmother's place earlier in the week, with a note saying that he'd understand if she didn't want to attend. She had wondered if that was his way of asking her not to come, but the look on his face when he opened the door for her completely wiped that thought from her brain.

Because the way he looked at her, his eyes ablaze with need the second his gaze fell on her, made Eliana's knees almost buckle.

Or was that her needy mind playing tricks on her? Making her want to believe Diego wanted her as much as she was burning for him?

'I'm glad you're finally here,' he said in a

low voice, and Eliana let out a breath she hadn't known she had been holding in.

'You are?' she asked, in spite of herself and her desire to make her composure appear resolute.

'Of course. Talking to you will give me a good excuse to avoid all my half-siblings. Ever since the funeral they've been overbearing.' He paused for a moment and laughed. 'It also means I can stop guarding the door.'

Eliana laughed with him, not letting the information he had just shared show on her face. Vanderson's death had hit him hard enough that his entire family was worried about him. Not for the first time she wondered how the two men had found their way into each other's lives.

'Before I let you in, I must warn you. Almost the entire Ferrari clan is here—including spouses and children. Enough people that I hope we'll become invisible. My family is also incurably nosy, so if they pester you let me know and I'll be your shield.'

Eliana had to laugh at his grave warning. 'Wait—how many half-siblings do you have?'

'Ten,' he said, and stepped aside to let her in.

The moment she walked across the threshold the muffled noise she had been hearing intensified around her.

'Ten?' She tried her best to keep the surprise out of her voice, but knew she hadn't quite managed to do so when she caught a strange expression fluttering across his face. It wasn't shame, but something akin to it. Was he embarrassed about his siblings?

'I told you my father was rather liberal with his interpretation of his wedding vows.'

This time she had no problem understanding his mood. A bitter edge wove itself through each word, and his resentment towards his father clear as day. Clearly while still married to Diego's mother, he'd had ten additional children out of wedlock.

'He's not here tonight, is he?' she asked, even though she thought she knew the answer already.

Diego laughed in derision. 'Not a chance in the world. He might be Vanessa's father, but I would be surprised if he even knew that she's just finished university. Ignacio Ferrari is not exactly...*involved* in any of our lives.'

'Good. Your siblings seem happy enough without his bad energy,' she said, with a playful chuckle underpinning her voice. 'And from the sounds of it, our new *princesa* will have enough aunts and uncles that she won't need grandfathers.' She patted her flat stomach affectionately and noticed Diego's eyes dart to her hand.

'*Princesa?* It's been a long time since my obstetrics rotation, but surely you can't know that at this point?'

Eliana shrugged. 'I'm only guessing from the feeling she's giving me.'

Some of the humour she had got to know so well over the last couple of weeks entered his eyes again. She much preferred this Diego over the one agonising about his painful past.

'Feeling? *Querida*, you are a woman of science. Next thing you'll tell me you've had the tarot read to determine the future of our child.' He tried to sound outraged, but his wide grin gave his true feelings away.

Her reply never crossed her lips, for a fire had suddenly burst to life right behind her navel, pumping heat through her entire body until her fingers felt tingly.

*Querida*.

A perfectly innocent endearment of familiarity. People used it all the time, to the point where it meant very little. But hearing it from his lips had catapulted her desire for this man in front of her up to the surface, despite her best efforts to keep her growing feelings buried.

He wasn't interested in her. No, he was here only because they were having a child together. It was their child that was behind all his interactions with her. She needed to get that into her head.

'Are you okay?' he asked when she remained

quiet, but before she could say anything they were interrupted by a woman's voice calling for Diego.

'Diego! The meat is almost ready. Can you…? Oh, who do we have here?'

Eliana saw that the woman stood almost as tall as Diego when she stopped next to them, and although her ebony skin stood in stark contrast to Diego's tawny hue, the high cheekbones and bright brown eyes immediately gave them away as siblings.

'This is Eliana Oliveira, the new chief of medicine at Santa Valeria. Avozinha thought it appropriate to invite my boss to the *churrasco*.'

His sister raised her eyebrows to look at him with a scepticism that intrigued Eliana. She didn't seem to believe him.

'She must have seen you two together if you got an invitation. You know Vovo doesn't like it that you always come to our family dinners on your own.' She turned to face Eliana. 'It's nice to see Diego has made a friend. I'm Gloria, his little sister.'

The woman stepped closer and air-kissed each of Eliana's cheeks before stepping away again.

'It's nice to meet you,' she replied, feeling a redness coat her cheeks at the way Gloria had emphasised the word 'friend'. Up until this moment she hadn't even thought about what her presence here might look like to other people. Would they think something was going on between them?

But there was, wasn't there? The memories of their kiss rushed back into her consciousness and she pushed them away.

'Well, don't hide away the first person you've brought home since Vanderson. Let me give her a tour.'

Eliana looked at Diego for a moment. He gave her a look of equal uncertainty before his sister took her by the arm.

By the time they sat down for dinner she had met every single Ferrari sibling, as well as their spouses and children.

Diego had groaned each time one of his family members had started to ask too many questions, or insinuated that he was usually not seen with a woman. But although he seemed exhausted by all their thinly veiled suggestions about their relationship status, Eliana saw the genuine connection he had with all of his siblings. Despite his father's wrongdoings, somehow his offspring had pulled through to the other side, forming a unique and beautiful family unit where they cared for each other.

Everyone seemed beyond excited to meet Eliana, which was a new feeling for her. No one had ever expressed this kind of enthusiasm on meeting her before. And what confused her the most was that they seemed excited she was here simply because Diego had brought her. Even though they didn't know anything about her, or their relationship, they wanted to get to know her.

It was that that caused a painful twinge in her chest. She had never known what it was like to be part of a family dynamic. Would she be able to give her child everything it needed even though she didn't know the first thing about family herself? Or was that where Diego came in?

She glanced to where he was sitting next to her, listening to the partner of one of his siblings. He seemed to know how to form close bonds much better than she did. His father hadn't spread his toxicity to his children, though clearly not for lack of trying. In Diego's interactions with his siblings she could see some hesitancy, though—as if he didn't dare let any of them get too close.

But they were all gossiping and laughing with each other without a care in the world. They had managed to pull through their rocky childhood. How come Diego believed himself incapable?

They wrapped up after dessert by toasting the woman of the evening, Vanessa, who had apparently just finished veterinary school, and then the Ferrari clan broke out into smaller groups again.

A warm sensation trickled down her spine when Diego laid his hand on her shoulder, prompting her to look up into his breathtakingly handsome face.

'Let's find a quiet spot. I think we both might have had enough questions and inquisitive looks.'

The smile spreading across his lips made her knees feel soft for a moment, forcing her to reach for the hand he was offering her. The contact didn't help with the weakness, and her heart was sent into overdrive when he didn't let go of her hand as they walked away from the noise to the other side of the garden from where the table had been set.

Only when they turned a corner did he let go, and point at a periwinkle-blue wooden bench that stood against the house's exterior wall. They sat down together, and the few inches of space between them felt like a cavern as Eliana raised her eyes to look at him.

Though she had enjoyed the conversation, and all the questions thrown at her, she'd noticed one particular topic was missing.

'You haven't told anyone about the pregnancy?'

'No, I haven't.' Diego stared straight ahead

for a couple of breaths. 'I felt like that wasn't a decision I should make alone.'

He hadn't wanted to make that decision on his own because they were in this together, she thought. Diego—though still surrounded by thick walls and shrouded in mystery—considered them a team.

Not a couple—he had insisted on that previously, and Eliana had forced herself to agree, even if she found resistance inside her. But a faint voice in her head kept calling out to him, tempting her to forget about the boundaries she had set.

He had made her a priority in that moment. Thinking about how she would feel before telling people news that was just as much his as it was hers.

'Thank you, I appreciate that,' she replied into the quiet, and smiled at him, giving herself permission to feel the warmth pooling in her stomach despite knowing that it couldn't ever be more than a fleeting emotion. But he cared about her—something she was not used to from anyone. Maybe she could trust him with more than she was giving him credit for…like her thoughts about Vanderson.

'I want to know more about my brother. You said you were close.' The words tumbled from her lips before she could decide against them. 'You still haven't told me much about him.'

He'd been near invisible in her life, but maybe Diego could shed some light on him. Had he grown up regretting his past actions?

The pain fluttering over Diego's face made her regret speaking those words, but as she took a breath, ready to take them back, he nodded.

'I know I've been avoiding the topic. His death was so…unexpected. It still leaves me numb sometimes. But you never had the chance to meet the real Vanderson, and I want you to know about your brother. How he opposed your father and how much he wanted to be reconciled with you.'

Reconciliation. A concept Eliana had thought about a lot when it came to her brother. And apparently, he had thought about it too. But then why had he never reached out?

She put those thoughts away for now. There were other things she wanted to know first. 'How did you meet? You didn't know him as a boy, or I would have seen you around.'

Diego shook his head. 'I met him during our mandatory military service. We were both training as medics, planning on attending med school afterwards. Our assignments often put us together, and we spoke a lot about what we wanted to do…how we planned on helping the less fortunate. Me because I had grown up poor, and him because he had seen what greed had done to his father's hospital.'

He paused for a moment, his hand balling into a tight fist, and Eliana resisted the urge to reach out to him.

'We decided we wanted to make a difference—which was when our idea for a free clinic in my old neighbourhood was born. Through his...your father, Vanderson was well connected, and he recommended me for a position at Santa Valeria once I had finished my medical training. We were waiting for Marco to retire, so Vanderson could take over. And he was also waiting for your father's retirement before reaching out to you.'

Eliana's mouth went dry and she swallowed hard. 'What had my father's retirement to do with Vanderson reconnecting with me?'

Diego sighed, a rueful smile on his face. 'Marco was a sad and spiteful person. From a young age Vanderson was forbidden to talk to you, and even after your brother had become an adult Marco threatened to disown him if he went against his wishes. Vanderson would have been ready to take that chance had it not been for the ownership of the hospital.'

This was information she had never heard before, and it stood in direct contrast to what she had believed to be true almost all her life. She had believed her brother to be her father's minion at worst, and apathetic at best.

'He really wanted to know me?' She didn't

know why she'd asked that question. It had sounded so desperate.

'Not being strong enough to be the brother you needed when you were growing up was the biggest regret in his life, and it pains me that he'll never get the chance to make it right.'

That confession took all the remaining air out of her lungs. She had never known what kind of person her brother was. A small part of her had always hoped that he would want to know her, but with each day that went by without her hearing from him, her hope had grown slimmer.

'Did you know he was married and had a child?' Diego asked, and grinned when she shook her head. He had his own family? Maybe those were the people the lawyers had spoken about. Marco and Vanderson's estates were closely linked. The estate lawyer had told her that there were other, unnamed beneficiaries of the will, which had made the estate complex enough to force Eliana into staying in Rio longer than she'd intended.

He reached into his pocket, retrieved his phone and unlocked it with a swipe before going through his camera roll.

'His husband's name is Alessandro, and their daughter's name is Daria. He owns a recreational facility near the beach, renting out surfboards and such. Daria has just turned five.

They adopted her when she was a couple of months old.'

The picture had been taken on a gorgeous summer day, with blue skies unfolding behind them. Diego, Vanderson and his husband plus child were seated at a round table, all of them smiling at the camera that, judging from the angle, Diego must have been holding.

Eliana's throat suddenly felt tight as she looked at the picture. It was serene, and full of the affection those four people had shared with each other. But more than that it made her realise that she had something she'd never known.

'I have a niece? And a brother-in-law?'

Her voice sounded strained in her own ears as she struggled with the sudden revelation. She had never even thought that her brother might have been married and had children.

It reinforced once more how close Diego had been to her late brother. How much did he already know about her? Was he nodding along as if he was hearing new information when he had already heard it from his best friend?

'So, did Vanderson tell you about my childhood? You must have already known about me before we met.'

Her voice was free of accusation, but she saw that he winced, nonetheless.

'He didn't tell me much. I think the guilt over his own behaviour sat too deep. But he told me how Marco had rejected you and kept you away from the family. That you grew up alone.'

An icy shiver clawed down her spine. That was a lot more than she usually told people. But Eliana found she didn't mind that Diego knew. With any other person the mortification would have been too much to cope with. But things were different with him. It was as if she wanted him to know.

'I can see he meant a great deal to you. No wonder you brought him here to meet your patchwork family.'

He'd not spoken about his half-siblings since they'd sat down. Now his gaze became distant as he looked up to the night sky.

'I like my siblings...even though I sometimes envy them for the relationships they've been able to build. While suffering the same father, at least they had their mothers to look out for them. My mother didn't care enough.' He heaved a drawn-out sigh. 'But Vanderson understood me like they never will.'

Diego envied his siblings? As she glimpsed more and more of the fragments of himself he hid behind those thick walls, she felt their connection solidify beyond the shared necessity of being parents together.

He understood her. He had made her the priority tonight and empowered her to make her own decisions. And he'd given her something of her brother she'd never thought she'd get.

'I wish I could've known him,' she said, and laid a hand on his thigh.

The small touch was enough to make him look up at her. 'Me too,' he replied, with a smile so sweet and full of longing it made her breath catch in her throat. 'He would have been excited about us. Shocked to his core, but also excited.'

'Since Vanderson was helping you, does that mean you now need *my* help to keep the clinic going?'

Diego's expression slipped for a second. A hopeful gleam entered his eyes, mixing with the intense fire she'd seen the moment he'd opened the door for her.

'That's not something I can ask of you. Not with everything between us being so...'

'Messy?' she asked when his voice trailed off.

'I would have phrased it with more delicacy if you'd given me a chance.' His voice was stern, but a smile was pulling at the corners of his lips when she glanced at him, chuckling herself.

'We'll find out soon enough when we need to compartmentalise work and parenting stuff. This can be our first test.' She paused, looking at him with intent. 'I think my father strayed very far from the path of putting patient care above anything else. If you tell me that Vanderson meant to change that, I'll want to continue on with that.'

She watched his entire demeanour change with each word she spoke, his posture relaxing and opening up, his expression one of such profound happiness and relief that Eliana almost gasped at the intense look he gave her. With a smile on his face, he wrapped his hands around her face and planted a short and hard kiss on her unprepared lips.

'I can't tell you how much this means to me—to my entire community. People like Miguel will be able to get the care they need when they need it.'

Shocked by the unexpected kiss—which she knew was a sign of gratitude and not of the burning desire she sensed coursing through her veins—she stared at him with a blank expression, blinking multiple times as she struggled to regain her composure.

Fires had erupted within her, starting in her core and spreading searing tendrils into every corner of her body. Their lips had touched for barely more than a second, but that was enough to thunder an almost impossible need for Diego through her.

His hands dropped from her face and he looked at her with wide eyes, seemingly surprised by his own action. 'I'm sorry... I shouldn't have,' he mumbled, although the narrowing of his eyes as his gaze darkened didn't show any of the regret he professed. Only the untamed hunger she'd seen in his face before.

It was a want that mirrored her own—and one that had led to the very reason they could never give in to one another. Not with a child involved between them. It would only lead to so much more heartbreak when they inevitably fell apart. Eliana wanted him. Everything deep inside her called out to him. But she needed safety more than anything else. Needed to matter to someone, to be their priority.

Though hadn't Diego shown her he'd made her exactly that today? Was it possible they could be something else even when they'd said they couldn't?

An awkward silence spread between them—the first one of the night—as they both grappled with their undeniable attraction to one another and their steadfast belief that they couldn't go there ever again.

Even though it kept happening.

'Have you told anyone yet?' he asked.

At his question Eliana looked down at her flat stomach, covering it with one hand and breathing a sigh of relief. The sooner they could move on from the tension brewing between them, the better.

'No one outside of the obstetrics department head. The first scan is soon.' She paused for a moment and looked up at him. A spark had entered his dark eyes, and his gaze was almost hypnotising her. 'Do you still want to come?'

'You want me there?' His voice was low, vibrating through her skin right into her core, raising the heat.

'You're the father—you have just as much right to be there as I have.'

'I'm not asking about my rights. Do you *want* me to be there?'

The tension between them came rushing back as he spoke those words, and she saw his eyes fill with an intent to conquer her.

'If you want to—'

'Ana.' He interrupted her, his voice low, filled with promises that made her heart beat fast against her chest. 'Do you want me?'

Eliana's mouth went dry and she swallowed. They had stopped talking about the scan. They were back to the tangible electricity filling her stomach with flutters. Did she want him? Want him how? At the scan? In her life? *Right now?*

What frightened her most was the fact that all those questions had the same answer.

'Yes,' she whispered, afraid that her voice would give out if she spoke too loudly, and watched him come closer...

The beast of unbridled desire within his chest had simply watched for most of the evening, rearing its head occasionally when he'd caught a glimpse of Eliana's smile or when her luscious scent had drifted up his nose.

From the moment she had walked through the door Diego had known that he would kiss her, that they would pick up where they had left off at the clinic. And this time he would make sure to follow through.

Kissing her in the back yard of his *avozinha*'s house had been a tactical error. He should have invited her to his place before drawing her into his arms. But he'd found himself unable to resist her any longer. Not after she'd said the one word he had been dying to hear from her lips.

*Yes.*

She wanted him. Just as much as he wanted her. That was all he needed to know to forget about where they were and who might potentially walk around the corner and catch them.

Eliana's warm breath trembled against his skin as he pulled her into his arms, his lips brushing against hers in a sensual invitation for her to get lost in the moment. It was an invitation she was clearly eager to receive, as she balled her hands around the fabric of his shirt and pulled him closer.

The passion swimming through his blood roared to life with that one kiss, sending heat cascading through his body. What was it about this woman that drove him over the edge with little more than a kiss? That made him keep coming back for more? That had allowed him to let his grandmother actually invite her to meet his family?

No woman ever got to meet any of the Ferrari clan.

Eliana opened her mouth and caught his lower lip between her teeth, giving it a short but intense squeeze that drew a groan of desire from his throat. She pulled back to look at him, an expression of want on her face. Her breath left her in an unsteady staccato, her chest heaving with anticipation.

Diego pulled her close again, deepening their kiss. This time Eliana let his tongue pass, moaning her mounting pleasure against his lips. His hands wandered over her back, finding the exposed flesh and brushing her with his fingertips. He remembered the softness of her skin beneath his hands that first night together, her taste as he'd explored her body at his leisure, drawing mewls of delight and release from her full lips.

How long had he been waiting for this to happen again? And how often had he told himself that he wasn't allowed to go there—ever? Only in this moment he couldn't remember why he'd been so against it. It was clear now that something special connected them—something that went beyond his understanding of relationships.

Was that why he always struggled to give in completely? Because he'd always be confronted by that crucial bit of information that he'd missed out on as a child? How to form a healthy and functioning relationship where both partners were equal. That wasn't what his parents had shown him.

This was lust burning in his chest—not some misguided emotional attachment. They had both said so themselves. Neither wanted a relationship that went beyond the way they would share custody of their child. If his parents had sought an arrangement the way he and Eliana were trying to right now, maybe things would have turned out differently. Maybe he would have known how to appreciate a tremendous woman like Eliana in more than one way.

His mouth left her lips, feathering light kisses down her neck and caressing her there. Need cascaded through him, reaching a boiling point when another enticing moan fell from her lips. They needed to go.

Diego brought a minimal amount of distance between them to look her in the eyes. They were smouldering with the same intensity he felt.

'My place is down the street,' he murmured, and excitement thundered through him when she grinned.

\* \* \*

If it hadn't been for the fire in her core, Eliana might have forgotten why she was there when she entered Diego's house and took in the view. The hallway was almost as large as the hotel room she was staying in, with polished stone surfaces and tasteful decoration in the few places it was needed.

But Diego had other plans for her. The moment they got through the door he slammed it shut behind him and was upon her not even a heartbeat later, capturing her mouth with his.

He pressed her against the cold wall and she felt his fingers leaving exquisite fires as they roamed her body. She let her head fall backwards, surrendering her entire self to Diego and his caresses.

This wasn't supposed to happen… But the voice that kept on warning her about it—about their relationship getting too messy—was growing faint and easy to ignore.

What was the harm? As long as both of them remembered that she would soon be leaving and that they weren't looking for anything permanent, maybe they could loosen the leash on their desire for just one night. At least this time there wouldn't be any accidents.

His hands had found the zipper of her dress. With a twist of her shoulder he turned her around, and she pressed her front against the wall while he pulled down the zipper with agonising slowness, leaving a scorching kiss every time he uncovered more skin.

'*Deus*, Diego, *por favor...*' she whispered, as unreserved need cascaded through her, bringing an intensity and wetness between her legs that made her knees buckle.

'What do you want, *amor*?' His voice was deep, filled with the restraint he was practising by undressing her bit by bit, taking his sweet time on this journey down her body.

'This is too much. I need you...*now.*'

The zipper stopped just above her bottom, and Diego peeled the dress from her back, folding it over at the front before flipping her around again. With one smooth motion he pulled on the dress again, making it fall from her body and pool around her feet.

The fire in his eyes made her breath catch in her throat. This was different from what she had seen in his face when they'd slept together all those weeks ago. Something about this moment was different from before, and it made her need for him burn all that brighter.

He kissed her, long and deep, tasting her mouth as if he had never kissed her before. Her thighs trembled when he pulled her against him, and the full length of his erection was pressing into her, urging.

'No,' he whispered when she slipped her

hands down to start removing his clothes. He took her wrist, wrapping his fingers around it. 'I want to be deliberate this time. I want to savour every moment, taste every part of you, until you have no more to give.'

'Diego...' Her breath came in bursts as his hands caressed her hips. He stopped for a moment when he stroked her stomach, drawing both of them back into the moment that had changed them for ever.

He glanced down, as if to check to see if he could find any trace of their child, and when his eyes came back to hers they were filled with a warmth that sent her pulse even higher.

'I was too focused on my own pleasure the first time around. I need to make it up to you,' he said close to her ear, raising the fine hair at the nape of her neck and on her arms.

Eliana looked at him for a moment, and in the next instant felt her feet leave the ground, making her yelp as she wrapped her hands around Diego's neck. He lifted her into his arms, carried her through the hall and down a corridor, into what she could only presume was his bedroom.

He let her drop on the bed, pouncing on her like a jaguar would jump on its prey, pinning her down. She shivered under the pressure of his body, writhing as his erection pushed against her again. It wasn't just her that wanted this. She was making him feel the same way, filling him with need and urgency. Eliana could see it in the tightness of his jaw as he lifted himself off her to trail gentle and warm kisses down her neck to her sternum, where he came to rest.

Eliana arched her back, pushing closer to him when his teeth gripped at the fabric of her bra, pulling the garment aside to expose her breasts to the cooling air of the Brazilian spring evening. The straps fell down from her shoulders as Diego found the clasp on the front, drawing the bra away from her body and throwing it on the floor.

Diego stopped for a moment, as if plotting his course, and a hungry growl was loosed from his throat. She propped herself up on her elbows, wanting to see what he was up to, but immediately fell back down with a long drawn-out moan when he sucked one of her peaked nipples into his mouth, rolling it around with his tongue.

A firework exploded in the pit of her stomach and her hips arched against his strong frame, as if begging to find any kind of release as the lines between pleasure and pain began to blur.

'Diego…' she whispered, unable to form any other coherent words, trusting that her voice would carry enough meaning for him to understand.

*Please, don't stop.*

He didn't.

His mouth left one breast to go to the other, lavishing it with the same attention and pleasure he had given the first one, before moving on down over her stomach, his lips and tongue leaving featherlight traces on her skin as if he was mapping her body so he could remember every detail.

Wasn't that what he'd said? That he wanted to remember everything about this moment? Eliana had thought it no more than a line from a man who had seen many women before her and would see many after her, too. But that was not how he made her feel in this moment—as if he was a trained lover going through the steps he had taken many times before. No, to her it seemed all of his attention was focused on her and on what made her writhe in pleasure. That thought alone was enough to renew the need inside her that settled into the wetness at her core.

What made this moment different from that night two months ago? It couldn't be that it was simply because they had started to get to know each other. To build a tentative friendship upon which they wanted to build the foundation of their co-parenting adventure. Was that enough to have such an impact?

Her thoughts were catapulted back into the present when the silk of her underwear scraped against her thighs as Diego moved them down in one smooth motion of his arm. His fingers brushed over her mound as he lowered his face to kiss her thighs, each time slipping just a bit further up, until she felt his breath right next to the place his hand had been caressing.

Her anticipation of what was going to happen next transformed into an eruption of untold pleasure when Diego parted her with one stroke of his tongue and lavished her with its attention.

Eliana fisted one hand into the linen underneath her as a trembling shook her body, and the beginning of a climax was already building inside her as her breath left her mouth in ragged bursts, mingling with the moans he coaxed out of her. Her other hand found Diego's as he caressed her stomach, and she gripped him as if she was holding on for dear life.

'Please, don't stop.'

This time she managed to articulate the words as the waves of her climax started to build, crashing through her with a ferocity that wiped any thought from her brain.

Diego's name clung to her lips as she gave in, losing herself in the pleasure that rocked through her. The muscles in her thighs tensed for a moment before they relaxed again, her breath still unsteady and coming out in bursts.

She felt him smile against her thighs as he kissed one and then the other, trailing small kisses up her stomach until he was on top of her, looking into her eyes with an intensity that brought a new surge of need to her core just as the first one was receding.

Eliana opened her mouth, wanting to say something, though she wasn't sure what. But he stopped her, laying a gentle finger on her mouth, tracing her lower lip before bending down and kissing her. Her mouth was filled with his taste, the warmth of his tongue, and she gripped at his shoulders so as to not drift away in the luscious cloud of ecstasy he had conjured around them.

'You are incredible, you know that?' he whispered against her neck, before his mouth trailed down again and goosebumps made all the little hairs rise on her body.

Her expression had changed for a fraction of a second, doubt clouding her eyes. Diego halted, looking at her intently, keen to know her thoughts. But before he could say anything her hands had found their way past his waistband. His button popped open with one flick of her finger, and one of her hands pulled at his T-shirt while the other wrapped itself around his shaft, stroking...

A low growl escaped his lips—a lot more feral than he'd intended to be. The moment he had seen the dress drop from her shoulders, exposing her incredible strength and a grace that shone from inside out, Diego had known he wanted to worship her all night. And that even then he wouldn't be worthy of a woman like Eliana. She had endured so much loss and rejection in her life, but instead of letting that experience harden her heart she had emerged from the pain with a softness and a kindness that brought him to his knees.

But now he was enjoying a glimpse of the other Eliana. The one he had met at the bar. Who knew exactly what she wanted and wasn't afraid to take matters into her own hands.

And what incredibly skilled hands she had.

Diego groaned again as she pulled his trousers down, and hardly noticed when she pulled his shirt over his head and threw it onto the pile of clothes already on the floor.

'Hang on,' he said, when Eliana hooked her leg around his waist and flipped their bodies so that he was lying on his back.

A wicked grin appeared on her face as she sat on top of him, his taut length straining against her. 'No. We've done it your way. Now we do it my way, Ferrari,' she replied.

And Diego closed his eyes with a primal moan when she released the tension in her thighs and let him sink into her in his entirety.

Her nails scratched along his bare chest as they moved their hips in harmony, and Eliana's small cries of pleasure were already threatening to undo him when he wanted this moment to last for ever.

Because this moment was perfection. They were permitted to be who they were—two people attracted to each other, who were finding their path towards their true feelings for each other. As long as they remained like this, they were allowed to be these two people.

The moment they finished Diego knew the spell the evening had woven around them would break, leaving them to cope with the reality of their lives. With the fact that they were not built for the type of relationships others had. Not after everything that had happened to them.

But right now he just wanted to feel this incredible woman crushed against his body as they lost themselves in their burning passion for one another.

With another groan, Diego pulled his upper body off the bed, slinging his arms around her torso and hugging her close to his chest before turning them around once more so he was on top of her.

'Ana, I—' He interrupted himself, pressing his mouth on hers again, wrapping her in an indulgent kiss as he sensed their shared climax approaching.

And with that kiss full of promise and tenderness he felt the release wash over him, as Eliana, too, cried out his name, writhing underneath him with a sob of pleasure.

# CHAPTER EIGHT

THE GENTLE BRUSH of fingers against her exposed back coaxed Eliana out of her slumber. She felt warm breath on the back of her neck, and she stretched her legs and toes as she enjoyed Diego's caress.

'*Bom dia, meu amor,*' he whispered near her ear, and sent sparks flying down her spine.

'You shouldn't call me that,' she mumbled back, but instead of pulling away she snuggled closer into his hard and warm chest.

*My love*. Such an endearment was way too intimate for what they were…which was something they hadn't defined. She had spent every night of the last week at Diego's, entangled in his sheets most of the time, but also talking with him about anything they could come up with.

Now he didn't reply, instead nuzzling into her neck, the kisses he traced on her skin making her shiver with renewed need.

'Don't you need to be somewhere? I'm sure

I told Suelen to make sure your surgical schedule is full.'

Through the thick fog of desire, Eliana grasped at straws. Anything to make him move away, even though that was the last thing she wanted him to do. And he knew she didn't really want him to go.

Diego chuckled into her hair, pulling her even closer to his chest. 'It's Sunday. We don't have to be anywhere if we don't want to.'

*No, don't say that.*

She needed him to be busy so she could find enough distance to get away. To think. Right now, all her emotions were tangled up in the visceral and deep connection they shared on more than just a physical level. While the sex was mind-bending, Eliana could see a pattern beneath it. There was a reason for it, and it had precious little to do with skill and everything with how she felt. For him, in particular.

And she must not feel anything for him. That wasn't part of the plan. The plan was to find an easy-going friendship so they could make decisions about their baby together.

As if he had read her mind, Diego slipped a hand down to her naked stomach, gently resting his palm on the smallest of bumps that was forming where their child was growing. It was that little bump that she should remember whenever her feelings for him were getting messy and tangled. Her baby deserved a stable home, even if it was only with one parent.

'You haven't felt anything yet, have you?' he asked.

Eliana shook her head and laid her hand on top of his. 'No, it's too early at the end of the first trimester. But at least I'm done with morning sickness.'

He hummed low, the vibration seeping through her pores and into her body, awakening a new wave of want for this man.

'I'm going to have to tell Avozinha. She'll be thrilled, and probably won't leave you alone once she knows.'

Diego had meant it as a jovial threat, but she actually found herself excited at the prospect of someone else partaking in the joy she had so far kept to herself. Even though everything leading up to her baby's conception had been an accident—and the situation with her Dr Dad was not in the least bit clear—she was genuinely excited to meet her child, and had felt sad that no one would be there to share that happiness with her.

Except now there was Diego, his *avozinha* and, by extension, the entire Ferrari clan. Her child would be able to know its extended family—people who cared about knowing their new niece, cousin or great-granddaughter. Despite Diego's claim that he wasn't close to his siblings, she could see they genuinely cared about one another. And now about her, too.

'Márcia was the one who raised you?' she asked.

Behind her, Diego stiffened for a moment, his lips still touching her skin. He relaxed after a few heartbeats, mumbling his response into her hair.

'She did. After one of my parents' countless breakups and subsequent reconciliations, they wanted to bring me back home after I'd spent several months with my grandmother. She refused to hand me over and instead told them to come back if they managed to go a whole year without splitting up again.' He let out a humourless chuckle. 'They didn't last half as long. So my *avozinha* ended up raising me and made sure to involve herself with my half-siblings too, so I could get to know them. It's thanks to her that I turned out the way I did.'

'You can tell her if you want,' Eliana said, wriggling around in his arms so she could look at him.

'Are you sure? She'll probably start making baby clothes straight away and drop them off at the hospital.'

She laughed at the thought of her office being transformed into a nursery. 'Maybe wait until I'm back in Belo Horizonte. Save the new chief the madness of finding baby sleepsuits in every drawer.'

They chuckled together, though this time she thought there was a strange sense of loss mixed into their laughter. Her departure was looming, and would take her an eight-hour drive away from Rio de Janeiro. She would leave soon, and they hadn't got any closer to understanding how they would work together as parents. Were they trying to put the cart in front of the horse? Was that why it was so difficult even to talk about it? And she knew a part of her yearned to stay here so her child could be close to its family.

'When are you leaving?' He tried to sound casual, but she sensed the tension in his muscles.

She shrugged. 'Soon. I've made my choice as Chief of Medicine, we're just finalising the handover, and then I'll have no more reason to stay here.'

*Except you.*

The words echoed in her mind, daring her to speak them, but they turned to bitter ash as she swallowed them. She couldn't let herself go there—not with all the mess around them. Diego was a man of enormous calibre and skill, and his compassion for his community ran so deep Eliana could only hope to feel so strongly one day.

But, especially after last night, she knew she

could never be a part of his world. Despite all the adversity he had witnessed as a child, he had managed to find his family, bond with them in a significant way that she never would.

Having grown up isolated from everyone around her, Eliana didn't know how to be a part of a family and doubted she could ever learn. Watching the Ferrari siblings interact with another had filled her with a yearning so deep, and it had hurt to know she would never have what they had.

'Who did you pick?' Diego asked, interrupting her thoughts mid-stream.

'Sophia.'

He arched his eyebrows in a surprised look. 'Sophia Salvador? The head of A&E? That's... actually a really good choice.'

'I spent so much time agonising over this decision, so your approval means a lot.'

Diego shot her a grin that made her heart skip a beat. She felt the heat rushing back to her core.

'Why was it a hard decision?' he asked.

'Because the hospital is infested with my father's people, who would be perfectly happy to stay the course it's on when what Santa Valeria really needs is a change for the better,' Eliana scoffed. 'The hospital should be known for the incredible talent of its medical staff—not for how nice the en-suite bathrooms of the patients' rooms are.'

She had made that exact speech in front of the board of directors as well, though they hadn't been impressed.

To her surprise, Diego laughed. 'You would get along well with Alessandro, Vanderson's husband. Vanderson could be a bit timid around his father, not wanting to draw too much attention to himself. Alessandro had no such reservations.'

'I would love to meet him,' she whispered.

She had only learned about him last week. With Vanderson's death, she'd believed her only link to her family was dead too, until Diego had dropped the bombshell around her brother-in-law and her niece.

Her child's cousin...

'You would?' There was an edge of surprise to his voice. 'I can take you to his shop. Daria might even be there, since it's the weekend.'

Her pulse quickened and her mouth went dry. She'd meant that wish to be a quiet desire, but had blurted it out before she'd been able to stop herself—something that seemed to happen way too often around Diego and his disarming smile.

Meeting her brother-in-law? The thought both terrified and excited her. But after seeing the dynamic between Diego and his siblings she wanted to see whether her child could have something like that as well—even if it was with a cousin rather than a sibling.

'I would like that.'

By the time they arrived at the Copa Cabana, where Alessandro ran his store, Eliana was a puddle of nerves, and Diego was fighting the need to chuckle by biting the inside of his cheek. Normally so confident and sure of herself, she seemed to be struggling with the thought of meeting a family member she hadn't known she had.

Although if he put it in those words, he could understand why she felt nervous. Diego himself had met so many mystery half-siblings and cousins he had never previously heard of that the situation bothered him very little—which was probably more a statement about his father's promiscuity than anything else.

They stood on the beach, a few paces away from Alessandro's store. A small café was attached to it, with some tables sprawled around the entrance. Behind the store was a five-metre-high climbing wall that made Diego smile when he looked at it.

When he'd been a more frequent visitor here, he'd sometimes do his workout by climbing that wall. Daria had often egged him on, asking him to climb faster and higher.

As if his thoughts had summoned her, a small

girl burst through the doors of the shop and bolted towards the pair. Diego smiled, going down on one knee so the girl could run straight into his arms.

'Tio! Where have you been? You said you would visit more often.'

Daria launched into a flood of sentences that he barely understood as they hugged each other, and he felt a twinge of guilt in his chest. He had only come to visit them once since the funeral.

'I'm sorry, *meu anjo*. You know how I get busy with work sometimes.'

Daria nodded gravely, as if she knew exactly how difficult the life of a surgeon was. Then she noticed Eliana, who now stood next to him.

'Daria, this is my friend Ana,' he said, and closed the gap between him and Eliana. 'Where is your *papai*?'

'Never too far away when she runs out of the store,' a low male voice said.

Diego set Daria down. She ran over to her father as he got closer to her. Alessandro came to a halt a couple of paces away from them but didn't even look at Diego. His eyes went straight to Eliana, and from the surprised and pained expression on his face it was clear that he had immediately spotted the similarities between her and Vanderson that Diego himself had missed that fateful night at the hotel.

'You're...his sister?' he asked, and Eliana nodded.

Tears sparkled in their eyes as they fell into each other's arms in an emotional display that robbed Diego of any remaining air in his lungs. He had thought that meeting Alessandro might be important to Eliana, but he had never imagined how emotional it would be for everyone—him included.

'Do you have time to sit down for a bit?' asked Alessandro, and Eliana looked over her shoulder to Diego, who shrugged.

He ushered them to one of the café's tables, where they sat down together, quiet for a moment.

'You could have given me a warning,' Alessandro said as he crossed his arms in front of his chest. 'You know I hate surprises.'

Diego smirked. 'That's why I didn't tell you.'

The man scowled at him, but his expression immediately softened when he looked over to Eliana. 'You really shouldn't put up with him... he's bad news.'

'Well...' She hesitated, her hand slipping to her stomach as she looked at Diego with a silent question: *Should we tell him?*

It was something Diego had thought about since he'd found out about her pregnancy. Eventually he'd need to tell the people around him that he was going to be a father. But their journey had been such an unconventional one he didn't know how to start explaining that he was having a child when he hadn't been in a relationship with a woman...ever.

Once someone outside of the two of them knew about the baby it would change everything. But Alessandro and Daria were the only people she had left that resembled her family; it was only natural that she wanted to connect with them by sharing their news.

Were they ready for that step?

There was only one way to find out.

Diego took a breath and gave her a small nod, which she acknowledged with a smile. Was she excited to be telling them?

'I know I've only just met you, so this may sound a bit strange. But Diego and I are actually having a child.'

Alessandro's eyes went wide with surprise, and his gaze darted between them as if he couldn't understand what she had just said. 'You two are...?'

'We're not together, no! This is an accident. We met some months ago now.'

She'd voiced her denial so rapidly it took Diego a few moments to register the hurt blooming in his chest. Which was ridiculous, since he *knew* they weren't together. He had set that expectation from the very beginning, so it shouldn't surprise him that she believed him.

Had *his* feelings changed?

They couldn't have. He didn't know how to love with every fibre of his being. Didn't know how to behave in the kind of family he secretly wanted to have. Alessandro and Vanderson had been the role models for something he knew he would never be able to achieve, no matter how much he desired it. So he had contented himself with watching from the side lines as their family came together and grew.

Being a minor character in their story was better than becoming a tragic failure in his own, right?

Except now here they sat, their roles reversed. He had made a child with this woman next to him, who had endured so much injustice and loneliness without letting it affect her heart.

She always tried to appear strong and independent when people were paying attention—a reflex no doubt born from the neglect she'd experienced during her childhood years. But whenever she thought no one was looking the guards came down and she became a much softer person. A person who would call their unborn child 'princess' because she felt a connection strong enough to know with certainty it was a girl.

He'd seen the same woman this last week as their passion had been transformed into something much more profound right in front of his eyes. He'd seen her come apart and put herself back together right under his hands, heard her whisper his name in the dead of the night as he pulled her closer into his embrace.

Everything in those moments had made sense in a way he hadn't experienced before. It had all just felt right, suddenly, and he felt like a fool for ever believing he couldn't have what he'd sensed last night. What he felt right now in this moment, as they told the first other person that they were having a child together.

Only she had rejected all those feelings with one phrase.

'I can't believe it. Of all the men you could have found in Rio, you've tied yourself to the eternal bachelor. That's material for a telenovela right there.' Alessandro looked at Diego. 'How do you feel?'

As if his world was falling apart right underneath his feet. Everything he'd thought to be true about himself had shifted since he'd met Eliana, and now he couldn't go on without her—didn't want to know what it felt like to be without her. She had found the thing Diego had thought he was missing. It had been inside him all this time, waiting for the right person to find it. Waiting for her.

'Better than you give me credit for,' he said, to distract himself from his own inner turmoil. 'I have you to show me how to be a good father.'

Alessandro laughed at that and looked down at Daria, who was sitting on a chair next to him and was busy enjoying her milkshake. She stopped drinking when she noticed her father looking at her and tilted her head, clearly oblivious to the discussion that had gone on between the adults.

'I think you're not giving yourself enough credit for turning out to be a decent man despite all the obstacles,' Alessandro said with a pointed look. 'I can think of a lot of different reactions to an unplanned pregnancy.'

Diego glanced at Eliana, who had gone quiet during their exchange, her hand still resting on the tiny bump that was starting to form.

'It wasn't how I planned to have a child, but I'm glad it happened the way it did,' she said. 'Diego hasn't shied away from taking responsibility. We're just trying to figure things out as we go along, while I'm still wrapping up things with Marco's estate.'

There was a softness in her words that caught Diego off guard. Was it affection? After she had rejected him so resoundingly he hadn't expected to encounter such warmth only a few moments later. Was she *glad* they'd had an accident on their first night together? That it had been with Diego?

'I mean, how else would I have met you?' she added, looking at Alessandro with a wide smile.

Their connection had been instantaneous, and Diego was happy for her. After the way Marco had isolated his own daughter from any kind of family life, she deserved to know some of her roots.

She halted for a moment, her eyes trailing over to the sea for a moment. 'I didn't see your name on any of the papers in my father's will. Vanderson was his only beneficiary, but after the accident...'

Alessandro shook his head with a sad smile. 'You're sweet to worry. But Vanderson had his own estate and that went to us as his next of kin. Me not getting along with Marco didn't affect us as a family.' Alessandro smiled, reaching over the table to grab Eliana's hand and squeeze it. 'Make sure Diego gives you my number so we can keep in touch. Daria will be thrilled to meet her little cousin in a few months. Isn't that right, *anjinho*?'

Daria beamed at all of them and nodded. Her excitement to meet her new cousin was palpable in her face. Diego heard a soft gasp coming from Eliana, and saw the shimmer covering her eyes as she looked at her niece with a big smile.

'I can't wait for you all to meet this little one.'

A noisy group of tourists walking towards the shop interrupted their discussion, and Alessandro stood up with a sigh.

'I have to take care of this.' He walked over to Eliana and pulled her into another hug. 'Let's grab some coffee when it's less busy, so we can have a chance to chat. I'm sure there are a lot of things you would like to know about Vanderson, and it would be nice to relive the memories I have of him.'

She nodded in agreement before hugging Daria as well and waving as they both scurried back into the store. When she sat down again, her face was unreadable.

'How are you feeling? Lots to process?' Diego asked, and looked at her for a moment before laying a hand on her thigh to give it a supportive squeeze.

'I like him. It's good to know that at least Vanderson had the chance at a normal life. Although no doubt my father left a lot of damage on him as well.'

*At least.* The words hung between them like a dark fog, suddenly rushing in to envelop everything around them. It sounded as if she had given up.

An invisible band had been constricting his chest since she'd spoken those words about her pregnancy, and he had now got to a point where his chest felt heavy under the crushing sensation. He couldn't hide his mounting feelings for Eliana any longer and had to admit to himself that he wanted more from her. More than he had ever wanted from anyone before and more than she was willing to give.

Which left him with no choice but to forget about how he felt. How he had fallen so hard without even noticing? She didn't want him the way he wanted her, and maybe that was for the best. How could he promise her a happy family when he had no idea how to make one? Better to make the best out of what they already had rather than try for something new.

'What do you want to do now?' he asked. 'The climbing wall is a lot of fun if you're feeling brave.'

She laughed. 'Making a baby from scratch has left me a bit exhausted, so I'll pass on the extreme sports for now. How about a walk on the beach instead?'

He smiled as he took her hand, their fingers weaving into each other's as they started their stroll, and a warmth rising in his arms from where their skin connected.

She would leave any day now. Eliana had said so herself. And Diego was determined to enjoy the time they had left, even if he was dreaming of what might have been if they had grown up differently.

The water sparkled in the light of the afternoon sun as they walked down the beach in a comfortable silence. The meeting with Alessandro had healed a part of Eliana's heart in a way only he could have done. With him she had regained a connection to her brother, and even though he wasn't here to explain, she was glad to know someone who could tell her who he had been besides what Diego had already told her.

Diego's support had been essential in this endeavour. It showed her he cared not just for his child but for her. Getting to know Alessandro—that would be for her alone.

She felt her already bleeding heart squeeze even tighter. Diego's affection meant so much to her when it really shouldn't. At some point would she have to admit that they might have gone too deep?

Eliana shook those thoughts away, instead focusing on the beach around her and the warmth his hand created where it touched hers, radiating heat through her entire body. It might be the last time she got to enjoy such a tranquil moment before she left Rio behind.

'Have you been here before?' Diego asked as they stopped to watch two people zip past them on a pair of quad bikes with frightening speed.

'Not really.' Her eyes followed the bikes as they wove through people. She heard excited laughter trailing after the drivers. 'I didn't like going out by myself when I lived here, and by the time I was older I had already moved away.'

'You haven't missed much. The Copa Cabana

gets so many reviews online every visitor comes here.' The bikes came zooming around again and he raised his hand, underlining the point he'd just made. 'I know a private beach that I—'

A loud bang drowned out the rest of his sentence and Eliana clasped her hand over her mouth as one of the quad bikes collided with a palm tree, sending the rider flying over the steering wheel and into the trunk before he fell on the ground unmoving.

Diego swore next to her and sprinted towards the person lying in the sand. She quickly followed him, scanning the people who were moving closer. When she spotted someone holding a phone, she pointed at them.

'Please call for an ambulance and say to the operator that there has been a motor vehicle crash on the beach.' Eliana didn't wait for a reply but turned around to find Diego kneeling beside the man, who had regained consciousness and was moaning in agony.

'What's the status? Anything I can do to help?'

Both the man's arms stood at unnatural angles. One had a dislocated shoulder, the other a potential fracture of the lower arm. A quick glance showed her the skin was still intact, though that didn't mean the breaking bone hadn't done some damage to the muscles and blood vessels in the arm.

Diego looked at his patient, assessing the damage before bending over the man again. '*Senhor*, do you hear me?' he asked, and the man nodded with a wince. 'We are both doctors and we're here to help. You've had an accident and crashed.'

Eliana knelt down as well, waiting for Diego's plan of action. Whatever the man's wounds were, she knew he'd been lucky that Diego was here to help with stabilising the fracture.

A small part inside her felt excited to be working with him. As chief at the hospital she'd spoken to many people working with Diego, and none of the other department heads had received such high praise. The compassion and care he gave each patient, no matter the severity of the case, was unparalleled, and after seeing for herself his interaction with Miguel, as well as the man in front of him now, she could see his staff had not exaggerated.

'We can't set the bone without an X-ray, but we can pop the shoulder back in and stabilise the arm with a sling until the ambulance arrives,' Diego said to her before turning back to the patient.

'Is he going to be okay?' His friend had stopped her bike a few paces away and now came running over.

Diego stood up for a moment, laying a hand on her shoulder. 'We have to get him to a hospital, but he is conscious. What I'm about to do will hurt without anaesthesia. Can you sit next to him?'

She nodded, her face as pale as the sand surrounding them, and dropped to her knees beside him.

'Have you relocated a shoulder before?' Diego asked Eliana as he came down next to the patient's head.

'I've watched several, but never done it myself.'

'Can you kneel behind his back once we prop him up? This will be rough on him, but it'll make things a lot easier for the ambulance.'

When Eliana nodded, he pushed the man's torso off the ground and she settled behind him, holding him upright while Diego took the arm with the dislocated shoulder between his hands.

'Most of the time you'll find that the tendons in the arm help the shoulder find its way back. All you have to do is pull.'

Eliana watched as he tightened his grip around the man's arm and pulled at it with a sharp but precise motion that sent a tremble through the patient's body accompanied by a stifled shout.

'Then follow the pressure of the tendons to bring the shoulder back into its socket.'

He got to his feet, asking one of the onlookers if he could borrow her towel and fashioning it into a makeshift sling, into which he carefully lifted the broken arm to stabilise it for transport.

'I know you're in a lot of pain right now, and the last thing you want is some doctor asking you questions,' he said, in a soothing voice that even managed to set Eliana at ease. 'But I have to ask one so we can make sure we're not missing anything. Are you feeling any nausea or sickness?'

The man's chest fluttered with each laboured breath, but he shook his head from one side to the other.

'We can't rule out a concussion, but at least he was wearing a helmet,' Eliana said, and Diego nodded.

His hand slipped inside his pocket, fishing out his smartphone. He turned the torch on with a flick of his finger, shining the light into the patient's eyes. 'Pupillary reaction looks good. Fingers crossed we have no spinal or head injuries.'

They both looked up when the sirens of an ambulance came closer and a red and white vehicle came into view. Two paramedics came running, with a gurney in their hands.

Eliana watched as Diego updated them on the patient's status and then took a step back as they readied him for transportation to the nearest emergency department. Her eyes flickered between the patient and Diego, who was now talking to the patient's friend.

'They're taking him to Copa Memorial for treatment. The ambulance can take you along if you want to accompany them.'

The woman's eyes were shining with tears at this point, and she looked around to the bikes. 'I want to, but...'

Diego followed her gaze. 'Did you rent them from the store with the climbing wall behind it?' He smiled when she nodded. 'The owner happens to be a good friend of mine, so don't worry about it. We'll sort it out. Go with him.'

The woman thanked them both with a sob in her voice and they watched her climb into the ambulance.

'You were incredible,' Eliana said, giving voice to the brewing thought within her. Not only had he kept the patient calm under chaotic circumstances, he'd been able to help with very limited resources.

Diego looked at her in surprise. 'I don't think so...'

Eliana laughed at the denial. 'I'm glad I got to watch you work before I leave. Now I know why your staff keep saying such nice things about you. Santa Valeria is lucky to have you to teach its staff the right way.'

He crossed his arms in front of his chest,

raising his eyebrows. 'Did the doctors in your hospital never help in emergencies?'

'Of course they did. What I'm trying to say is that I love your compassion and your dedication to doing the right thing. And after speaking to everyone at Santa Valeria I know that more people who think and act like you are needed.'

His brown eyes grew darker, narrowing on her and sending a shiver crawling down her spine. There was an unspoken desire written in them, something neither of them wanted to acknowledge. Speaking of it would undermine every boundary they had established between them—every agreement they had made for the good of their baby.

So Eliana bit her lip, swallowing the words rising in her throat, and looked at the quad bikes instead.

'Let's get these bikes back to Alessandro,' she said, needing to break the sudden intensity between them.

# CHAPTER NINE

THE MORNING LIGHT filtering through the half-drawn curtains fell onto Eliana's face. She tried to turn around but met surprising resistance in the form of Diego, who had his arms wrapped around her waist and was pulling her into him even as he slept.

She looked down at herself. Her naked body was wrapped up in his sheets, her bare back hot where it connected with his chest. Their one night together, which should have been a one-off lapse of judgement, had extended into the last three weeks, with them spending both days and nights together.

The way they had been living was so far removed from what their lives would look like once she left—which would be soon. And they were nowhere near figuring out the arrangements for their co-parenting journey. Instead of focusing on that, they had given in to the tension that had been building between them for weeks.

Misguided tension.

Nothing about their situation had changed. Eliana was still going to leave, handing the hospital over so she didn't have to be involved any more. The city reminded her too much of Marco and what he had done to her. And although spending time with Diego opened her heart in ways she had never experienced before, there was still a sneaky voice in her head, whispering words of caution and poisoning these moments they were sharing together.

He'd shown incredible kindness and dedication to his community. But she'd also glimpsed the ruthlessness with which he had gone about it—taking resources from the hospital as well as smuggling people in. Diego had always acted for the right reasons and was ready to put his own career on the line for it, but would he do the same for her? Would he consider her part of his people when her struggle had been so different?

The doubts gnawing at her heart with their sharp claws and teeth did little to help her relax back into slumber. Every time she closed her eyes her thoughts started to whirl around in her head, corrupting what had been three weeks full of pleasure, laughter and closeness.

With a soft sigh on her lips Eliana turned around—and gasped when she stared right into Diego's warm brown eyes.

'Good morning,' she said, when his eyes narrowed as if he had caught every thought that had just wandered through her head.

'Do you want me to let you go?' he asked in a calm voice, and Eliana got the impression that he wasn't necessarily talking about his arms around her waist.

She took a breath to steady herself. His gaze was throwing her off balance, to the point where she couldn't quite remember exactly what she had been afraid of.

'I have to go to the hospital. My first scan is later today, and I need to get some things done before that,' she said, to wriggle out of telling him about her thoughts. 'As a matter of fact, you need to be in the hospital, too. The mayor's wife is getting her hip replaced today, and she's insisted she will only have the best surgeon touch her.'

Diego groaned, but the sound was very unlike the sounds that had filled her ears throughout the night as he came back for more of her.

'It's a hip replacement. Any second-year registrar can do that. You're just wasting money, putting the head of orthopaedics on this.' He sighed and released his grip around her to scrub his hands across his face. 'That money would be better spent on something ground-breaking—like fixing curved spines. A doctor from Peru has contacted me about a patient who has a fifty-degree bend they can't fix with steel rods.'

Eliana took the opportunity to roll out of bed, stepping out of Diego's range so he couldn't grab her again. 'Write down a proposal and we can talk about your curved spine. But until then I expect you to give the mayor's wife the very best care. From what the accountants tell me, she's a huge benefactor of the hospital.'

Eliana bent down to pick up her clothes, and when she looked back up Diego's face had changed. The humour in his eyes had died, leaving nothing but an icy tundra where she had just seen warmth and compassion.

'Don't tell me you're putting people with deep pockets ahead of patients who actually need help?'

The accusation came out of nowhere, and Eliana's chest constricted for a moment. She was surprised by the ferocity with which he'd spat those words at her.

'You know I'm not. But big donors are part of the ecosystem, too.'

Diego snorted in derision. 'That phrase comes straight out of Marco Costa's playbook.'

The ice in his gaze took over her body, trickling down her spine and through her body as if someone had poured cold water all over her.

'Do not compare me to that man,' she said, fighting to keep her voice even. 'You don't know what he was like as a person. You only ever interacted with him when you were trying to bend the rules in your favour. Any chief would be annoyed with you over that.'

Her chest heaved as she stared at him, looking for the man she had got to know so much about in the last few weeks, believing she might be able to trust him with the thoughts dwelling inside her. But his expression was unreadable.

'The same goes for you,' he said. 'If you're suddenly so concerned with profits I might have made a mistake showing you my clinic.'

His voice had dropped low, but instead of it causing the usual goosebumps of pleasure to coat her skin she felt the hairs on her arms stand on end in warning.

'Where do you think the money for expensive Peruvian surgeries comes from? All this because you think yourself too good to do a hip replacement?'

Eliana stared at him, waiting for a reply that didn't come. How could Diego accuse her of being like her father when she had worked so hard to support his vision of Santa Valeria's future?

'I don't want to waste my time appeasing rich people when there are others who need my help,' he said, with such quiet fury that Eliana glared at him.

Sprawled out in the bed like that, he would have been a breathtaking picture of masculine sensuality if she'd been able to see past his almost irrational response to one surgery. It wasn't as if she'd cancelled his entire surgical schedule and asked him to focus only on the mayor's wife.

'You are helping the hospital by doing this. The hospital you have, in essence, been *stealing* from for the last few years.'

He sat up, opening his mouth to speak, but she stopped him with a shake of her head. She knew she would regret letting this conversation go any further than she already had.

'I'm going to leave and let you contemplate who you just compared me to.' She paused for a moment; her hands balled into tight fists at her sides as she sensed the anger rising in her. 'I have the scan today, at two in the afternoon. It's at the hospital, so I'll see you there.'

Despite feeling wholly justified to uninvite him, she realised she needed to be the bigger person. He was still the father of her child.

Without giving him a chance to rope her into any further argument, Eliana took her clothes and fled the room, getting dressed in a hurry before leaving the house with tears of deep hurt stinging her eyes.

'You're an idiot.'

Diego looked up when the voice of his sister Gloria ripped him out of his contemplations.

He had been ready to leave for the hospital when his *avozinha* had called, asking if he could take her along. Miguel had just received his new leg, and she wanted to pay him and his mother a visit.

In typical Márcia fashion, she had been nowhere near ready when her grandson had pulled over to pick her up. So he had come inside to make himself some coffee as he waited. He'd need a lot of caffeine if he wanted to get through the day in one piece.

'Good morning to you, too,' he said, in a low voice that conveyed his overall annoyance with the way his day had started.

'I can't believe you finally bring home a woman and then you mess it up within a month.' She paused to look at him.

'How could you possibly know about that?' The accuracy with which Gloria had pinpointed the source of his annoyance was bordering on spooky.

'You were happy when we last saw you. Not just content, but actually smiling and engaging. None of us had ever seen you that way, so it was easy to guess what was different since you did us the favour of bringing her here.'

Diego crossed his arms, narrowing his eyes at his sister. 'Did you call the council of siblings to discuss this?'

Gloria chuckled—which didn't help his sour

mood. He didn't need anyone butting into his affairs.

'No, Albert saw you two interlocked. He said it looked like you were eating something off her neck.'

Diego glared at her, the exasperation in his chest fading away as he was confronted with the truth he'd been struggling with. He wanted to pretend that Eliana's exit that morning didn't mean anything to him.

'Our nephew saw us?' he asked.

Gloria nodded and couldn't hide her grin. 'You made out with someone in Avozinha's garden while the whole family was here. You couldn't have done a better job if you'd wanted to be caught.'

He hadn't thought about being caught when he had kissed Eliana in the garden. That moment had been about releasing something that had been dwelling inside him ever since they'd met during that surgery. Just moments before they had heard that they were having a child together for the first time. Such news should have made him wary of the woman involved, but instead they had grown closer.

'I'm still waiting to know why I'm the idiot here.' He cast a suspicious glance at his sister, who shook her head with a click of her tongue, as if the answer was the most obvious in the world.

'Because I was out walking Pelé when I saw Eliana leave your place in what looked like a hurry. Now, a woman you take to meet your ridiculous family must be special, because in all the years of our urging you to bring someone the best you could do was Vanderson. And no one ever caught you two making out.'

Diego grimaced, his thoughts still catching up with what Gloria had just revealed. The night at his grandmother's house had not gone as he had planned—which might be something of an overstatement. There hadn't been much planning going on after he'd kissed her. All he'd known was that he had to have her in his house. Not just to sleep with her, but to watch her fall asleep. To have her warm body next to him while he drifted off.

In a completely uncharacteristic move, Diego had found himself yearning for more than just a physical connection. And throughout their nights together, he had started to think about their future—if there could even be a future for them together. He had been close to talking to her about it, to discussing with her the blooming feelings in his chest that he had never felt before.

Until Eliana had mentioned his scheduled procedure on the mayor's wife and a wave of deep-seated anger had come rushing into his chest, banishing any other emotion that might have been there for the duration of a few heartbeats. Marco had done that sort of thing—constantly cancelling essential or even urgent surgeries so he could do a routine procedure that any registrar could handle on people who were important and brought in significant donations. They had been put ahead of people with genuine needs who needed his steady hands and exceptional skill to help them.

It wasn't a trend Diego wanted to see continue under the new leadership, so when she had mentioned it something inside him had snapped.

He'd stared at the ceiling after she'd left, his rage subsiding with each breath and being replaced with a feeling of profound unease.

His words had hurt her, and he had meant them to have that effect, but as he'd lain there regret had crept in. The hospital needed big donors to keep going—he understood that well enough. And none of his urgent patients had been bumped further down the line for him to do this procedure. Had his anger been an overreaction because of the issues he'd experienced in the past?

'She's pregnant, Gloria,' he said now, letting go of the weight he'd been carrying around. 'We're having a child.'

Her eyebrows shot up. 'Then you'd better get your act together, big brother.'

A thought occurred to Diego that made him

shiver. 'You haven't told Avozinha that we've fought, have you?'

'I'm not that cruel. I didn't tell her about the kissing *or* the falling out.'

He looked over his shoulder when he heard rustling coming from the house and spotted his grandmother packing her bag. 'I don't know which would be worse. And don't tell her this either,' he whispered at his sister, who shot him a grin before he got up and ushered his grandmother to the car.

He glanced at the clock as they drove, wondering if he would be able to see Eliana before his surgery. He didn't want the shadows of this morning haunting them throughout the day, and he needed to let her know he hadn't meant to sound as harsh as he had. That it had been no more than a reaction from the past.

He didn't know how to handle the feelings he'd started to have for her. For the family they could surely have together if they wanted to.

Diego shoved his thoughts aside as he went into the scrub room to change for surgery. Whether he liked it or not, the mayor's wife was now his patient, and she deserved him to be on top of his game just like anyone else.

Nerves made Eliana's stomach turn inside out as she settled down on the exam table. When she'd arrived in the obstetrics department the receptionist had asked her to go through to a room immediately. A fact she was grateful for. While her pregnancy wasn't exactly a secret, she didn't want to invite any questions from the staff if they happened to pass by and see her there.

She had told the receptionist to keep an eye out for Diego and send him through if he arrived, and was glad that she hadn't had to specify why she wanted to see him.

Dr Felix sat on a stool next to her, looking at the patient chart on a tablet in front of her and asking all the routine questions. Eliana answered them, her eyes darting back to the door, hoping that at any moment Diego would burst through it, apologising for his delay.

A small voice in her head told her that he wouldn't come. Not after the way they had parted this morning. But she ignored the doubt growing inside her, wanting to believe that he wouldn't not show up just because they'd had an argument. As co-parents, that would probably happen more often than they wanted. Would he always bail when they were standing on opposite sides?

That thought struck fear in Eliana's heart. The thought of getting to know his family—and getting to know her own family through him—had filled her with a warmth that made her heart beat faster. Somewhere along the line her feelings for him had become a lot more tangible than she had anticipated. Wanted, really. But would she even fit into his life? Did he want her to? Her intention to leave Rio remained the same. And Diego hadn't asked her to reconsider, either.

She had found a replacement chief of medicine. The lawyers were all but finished dealing with the estate of her father. After that she would be heading back to Belo Horizonte, leaving Rio and all its painful memories behind her. She'd need to forget about whatever feelings she had for Diego because they clearly were not meant to be.

She couldn't even count on him to come to the scan of their unborn child.

'Both you and the baby are in perfect condition, Dr Oliveira,' Dr Felix informed her, bringing her thoughts back into the room. 'I'm having a look at the results of your prenatal blood tests right now, but unless I see anything concerning you can just come back in a few weeks for your sixteen-week check-up.'

'Oh, I probably won't be here by then. I'm heading back...back home as soon as my business here is done.' She stumbled over the word *home*, her heart skipping a painful beat. She had grown more attached to this place than she was ready to admit.

'I'll make sure to send you a copy of your file so your new doctor has all the information you need.' Dr Felix smiled at her, then looked back at her tablet. 'Are you ready to know the sex of the baby?'

Eliana's eyes went wide with surprise. She had forgotten that they had done a blood test that would tell her the sex of her baby even at this stage. Again her eyes darted to the door, which remained stubbornly closed, and her chest constricted. He really wasn't coming.

Dr Felix noticed her gaze, following it with her own. 'Waiting for the father?'

'Yes, but I think he might be stuck in surgery.'

She didn't believe that, but it was a better excuse than the fact that he'd bailed because they'd argued and he didn't want to operate on the mayor's wife. The surgery must have ended hours ago.

'We can keep this information from you a bit longer if you want to wait.'

The problem was that Eliana wasn't sure.

Part of her did want to wait—desperately. Despite all the barriers, all the walls and traps she had set around herself, Diego had danced around every single obstacle and planted himself in her heart. She wanted him to be a part of this moment, to be a part of her family—wanted to share the highs and lows of her pregnancy with him.

But he had accused her of putting profit over patient care, just as her father had done. And to hear that he thought so little of her after all the time they had spent together had crushed her heart into tiny pieces.

Dr Felix had clearly sensed her hesitation. She picked up a small piece of paper from her desk, writing something on it before putting it in an envelope, which she handed to Eliana.

'These are the blood test results. You can open it together if you want to find out.'

Eliana took the envelope with a grateful smile and jumped off the table, pulling her blouse back into place.

As she walked out of the obstetrics department she grabbed her phone to look at the surgical plan for the afternoon. Perhaps Diego had been pulled into an emergency surgery...

Something was definitely off when Eliana arrived at the orthopaedics department. The staff's whispers died down the second she got close enough to decipher some words, and picked up as soon as she was far enough not to overhear their chatter. A pang of terror grabbed at her heart. This had something to do with Diego. She had known that the instant she had arrived, even though there was nothing to indicate that.

'Where is Dr Ferrari?' she asked a passing nurse, who looked at her with wide eyes.

'He's in the VIP room. It's the mayor's wife. She...'

The young woman's voice trailed off, and Eliana shuddered, her suspicions confirmed.

Something had happened during surgery.

All thoughts of him missing her appointment were wiped from her brain, all her attention immediately on the critical patient they had in their care.

Whatever she had feared finding in the patient's room, the reality was a lot worse than she had imagined. The sound of a flat beep drifted into the hall before she arrived, filling her with a sense of dreadful foreboding. A flat heart monitor was never a good sign. Neither was the fact that the room beyond was too quiet.

Eliana braced herself as she entered the room, analysing the scene in front of her. A female patient lay in a hospital bed, her chest cracked open in what looked like an emergency thoracotomy—something a surgeon would only do if they had no other option and other measures to stabilise the patient had failed.

What had happened that Diego had needed to crack open her chest? Blood clot? They were common in women her age and could happen at any time.

A junior physician hovered around the bed,

picking up the different instruments that had been used in the emergency procedure and putting them on a cart. And behind him, slumped in a chair, sat…

'Diego?'

His face looked hollow. With his head tilted backwards, she could see the blood that covered the front of his scrubs as well as parts of his arms, where the gloves had stopped. In the hurry of the emergency he didn't seem to have put on a gown for extra protection.

Eliana looked at the registrar, still fumbling with the instruments. 'Are you from the cardio department?' she asked. He nodded, clearly intimidated by the presence of the chief. 'Tell the head of Cardio I'll need to speak to her before we break the news to the mayor.'

She dismissed the young doctor with a nod of her head before turning back to Diego, who had sat up slightly.

'What happened?' she asked, doing her best to sound unemotional. Seeing him covered in blood had sent pangs of terror through her body until she'd realised that it wasn't his.

'Are you here to admonish me for letting your VIP patient die?' he said in a quiet voice, resentment giving his tone an uncomfortable edge.

Eliana remained silent, not rising to the bait he'd laid out. Instead, she squatted down in front of him to be on the same eye level.

Diego took a few breaths. Tiredness was etched into every feature of his body. She could tell that he had fought tooth and nail to keep his patient alive.

'My best guess? Pulmonary embolism. Even if we'd have caught it early, it would have been too late. I was about to leave when the post-op nurse paged me to check in on her.'

Eliana glanced back at the patient. That had been her first thought as well. A blood clot that had travelled all the way to the lungs, blocking off the flow of blood. She would have probably cracked the chest open too, and tried to manually aspirate the heart.

Looking back at Diego, she put her hand on his knee. The emergency had clearly taken a lot of energy out of him, and she suspected he might have tried even harder knowing the patient was important to her. Or did she simply wish that to be true?

Whatever the reason, the Diego in front of her looked utterly broken, and no matter how angry she was at him for missing their appointment, the part of her that cared for him a lot more than she was willing to admit wanted to take care of him.

They could have their difficult conversation later.

'Come on, let's get you cleaned up.'

She took him by the hand, and together they

walked back to her office, where she shoved him into the adjacent bathroom so he could shower.

Diego heard two muffled voices on the other side of the closed door when he stepped out of the shower after what seemed to be hours. He stopped, listening and trying to understand what was being discussed. One of the voices belonged to Eliana, but the other one was harder to pinpoint.

His question was answered a few moments later when he heard a third voice coming out of the speaker of a phone. The mayor. So the other person must be the head of cardiology.

Dread came rushing back into his system when he thought about the surgery. Hip replacements were routine work. Diego had done hundreds in his career, and his mortality rate lay way below the already tiny rate of hip fractures and related surgeries.

Low, but not zero.

Diego leaned against the door, closing his eyes as he shook off the thought of the last couple of hours. Losing a patient was never easy, but this one really bothered him—mainly because he hadn't even wanted to do the surgery, but had had to concede in the end that Eliana would have to ask for his time in such cases to garner support from wealthy benefactors.

It was something Marco had done constantly as well. The difference between those two, though, lay in what they'd intended to use the money for. Eliana wasn't lining her own pockets with the funds she'd drum up through such procedures—a fact he now realised.

He hoped it was not too late to apologise for his barbed words earlier today.

If only he could have given her a good outcome.

He'd let her down.

Diego knew this wasn't really true—that he had done everything he could to save the patient's life, and sometimes that wasn't enough. Despite knowing all that, he felt like an abject failure.

'You can come out now.'

Her voice rang a lot clearer than before, and a moment later the door opened. Eliana stood in front of him, holding a fresh pair of folded scrubs.

'I brought you some spare clothes.'

He took them with a nod of gratitude and slipped into the clothes before stepping into her office, where he stood for a moment.

'I just spoke to the mayor. He's still processing the news, but thank you for all the effort you put into saving his wife,' she said, and sat down behind her desk, pointing at the chair across from her.

Diego didn't take her up on the invitation but instead elected to stand, leaning his hip against her heavy desk. 'I'm sorry for how it turned out.'

'I know.' Eliana smiled half-heartedly and shrugged. 'He'll come to understand...just like every other spouse in such a situation.'

'Except he was more important to you.'

Eliana let out a sigh. 'He wasn't any more or less important than anyone else. There's a difference between rolling out the red carpet for someone and blatantly preferring them due to their status.'

'I know. I realise that now. And I don't know why I brought it up again. You don't operate in the same way Marco did, and I shouldn't have said otherwise.' He stopped for a moment, relaxing the arms he had been crossing just a moment ago. 'I apologise.'

His apology seemed to throw Eliana off guard, for she stared at him for a couple of heartbeats before finally nodding. 'Thank you. I appreciate that acknowledgement.'

They stayed quiet for a few moments.

Then, 'You missed the scan.'

The sharp tone in her voice was back, though he could see the restraint on her face.

The scan? Diego hesitated for a moment as the sequence of events this afternoon came back to him. With the urgency of the moment her appointment had completely slipped his mind. Guilt bloomed in his chest, mingling with the already heavy shroud of losing his patient. How could have forgotten about the first chance to see his child?

'Are you angry I missed the appointment? Ana, I had to attend the Code Blue of my patient.'

Eliana huffed, her eyes narrowing with a dangerous sparkle. 'I'm not angry that you had to see to your patient. What concerns me is that I had to remind you about the scan now. You didn't even ask if I'm…if *we* are okay.' She took a deep breath, seemingly steadying herself as she looked away for a second. 'I thought we were in this together.'

He paused. Her answer had not been quite what he had expected. She wasn't angry that he had missed the scan. She was angry because he hadn't asked about it.

'This isn't the last time I'm going to miss things,' he said slowly as he collected his own thoughts. 'If you take our kid away from Rio I won't be there for a lot of things. I want to be involved, and I'm sorry I couldn't make it this time, but you're the one carrying our child away from here.'

Diego's pulse quickened, his mouth suddenly dry as he stared at her confused expression. The truth of his feelings for her had started to coalesce—to the point where he could no longer deny it. He wanted her to stay—wanted them to be a family. Because he had fallen for her without even realising, and the thought of watching her leave hung over him like a dark fog.

'Diego...' She looked away, scrubbing her hands over her face. 'I'm still leaving as soon as my business here is done. I can't stay in Rio.'

'Why not?' He knew she struggled with her past, growing up alone and isolated. But was that enough to rob them of the chance of becoming a family? Wouldn't she try for him?

'Because there's just too much pain here. Even being back at this place brings unease to my stomach.' She lifted her hands, indicating the hospital around her. 'Everywhere I go I can feel the stares, hear the whispers about what Marco Costa did to my mother. I hear what a good woman she was or what a poor woman she was, depending on the person I speak to. That's all she'll ever be—a scandal. And that's all I'll ever be here as well.'

Diego's heart broke in his chest as the flood of words escaped her lips. Words she had spoken for the first time, judging by the sad but also strangely relieved expression on her face. So that was where her insecurities came from. She didn't believe she was good enough to be here, when nothing could be further from the truth.

'You've already shown yourself to be way more than the circumstances of your birth,' he said into the silence spreading between them. 'The mayor's wife just died in your hospital. You knew exactly what to do and you did it calmly. Like the true leader of a hospital would.'

Eliana scoffed. 'I wouldn't be so sure about that. Internally, I've been freaking out ever since I saw her in that room.'

'But you didn't let that affect you. Despite feeling overwhelmed, you remembered to care for the immediate family of the patient first rather than let yourself be carried away.'

Seeing the flaws in someone's actions rather than acknowledging every right step they took was something he was very familiar with, and he knew it took a lot of energy and self-confidence to snap out of it.

She looked at him with furrowed brow, digesting his words. 'I was never meant to be in this position.'

'You don't know that,' he replied, and reached out to brush his knuckles across her cheek. She didn't move away. 'Maybe this wasn't your plan, but neither was this baby—and look how that's turned out. You care so much for it that you want to carry it away from the place that caused you so much pain.'

His hand slipped down her neck over her arm and finally reached her stomach, where he rested his palm, fingers splayed across her abdomen.

Eliana looked down, taking a deep breath. 'You want me to stay?'

'I do, yes,' he said in a low voice.

'Why?'

His heart slammed against his chest as the truth rang clear in his head. 'Because I'm falling in love with you and I want us to try and have what we both weren't able to have growing up. We can be a family.'

It had taken him this long to realise that he wasn't doomed to repeat the mistakes of his past. Just because his father hadn't stayed true to his mother, it didn't mean that needed to be *his* life, too. He was free to love Eliana to the best of his abilities. Showing up to do his part every day. Choosing her and their child until the end of eternity.

Her eyes went wide in surprise, and he saw a slight flush colouring her cheek at his unexpected confession. Well, when he'd come in this morning, he hadn't thought they were going to have this conversation either. Hell, he hadn't even made up his mind whether to tell her about his feelings or if he should just let her go.

'Diego... I thought we had agreed to be friends,' she finally said after an extensive silence—and all the air left his lungs at once, as if someone had kicked him in the stomach.

Despite feeling utterly deflated, he managed a chuckle. 'I think we left the friend zone behind when we started making out whenever no one was watching.'

The blush on her cheeks intensified, and under any other circumstances Diego would have enjoyed the sight. If only she hadn't just rejected him.

An invisible hand reached inside his chest and squeezed his heart to the point of physical pain. Any more and he knew he would break.

'I'm not going to stay here,' she said. 'I can't. Not when I don't even know if you'll ever be able to put me first.'

'What? You doubt me because I missed this one appointment?' The accusation hurt in the depths of his chest, pulling the already suffocating band even tighter.

'No, I doubt you because you've kept things from me. Important things about your dealings in this hospital,' she said in a strained voice, as if she was willing herself to remain calm. 'But your motives are pure, and I've been working hard these last couple of weeks to give you the funds you need. I love how much you care about your community. But you're so used to doing things only the way you do it. I don't know how I would fit into that—how you see us as a family.'

She paused and shook her head.

'I'm not even sure you would have told me about the clinic if I hadn't stumbled upon Selma in the emergency department.'

Diego lifted his eyebrows. He opened his mouth to defend himself, but closed it again after a second of silence. Eliana wasn't wrong, and he didn't have any intention of stopping. Didn't feel bad about it either. Those people out there needed his help, and it wasn't *his* problem that the system was so fundamentally broken that he needed to resort to these tactics.

'I do what I have to do to help my people,' he said through gritted teeth, and saw her recoil.

'I'm not saying that anything you do is wrong. If more doctors were like you we wouldn't even need a free clinic. I just wish I could see the same tenacity in you when it comes to me and our child. But between your work and your mission I don't think we're as much of a priority as we should be.'

An icy shiver trickled down Diego's spine as he grappled to understand her words. 'You don't think you're a priority for me?'

The implication of those words shook him to his core. If his actions had made her feel that way, he really wasn't any better than his father. He truly didn't know how to be a part of a family, no matter how hard he tried.

His face must have shown the darkness of his thoughts, for Eliana lifted her hand to reach out to him, but stopped a few inches before their bodies could touch.

'I'm...sorry.'

He could see the conflicting feelings in her expression, and it was those warring emotions that almost made him believe she didn't mean what she'd said. But he had no choice but to believe her, even though he wanted the opposite to be true.

He pushed himself onto his feet. 'Don't be,' he said curtly, as the pain of rejection started to well up inside his chest again. 'Let me know about the baby. I can drive up for the next scan.'

He turned around, but stopped in his tracks when Eliana called out to him. 'Are you going to the dinner tomorrow? I've invited all the department heads to talk about the future of the hospital. I need you to be there.'

The future? Diego had rarely been less interested in the future than in this moment.

'If it's about work, sure,' he said with a throwaway gesture, before leaving the office and closing the door behind him.

# CHAPTER TEN

The Dinner was the last thing Eliana was in the mood for. Diego's unexpected confession had rocked her to her very core, and she felt the entire world had changed around her.

It couldn't be true. How could he love her when no one had ever done so in her whole life?

What had he been thinking, asking her to stay?

Her heart had been shredded into a million tiny pieces when she'd rejected him. Everything inside her had wanted to shout yes, to wrap her arms around him and never let him go. She'd wanted to be the kind of brave person who could forget about all the dangerous and hurtful things looming in the shadows of their romantic relationship.

His focus was so singular, she was afraid to find out what would happen if he fully focused on her, as she had demanded. But with the needs of his community, the grand plans he wanted to achieve, would he even be able to look out of her? For their child?

All the years of only depending on herself, without her father's love and support, had thickened the walls around her to the point where she could not trust anyone to come in. What if she let him in, let him see everything inside her, all the pain and chaos, and he realised what he was in for? What if he left? Eliana couldn't do that to her child—not when she had grown up on her own.

As much as she wanted to accept his love, to dare to hope, she couldn't be selfish. Her child needed her father more than she needed her lover.

Eliana took a deep breath, pushing the thoughts away. Tonight she had to be the chief one last time.

Her dinner for the hospital's department heads was being held at a restaurant Suelen had selected. They were to be seated in a private dining room so they could all talk freely with each other. But the first thing Eliana noticed was the empty chair and who it belonged to—Diego.

Her nerves lay blank from the conversation they'd had yesterday, and dread turned her stomach into knots when she sat down next to Sophia, who was looking at her with a degree of concern. Outside of Diego and the obstetrician, she was the only other member of hospital personnel who knew about her pregnancy. She also knew that it was Diego's child.

'I'm fine,' she said to the older woman, who had raised an eyebrow at her.

'Doctors make the worst patients—especially when it comes to high-ranking ones such as yourself,' Sophia murmured, her voice audible only to Eliana.

She smiled at the words. 'Thankfully, I will have you to deal with all my work very soon. Just send me an occasional email with updates—that should do it. I trust your judgement, or I wouldn't have picked you.'

'Should those emails contain a detailed Ferrari Report, or would you rather not read about him?' Sophia's tone was playful on the surface, but alluded to a lot more than Eliana wanted to discuss.

Was he not going to show up after her rejection yesterday, even when she had asked him to come?

Her mouth went dry and she reached for her glass of water, taking a big gulp. She had arranged this dinner in an attempt to reach out to him one last time—even though she was rejecting him she still cared for him, and she wanted him to know how much their time together had meant to her. How much she admired his indomitable spirit and sense of community.

One last gift for the man she loved but couldn't be with.

'I want to say that won't be necessary, but I don't want you to call me a liar,' she said with a sad smile.

'What happened?' asked Sophia.

Such a simple question, and yet Eliana didn't know how to answer it. What *had* happened?

'At the beginning we were just two people who met in a bar and never planned on meeting again. Until we got the news of my pregnancy from you. Then everything changed. We thought we could be friends but…' Her voice trailed off. But what? They'd fallen for each other when they really shouldn't have done?

Eliana still wanted to give in to his lure. She was standing at the edge of a cliff, ready to fall for him. But what if he didn't show up to catch her?

'For what it's worth, I've known Diego ever since he started working at Santa Valeria. He's a good man, and does great work with his pro bono efforts. But he takes himself a bit too seriously.'

Sophia shrugged when Eliana raised her eyebrows in a silent question.

'I don't know how to say it better. He just… gets too much in his head sometimes, and that leads to impulsive decision-making. It makes him a brilliant doctor in times of crisis, but

I'm not sure how well that works in personal matters.'

Eliana went quiet for a moment, thinking about what she had said, and then the waiting staff arrived with the wine she'd ordered for the table—excluding herself.

The twinge in her chest resurfaced as she looked at the empty chair one more time. He really wasn't going to come. It shouldn't surprise her—not after she had rejected his advances. But she'd really thought that he would come, for the sake of what they had and in spite of what they wouldn't have in the future.

'Thank you for joining me, everyone,' she said, and drew the attention of the room to herself. 'I guess I could have sent an email, but I didn't want to miss the opportunity to talk to all of you personally before leaving. As you all probably already know, I have finally made my choice for the new chief of medicine.'

She paused and raised her glass.

'I'm pleased to announce that Sophia has agreed to become the new chief of medicine and will usher Santa Valeria into a great new future.'

Glasses clinked all around, followed by a brief silence as everyone sampled their beverage. Eliana cleared her throat, suddenly feeling tight and constricted. She had practised these words believing Diego would be there to hear them, and understand their significance. Did it even make sense for her to say them?

'On top of that, I've also worked on establishing a more robust way of enabling you and your teams to help the less privileged communities here in Rio.' She paused to look around the room, her eyes once again resting on the empty chair. 'When speaking to you, I've heard many of you express interest in doing more pro bono work. So, starting immediately, a percentage of Santa Valeria's profits will be put into a newly established charity whose leader you can petition to release funds for pro bono projects. It will be led by Diego Ferrari,' she continued, and paused when she felt her voice wavering for a moment, 'who sadly could not be here tonight.'

Glasses clinked again, and Eliana sat back down on her chair. The cheerful atmosphere in the room was not managing to penetrate her gloom. But at least she had done something good while she was here in Rio, even if things hadn't turned out as she'd expected. With the new charity, Diego would have the right tools to keep going with his free clinic and help his colleagues bring in a significant number of cases from less wealthy patients.

She had done it because it was the right thing to do, but he had been the one to inspire her action. And now he couldn't even show up at the dinner.

* * *

'All right, this should be enough to hold you over.' Diego handed the patient a small paper bag with the required medicine in it and sighed with relief when the man closed the door behind him.

He let himself fall into the rickety chair behind the reception desk, burying his hands in his palms as he let out a groan of exhaustion. The plan had been to quickly stop by here and drop off some supplies someone had donated before heading to the dinner Eliana had organised for the leadership team at the hospital.

But when he had arrived at the clinic some people had already been waiting, needing to see a doctor right that instant. The patient they'd brought had been struggling with a nasty infection on his calf that Diego had needed to lance straight away, or he would have risked going into sepsis. By the time he had drained the fluids and packed the wound with antiseptic paste, hours had come and gone. But at least the patient had been saved and wouldn't lose his leg.

Diego glanced at his wristwatch, the weight of it still unfamiliar on his arm. He had worn it for the occasion of dinner tonight, along with a suit—the jacket of which he had tossed aside without much care when the patient's brother had hauled him in.

Just before midnight. There was no chance

they were still at the restaurant. Another emergency had prevented him from fulfilling the promise of his presence.

Maybe it was for the best. After all, hadn't he proved Eliana's point by skipping her dinner? When that patient had lain down on the table, a quick glance at his wound had told him the infection was severe enough that he needed immediate treatment and nothing else had mattered.

Should he have sent a message to let her know he was held up? The thought had swirled in his brain as he'd started the procedure, but he'd decided not to act on it. She would just see it an excuse after the way they'd left things. Hurt had stopped him from picking up the phone, and he had chosen instead to immerse himself in the urgent patient waiting at his door.

But he cared so deeply for both Eliana and their child. Hearing from her mouth that she didn't think he considered them a priority had thrown him into a dark pit.

Diego wasn't someone to give up. Ever. That was why he'd managed to keep the free clinic alive for as long as he had.

What was different with Eliana that he felt unable to pick himself up and fight? Their conversation yesterday had crushed him. He'd left her office feeling numb, as if walking through fog, trying to understand what had just happened. Why had he not stayed and argued more?

Because she was right.

Tonight would have been the perfect opportunity to prove her wrong, to show her that he cared about her above all else. But even though the thought had been on his mind he hadn't picked up the phone to get in touch with her.

Why?

Because Diego was afraid to feel how deep his love for her ran...how much it would destroy him to truly lose her.

Or might he resemble his father, after all? What made him think he could love her when he knew nothing about the concept? Fear paralysed him. What if he really was like his father? Maybe it was best she learned now before they got in too deep.

He pressed his palms against his eyes, willing his thoughts to stop chasing each other. The door of the clinic opened again. Diego swore under his breath. Had he not locked it after the patient and his family had left?

'We're not open right now, so if it's not an emergency please come back in the morning,' he said, without taking his hands off his face. Profound tiredness was digging its vicious claws into him, and he just wanted to rest.

'I thought I might find you here.'

Eliana's voice was coated with ice, sending a shiver down his spine.

He sat up straight, looking at her with a surprised expression. 'What are you doing here?' he asked, before he could think better of it.

'Me? What are *you* doing here?'

She looked at him, and there was a different kind of fire burning in her eyes than the one he was used to seeing.

'But of course you're here. Because you are Diego. You would give an arm and a leg to help your people, but you can't show up for me when it counts.'

Diego rose from his chair, meeting her gaze and not flinching at her bitter tone. 'I don't get to decide when emergencies come in,' he said, with a veiled expression. Agitation flared in his chest, mixing with the guilt he'd been carrying around since yesterday and creating an explosive fire.

'That's not the point. I was never angry with you for looking out for your patients. I know what it's like—I've been in your place.'

'*Have* you, though? Have you *really* been in my place? Have you watched friends die and families fall apart because of the inadequate health care that exists for people who live in the *favelas*? Because that's what I see every time someone comes through these doors. I clawed myself to the top from the very bottom so I could help them avoid such a fate. How could you possibly know that when you grew up in the best private school in this country?'

The words burst from him like a geyser that had been blocked by a boulder for far too long.

Eliana stared at him silently. The only indicator of her emotional state was the raised pulse he could see hammering against the base of her throat as she swallowed.

'You don't even know half the things I had to go through, growing up the way I did. I might have had plenty of food and clothes to keep me looking the part, but I was alone. You had your community to bond with and carry you through the hard times. I had no one.'

The last words came out as a whisper, and regret wrapped itself around Diego. He hadn't meant to throw his own internal turmoil at her.

'Why don't you tell me?' he said. 'You no longer have no one. You have no idea how much I—'

'No,' she interrupted him in a voice made from stone. She took a shaky breath, her golden-brown eyes trained on him. 'You do *not* love me. If you believe that I don't understand your pain because I grew up surrounded by my father's wealth, you cannot truly know me. I've told you so much already, but you still don't understand.'

Hurt was etched into each of her words—

a pain that resounded so intensely within him that it stole his breath. How had they got to this place where they had stopped understanding each other? It seemed as if the last few weeks had only been a mere dream of two people who were too different to tread the same path.

'Don't say that I don't love you,' he whispered, feeling the weight of her words settling on his chest and breaking his already crushed heart into pieces. 'I know it's true, whether you want to hear it or not.'

He might deny many things, but his feelings for her were genuine—even if they had landed them in this painful place.

'I thought I could do it,' she said. 'I really believed I could be in your life without hurting so much…without all this pain. But I don't think I can—'

Her voice finally broke, after wavering throughout her sentence, which prompted Diego to get off the chair and take a step closer to her.

She immediately shook her head. 'I waited for you at dinner, praying that you would show up despite the conversation we'd had. I wanted to be wrong about my reaction yesterday. I let you in…told you what it was like being on my own, having no one to trust.' Her throat bobbed when she swallowed a deep breath, her voice straining with each word. 'I asked you to show up when it counts—and you didn't. And you still haven't even asked about the scan.'

Her words hit him like a blow to his solar plexus, knocking the air out of his lungs as he slipped deeper into the dark pit he'd thrown himself into last night. After everything they'd discussed, all the things they had been through, he hadn't asked her about their child. He really wasn't any better than his father.

'I don't know what to say,' he rasped, his throat thick from the onslaught of emotions mixing in his chest. 'How is—?'

Eliana shook her head. 'I don't need you asking any more. I think we've reached the end of our road here, Diego.'

Her hand slipped into her handbag and retrieved an envelope. It looked bent, as if she had been carrying it around for a while.

'What is it?' he asked, flipping the envelope to examine its back. There was nothing written on it.

'Something you should know,' Eliana replied, with a rueful frown pulling at the corners of her lips. 'I'm leaving tomorrow. I know we have yet to figure out how we want to do things with the baby. I will be in touch as I get closer to my due date. But for now, I think I need some distance.'

'Ana, *por favor*...' He put the envelope down and circled the reception desk with two large strides, wrapping his hand around her upper arm as she turned to leave. 'Please don't go.'

'I have to—don't you see? Things shouldn't be so painful if they're right...if they're meant to be.'

She turned her head to look at him, and the pain in her eyes almost made him recoil.

'Maybe we were just kidding ourselves from the very start.'

'Ana...' He whispered her name and his hand went up to her cheek, only for her to flinch away before he could touch her.

'I have to go,' she said as they looked at each other, and she freed herself from his grasp, fleeing through the door before he could find the words that might persuade her to stay.

With a sigh that didn't even contain half of the pain and anguish welling up in him, Diego fell back into the chair and buried his face in his hands, his entire being crushed by what had happened in the last hour. She was gone, driven away by his inability to find her the space in his life that she deserved.

He was just like his father.

In the end, he had failed to be different.

A heavy blanket of sadness fell on his shoulders and he sat up straight again, his eyes falling onto the envelope he had put down as he'd tried to stop her leaving. He picked it up, turning it around in his hands a few times before opening it.

Inside he found a small flashcard with one word written on it: *Princesa*.

# CHAPTER ELEVEN

DIEGO LOOKED AT the equipment being unloaded off the truck and taken into his clinic and felt the familiar twinge of regret in his chest. He had gone back to the hospital the day after that night in the clinic to find a summons to the office of the new chief of medicine.

There, Sophia had told him what he had missed when he'd skipped dinner—the announcement that he would oversee a new charity dealing with everything related to community outreach and pro bono procedures at Santa Valeria. It was a position he wouldn't have dared to dream of even with Vanderson in place. And Eliana had made it come true without even thinking twice about it.

Thinking about her still felt as if a searing hot dagger was being poked between his ribs, leaving him feeling hollow. Weeks had passed since he had last heard about her, although he'd tried to get in touch with her to thank her for the new job and to hear about their baby. His daughter.

That was the only thought that managed to pierce through the darkness he surrounded himself with, making his chest swell with unbridled joy and anticipation of the day he got to meet her.

A lot of the things said that night had been born out of fear—he realised that now. Fear of the unknown. Fear of trusting his heart over his head. Fear of losing the only woman who had ever meant something to him.

She alone had managed to sneak around his defences, making herself a cosy nest inside his heart. But his first reaction had been to treat her like an intruder, and the result of that reaction would be something he would regret for the rest of his life.

'Could you at least try to look pleased about this?'

Diego turned around when he heard his *avozinha's* voice behind him. 'I'm thrilled. With the extra staff and equipment we can service a much wider area of the Complexo do Alemão. We've even got our own patient transport van now.' He pointed at the roomy van parked near the entrance.

'You'll need to sound more convincing for me to believe you,' his grandmother muttered, while shaking her head at him. 'But you've been moping around like a sad puppy for the last four weeks. I guess you'll tell me it has nothing to do with Eliana and your baby girl being so far away.'

Diego sighed, rubbing his temples in a futile attempt to stop the emerging pain. 'I'm not moping. Am I sad she's gone? Yes, of course. I missed the first scan, and I wish I could be there for the next.'

Eliana had left almost four weeks ago, meaning she was well into her second trimester now and would soon have her next routine check-up. It pained him to think that he had yet to see his daughter, even if it was only through the screen of an ultrasound.

Throughout his life Diego had made many questionable choices and mistakes, letting the shadows of the past haunt him to the extent that it had sometimes immobilised him, rendering him incapable of deciding. It was that kind of primal fear that had made him stand back as Eliana walked out of his life for good.

'Have you told her you'd like to be there?' Márcia asked, and he scoffed at that.

'She's not taking my calls.'

'Can you blame her after the things you said to her? To think that you didn't even ask about the baby…' Avozinha clicked her tongue with a disapproving head-shake.

He drew his gaze away from the X-ray machine now being delivered to look at her. 'What? Who told you that's what happened?'

'You should know by now that your grandmother knows everything. I really thought I'd raised you better, my *netinho*.'

Diego's ears suddenly pricked. Little grandson? She had stopped calling him by that diminutive ages ago...only used it now when...

'Okay... I'm in trouble, apparently.'

'Of course you're in trouble!' Márcia raised her voice at him. 'How can you believe you are *anything* like your father? My son turned into a selfish and egotistical man, despite my efforts to raise him as a good person. But he used to be kind and sweet—qualities I see in you to this day.'

Diego stared at her, his mouth slightly agape. How could she possibly know that this was what he had been struggling with? That these were his innermost thoughts—the fear that he would turn out precisely the same because he hadn't been taught any better. But...

'He didn't teach me anything,' he whispered, and the revelation struck him like a ton of bricks falling on his head. 'He wasn't around enough for me to learn *anything* from him. He didn't teach me.' He looked at his grandmother in disbelief. '*You* did. You raised me to be better than him.'

Márcia shrugged, but gave him an encouraging smile. 'Glad you got there in the end.'

Diego froze, unsure what he should do next.

How could he ever have believed he would turn out like his father when that man hadn't spent enough time in his life to influence him? No, all the things he had learned had come from his grandmother and all the half-siblings he'd grown up with.

His mistake seemed so incredibly foolish now, and his outburst in the clinic a couple of weeks ago silly. He was in love with this woman—what else was there to know?

'She has her next scan tomorrow. If you leave now you can get to Belo Horizonte with time to spare,' his grandmother informed him.

He grabbed her by the shoulders, planting a kiss on her cheek before realising what she had just said. 'How do you know that?'

'Just because you were having issues talking to her it doesn't mean I missed out on bonding with the mother of my next grandchild.'

She said it so matter-of-factly that Diego had to laugh.

'Text me the name of her doctor,' he said as he turned around to leave, heading straight for his car so he could be in Belo Horizonte just after nightfall if all went well.

Eliana sat in the empty waiting room, softly talking to her growing bump. She had her hand draped over it, as if wrapping it in a protective cocoon as she waited to have her scan.

Even though she was well into her second trimester she had yet to feel any movement from her tiny daughter. A fact that—according to the several online pregnancy communities she had found—wasn't anything to worry about. Most women in their first pregnancies didn't notice anything until the twentieth week. Eliana was just past sixteen.

It was at moments like this, when her nerves got the best of her, that she wished Diego was here. At least she could have shared the worry with him, if nothing else.

The thought that she had made a mistake gnawed at her more and more. Their last encounter had been charged with her fears—driven by them as she pushed him away and in doing that losing any chance of a future where they might have been a family. Where he might have sat here with her, holding her hand, as they found out more about their child.

And why? Because her insecurities had overwritten sensible concessions in those moments. For her entire life she had been irrelevant, with no one caring where she was or how she was doing. The damage caused by her father's neglect ran a lot deeper than she'd understood before she'd met Diego and got pregnant.

Because of her past pain she had demanded to be prioritised over things he didn't have any control over. For the first time in her life she'd had someone who truly cared for her, cherished her beyond any doubt, and instead of taking his feelings and actions at face value she had pushed him away—too afraid to deal with a reality where Diego wasn't going to abandon her.

It was an action that seemed so foolish now that she'd had time to process it. Why had she felt the need to leave Rio de Janeiro behind her as fast as she could? It wasn't the city's fault that her father had been a neglectful wretch. And Alessandro and Daria lived there—the only family she had remaining. Along with Diego's big family. All her daughter's aunts, uncles and cousins lived there, and so did Márcia, who was already more involved as a grandmother than Eliana ever could have hoped, and checked in with her almost daily. Not to mention Diego himself—the man she loved with all her heart.

Eliana had made a mistake, running away. She was at the point where she had to admit that.

Not for the first time in the last couple of days she took out her phone, checking flights back to Rio. She was still fine to fly, even with the pregnancy, though she'd have to choose soon.

Would Diego even take her back after the fight they'd had? Her heart squeezed inside her chest, sending a stabbing pain through her body.

She could sit here and wonder if he would, or she could go back and find out.

Her finger hovered over the flight, ready to buy the ticket, when the receptionist came into the waiting room to call her. 'Dr Oliveira, we're ready for you now,' she said, in a soft voice that sounded almost swoony. 'Dr Ferrari has just arrived and he's gone through. Your husband is...'

The receptionist waved her hand in front of her face, but Eliana's mind had gone blank after hearing his name so unexpectedly. *He was here?* Her mouth went dry and she suddenly felt both heat and chill rising within her, creating an intense storm as they met in her midsection.

She held her breath as she opened the door, and gave a soft cry when she saw Diego sitting in a chair with the sort of casual nonchalance she was so used to seeing from him. As if he belonged in this chair, in this place...

'Diego, you—'

He stood up from the chair and took a step towards her. 'I made it this time. No emergencies or last-minute patients.'

Her mind was still reeling from his sudden appearance, her lips parting without any words leaving them. She stretched out her hand, wanting to touch him, to kiss him, and tell him what a fool she had been.

But they were interrupted by her obstetrician Dr Porter entering the room, and after some brief introductions he started the scan and check-up.

Diego slipped his hand into hers when she winced at the chill of the gel on her stomach, and they both looked at the ultrasound picture in awe as Dr Porter showed them their daughter. He squeezed her hand as they looked at the screen together, feeling the magnitude of this moment. They had made this little life. Together.

'Okay, both mother and child are healthy and looking good. Have you experienced any discomfort? Unusual bleeding? Anything?'

Eliana shook her head, still speechless from seeing her daughter through the ultrasound, overwhelmed by the unconditional love she'd experienced at the sight of their child. Glancing at Diego, she saw he had a similar expression, and they looked at each other with a small smile, knowing each other's thoughts without having to say anything.

They walked out of the doctor's office and into the car park in silence, only stopping when they got to Diego's car. Then they turned to each other, deeply lost in the other one's eyes for a few heartbeats, before they hugged each other.

Tears started to coat her eyes, falling down her cheeks as relief washed over her. How could she have let him go?

'I'm so sorry, Diego,' she whispered into his neck, prompting him to take her face in both of his hands so he could look at her.

He swiped over her cheeks with his thumbs, brushing the tears away. '*You're* sorry? I have to apologise for *everything* I said. I was hurt and confused. I wanted to be with you, but I didn't know how. I lashed out. But if you let me I will try to make up for that for the rest of our lives together.'

'I thought you were putting me in second place. I couldn't deal with being part of a family. I didn't think I knew how to be with someone like you...someone who has radiance and love all around you. I'm still not sure I know how to be a part of it, but I want to try. If...' She swallowed the lump that had suddenly appeared in her throat. 'If you'll have me back.'

Diego looked at her for a moment, the brown of his eyes darkening. He looked like a predator that had just spotted its next meal. She held her breath as he remained quiet, then he dropped his head towards hers, brushing his lips against her in the kiss Eliana had been longing for since she'd left Rio de Janeiro a month ago.

'I love you, Ana. There's nothing in this world that can change that—nothing anyone can do or say to change my mind. And I promise to show you that every day until for ever.'

Eliana smiled as relief and joy collided in her chest, igniting the firework in her heart that had been waiting to explode ever since she'd met him that night at the hotel bar all those weeks ago.

'I love you, too—*ah!*'

She suddenly went rigid, and concern washed over Diego's face. 'What's wrong, *amor*? Is it...?'

But then she smiled again, even bigger than before. 'I can feel her... I think she just kicked me a little bit.'

Diego's eyes went wide in wonderment and he looked down, placing his hand on her protruding belly. '*Eita, princesa*, that's not very princess-like,' he said with a grin, and pulled her closer to him again. 'Oh, I almost forgot. Avozinha gave me this to give to you,' he added, and his hand vanished into his pocket, retrieving a small velvet box that he handed to her.

'She wants me to have her jewellery?' Eliana raised an eyebrow—and gasped a second later when she flipped the small box open. Her eyes snapped back to Diego, who was now kneeling in front of her.

'She thought her engagement ring would look good on your finger, and I think she's right. Will you let me show you how much I love you by becoming my wife?'

The tears she had just managed to get under control started to fall down her cheeks again as she nodded with a sobbing smile, pulling Diego off his feet and into her arms. 'Yes,' she whispered in his ear, and squealed as he wrapped his arms around her even tighter.

Eliana knew they still had challenges ahead of them, but whatever was coming at them they would deal with it. Together.

# EPILOGUE

ELIANA FOUGHT TEARS as she looked in the mirror. The day was finally here: she was going to marry the love of her life.

She was surrounded by his sisters, who were laughing with her, and sharing advice from their own weddings, as well as cooing at her daughter Alice, who was lying in a small cot in the room, observing the proceedings through wide eyes.

She and Diego had debated for a long time whether they should get married straight away or wait for their child to be born. An urgency to tie the knot had filled them both, and neither had wanted to show any patience, but in the end Eliana had decided to wait. As a first-time mother she'd found the stress of pregnancy challenging, and she hadn't wanted to add to that.

The same day he'd come to pick her up in Belo Horizonte they had returned to Rio together, to forge a better future for Santa Valeria.

Eliana had been happy to leave Sophia to deal with the daily task of being the chief of medicine, freeing up her own time to help Diego build on the clinic, sharing the burden and the joy with him. She much preferred practising medicine over sitting in a stuffy office with endless paperwork. And bit by bit they were building the hospital they'd envisaged.

Now the day she had been so looking forward to had finally arrived, and she was sharing it with the people surrounding her. The Ferrari clan had welcomed her to the family with open arms, as if she were a long-lost sister, just waiting to find her family again.

'Don't cry! We've just got your make-up done,' Gloria said with a laugh as she put her arm around her shoulder, squeezing her full of sisterly love.

'Pick a random point on the ceiling and focus on it. That's what helped me,' chimed in Bianca, another one of the Ferrari sisters.

Eliana tilted her head backwards and looked at the ceiling above her head, willing the tears of joy to recede at the very least until they'd had all the pictures taken.

The door behind them opened, and all the women whirled around. Alessandro entered the room, followed by his daughter Daria, who was wearing the same dress as the bridesmaids.

'Is he ready?' Gloria asked, giving voice to the question everyone wanted to yell at him.

He nodded. 'I'm here to pick up my lovely sister and take her to the altar.'

The tears she had just managed to fight off started to well up again. It was finally happening. She was going to get married to Diego.

She took Alessandro's arm and let him lead her down the stairs, through Diego's *avozinha*'s house and into the garden, where they had set up chairs for the guests and a beautiful wedding arch. Her heart skipped a beat when the arch came into sight and the guests rose from their chairs.

And there he stood, at the end of the silver-white carpet they had rolled out, looking at her with an intensity she had got to know so well over the last year. His excitement matched hers as she walked down the aisle to meet him, her soulmate. Alessandro kissed her on both cheeks when they got to the end, before handing her over to Diego with a stern but warm look in his eyes.

'Are you ready for the rest of our lives?' she whispered when Diego leaned in to kiss her as well.

He smiled and grabbed her hand. 'Since the day I met you.'

* * * * *

# MEDICAL
## Pulse-racing passion

### Available Next Month
All titles available in Larger Print

**Dr Finlay's Courageous Bride**  Marion Lennox
**Marriage Reunion In The ER**  Emily Forbes

---

**Stranded With The Paramedic**  Sue MacKay
**A Family Made In Paradise**  Tina Beckett

---

**How To Resist The Single Dad**  JC Harroway
**A Date With Her Best Friend**  Louisa Heaton

---

Available from Big W, Kmart, Target,
selected supermarkets, bookstores & newsagencies.
OR call 1300 659 500 (AU), 0800 265 546 (NZ) to order.

Visit millsandboon.com.au

6 brand new stories each month

# MEDICAL
Pulse-racing passion

MILLS & BOON

Keep reading for an excerpt of a new title
from the Western Romance series,
A COWBOY THANKSGIVING by Melinda Curtis

## *PROLOGUE*

THERE WERE TIMES when twelve-year-old Beauregard Franklin Monroe felt like he was on top of the world.

This wasn't one of those times.

It was Thanksgiving week, a time when the Monroes gathered. A time when the younger generation competed in the Monroe Holiday Challenge—a five day event that culminated on Thanksgiving morning, followed by the crowning of this year's winner.

And this year's loser.

Sadly, for some unknown reason, Bo was often the year's biggest loser.

How could that be? Bo was athletic and large for his age. Everyone competing, except for his brother Holden, was younger than he was. He blamed it on his continuing growth spurts and clumsiness, a weak excuse at best.

But here it was. Thanksgiving morning. The last day of competition before the grand feast. And there was only one Monroe beneath Bo on the leaderboard—his cousin Sophie. Something had to change.

Before he'd eaten breakfast, Bo had taken time to write in the small notebook his Grandpa Harlan had given him.

*Run fast. Play hard. Pick myself up when I fall.*

The notebook was a secret between his grandfather and himself. A way to be your own cheerleader, Grandpa

Harlan had said. To create the life you want, he'd said. To get where you want to be.

Right now, Bo wanted to do better in the holiday challenge.

"What are we doing today, Grandpa?" Bo shouldered his way to the front of the pack, ahead of his two siblings and nine cousins. The sun was out in Philadelphia, but the cold air chilled his fingers and nose.

"There are six pumpkins hidden in the woods." Grandpa Harlan addressed all his Monroe grandchildren. "Each pumpkin you find and bring back earns you a point. One pumpkin has a leaf drawn on it. That one earns you two points. Got it? And...go!"

Bo didn't linger. He bolted into the woods. But he wasn't fast enough to leave the pack behind. Holden tripped him. Cousin Shane elbowed him when he stumbled. Cousin Olivia knocked his cowboy hat off as he righted himself. And in the process, Bo careened into Cousin Sophie, who fell. Twin cousins Laurel and Ashley stopped to help her.

Bo ran on.

*Finally, I won't be last.*

Bo thrashed through the underbrush and tripped, falling on a pumpkin the size of a basketball hidden beneath the branches of a bush. Finally, his two left feet were good for something. And... Holy cow! This pumpkin had a leaf drawn on it with black marker. Two points! He wrapped his arms around the orange prize and stumbled back to Grandpa Harlan. If he hurried, he could return to the woods and try to find another.

His grandfather knelt next to Sophie, examining her scrapes, which were bleeding a little. Laurel and Ashley hovered nearby, sending Bo dirty looks.

Bo placed the pumpkin at their feet. "I found one." He danced around as if he'd just scored a league-winning touchdown. "I found one! I'm not last. I'm not going to get another loser trophy."

"Stop right there." Grandpa Harlan straightened and put a hand on Bo's shoulder. "You knocked Sophie down." His tone of voice didn't ring with approval.

Bo hurried to defend himself. "The only reason I bumped into Sophie was because Olivia pushed me." He tipped his cowboy hat back, tugged down his sweatshirt and tried to smile innocently. His mother always said his charm and good looks got him out of trouble at school. She considered them mixed blessings. But with a combined total of eleven siblings and cousins, Bo had to work with what little he had. "It's not my fault. Blame Olivia."

"But you didn't stop to make sure your cousin was okay." Grandpa Harlan helped a still crying Sophie to her feet. "As the Grand Poo-Bah of the Monroe Holiday Challenge, I hereby award your pumpkin to Sophie."

Laurel and Ashley cheered.

"But..." Bo's shoulders slumped. "I would have helped her up if I'd have known that was a rule." He glanced at Sophie's scrapes, which looked painful, and those tears of hers, which were real, and felt remorse. "I'm sorry, Soph."

"I won't reverse my verdict." Grandpa Harlan softened his decision by righting Bo's cowboy hat. "I hope this is a lesson you take to heart, Bo. No matter what else goes on, people always come first."

Take it to heart? He'd never forget this feeling of letting Sophie down and being a failure.

Five of the competitors, including Holden, Shane and Olivia, emerged from the wood, each carrying pumpkins and wearing big smiles that said they hadn't come in last.

"I'm cursed." Bo trudged back to the house where he'd

receive the biggest loser trophy served with his pumpkin pie. "I hate the Monroe Holiday Challenge. I'm done playing."

But he knew that was a lie. Because if there was a chance that he wouldn't come in last in the competition, he was going to take it.

As for the rest of his life?

He was going to try his best never to be last at anything else. Ever.

## *CHAPTER ONE*

"Good news, Bo. We're bringing back the Monroe Holiday Challenge this Thanksgiving."

Bo Monroe had just taken a sip of his beer when his cousin Shane made his announcement. He nearly sprayed said beverage into the firepit in the backyard of the Bucking Bull Ranch. Instead, he managed to swallow and say in a choked voice, *"Why?"*

A steady stream of snowflakes fell with a soft pitter-patter on his straw cowboy hat. It was a week before Thanksgiving and snow had been falling in Second Chance, Idaho, since October.

Or so he'd heard. Bo and his dog Spot had just arrived from Texas for a visit and Bo had accepted an invitation to have a beer with Shane and Jonah after a family dinner. Spot, his Harlequin Great Dane, was hanging out with the rest of Shane's family indoors, probably curled up in front of the fire since the dog was a born and bred Texan, unused to temperatures below fifty.

"You want to know why we need to bring back a beloved holiday tradition?" Shane sat at Bo's right. He grinned from ear-to-ear, and considering he'd been in a near-fatal car crash a few months ago, it was good to see him smiling again. But not over this. "Because none of you want me to hold the Holiday Challenge crown forever."

Bo's competitive streak agreed. It was his pride that didn't want to compete.

"You've held the crown for over twenty years. I'm willing to let you hang on to it forever." Jonah shrugged deeper into his jacket in the chair to Bo's left. Born and raised in Hollywood, Bo's script-writing cousin hated the cold as much as Spot did. Jonah wore a blue parka, fur-lined hood up over his short red hair. "I hated those challenges. And most of us hated Olivia, Holden and you, Shane, for winning."

Bo nodded.

"But this time things will be different," Shane promised, sounding like a CEO at a shareholders' meeting, which was fitting considering he had been a CEO up until last January. In deference to the cold, Shane wore a thick, stylish blue jacket, a knit cap and gloves. He might be living on a ranch, but he was not, and never would be, a true cowboy. "We have to do this before we're too old."

Thinking of age and physical prowess, Bo sized up Shane, making a mental tally of his cousin's corporate softness.

*I could take him... If I wasn't cursed in the challenge.*

"I don't know about Bo, but I'm not up for a physical competition." Jonah stretched one leg toward the fire, groaning like it pained him to do so. "I pulled a muscle climbing the ladder to the hayloft."

"And what were you doing in the hayloft?" Shane teased.

"I was helping Emily move hay." Jonah tried hard not to smile but ended up grinning back at Bo, still riding his wave of post-engagement bliss.

Although Bo was happy for his cousin, that bliss stung a little.

Over a year ago, he and Jonah had been in love—or thought they'd been in love—with the same woman—Aria. They'd both lost her. A blessing of sorts, as it turned out.

Jonah had quickly moved on, writing a script about the experience as a form of therapy before landing the heart of Emily, a diehard cowgirl and former rodeo queen. Bo had been picking up the pieces of his heart at a slower pace, taking into consideration Aria's last words to him...

"Look at us together. We're perfectly matched in the mirror," Aria had said in a voice that was as delicate and refined in tone as her polished good looks. "You may be an engineer, Bo, but you have no ambition, no life plan. And nothing to indicate you want a wife and family, except for those scribbles you make in your notebook every morning. And Spot, I suppose." She'd scratched his dog behind the ears before handing Bo his leash and dog dish, items she'd used while dog-sitting. "And even Spot has to deal with your long absences from traveling and working on an oil rig."

Spot had stared up at Bo with the same accusation in his big brown eyes.

*Even my dog thinks I stink at relationships.*

After that, Bo had taken a hard look at himself and realized that—on paper, at least—he looked like he wasn't interested in long term relationships or happily-ever-after. He was determined to change that impression.

"Listen," Shane said, voice rising above the soft hiss of falling snow and the crackle of flames. "I've been telling my boys about the challenge and they're excited."

Bo and Jonah exchanged looks and then simultaneously said, "No."

"I reject your rejections." Shane wasn't the type to give in easily. "The boys have come up with a list of games to play, ones with a cowboy twist." The boys Shane referenced were the ones he was going to adopt in January after he married their widowed mother, Franny, at New Year's.

"Are these games Franny approved?" Bo shook his

head, dumping a bit of snow from his hat onto his shoulders. "Forget I asked. *I* need to approve the games. You all owe me that much."

Jonah gaped at Bo. "I can't believe you said that. You're actually considering playing?"

"Only if I have a chance to win." Or at least not come in last.

"It was never about winning," said Shane, the family's most frequent winner. "And this time, it won't be cutthroat. It'll be fun. We'll have teams of three instead of competing one-on-one—two adults paired with a kid. I bet that boy you're picking up tomorrow will enjoy it, Bo."

That boy was a relation of a friend of Bo's, Nathan Blandings, an army engineer who'd been unexpectedly deployed overseas. Nathan had called a few days ago and, over a bad connection, asked Bo to host the young orphan for the week of Thanksgiving. Bo wasn't usually the man someone chose for such a job, him being a bachelor and all. Nor was he usually the man who accepted such a request, having an active social life. But he hoped the experience would give him perspective when it came to settling down and contemplating how to raise his own kids.

"Fine. I'll take Max." Hopefully, the kid was a budding athlete with the will to win.

"If only you had a significant other..." Shane began.

"Back off." Bo crossed his arms over his chest, trying not to look as wounded as he felt. "Not everyone finds love as easily as you two."

"Dude, we aren't the ones compared in appearance to underwear models." Jonah chuckled. "And yet, of the twelve Monroes who inherited Second Chance, everyone found love here, except you."

*I'm even last in love.*

Bo slumped in his folding chair. It was true. He couldn't

go anywhere in town without seeing a happily partnered family member. They all had someone to confide in, to share private jokes with, to cuddle up with on a cold winter night.

*And I have Spot.*

Who was a bed hog.

Shane cleared his throat. "Bo, I know you attract a lot of attention just stepping into a room."

"Being too pretty is a curse," Jonah mocked mournfully.

Bo pressed his lips together to keep from sneering at Jonah.

"It's not all about physical attraction." Shane stared at the falling snowflakes dreamily, like a man staring at the woman he loved. "I saw something in Franny the moment we met. There was a sadness in her eyes. I had to find a way to chase those blues away, even if I didn't know why I was doing it. Turns out it was because she was meant for me. That's the kind of person you need to find."

Bo kept silent, not understanding how someone could be meant for someone else or how you'd know it instantly.

"If we're handing out love advice…" Jonah felt the need to chime in. "I was attracted to Emily from the start. She's my kind of pretty and my kind of talker. Admittedly, Em was mistakenly attracted to you at first." He clapped Bo on the back. "But she eventually fell for brains over beauty. Truly, it's what's inside that counts. Her values match my values, her sass can handle my sarcasm. *That's* the kind of person you need to find, Bo."

Although it was true that women were often drawn to, or in awe of, Bo's physical appearance, Bo found that to be a turn-off. He was more than a pretty face.

He shook his head, shaking off romantic notions, along with another dusting of snow. "That's enough, guys. I don't need love advice. I have a plan for love." As any good engineer would, once he applied his smarts to the situation.

His cousins stared at Bo as if he'd bought a ten dollar ticket on a two dollar ride.

"I'm getting my house in order. Literally." Bo warmed to his topic, leaning forward. "I made an offer on a home in Houston. And I want to find a place up here before I leave next weekend." Not to mention, he'd accepted a full-time job at an oceanographic oil company that offered generous health and retirement benefits. "I've got a life plan, one that is specific about the kind of life I want to lead and the woman I want by my side." There would be no more falling for complicated, high maintenance women or women with messy relationship histories. "I've got a clear vision of my future. When my plans are in place, I'll look for love. And mark my words, the next woman I fall for isn't going to be able to resist me."

His cousins' mouths hung open.

In awe, Bo assumed.

FRIDAY AFTERNOON, Bo stood in baggage claim at the Boise airport holding a sign with a name printed in bold, black letters: *Max Holloway*.

He scanned the approaching crowd for someone wearing an airline uniform and holding the hand of a young boy.

A little girl wearing a bright pink tracksuit and thick, round glasses ran up to Bo, brown, corkscrew curls straining the bands around her ponytails. "Hi." She tucked her thumbs beneath her purple backpack straps. "I love cowboys."

"Is that so?" Bo tipped his cowboy hat and spared a smile for the overly friendly girl before continuing his search for an escorted minor in the crowd.

"For Max Holloway?" A woman with light brown, curly

hair and thick, round glasses wheeled a large, yellow suitcase to a stop in front of Bo's booted feet and set a car seat by her side. She wore blue slacks, a white button-down blouse and a blue blazer. So much blue. She had to be an airline employee of some sort.

But if she was, where was the little boy?

"I was expecting Max?" Bo stared at the little girl, who seemed nothing like a Max and too small to be traveling alone, much less compete in the Monroe Holiday Challenge.

"It's *Maxine*," the woman said in a no-nonsense voice.

"Okay." Max was Maxine and an adorable little tyke. Plans for the holiday challenge would need to be adjusted. Even the lines he'd written in his notebook this morning—*be positive, beat Shane*—seemed a stretch. Maybe he'd use this as an excuse to drop out or at the very least get paired with someone who could help him win. Smiling, Bo handed the woman his placard. "Do I need to sign anything before taking custody of Maxine?"

The woman gave him a disapproving once-over. The airlines had chosen her well. She didn't seem like the type to put up with drama—be it lost luggage or awkward transfers of minors traveling alone.

The urge to win her over surged within him, strengthening his smile.

"Right. You need identification." Bo took out his wallet and showed her his driver's license. "Are you looking forward to Thanksgiving?"

"Yes." The airline employee stared at him steadily through her thick glasses. Her eyes were the color of his favorite, oak-aged whiskey. She glanced at his ID. "Beauregard Franklin Monroe."

*Beauregard...*

What had his parents been thinking?

"Not everyone can grow into an old school name like Beauregard." Grinning at the little girl, Bo twirled an imaginary handlebar mustache. "But you can call me Bo." He tucked his wallet in his back jeans pocket, propped the car seat on the yellow suitcase, took possession of the little girl's hand, and then navigated through the sea of travelers. "Do you like dogs? Spot is waiting for us in my truck. You'll love him. I feel like ice cream before we make the drive over the mountain to Second Chance. What do you think?"

The little girl blinked up at Bo with eyes the same color as those of her airline chaperone. "Don't I have to eat my vegetables first?"

"Of course not," he said cheerfully. "It's the holidays." That's what his Grandpa Harlan used to say, much to his mother's chagrin.

"Vegetables first," said the woman behind him. "Always."

Bo stopped just before the exit. He hadn't realized the airline representative was still tagging along. "Sorry. I didn't sign for her, did I?"

The woman wasn't carrying a pen. She didn't have a sheaf of papers. But she was frowning at him in the worst way.

"Mama, just once I wanna have ice cream before vegetables." The little girl smiled coyly. "Please…"

"Mama?" Bo took a step back, earning another frown from the woman.

"I think there's been a mix-up." The woman gestured from the little girl to herself. "Nathan said you'd take us in for Thanksgiving." At Bo's blank look, she added, "*Us*, as in two."

"No. Nathan said…" Bo trailed off, trying to remember. *My…(unintelligible)…needs a place to spend the holi-*

*days. Max is an orphan and...(unintelligible)...can't spend with them. (Unintelligible)...you owe me.*

Shane and Jonah were going to have a good laugh over this misunderstanding. They might even try to make a team out of them.

*Not a chance.*

Bo drew a deep breath, determined to make the best of things, such as they were. "To be honest, we had a bad connection and I'm not sure what Nathan said exactly." Bo forced himself to chuckle, although he felt like nothing was funny. "All I got was that some kid named Max needed a place to spend the holidays. And then came the email from Nathan with the flight number and arrival time, plus the name Max Holloway."

The woman straightened her jacket and righted her glasses, all the while keeping a close eye on her little girl. "Is that all?"

"Yeah. That was the gist of it." He forced another mirthless chuckle, a little ha-ha-ha that would never pass for Santa's ho-ho-ho. "It's all good. There's plenty of room in Second Chance for both Maxine and you." Whoever she was.

"That's Luna," the woman informed him in an exasperated voice, pointing at her daughter. "And I'm Max."

*She was the orphan?*

"And to think, I used to like surprises," Bo muttered.

"I like cowboys, and Mama likes books." Luna pushed her glasses up her nose. One of her ponytails was askew over her ear, as if she'd fallen asleep in Maxine's arms and shifted her head to-and-fro to get comfortable. Which was adorable but wouldn't help him win any reindeer games. "Are you a for-real cowboy, with a horse and everything?"

Bo drew back in mock surprise. "Miss Luna, I'm a Texan. Now, I'm currently horseless, but—"

"Well, shoot." Luna scuffed the sole of a little red, sparkly sneaker on the carpet. "You aren't a real cowboy. You just look like one."

"I'm a Texan," Bo repeated, feeling a frown crease his brow as he defended his adopted home. "Wearing boots and cowboy hats come second nature to me."

Luna eyed him up and down. "Do you have cows?"

"No."

"Do you live on a ranch?"

"No."

"You're not a real cowboy." The little thing had the nerve to look disappointed.

In Bo!

Except for Aria, Bo was never a disappointment to the ladies.

He swallowed the compulsion to explain his life plan to a pre-schooler. "Help me out here, Maxine."

"You're on your own, Beauregard." Maxine took possession of her daughter's hand and stepped around Bo, poised to take the lead. "Which way?"